Witch'd

A Novel by
Gabriel Mero

Pages Promotions, LLC
Birmingham, Michigan
www PagesPromotions com
Info@PagesPromotions com
© 2022 Gabriel Mero
Edited by Diana Kathryn Plopa

Print ISBN: 978-1628282689
E-Book ISBN: 978-1628282696
Library of Congress Control Number: 2022915753

Dedication

For anyone who has ever felt that they're not good enough – you are.

Acknowledgements

There are many people without whom this book would not be what it is today.

My grandmother, June Yonkey, who taught me what it is to be strong. Whenever I want to give up, I think of you, and I push through.

My mother, Betsy Hebert: you instilled in me a love of reading and horror movies. Although I don't get to see you as much as I would like, you are in my heart always, and I wouldn't be who I am without you.

My aunt, Julie Vitale: your unconditional love and support have meant the world to me.

My cousin, Megan Kozubal: you are one of my very best friends. Whenever I need support, you are there for me and I am eternally grateful.

My editor, Diana: you took something that was mediocre and helped me turn it into something amazing. Thank you!

My dear friend, Chelsea Gouin: you have been my number one fan since we met Freshman year in French class. When I feel like my writing sucks, you make me believe it's worth something.

Kayla Borbolla: your expertise in The Craft is second to none. Thanks for all your help; the magic wouldn't happen without you.

Amanda Sharp: your friendship has been such a blessing in my life. Thanks for always having my back and for inspiring such an awesome character as Amethyst.

Erik Szyperski: thank you for the countless hours you patiently listened while I bounced ideas off of you and for your support in my writing.

Last, but certainly not least, to my babies, Clara, Alistair, Romana, and Cersei: you guys are the light of my life and I love you all with my whole heart. You guys might not live forever, but you'll live on in my heart and in this book.

Prologue

A sigh of pure exhaustion escapes my lips as I collapse onto the small twin-sized bed. The mattress is memory foam and oh, so deliciously comfortable. As soon as the bed settles, my cat, Romana, scurries onto my chest, her orange tail swishing with delight as she purrs.

It's been a long few weeks. The move from suburban Michigan to this sleepy New England town was spur of the moment. My stepdad, Don, is a real piece of work. He and my mom have been together for as long as I can remember, but I've never liked him. Between him trying to force me into being a jock – skating lessons for hockey, as well as one season of tee-ball, and two of soccer, and the near-constant mental and occasional physical abuse that he doled out, being away from him is hardly breaking my heart. Living with him was not a total nightmare, though. He tried to make up for what he lacked in love, affection, and acceptance with things. He has a good job, so I had every toy, book, DVD, and game system I wanted. I never went without food, never went without heat or running water, never went to school looking poor. The truth is, I think he could always tell that I'm not a cookie-cutter clone. I'm different.

Things between Don and my mom were never perfect. They've been fighting since day one. A bossy control freak should not date a fiercely independent woman. All my life, it was fight, pack the car, make up, repeat. I suspect that the two of them secretly love drama. Why they ever decided to get married, I'll never know. I guess my mom figured that by getting with him, she and I would be well provided for, and our lives would be less stressful. *Guess again.*

Things really took a turn for the worse after my brother was born. When he was about two and a half years old, he was diagnosed with Autism. Typically, that would bring a couple closer together, I'd assume, anyway, but in this case, it drove them irrevocably apart. I suspect that being the arrogant asshole he is, Don thinks that his genes are as perfect as he is, so the taint must've come from my "white trash" mother. After all, her son from her first marriage—that's me—is a nervous wreck and... different.

The fights became more frequent and more intense. I'd lie in bed at night trying to sleep for school the following day, and I'd be kept awake by their loud voices and swearing. My heart would pound in my chest and ears, my breath short. It wasn't until the night that I heard the meaty *slap* of a palm hitting skin that I threw back the covers and raced down the stairs.

My mom lay on the ceramic tile in the kitchen, her hand to her cheek. Don loomed over her, his face red and spittle flying from his mouth as he screamed obscenities at her.

Not waiting for my common sense to take over, I unlocked my cell phone and dialed 911. Don heard my voice telling the operator our address and that I'd seen him hit my mother. Catching wind of what I was doing, he ripped the phone from my hand and whipped it against the wall. I watched as the screen shattered and sprayed glass all over the floor.

"Nice try, you little fucking faggot. Can't even protect your mom like a real man, can you?"

I felt my blood boiling as I clenched my fists. The truth was, it wasn't even a fair fight. I'm five feet eleven inches and about one hundred forty pounds, while Don is about two hundred fifty pounds and six feet tall. In my hyperbolic mind, he could punch right through my abdomen.

My mom got to her feet and shoved me away. "Go back to bed," she hissed. I could tell that she was springing like a cat about to pounce on its prey. I watched in amazement as she launched herself at him and punched him right in the face. He staggered back, knocking the black leather sofa over with him. My mom packs quite a punch for a tiny woman of five foot three and one hundred fifteen pounds.

The police showed up in a matter of minutes and broke it up. My stepdad wasn't arrested because my mom didn't have a scratch on her – he had a gouge just below his eye from her nails – but they did threaten to take my brother and me away if they didn't separate.

And so, mom, my brother, Brent, and I packed up and headed east. My grandmother lived in New England – I hardly knew her because Don had never liked her, especially once he found out she'd given me a Star of David necklace and was teaching me about Judaism, and so we stayed away—was more than happy to let us come stay with her until my mom got back on her feet. It was a long car ride, and my nerves were shot, but at least I was able to keep my cat. If I'd had to get rid of Romana, I would've been devastated.

We've been here a couple of weeks now, and while the peace and quiet is refreshing and new, it doesn't quite feel like home. How could a town with a name like Willows Crest feel like home? It sounds like the name of a teen soap.

My nerves have settled down a bit since the move, but they are working overdrive tonight. Tomorrow is the first day of my freshman year at Burnham University – new town, new school, no friends. Just what every twenty-year-old wants.

Romana settles on my chest, and I scratch her chin affectionately. "Who's Daddy's baby?" I coo.

She rolls onto her back and stretches a paw out toward me, yowling as if to say, "Me! I am!"

My heart swells with joy at this. I've never been a people person. People lie, cheat, and steal. An animal will love you for life as long as you're nice to them and care for them. Especially cats. They don't give their love away freely.

My thoughts are interrupted by a light knocking on the door. "Come in," I call, sitting up.

The door opens to reveal my grandmother, Ginevra. She's holding a coffee mug with steam billowing out of the top. My grandmother is an interesting woman. She has lived in America all her life, and yet somehow, she speaks with a slight British accent. A posh British accent. She has dark curly hair, which she piles on her head in a chignon, and favors baggy, free-flowing robes and gowns. She reminds me of an old Bohemian woman.

"I thought you might like a cup of tea," she trills, smiling. The truth of the matter is, tea is like crack to me. It's one of the only things that can calm me down when I'm stressed out. I've tried a copious amount of teas over the years, but my absolute favorite is Earl Grey. The first few times I had it, I thought it tasted like black pepper. I started letting it steep for longer, and the bergamot flavor really came out. It's been true love ever since.

"That's so nice. Thanks, Grandma," I say, accepting the steaming mug from her.

She sits on the bed, beside my legs, and reaches out to pet Romana. Romana is a nervous Nellie, much like I am. She doesn't really like anyone except for me. I'm quite surprised to see that she sniffs Grandma's wrinkled hand and rubs her head up against it.

"I know you're anxious about tomorrow, bubala," Grandma says, as if somehow reading my mind. She has a habit of doing that.

"Yeah," I confess, sighing. I really wish that I could be a normal, non-anxious person. It really sucks worrying about every minute detail all the time. I graduated back in 2009, and although I'd been pressured to go to college, anxiety had left me practically paralyzed. Two years , I'm looking to try again. New town, new me.

"It'll be all right, I promise. It's an adjustment, yes, but this is a good change for you."

"Is it?"

She smiles sadly. "I'm so sorry you had to live with that for all those years. He has completely destroyed your self-image, hasn't he?"

"It's kind of hard to feel good about yourself when someone is constantly degrading you," I say quietly. I've never really talked to anyone about how Don treated me. Not my friends, not my mom. I guess a part of me was always afraid of what would happen if he found out that I told.

Grandma leans over and takes my right hand in both of hers, and squeezes tightly. "Those days are over, all right? He can't hurt you anymore. You're safe now. I'm going to do everything in my power to help build you back up, bubala. You'll see that he was just a sick bastard. His opinion of you is inconsequential."

I feel my eyes start to sting with tears, and I blink, trying to clear them. I'm not super comfortable showing emotion in front of others, let alone crying in front of them.

My Grandma seems to sense this and stands back up. "I'm so happy you're here. Now, drink your tea and get some sleep. You have a big day tomorrow. You don't want to miss your first day."

"Okay," I say, sipping my Earl Grey. Its citrusy warmth cascades through my body, instantly combatting my over-dramatic nerves.

"Goodnight," she says, flicking the light switch off.

"Goodnight, Grandma."

She smiles again and shuts the door behind her.

I settle back into bed and drink my tea as Romana nestles up next to me. *I could definitely get used to the serenity around here.*

I feel myself getting sleepier and sleepier with each swallow of Earl Grey. I set the mug aside and pad across the room and into my bathroom for a quick shower, and to wash my face, take my contacts out, and brush my teeth.

Romana is still in bed when I come back into the room. I slide under the covers and tuck them up under my chin before switching off the lamp on my bedside stand. I'm far too sleepy to attempt to read tonight.

I settle in on my side, Romana alongside me, purring happily, and I slip into sleep.

I'm dreaming. I know I am. I'm back home in my tiny white bedroom, devoid of personality. I can't see anything, but I know it's my old room by the king-sized mattress I lie on.

I can't hear the fighting, but I know it's happening. I lie there immobile, staring into the darkness around me. I tentatively reach out for Romana –comfort—but she's not beside me. Where else would she be?

I sit up and call for her, but she doesn't come to me.

I switch on the light, and she's nowhere to be seen. Where is she?

Downstairs, I hear her cry out.

I'm on my feet and down the stairs in a flash. Don has her by the scruff of the neck.

I rush over and snatch her from him, holding her tightly to my chest.

"She's fucking going," Don bellows.

"No!" I cry. "Please! She's all I have!"

"You're not going to have powers in my house. She's going."

Powers? What is he talking about?

Don opens the front door to reveal two people from the pound, holding out a cage.

I shake my head furiously and hold Romana more tightly.

I feel Don's hands prying mine away from Romana, and no matter how hard I try, I cannot overpower him.

"Please!"

He wrenches her from my arms, and sobbing I collapse to the ground. Romana cries out in fear before she is shoved into the cage. Before I can react, the door is slammed. She's gone.

Don stands over me, a malicious grin alighting his chubby face. "You'll never get away from me," he said, his voice echoing louder and louder.

I jolt up in bed, Romana's name exploding out of my mouth. My chest rises and falls as my heart hammers against my rib cage. Tears stain my cheeks, and sweat makes my sweatshirt cling to my skin. Romana butts me with her head, and I collapse, relieved. *It was just a bad dream.* I kiss the top of her head and will myself to calm down. *Everything is okay. I'm safe.* I don't sleep again for hours.

Gabriel Mero

Chapter One

When my alarm goes off at 7:45am, I groan. *How is it time to get up already? It feels like I just got to sleep.*

I'm not a morning person, never have been. I'm grumpy and sluggish if I don't get at least ten hours of sleep. I suspect that part of it is due to my anxiety and depression and the fact that I honestly love to sleep. I love the warmth and comfort of a bed. I love the temporary reprieve from the chaos that seems inexorably drawn to me.

I reach out, and my fingers find my new phone—a welcome gift from Grandma. I fumble with it, struggling to see without my contacts. I hate wearing my glasses but grudgingly slide the thick black frames onto my face. I hit the center button, and the tiny screen illuminates. No texts. Not one of my friends has bothered to check in on me from back home. I angrily shut my alarm off. *No snoozing for me today.*

I normally sleep on my side, with Romana curled up against my shoulder, but strangely, I find that I'm lying on my back. I've never been able to sleep on my back unless I have the flu. Romana has nestled into the cleft between my legs, her sides constricting and expanding as she sleeps.

I hate to wake her, but I can't miss my first day of school. "I'm sorry, baby," I murmur, moving my legs. Romana looks at me in confusion and moves to my side. I scratch her ears as I sit up, yawning. *Ugh. I hate mornings.*

I'm grateful that it isn't winter yet. There's nothing I hate more than being forced out of a perfectly warm bed to brave numbing cold. I've always been extremely sensitive to the cold. *What are winters in New England like?*

I force myself onto my feet and across the room. I cross the hall and step into the bathroom. I lock the door behind me and flick the light on. I'm surprised to see a steaming mug of Earl Grey sitting on the sink beside my contact case. *Wish fulfillment?* I wonder, taking a sip. It's the perfect temperature.

As the shower warms up, I prep my inspirational playlist. I listen to the same playlist I've listened to for the last two years or so: "Fantasy," "One Sweet Day," and "Always Be My Baby" by Mariah Carey. *Oh, yeah, Don was delighted that his "son" was a huge fan of the Songbird Supreme.*

After getting out of the shower, I quickly apply my moisturizer before plugging in my blow-dryer. My hair has always been difficult to style as it has a will of its own, but shockingly, I can get it into a messy quiff as long as I keep the top thinned and trimmed and the sides shaved down. My hair is kind of my thing.

Once the top of my hair is standing straight up like I've just had a scare, I lace my fingers with hair wax and work them through my locks. Satisfied that every almost black hair is in place, I apply a thick layer of hairspray and finish the last of my tea.

I stare at my reflection, chewing my lip, contemplating my mirror image. I have a thin, narrow face with a square chin. My alabaster skin hangs tight over high cheekbones. My nose has a long thin bridge – complete with a hump – but ends in wide bulbous nostrils. My eyebrows are relatively thick black caterpillars over wide, blueberry blue eyes. I've never found myself particularly good-looking. Still, I have to admit that it could definitely be worse.

Satisfied that I look passably decent, I go back into my room and throw open the doors to my tiny closet. My myriad collection of shirts hangs on hangers, while my comparatively small collection of jeans are neatly folded on the top shelf.

I reach up and pull down a pair of black skinny jeans. They're my favorite pair. They're made of a stretchy material and are extremely comfortable.

I quickly decide on an old Tegan and Sara shirt. I've never seen them in concert, but it's on my to-do list. I grab a flannel over shirt just in case; I get cold easily and have learned that it's better to be safe than sorry. I pull on my favorite black

Converse high tops to round off the ensemble. I look like a cross between a lumberjack and the lead singer of an early 2000s emo band.

With my outfit complete, I slide my messenger bag over my shoulder and take a deep, calming breath. *You're going to be fine,* I assure myself, wishing that I could actually believe it. I give Romana a quick peck—to which she meows—and head out. I can't be late on my first day.

I go downstairs and deposit my empty mug in the kitchen sink, running some water into it. I'm surprised to see my Grandma sitting at the kitchen table, smiling.

"I'm sorry, was I too loud in the bathroom?" I ask, second-guessing the Mariah.

"Not at all, bubala," my grandmother replies with a warm smile. "I'm not much of a sleeper nowadays."

I nod, checking the time on my phone. If I don't leave soon, I will miss my bus.

"How was the tea?" Grandma asks.

"Are you the one that left it for me?" I inquire.

"I was up anyway. I figured you could use a boost for the day."

"It was much needed, thanks."

Grandma's smile falters, and she leans forward in her chair. "Did you sleep well last night?"

I remember my dream and shiver. I don't ever want to have a dream like that again. "I had a bad dream," I confess.

"I heard you shouting the cat's name."

"In the dream, Don was taking her from me, sending her away." My eyes start to tear up at the memory.

"You and Romana have such a sweet connection," Grandma encourages. "Not every person can bond with a cat like that."

"I've had her since the day she was born. I'm basically all she knows."

Romana's mother, Clara, had snuck out before I could get her neutered and got pregnant. I'd found homes for three of the five kittens, but bonded with Romana and her twin brother, whom I'd named Alistair. Don refused to let me keep three cats, so I'd grudgingly split up my happy cat family. I'd been devastated when Clara went missing, but deep down, I'd been relieved that it wasn't Romana who'd gone outside and never came back.

My Grandma stands up and comes to stand by my side. She opens up her hand to reveal a key fob. I knit my brow in confusion. "Take my car to school," she says. "I rarely use it, and you shouldn't have to waste money on the bus."

I don't know what to say. Don never trusted me with his Escalade. Not once. I've only ever driven my mom's Lincoln Continental.

"Thanks, Grandma," I manage, shocked. I'm not really used to people being nice to me. My mom and I get along pretty well, but we tend to bicker.

"Of course, darling. Be safe."

"I will," I promise.

"And, don't forget to pop in and thank Lilja for getting you in."

"I won't."

Once outside, I stand before my grandmother's pearl white Buick. It doesn't have a scratch on it, and all I can think is that something horrible will happen, that I'm going to be the one to scratch it. *Just breathe,* I tell myself.

I thumb the button, and the key folds out. Not too complex. I climb into the driver's seat and am delighted when I turn the key in the ignition, and the engine purrs to life. I let it warm up for a few minutes while I plug in my aux cord. I scroll through my music library, tapping my thumb against my lip. Mariah Carey, Idina Menzel, Alanis Morissette, Katy Perry, Demi Lovato... Madonna! I delightedly select Madonna's *Ray of Light* album and pull out of the driveway to the thunderous beginning of the opening track, *Ray of Light*.

I feel the tension wane a bit in my body, and I rock out on my way to my next adventure.

Because I drove to school instead of taking the bus, I was one of the first students to arrive. I can feel myself relaxing as I take in the barren parking lot. I get very stressed when I can't find a parking spot. It's actually surprising that I took my grandmother up on her offer to use her car—driving really flares up my anxiety. I spend the whole time stressing that I'm going to get into an accident or kill someone, or something will happen to the car, and I'll be stranded.

I park and switch the engine off. The clock tells me that I have half an hour until my first class begins. *Should I go in and find it, or wait in the car until more people arrive?* I look into the rearview mirror and see that an army of cars is heading my way. The buses can't be far behind. *Guess I'll go, then*, I muse.

I lock the car behind me and sling my messenger bag over my shoulder. It's the end of summer, so it isn't cold despite it being 8:30 in the morning. *Good. I hate the cold.*

I hurry into the building and try to get my bearings. As I expected, I'm totally lost. My high school had four different wings and three floors, but I'd gotten around just fine because each hall was uniform. I feel a pang of sadness that I won't be with my friends from back home. What few friends I did have will soon forget all about me. I'll be lucky to make new friends in Willow's Crest; severe social anxiety doesn't help one make friends.

My first class of the day is British Literature. Many people recommended that I start by taking my prerequisites, and I have. Still, I have no social life to speak of, so I decided to take a few extra classes. I'm already two years behind on my schooling anyway. If Don had had his way, I'd have gone right into college the fall after I graduated. But the uncertainty of whether or not he and Mom would stay together—the fighting had grown exponentially—and general anxiety had stopped me. So now, at almost twenty-one, I am finally tackling this fear.

When I was little, I had this absurd vision that in high school, I'd look like Greg Brady—complete with bell bottoms—and that college would just be me, a small group of students, and a professor sitting in a treehouse on campus. I don't know why that's how I saw it all, but the real thing is much different. As I take in the vastness of the campus, I can't help but wish that we were, in fact, meeting in a tree house.

I look up as a figure emerges from one of the doors and catches my eye. It's a woman with a mess of curly brown hair and penetrating brown eyes hidden behind cats eye rimmed glasses. Her pale skin hangs tightly over high, sharp cheekbones, ending in a wide, square jaw, the kind I've always secretly wanted. From the description my Grandma gave me, this must be Lilja Edwards, the Dean of Admissions.

"Ms. Edwards?" I croak, my voice getting caught in my throat.

"You must be Graham." She pronounces my name perfectly in her cultured British accent. Like my mother, I detest the American pronunciation of my name; it's just so bland and simple. *Gray-am* is so much more sophisticated.

"How did you know?" I hoist my messenger back up onto my shoulder self-consciously.

"This is a small town, and everyone knows I prefer to go by Lilja. Ms. Edwards makes me sound like a school marm."

I can't resist a laugh at her vanity. Something about her suddenly puts me at ease, and I feel the way I used to around teachers I'd known forever, like Mrs. Sawyer back home. I'd had her for English in eighth and ninth grades and then continued to visit her in the morning until I graduated. I've always felt more comfortable around adults and children than people my own age.

"I just wanted to thank you for pulling strings and letting me in past the enrollment date."

Coming to Willows Crest was a last-minute decision, and I missed the cut-off by months. I could have just waited and started classes in the winter semester, but Grandma had insisted that she could make it happen for me now.

"Oh, don't mention it." Lilja waved a dismissive hand. "Anything for a relative of Ginevra's. We go way back, you know."

"Yeah, she said that..." I regard her once more and note that she looks to be in her mid-forties, while my grandmother is in her early seventies.

"We went to school together."

"How?" I blurt before I can stop myself. Obviously, they didn't go to grade school together because of their vast age difference. If Lilja were a medical professional, I could assume they'd gone to nursing school together or something, but that isn't the case, either.

"Let's just say it was a long time ago."

"If you're the same age as she is, kudos to you. You don't look a day over forty!" I know this is supposed to be a compliment, but as the words are tumbling out of my mouth, I also see how they are degrading, too. Before I can apologize, Lilja speaks.

"That's very kind of you to say. I won't tell you how old I actually am, but forty is a milestone I passed ages ago." Her chuckle is throaty, and I relax, knowing I haven't offended her. "Your grandmother is like a sister to me," she says out of the blue.

"She's a great woman."

Lilja suddenly takes my hands in hers and looks deeply into my eyes. "I hope you'll be happy here, Graham. This is your chance to start over, to find yourself. Don't be afraid to come to see me if you need any help."

"I will, thanks." I don't know what else to say. I notice that she's wearing a necklace or rather a small glass jar filled with what looks like herbs. "I like your necklace."

She looks down at it. "Oh, this? Thanks. It's just a little something I made at home."

I notice that the hallways start to fill with bodies as the other students start to trickle in from outside.

Gabriel Mero

"Well, I should get to my first class. Wouldn't want to be late on my first day." I know I sound stupid, but I can't help myself.

Lilja purses her lips and waves dramatically at the hallway. I guess this is her way of dismissing me. I shoot her a tight smile before I take off toward my class. As strange as Lilja is, I feel like I have a kindred spirit in her. People have called me weird my whole life; I've never tried to be anything but myself, but I wouldn't mind being labeled as eccentric. Eccentric is like a nice, cool version of weird.

Being a worrier, I have been studying the campus map religiously the last week. At night, when sleep evades me, I've been mentally plotting every inch out so that I won't get lost. This comes in handy, as I easily find the lecture hall for British Literature.

As I enter the auditorium, I see that the only person in the room besides me is a short woman with glasses and spiky hair. Professor Perrou, I assume. She sees me and smiles. "Welcome," she calls up to me. "Sit wherever you'd like."

"Okay." I plop down into a chair in the first row, as close to her as I can get. Sure, I've always kind of been the teacher's pet, but I also have terrible vision, even with glasses and contacts, so the closer I sit to the front, the easier it is for me to see everything. Plus, I've always felt safer up front, free from the bullies. *Are there bullies in college?* I can't help but wonder.

I hear someone sit in the chair next to mine, which breaks my thoughts. I pretend to be thoroughly engrossed in my papers. It works for five seconds before she speaks.

"Hey," a warm voice says.

Please don't let her be talking to me, I think, as I cautiously cast a furtive glance her way. Sure enough, the girl is looking at me expectantly. She has glasses and dark hair that is pulled back into a braid. She looks harmless. "Um, hey," I grudgingly say.

"It's nice to see that I'm not the only one who likes to be early," the girl continues.

"I hate to be late." I hope she'll take the hint and leave me be.

"Me, too. I'm early for everything."

No such luck. "Same." I don't want to seem rude, but I am hopeless at small talk.

"I haven't seen you before. Are you new?"

"Yeah."

"I'm Amethyst."

Damn, she is persistent. "Graham."

"Oooh, I love how you pronounce that. It's hot."

I feel my face flush scarlet, and she laughs.

"I'm a junior. What year are you?"

"Uh, freshman."

"Nice! Isn't college great? It's like high school just with better sex, more drugs, and legal alcohol."

"Sure…" I have never partaken in any of these activities, though not from lack of desire. I've had a few crushes, but when you're into teachers, it doesn't usually play out as the fantasy would have you believe. I'm not a drinker, not after seeing how alcohol ruined my dad's life. As for drugs, I'm a control freak, so I stay away from the heavier stuff, though I would try pot with someone I trust.

"So, what's your major? Mine is veterinary medicine."

"I haven't decided yet," I confess, examining my cuticles as if they're the most fascinating thing ever. Having an undecided major is a mark of shame on me. At least that's how Don always made me feel.

"Don't worry about it. You have plenty of time to decide. You'd be a sexy writer or something. Maybe grow a little bit of beard, wear just a smidge of eye liner like Johnny Depp in *Pirates of the Caribbean*."

Her narrative is aggressive, unbidden, and it makes me laugh. *Me? Sexy? Not likely.* I am certainly no Johnny Depp, though, to be honest, I have never seen him as attractive.

Before either of us can say anything else, Professor Perrou calls for quiet. *Quiet? When did class even begin? When did the auditorium fill up with students?*

Professor Perrou talks for about forty-five minutes before she dismisses us, and we all rise. I hope that Amethyst will just walk away, but she lets me down once again.

"Let me see your schedule," she says pointedly.

I can't refuse without looking like a total douchebag, so I tentatively hand it over. Her eyes scan the paper hungrily as if she's reading a sordid celebrity tell-all, and then she grins widely. "We have Philosophy together!" she exclaims

"Oh?" I say.

"Thank God. Most of the people that go here suck. You seem pretty cool."

"I do?" I can't mask the incredulity in my voice.

"Of course. For starters, you haven't told me to shut up yet."

"Does that happen a lot?"

"Oh, yeah. I'm Italian. I have a loud mouth, and I speak my mind; it drives people crazy."

I don't want to admit it, but she's starting to grow on me a little. She seems to be an outcast, too. If I don't make at least one friend, it will be a long four years here.

"I should get to class; I don't want to be late on the first day. I'll, uh, see you in Philosophy, I guess," I say, standing.

"Deal."

She walks away with a goofy grin on her face. *Maybe she's just the person to bring me out of my shell a bit.* I hurry off to French class, hoping it isn't too hard to find.

I took French every year from seventh grade until I graduated. I have a natural affinity for languages, I guess because I took to it like a fish to water. Back home, when Madame Benedic called in, she would leave specific instructions for the substitute that I would know how to teach that day's lesson. I was honored to get a moment in the spotlight, though it did little to help me gel better with my peers. I haven't used my French skills much since graduation, so I'm a little rusty, but I'd like to flex my Francophile muscle and get back into shape, so to speak.

The first few minutes pass by relatively painlessly, except for correcting the professor on how my name is pronounced. It's all so predictable: the apologetic smile and affirmative head nod, the snickers from the bullies. I'm over it.

Madame Colbert makes us sit in alphabetical order by last name and then come up with an adjective that describes us that also starts with the first letter as our name. Being in the middle of the alphabet, I sit through Polite Peter, Athletic Aaron, Burnout Brad, Cuddly Cailyn, et al. As it grows nearer to my name, I feel my pulse quicken, and my mind races to come up with an adjective for myself. *Giggling? No. Giant? Hardly? I'm into Star Trek, Star Wars, the Lord of the Rings, Doctor Who,* and things of that nature… *perhaps geeky? Would that be like waving a red flag before the angry bull of the bullies?*

The girl in front of me – Jumping Jessica – takes her turn, and I take a deep breath to steady my hyperactive nerves. "I'm Geeky Graham," I say, instantly regretting it.

There are a few giggles – of the unkind variety – as well as someone saying, "more like Gay Graham," under his breath. This is met with more exuberant laughter.

I feel my cheeks burning but pretend not to have heard it. I have a soft voice; I can't help that. *I'm not gay; I can't be. That's not an option for me.*

Madame Colbert shoots the culprit – Raging Ryan – a death glare. "This is a bully-free university, Monsieur Matthews. If I hear more cruelty like that from your mouth, you'll be talking to the Dean about your homophobia," she says authoritatively.

"Sorry," Ryan mutters, looking like he'd much rather punch me than actually apologize.

After a few moments of silence, we continue the game, and I zone out until we're dismissed. I quickly jump to my feet and try to hurry out the door, but I hear Madame Colbert's voice calling after me. Monsieur Norris?"

Fuck. I stop and turn back toward her. She motions for me to come to her desk, and I swallow past a dangerously dry throat. *Here we go...*

"I just want you to know that you're safe in my classroom. I take the anti-bullying rules very seriously," she says quietly so that my classmates can't hear her.

"Thanks, I... appreciate that," I choke out. "But I'm not gay."

She nods in understanding. "Regardless, I will not tolerate such behavior in my classroom."

"Good," I say.

She pats my bony shoulder comfortingly. "Have a good rest of your first day, dear."

"Thanks, you, too."

I have an hour and a half to kill before my Philosophy class, so I go out to the car and spend it reading.

I find the Philosophy room at the other end of campus. All this walking back and forth across campus is definitely going to help keep me thin. When I enter the classroom, I'm not surprised to see Amethyst in the far left corner, her leg up on the desk beside hers. She's wearing an ecstatic smile that I find endearing. No one has ever looked even remotely that happy to see me before.

"I saved us seats in the back so we could talk," she says as she removes her leg from the seat.

"I'm not really good at multi-tasking" I confess. "Maybe we should keep the talking to a minimum." Her smile falls, and I feel bad for being so rude. "It's nothing personal," I say with a slight smile. "My grades are just really important to me. Even when I pay attention, I barely pass math. I get, like, a C. Philosophy should be easy, but just in case..."

"Math sucks," she agrees, seeming to accept my answer. "But, yeah, I get it. Grades are important to me, too."

The philosophy prof is a lanky old man named Professor Shuck. I'm not big into philosophy, but he seems nice. When he mispronounces my name, he apologizes profusely.

Professor Shuck hands out a class syllabus detailing what we will learn this semester and what materials we'll need for the class. I know that money is tight for Mom, so I'll have to look into a job. I'm not very good at saving money – I like things too much – but I don't want to make things any more difficult for her than I absolutely have to. Don used to give me $100 for every 'A' I'd get on my final report card at the end of each year. I have about $100 left from June. That'll get me my school supplies.

We're dismissed again, and I prepare to trek across the campus to the car. I have no more classes today and am desperate to crawl back into bed and nap. Amethyst stands up and holds out her hand. "Give me your phone," she orders.

"What?" I asked, surprised.

"You heard me. If you're going to make me pay attention in this bullshit class, then you're going to give me your number so we can talk at home. You're my friend, whether you like it or not."

"No offense, Amethyst, but you don't even know me."

"Well, I'm trying to." She snaps her finger, and I dolefully hand her my phone. She replaces mine with her own. I enter my name and number and hand it back as she's finishing with my phone.

'I'll text you later," she says, sliding her phone into the pocket of her jeans.

"I'll answer if I'm by my phone. I'm probably going to take a nap."

"Deal. Unless I can convince you to come hang out with me this afternoon."

"Oh, I can't. My mom needs me home to get my brother off the bus. "

"Cute and responsible. Damn."

I laugh as we make our way out.

We part ways in the hallway, and I turn back and watch her retreating form. I have never had someone fight so hard to be my friend. *My friend*. She seems genuine. Maybe things won't be so bad here in Willow's Crest.

Gabriel Mero

Chapter Two

Well, so far college has not been nearly as terrifying as I had thought it would be, but a part of me is disappointed that there are still no treehouses. Stupid childhood imagination. I'm hoping that Amethyst will lose my number or something; I hate talking on the phone unless I'm extremely close to the person. So, basically just Mom.

I hurry to the Verano and hit the road ahead of the buses. I weave my way through the quiet side streets, anxious to get home and take a nap. I wasn't lying to Amethyst when I told her that I had to be home to help with Brent. Thankfully for me, his school doesn't have a half-day, so I can squeeze in a quick cat nap before I have to take responsibility for him.

When we moved here, my mom was able to transfer to the Kohl's here in Willows Crest. Without Don's impressive income, she has to be financially independent for the first time since she was twenty-six. She works the overnight shift, so I take Brent in the evening while she naps, then she feeds and bathes him. When she leaves at 9:30pm, I put him to bed and then head up to my room. Grandma is more than happy to help, but he isn't used to her yet, so the responsibility falls on me. I don't really like kids, and the last thing I want to do is be tied down with a special needs kid, but we all have our cross to bear.

I pull the Verano into the driveway and unplug my aux cord. It won't play unless it's plugged into my phone, and something tells me my grandmother won't understand that and will think her radio is broken.

When I open the front door, Grandma is sitting in the parlor watching soaps on television while her hands expertly crotchet an afghan for someone at her Temple.

"How was your first day, bubala?" she calls out to me.

"It wasn't totally torturous," I confess. "I made a friend, kind of."

"That's great! I'm so proud of you. I know you don't have it easy with your anxieties."

"Yeah," I agree. "Lilja was nice. How old is she, anyway? She looks so young!"

"She's had work done," my grandma replies with a snicker. "She's been nipped and tucked to within an inch of her life."

Could Lilja really be my grandma's age? I know that plastic surgeons can work wonders, but can they really make you look almost thirty years younger? Lilja doesn't even move like a woman in her sixties or seventies.

"I'm going to go take a nap. I'm exhausted from last night."

"All right. Your mom hasn't awoken yet."

Mom doesn't normally get up until two o'clock. The benefits of working ten to seven.

I take my shoes off and set them on the mat by the door before I pad on stockinged feet up the stairs to my tiny bedroom. It's located at the end of the hallway, secluded from the other two rooms. At least I have some privacy.

As soon as I open the door, Romana looks up, and, seeing me, jumps to her feet, tail swishing excitedly. She doesn't leave my room. Neither Don nor my mother is a fan of cats. The conditions of me having Romana were that she stay in my room and that I clean her litter box and vacuum daily. The most important rule being that she does not damage anything by sharpening her claws. I'd refused to have her declawed; it's convenient but cold-heartedly cruel.

"Hey, Momana," I coo, using my pet name for her. I imagine cats hate it when their owners baby talk to them, but she's so cute, and I can't help myself.

In response, she vocalizes and starts to purr. I sit on the bed next to her and scratch her head. I hate to admit it, but I miss her very intensely when we're not together.

After a few minutes, she jumps off the bed to eat. I change out of my school clothes into my standard bed wear: a hoodie and athletic pants or pajama bottoms. I like to be warm and comfy when I sleep.

I lie back and pull the blankets up to my shoulders. The sudden warmth is Heaven. I hate being cold. I close my eyes and feel a calmness flow through every inch of my body. Romana leaps back onto the bed and lies down on my legs, bringing extra warmth to me.

I don't know if I fall asleep or not. Everything goes still and quiet, and I feel like I'm floating... until I hear a jingling.

I crack open my right eye, and thanks to keeping my contacts in, I'm able to see that the noise is coming from my phone. Someone is calling me. *Who?* No one ever –thankfully—calls me.

I pick my phone up and squint at the screen. It's aglow, and AMETHYST is displayed. For a second, I debate whether to ignore the call, but then I ascertain that Amethyst would just continue to call until I do answer. She's persistent. "Hello," I say sleepily.

"Hey, bitch. What's up?" I can hear a clinking in the background and then, after a few seconds, the sound of Amethyst exhaling.

"I was just lying down to take a nap." Honesty is always the best policy.

"Oh, shit. Sorry," she giggles.

"It's fine." I stretch, causing Romana to move up to my chest. She doesn't often lie there. I sit up, and she stays.

"So, what are you doing?"

"…Just sitting in bed, petting Romana."

"Who's Romana?"

"My cat."

"I *love* cats!" she exclaims. "I have one. I call him Sid Vicious because he's a little asshole. Every day, I tell him I'm going to find a way to make him live forever."

I kiss the top of Romana's head. The thought of losing her makes my chest and throat constrict.

"Can I see her?" Amethyst asks.

"Yeah, one sec." I pull the phone from my ear and take a quick picture with Romana. I ignore how tired I look and how shitty the quality is. I could have taken a nicer photo on my digital camera. After I hit send, I let Amethyst know it's coming.

"Aw, she's so adorable! You're sexy as fuck, by the way."

I blush and barely mutter, "thanks."

"Sorry, I know I'm a bit forward. I'm not flirting with you, though, not really. It's just my personality."

"Okay," I laugh. My phone vibrates, and I see that I have a text from Amethyst. It's a picture of her and a white cat with orange spots in random places. "Sid Vicious, I assume?"

"Yeah."

"He's cute."

"Thanks, I think so." I hear her exhale again. "So, I was wondering what you're doing after class tomorrow."

"I don't have anything *planned*, but I need to be home by six, so I can watch my brother."

"Gotcha. How old is he?"

"He's nine."

"Cool. I always say I want a kid, but I want to skip all the baby shit. If I could get one that was like, eight or nine, I'd be fine."

"He's certainly a handful. My stepdad has turned him into a spoiled brat. And to top it all off, he's Autistic."

"Shit, I'm sorry…"

"It's… whatever," I assure her lightly.

"Well, it's awesome of you to help your mom with him."

"I guess." It's not like I have much of a choice, but I know what she means.

"If you want to do something tomorrow after class, that would be cool. I don't really have any friends to do anything with. We could go shopping or something."

"I think I have just enough money to get my supplies and that's it. I need to look into getting a job."

"Dude, my uncle owns a video store right here in town, and we're looking for another manager. I could get you an interview if you want."

"Really?" I'm taken aback by her bountiful kindness. None of my friends have ever done anything like that for me before. I usually get the friends that use me for money and attention until they find someone better. My guard is always up.

"Yeah, no problem."

"Thank you!" I've never had a job before, but working at a movie store can't be too complex, I suppose. It dawns on me that I'd have to deal with customers and anxiety burns like fire in my stomach. I don't want to be a freak, I want to be able to get a job and live a somewhat normal life. Surely, I can work around my anxiety enough to pull this off. I'd only be working part-time, so we should be able to work that around my mom's schedule. "I appreciate that."

"You're welcome. I don't know if you have a car or not, but I could come get you."

"My grandma lets me take her car sometimes."

"Well, I'm here if you need me. So would you be interested in hanging out tomorrow? I can drive us and have you home by six"

Turning her down would be extremely rude, especially considering how generous she's been, and I do think of her as a friend. "I'll have to check with my mom and let you know."

"Of course. I'm here to help."

"I'm not used to friends actually being friends," I confess.

"Well, get used to it, bitch."

I laugh just before I hear a knocking on my door. "Yeah," I call, and my mom shuffles in.

"Listen, Amethyst, I have to go. My mom wants to talk to me."

"No problem. Text me."

"Okay."

"Bye."

"Bye."

I end the call and turn to see my mom regarding me with a confused look. She has dark brown hair that's bedraggled from sleep. She's pretty, with a nice figure and a bad temper. We have the same thin lips and blueberry colored eyes. She has more a stereotypical Jewish nose than I do, of which I'm envious.

"You're talking on the phone?" she's perplexed.

"Just my friend Amethyst."

"Amethyst? What the hell kind of name is that?"

"Be nice. She's trying to get me a job."

"A job? I can't be shuttling you back and forth to work, and I need you here for Brent," she says, getting riled up.

"I'll talk to the owner and see if maybe I could work on the days you have off. If it's close enough, I can walk."

My mom comes and sits next to me. Romana burrows deeper against me. She isn't too keen on my mom.

"I'm sorry. I'm tired and stressed out. If you want a job, we'll try to make it work."

"I don't *want* a job," I correct her, "but I need new clothes, and I know money is tight."

"It is," my mom agrees, sighing. I know this whole move had been rough on her. After Brent was born, she quit her job and became a housewife. As her relationship with Don began to deteriorate, she consoled herself with dolls. That was fine when Don was paying the bills, but now he's obviously cut her off, and she's in way over her head.

"If you want to go get some more sleep, I'll get Brent off the bus for you," I offer.

"I can't sleep anymore right now, but thanks."

My stomach growls gregariously, and I exhale. I haven't eaten since about nine o'clock last night.

"You didn't eat yet?" my mom asks.

"I wasn't too hungry when I got home. I figured I'd take a quick nap and then make some macaroni and cheese or something."

"We're going to have to get food for Brent once he gets home. We'll have to see if he wants McDonald's or Burger King."

When Brent was younger, he'd eat cottage cheese and mashed potatoes. Somewhere along the line, he switched to strictly fast-food French fries. It's not at all healthy, but what alternative do we have? We're lucky that he'll eat a rice cup and some chips for lunch at school.

"Arby's sounds good to me," I say with a devilish grin. I've been craving a Philly Beef and Swiss for weeks. They don't exactly have them anymore, but the French dip is close enough to sate my hunger.

"You're a little con artist," my mom jokes. "When you were little, I'd get one for myself and one for you. You'd scarf yours down and then sit there and stare at me like a dog until I got pissed and just let you have the rest of mine."

"I was a terrible child," I agree. "Oh, I forgot to tell you. Amethyst wants to go shopping tomorrow. Can I go? She promises to have my back in time for you to go take your nap."

"Who's this Amethyst?"

"Just a girl I met in my British Literature and Philosophy classes."

"Oh." My mom gives me a knowing look.

"We're friends," I clarify, suddenly feeling incredibly awkward.

"As long as you're back in time for me to lie down, I don't see why not," Mom relents.

We walk out of the room and downstairs to the kitchen. I make a peanut butter and jelly sandwich and pour myself a tall glass of milk.

"Beverly," my grandma says, coming into the kitchen at the sound of our voices. "I've got a funeral dinner at Temple I volunteered to work, and then I need to run to the grocery store. Is there anything you'd like me to pick up?"

"Not that I can think of right now," Mom replies. "I'm taking Graham and Brent out for dinner before work. If I need something, I can always run and do it then."

"I wish we could get Brent to eat something besides fries. He's not getting any nutrition. He's going to end up sick." Grandma notices that I'm scarfing down my sandwich. "I don't suppose you've eaten today, either," she says to me.

"No." Back in eighth grade, I started getting an upset stomach quite frequently. I went to a few doctors, but nothing was ever diagnosed. I'd decided that it was best not to eat before or during school. After all, I can't be running to the bathroom if my stomach is empty, right? Sure, I got accused of being anorexic, but I didn't care.

"Both you boys are going to end up in the hospital with malnutrition," Grandma says, shaking her head. She takes her keys out of her purse and leaves. Mom rolls her eyes and starts running water for dishes.

When Brent gets off the bus, we get into my mom's Lincoln and drive across town to the business district. My mom asked Brent where he wanted fries from, and he said McDonald's. Lucky for me, Arby's is a few driveways down.

As soon as we get back home, I tuck into my curly fries. They are greasy and delicious. Ever since I was a kid, I've always eaten my fries first. Mom thinks I'm weird, but then again, she thinks I'm weird for dunking my donuts and cookies in milk.

We eat dinner in relative silence. Mom reads a Stephen King novel, and Brent watches *Spongebob* on his little TV. He likes to find the scenes with explosions and then watch them with the volume blasting. Then he repeats it over and over. I know he can't help it, that it's a quirk of his affliction, but it's annoying. I often feel like I'm living in an insane asylum.

I watch Brent as I eat. He's tiny for his age, with a head of curly blond hair and big, bright blue eyes. He doesn't really look like my mom, but he doesn't look like Don, either. Don was adopted, so we don't know what his parents looked like.

As soon as I've finished eating I move into the family room, where my prized Playstation 2 awaits. I know newer systems have come out since then, but why mess with a good thing? I don't like to spend too much time gaming, but it is effective in helping me shut out the outside world for a bit.

Mom and Brent come in a few minutes later; Brent makes Mom watch annoying videos on Youtube with him. I'm just grateful it's not me, for a change.

"God, that game looks so violent!" Mom exclaims, frowning in disgust as she looks at the TV.

"It's *BloodRayne*," I mutter as if that should mean something to her.

"You're just slashing and hacking those guys up. There's blood everywhere!"

"They're Nazis, it's not like they're good people."

"Fair enough." At around six, Mom stands up. "I have to go lie down now," she announces. I don't respond, because I'm engrossed in decapitating Nazis. "Graham, please pay attention to your brother. You know, check his diaper, make sure he doesn't need anything."

"I'm not twelve," I reply, rolling my eyes. "I've been doing this for years. I know how to take care of him."

"I know." She smiles sadly, goes to take her nap, and I tune my ears to listen to Brent. He's happily clicking away at the mouse and giggling over Lofty from *Bob, the Builder*.

We stay in the family room until Mom gets up at a little after eight. It's dark outside now, and the room has taken on an eerie ambiance. Both Brent and I have been so focused on our entertainment that neither of us has bothered to turn on any lights.

While Mom gives Brent a bath and gets ready for work, I watch a few episodes of *That '70s*

Show on Netflix.

Mom leaves for work at 9:30pm. I always feel an odd melancholy when we say goodbye. It's dumb because she'll be back in ten hours. I shut the TV off in her room and lie in the total blackness, waiting for Brent's breathing to grow steady. Mom is okay with me sleeping in her room, but I prefer my own bed. Plus, I'd miss Romana.

After twenty minutes or so, I ease out of bed and move my pillow to prevent Brent from rolling off the edge. I slip out of the room. On my way upstairs, I can hear Grandma's television humming through the walls. She often falls asleep with it on. I would switch it off for her, but I only have enough energy to get upstairs, brush my teeth, and take my contacts out.

By the time I get back to my room, it's after ten o'clock, and I am tired beyond belief. I take my glasses off and crawl in bed. My anxiety flares up, and I double-check to make sure that my phone is indeed plugged in and charging and that my 7:45am alarm is set.

When I switch my bedside lamp off, I roll over to my left side. Within seconds, I can feel Romana propped up against my shoulder. This has been our nightly ritual since she was a kitten.

I will myself to sleep, but despite my fatigue, my mind wanders to last night and the traumatic dream I had. *Please don't let me have a dream like that again tonight,* I beg silently. If the dream itself weren't traumatic enough, it also deprived me of precious sleep. If there's one thing I can't go without, it's sleep.

I feel myself relaxing and surrendering to the calm.

Chapter Three

When my alarm goes off, I am not as irritated as I usually am. Surprisingly, I slept very well last night. I didn't have any nightmares. In fact, I didn't even dream, at least not that I can recall. My first class isn't until nine-thirty, but I have to be up to get Brent off to school if Mom is late.

I go through my normal morning routine, and then as I'm heading out of my room, I fill Romana's food dish and give her a loving peck.

Downstairs, the house is dark and quiet. Brent is still asleep. Grandma is either asleep or at Temple. Mom isn't home yet; she got out at 7:30, so she should be home at any time. I glance at my phone, it's 7:55. I have about fifteen minutes to catch the bus.

By the microwave, I see a piece of paper strategically laid out. It's a note.

Gone to Temple. Back in the afternoon.

Xoxo Mom/Grandma

Okay, so Grandma isn't home. I already know that Mom won't let me borrow her car for school, so I'll either have to try to catch the bus or walk. It's honestly not a terrible walk, but I have no idea just how long it will take. My stomach twists up into nervous knots, and I hate myself a little. *Why can't I be a normal person? Why do I have to be ruled by near-constant anxiety?*

I hear the front door open, and I feel the tension in my gut loosen exponentially. My mother comes into the kitchen, looking exhausted and looks me over.

"What's wrong?" she asked, eyes wide. "Is Brent okay?"

"He's fine," I answer. I see Mom visibly relax. "Grandma isn't home, and I'm about to miss the bus, I was just getting all worked up."

"You poor kid. You're just a bundle of nerves."

"Yay me," I quip, sliding my messenger bag over my shoulder. "I'd better go before I miss the bus."

"All right. Peace."

"Bye."

As I walk out the door, I pop my earbuds in and turn on the *Rent* soundtrack; it's been a staple in my life since the movie came out my Freshman year of high school. By now it is as familiar to me as my own body.

The bus stop is a few blocks away. I'm surprised when I get to the corner, and I'm the only one there. Either everyone is rich enough to have cars, or I live in a relatively unpopulated area, or I've missed the bus. My nerves set in again, and I repeatedly tap my shoes on the cement as the guitar on the album blares to life.

After a few minutes, I see a big gray bus approaching. Once again, I almost instantly relax, though my mind does whirl in a mental hurricane when I think about what happens *after* I get on the bus. Where am I going to sit? Am I going to have to sit with a stranger?

These thoughts eddy in my head as the bus hisses to a stop before me. Slowly, I step up, nodding to the bus driver before seeing the first seat—directly behind the bus open. Grateful, I collapse into the seat and close my eyes, letting the music take over. My mind and body go on autopilot.

****

As I'm walking out of my American History class, Amethyst manifests by my side. "If we don't hurry, we'll be spending most of our lunch in line," she says.

"I don't eat," I inform her, looking down at my feet.

"I can tell that by looking at you," she laughs. "Eating is good for you, but I'm not your Mom, I won't make you. Do you want to go grab us a table, then?"

"Sounds like a plan."

My high school didn't have a cafeteria. Lunch was held in the commons. We also had three lunche periods to accommodate the large number of students in the school. Burnham University has a proper cafeteria like we had back in elementary school. Instead of the round black tables back home, Burnham has the traditional long brown ones.

I sit down at a vacant table in the front row. I can see Amethyst waiting to pay for her wrap and fries. She waves exuberantly as I pull my sketchpad out of my messenger bag. Back in high school, during lunch, I used the half-hour to work on homework from my previous classes, but I don't have any homework yet. I can't read my book because Amethyst would be upset, so I decided to draw.

I've been drawing for as long as I can remember. I wouldn't say that I'm exceptionally talented at it, but I'm better than most untrained people. Since kindergarten, I've taken art classes, and it has helped me immensely. My art teacher back home – Mrs. Rinke – taught me so much. She taught me how to do shading properly, that the eyes are placed in the exact center of the head, and that the distance between the eyes is equal to the width of one eye. I'll never be good enough to make a career out of it, but it's a fun hobby.

Amethyst sits down across from me, her tray exuding the delicious smell of greasy fries. My stomach grumbles hungrily, and a wave of nausea washes over me. I will the bile not to come up.

"Are you sure you don't want a bite of my wrap? It's chicken bacon ranch," Amethyst says, holding the unbitten half out toward me.

"No, thanks," I say. "I'm Jewish, so no pork."

"You're Jewish? That's so cool! I've never met an actual Jew before. I'm an atheist."

"It's pretty cool. I think my favorite part about Judaism is we believe that Heaven has an open door policy; no matter your faith, if you're a good person, you can get into Heaven."

"I love that. So, why don't you eat?" Amethyst queries, plopping a golden fry into her mouth.

"I have issues," I reply. I don't really want to go into detail. It's embarrassing to admit that I have a spastic colon.

"Anorexia?" she guesses, her voice devoid of judgment. I appreciate that more than I can possibly fathom.

"I wish it were that simple," I laugh bitterly. "It's my stomach."

"Say no more." Amethyst holds both hands up in surrender. I smile gratefully that she doesn't want to delve deeper into my neuroses and gastrointestinal ailments.

I flip through my sketchpad to my last semi-completed drawing. It's Piper and Phoebe Halliwell and Paige Mathews from Charmed. It's one of my favorite TV shows, and I like to draw the book and DVD covers. I start to darken the pencil of Piper's long hair.

"What's that?" Amethyst asks, peering up over the rims of her glasses. I can't help but wonder if this technique actually helps her see better or if it's just a force of habit. I move the pad so that she can see it better. "Wow, that's really good!"

"Thanks." I'm pretty sure even my ears turn red at the compliment.

"My mom loves that show. She has them all on DVD. One episode per disk." She rolls her eyes dramatically.

"One episode per disk? My sets have at least three episodes per disk. Mostly four."

"She has burned copies."

"Oh, okay."

"She didn't know that you can put more than one episode per disk." Her face goes dark as if recalling something bad. "When I was sixteen, she, uh, got in a car accident. She suffered major brain damage. I've been on my own ever since."

"I'm sorry," I say sincerely. I can't imagine having something terrible like that happen to my mom.

"It's fine. She lives with my grandparents."

"Where do you live?"

"I have my own apartment in town."

"That's pretty awesome." I'm impressed.

"So, you never told me where you lived before."

"Chesterfield, Michigan."

"Where's that?"

"It's a suburb about a half-hour south of Detroit."

Amethyst knits her brow. "If you're from Detroit, then why are you white?"

I burst out into laughter. Amethyst is paraphrasing a quote from *Mean Girls*.

"I'm actually from Detroit."

"Really? What are the chances of that? We are both from the Detroit area, and now we're here in Willows Crest."

"Looks like we were destined to be friends. It's Bashert." I smile at her.

"So, you like witches?"

Like is an understatement. I have loved witches for as long as I can remember. Some of my earliest memories are watching *The Wizard Of Oz* and idolizing the Wicked Witch of the West. Since then, if it involves witches, it's great by me.

"Love," I answer simply.

"I'm a witch," Amethyst states matter-of-factly.

"That's cool." I have always wanted to try witchcraft for real, but I have been halted by the ingredients and tools needed for most spells.

"Are you into witchcraft?"

"I think it's interesting," I reply. "I tried a few spells back in middle school."

"What were they? Did they work?" She looks at me intently.

"Simple stuff, really," I shrug. "Make it rain, stop the rain, warm myself up, lose weight. One time I did a stupid one on my little brother to give him the mind of a frog... and before you ask, no, he doesn't hop around our house and eat flies," I snicker.

"Did the others work?"

"I like to *think* that they worked. Who knows? Maybe when I did the rain ones, it was supposed to rain or stop raining. The heat one, I remember that one perfectly. It was winter, and I was walking to my bus stop. You know about cold Michigan winters." Amethyst nods in agreement. "I was getting colder and colder, and I remembered this spell I'd seen online. I chanted it five times and suddenly felt this intense burst of warmth in my chest." I shrug again. "But whether the spell actually worked or it was psychological, who can say?"

Amethyst slides the last of the wrap into her mouth, chews, and swallows. "I think they all worked, except for the frog one. I know this sounds crazy, but when we met yesterday, I felt an intense power within you."

"Intense power in me? Come on," I laugh. "I suffer from extreme anxiety. The only power I possess is the intense power to make myself a nervous wreck."

"You have to be more confident." Amethyst encourages. "You're seriously so much more than you think you are." I frown at her questioningly, and she smiles. "I'm an empath. I can feel your self-doubt."

I don't know what to say. I check my watch. It's getting time to head to my next class. I have never been so thankful to be interrupted.

The rest of the day goes by normally. I'm that weird guy that actually likes school. I feel comforted by the structure and the routine of it all.

I meet Amethyst outside of her last class for the day. She asks if I'm ready to go shopping.

"Sure," I say, slipping my plaid overshirt on in case it's cold out.

In silence, we walk out to the parking lot, and as soon as we're outside the building, Amethyst lights up a cigarette. She offers one to me, but I politely decline.

"I hope I didn't freak you out too badly earlier," she says, turning the car on.

"Not at all. I'm open to things. To be honest, you're the only person that I've told that to. Anyone else would call me crazy if I told them that I used to do spells."

"Why did you stop?"

"A lot of the spells I saw required candles and spices and stuff. I couldn't ask my mom or stepdad to get them for me. My stepdad gave me enough shit about liking *Charmed*."

"Why?"

"He felt that it was a show for women and that witchcraft is for teenaged girls."

"Fuck him."

She pulls into the Walmart parking lot and shuts the engine off. We walk in and stop at the Subway first to get frozen drinks. I love frozen drinks! Content, we head back to the office supply section.

As we're sifting through the supplies, I realize that this is the first time I've gone shopping without my mom or Don. *How pathetic is that?* I don't know Amethyst too well yet–it's been a day—but I feel safe and comfortable around her.

We grab folders, notebooks, binders, pencils, and pens. Neither of us is entirely involved in the process. We're grabbing what we need and throwing the stuff into the cart, mindless as automatons.

We stop in the clothing section and Amethyst grabs a few blouses before steering me toward the men's section.

"Now that we're friends, I have to say, the whole emo lumberjack thing is tired. The flannel? What are you, a lesbian? Let's get you something more your style."

"How do you know what my style is?" I ask, trying not to be offended at her brutal honesty.

"I'm an empath, remember? I can feel your emotions, I can read who you are deep in inside, all the things you try to hide or don't want to admit."

My throat goes tight and my heart races at this, but I don't know what to say. Can she really see all the parts of me that I try to hide?

She stops next to a rack and hands me a purple short sleeved button up shirt. "This is so you. You can wear a tank top underneath it if you want, or not. But purple is your color.

"Thanks." I look at the shirt and see that it has small red blossoming flowers on it as well. It doesn't look bad, honestly, it's just not something I'd have picked out on my own. The price tag says $36.99. I have enough to get it, so I set it on my pile of notebooks in our cart.

I want to go look at the DVDs and books, but I know I don't have any extra money, and I don't see the point in torturing myself.

"Is there anything else you need while we're here?" Amethyst asks, glancing at a celebrity tabloid as we head back the way we came in.

"I'm good for now, thanks," I assure her.

We get into a checkout lane and purchase our goods. I'm sad to see a huge chunk of my very limited funds going out the door.

Back at the car, Amethyst lights up another cigarette. She and my mom will love each other when they eventually meet.

"Where do you live?" she asks me as we pull out into traffic.

"It's on Roseland Drive."

"Holy shit," she whispers.

"What?" I demand, my heart suddenly beating faster.

"We're practically neighbors. I can totally give you a ride to class on the days your grandma needs the car."

"That would be nice, thanks."

She waves it off. "If you get the job at the video store, you'll be working with me, so I could take you home afterward, too."

"I've never had a job before," I confess.

"So? My uncle will love you."

"I have, like, no people skills."

"It's a movie store; all you have to do is say "hi," ring them up, and tell them to have a good day. We're not extremely busy. Since Netflix, Hulu, Vudu, Amazon Video, and Redbox, video stores are pretty much obsolete. Most of the time, we'll be cleaning shelves and looking for missing movie covers."

"Missing movie covers?"

"People let their bastard kids run loose in the store like savages. They put their grimy hands everywhere and move the cases. It's annoying as fuck, but it's a job."

I silently agree.

She pulls into the parking lot of a nondescript building. If it weren't for the small showcase with the old-fashioned film reels and popcorn display, I'd have no idea that it was a video store.

Amethyst puts her cigarette out on the pavement and leads the way inside. She's greeted by a short middle-aged man. He smiles warmly and gives her a hug. "Uncle Vito, this is my friend Graham," she introduces me with a flourish.

Normally I'd be a bundle of nerves, but with Amethyst here, I feel grounded. I shake Vito's hand, Don's voice in my head barking that a man has a firm, confident handshake, and maintains eye contact. "I've heard so much about you," Vito says and leads us out of the main room and into a cozy office. He sits at the desk, and I sit across from him.

"You have?" Honestly, I'm not surprised that Amethyst has talked about me.

"I told him you're a great person and that you're perfect for this job," Amethyst interjects.

"Do you have any work experience?" Vito inquires.

"No," I confess. "I help take care of my Autistic brother in my spare time. Unfortunately, it doesn't pay. I know my generation isn't known for its exceptional work habits, but I assure you that I will be on time every day. I'll even be early if at all possible. I'll stay as late as you need me to, as long as my mom doesn't need me at home."

I hear the words coming out of my mouth and I am astounded. *Where is all of this coming from? I don't sound like me. I sound like Don. Maybe all those years with him weren't completely terrible…*

Vito chews his bottom lip in contemplation. "How old are you?"

"I'll be twenty in October."

Vito nods and glances up at Amethyst. He sighs. "All right, I'll give you a shot. Any friend of Amethyst's can't be too bad."

He reaches into his desk and roots around for a minute before pulling out a stack of papers. He slides them across the desk to me. "Those are your W-2s. I'll need those back from you as soon as possible."

"Is it all right if I take them home with me? I've never filled one of these out. I'll have to have my mom help me." It kills me to admit that last part.

"Of course. Just bring them back when you start."

"When do I start?" I ask.

"How does Friday sound?" Vito suggests.

"Sounds great to me," I nod in affirmation.

We shake hands again, and Vito leads the way back into the main store. He goes up to the computer and hits a few buttons. He asks for my name, address, and phone number. "I'm setting you up with an account," he explains over his shoulder. After a few more seconds, he exclaims, "Done."

"Let's go pick out some movies," Amethyst suggests, walking past the counter and into the store proper. "We get them for free."

My eyes take in the plethora of movies lining the shelves. I've always loved movie stores. I don't know if it's being around so many movies or the explicit promise that you'll leave with a new story or an old favorite. It's akin to my love of bookstores.

The store is small, but the selection is impressive. I gasp in excitement when I spot *Scream 4*. I'd wanted to go see it in theaters, but my mom hadn't been convinced that it would be good, since she'd hated the third one. Don hates horror movies, so I didn't end up getting to go.

"I've seen it. It's really good," Amethyst intimates.

We check our movies out, say goodbye to Vito, and get back in the car. It's getting to be time for me to go.

Amethyst expertly navigates to my street, and I point out the two-story colonial that my Grandma built after her original family home burned down in the late 70s.

"I love it," she purrs, looking up at it appreciatively.

"Do you want to come inside?" I ask.

"Normally, I'd say yes, but my mom is staying with me for the week," she explains.

I open the door and get out, ensuring I have my messenger bag, papers, and supplies.

"Thanks for hanging out with me," Amethyst says, smiling sadly.

"Thank you for taking me and for helping me get the job," I reply.

"Hey, that's what friends are for."

I smile and shut the door. "Have a good night."

"You too."

I walk up the driveway and onto the front porch. I look back and wave before Amethyst honks the horn and drives away.

Inside, I'm greeted by my mother. "How'd it go?" she asks.

"I got the job."

"Good for you!" She lightly punches my shoulder.

"And I made a friend. I definitely made a friend." Hearing those words come out of my mouth makes me grin from ear to ear.

Gabriel Mero

Chapter Four

By the time my last class ends on Friday afternoon, I feel like I'm going to throw up. *Why the hell did I think that I could work at the video store? I'm going to mess something up terribly and get fired, and then Amethyst will hate me for making her look bad.*

I rarely got compliments during the fourteen years that I lived with Don. He focused solely on the negative and in the most savage way possible. He couldn't reprimand me without turning me into his own personal punching bag. It's no wonder that I'm a nervous basket case. I don't want to be the victim. I really don't. I don't like people who allow themselves to be victimized. I believe in being strong and owning your shit, and yet...

Amethyst is waiting patiently by the doors for me when I arrive. I don't have a lot of homework for the weekend –thank God–but I do have a lesson review in Remedial Math and a weekend reading lesson in English.

One thing I miss about high school are the lockers. I hate carrying all of my stuff with me or having it in the car. My mind isn't always the most coordinated, so I am constantly checking and double-checking myself; it's exhausting.

"How are you feeling?" Amethyst can clearly sense my nervousness. Maybe she really is an empath.

I groan loudly. "All I can think about is that I'm going to mess something up and end up getting fired."

"You'll be fine," she assures me as she opens the side door leading out to the western parking lot. Outside, she lights up a cigarette, and the smoke wafts my way, recalling distant memories of visiting with my dad as a kid. He smoked a lot, and every time I smell cigarette smoke, I automatically think of him.

I haven't seen my dad in years. Actually, the last time I saw him was at my graduation. It was awkward, but thankfully he didn't stick around long after the ceremony. He was never willing to make the drive to come see me. He'd call once in a while to talk, say all the things a Dad is supposed to say, then he'd promise to call the following Sunday and promptly forget for a month or two. Every birthday and Christmas, I'd get a card with $50. He was mostly nonexistent, but at least he made the attempt sometimes... I have no idea where he is now.

"I know I sound neurotic," I continue, standing upwind of Amethyst and her distracting smoke.

"Not at all. It sounds like your stepdad was a total dick to you. He completely shattered your self-confidence and made you feel like you're not good enough."

"Yeah."

"Well, he's wrong. You are amazing, and anyone who tells you differently will have to deal with me. I'll kill them."

That makes me giggle, and I hop into the passenger seat of her car. "I appreciate that, but to be fair, you've only known me for like, three days."

"Three glorious days, and that's enough to see that you're awesome."

I stare out the window and worry my lip with my teeth. "I'm just so scared of messing up and you hating me for it."

"Why would I hate you?"

"Because you vouched for me."

"All I did was bring you in for the interview. You got yourself the job."

I don't quite believe her, but even if she did have a hand to play in it, she'd never admit it. Amethyst has made it her goal to cure me of my low self-esteem. I love her for that.

We park, and I start fidgeting. It's showtime. I feel like an actor that has just walked on stage to a full house only to realize he's forgotten all of his lines.

"Relax, breathe," Amethyst soothes. I don't point out that I *am* breathing already.

We go inside and tuck our belongings under the front counter. Vito greets us warmly, hugging Amethyst and shaking my hand. "I just got done putting the new releases for next Tuesday into the system. If you two could clean the cases and put the labels on them, that would be great," he says.

"Do you want us to put the disks in them, too?" I ask.

"Please."

Vito goes into the office to grab us some empty rental cases. Amethyst opens the drawer and pulls out a squirt bottle and some cleaning cloths.

Vito returns with a stack of cases that towers over his head. Instinctively, I reach out and help him before they scatter everywhere. He smiles gratefully and sets them on the floor. "I'm going to go have dinner with my family. I'll be back at close to lock up the shop. If you need anything, call me."

As soon as he leaves, I turn to Amethyst. "He closes at the end of the night?"

"The manager, Derrick, used to, but he shafted us and quit spur of the moment."

"Why?"

"He felt he was entitled to more than $10.50."

"We make $10.50?" That seemed like an extravagant amount of money for such a simple job.

"We make $9.25," Amethyst corrects me. "Derrick made more, obviously, because he was the manager." She sighs. "I feel for Vito. He opens at eleven, works until three when I can come in, then goes. He comes back at nine to close the place up."

"That does sound like a lot of running around." I start removing disks from DVD cases and placing them inside the empty rental cases. "How many people work here?"

"You and me, basically," she says, spraying the cases and wiping them. "On the days we don't work, he just works an open to close."

"Wow."

"But not for long. I can tell you'll do well, and then you can be promoted to manager."

"What?" I sputter. "No! You've been here longer, and you're his niece. If anyone gets it, it should be you."

"I'll take the pay raise, but I don't want the responsibility."

The door opens, dinging. We look up from our tasks and see a middle-aged couple walking toward us.

"That's all you," Amethyst says under her breath.

"Hi!" I say too enthusiastically. The man and woman look at me like I've suddenly grown a second head. "I suck at this," I whine to Amethyst.

"It was a little much, but too much is better than too little. Just try to find somewhere in the middle. You don't want to be too nice and scare them off, but you also don't want to be aloof or rude and make them think they're bothering you."

I nod, trying to process it all. I feel like my synapses are working overtime.

The couple take a few minutes to wander through the store before coming back to the desk with a stack of movies.

"Sorry about before," I say lamely. "It's my first day, and I'm a little nervous." I think that being honest will get you somewhere in life.

"I just assumed you were really friendly," the husband replied, laughing. His Sam Elliot-esque mustache bounces with the movement.

Amethyst has been coaching me on how to ring a customer up for the last day, and now, she politely stands back to let me try it on my own, but she stays close. Her presence is a huge comfort to me.

"Uh, what's the last name?" I ask, clicking on the small gray box at the bottom of the screen.

"Deshais," the man replies. "D-E-S-H-A-I-S."

I type it in, and Greg Deshais pops up under the customer ID.

"Greg?" I ask, just to be sure.

"That's me."

I slide his movies over to me and punch in the numbers on the labels. After entering each one, I glance up to make sure that the correct title is on the screen. Once all four movies are entered, I find the button that has a hand and money. I click on it, and the payment screen pops up with the total and accepted payment methods. "Uh, that'll be $10.60, please," I say, trying to keep my voice steady.

Greg hands me a $20 bill.

"Out of $20?"

"Please."

I hit cash and then $20. Another screen appears with the correct change. I count out the $9.40 and hand it to him. "The black cases will be due back tomorrow, and the red cases will be due on Monday," I say.

"All right. Take it easy," he nods at me.

"Thanks, you, too." His wife smiles at me warmly, her eyes crinkling sincerely.

As soon as they are out the door, I whirl around to Amethyst, who is beaming.

"You killed it!" she enthuses, giving me a high five. "See?"

"I was pretty good, wasn't I?" I can feel pride swelling in my chest.

"I'll keep working on these cases if you want to ring everyone up tonight."

"Okay," I nod. "I can do this." As pathetic as it is, I feel like I'm on top of the world. I feel invincible.

By eight o'clock, Amethyst has finished the cases, and we've moved on to arranging the shelves. It honestly isn't too bad; a few misplaced covers here and there, but nothing terrible.

I walk back to the counter and take a quick sip of my Earl Grey. Vito has a microwave in his office, and I couldn't resist a good cup of comfort. As I swallow the citrusy tea, I realize just how badly I need to pee. "Is there a bathroom in here?" I inquire.

"No, you'll have to go out in the back alley." My eyes widen in shock, and Amethyst roars with laughter. "I'm just kidding, dork. There's a bathroom in Vito's office."

I nod and dash inside. The bathroom is across the room and, honestly, looks like a closet. I quickly do my business and wash my hands. When I come out, Amethyst is zipping up her hoodie.

"I'm going out back for a cigarette," she says, pulling her pack of hand-rolled cigarettes out. "There's a customer in the store."

"Okay."

"I'll be right back." Amethyst goes out the door, and I go to stand behind the counter. I peer into the store and see the back of a guy.

Satisfied that he's preoccupied, I fish my phone out of the pocket of my jeans and check to see if I have any text messages. I honestly don't know why. Mom, Grandma, Vito, and Amethyst are the only people who have my new number. I'm connected to my old friends on Facebook, but I haven't been able to bring myself to go on yet. The idea of seeing my "friends" going about their lives without me is a painful thought.

I shake my head and slide my phone back into my pocket. Suddenly, movies slam down on the counter, and I gasp, hand flying to my heart. I was not prepared for that. "Sorry," I murmur, "I was just checking…"

The rest of my sentence dies in my throat as I look at the guy across the counter from me. He's about five foot nine, with a slim, sinewy physique. Decent biceps bulge out of a tight black shirt, and I can see that his arms are covered in tattoos. His styled hair is jet-black, and his brown eyes seem to pierce my soul. It's hard to guess his age. He looks both young and old, simultaneously.

A strange feeling comes over me, and my mouth opens and closes several times with nothing coming out. *What is happening to me?* He continues to stare at me, either oblivious to my inability to think or speak or waiting for me to get my shit together.

He's the kind of guy that women go nuts over, and as I take in his thin lips, I can't help but wonder what they would feel like pressed against mine or kneading the soft, sensitive flesh of my long, pale neck.

No!

I shake my head and clear my throat, my face flushing. "I-I'm sorry," I stammer, looking away.

"It's all right," the guy says, chuckling. His voice is deep.

"What's... what's your last name?" My thoughts are cloudy as I try to function. *What the hell is going on with me?*

"Mayfair."

I'm more than happy to look away from him as I type his last name into the system. An account for Erasmus Mayfair comes onto the screen.

"Erasmus?" I croak.

"Mhm."

Who names their kid Erasmus? I wonder as I enter the numbers into the computer. I glance to check that the title is correct and frown. A small gray box shows that the title does not currently have an active status.

I glance up at him. He's staring at me intently.

"It says the title doesn't have an active status," I force myself to say. "It's my first day..."

"I didn't think you looked familiar," he replies calmly.

"It'll just be a minute. My coworker went out for a cigarette."

"No worries."

His voice has a musical quality that makes me want to surrender myself to him, no questions asked. But I can't. I won't. *I'm not gay.*

Amethyst comes in and sees us. "Hey, Erasmus! How have you been?" she asks.

"Not bad. You?"

"Same. Working here."

"His movie has an inactive status," I interrupt, my voice sounding reedy in my head.

Amethyst squeezes in next to me and clicks on an icon that looks like a magnifying glass. She types in the number, and the movie pops up. She hits a pencil icon, and all the copies of the title are displayed. She selects the specific copy. The status says sold. She makes a *tsk* sound before making it into an in-store copy.

While Amethyst works, I can feel Erasmus' eyes on me, almost searing my flesh. It takes all of my willpower to keep my eyes on the screen and not stare into the tantalizing depths of his eyes. Amethyst fixes it and explains it to me, but I don't hear her words. My heart is thumping in my ear, drowning everything else out. She waves her hand in front of my eyes, and I snap out of it.

"Sorry," I shake my head again. "$3.18, please."

Erasmus hands me a $5 bill, and when our hands touch–ever so briefly—I feel as though I've been struck by lightning.

"$1.82." I hand him the change. Again, our skin touches for a mere second, and my body floods with light. "It's due back on Monday."

"Thanks."

Our eyes meet again, and I struggle to will my lungs to fill with air as I inhale. Something freaky is definitely going on.

He nods at Amethyst and departs.

"Don't worry, he has that effect on most girls," she says when he's gone.

"Huh?"

"He's fucking hot."

"I'm not gay," I rasp.

"Oh. I'm sorry. I kind of assumed you were..."

"Well, I'm not." Face blazing, I walk away to go wash shelves.

I'm quiet for the rest of the shift and most of the ride home. *Seriously, what was that?* I wouldn't call what I felt for Erasmus attraction, per se, but....

No. I can't be attracted to him because that would make me gay, and I'm not gay. Don's pontifications about how disgusting being gay is and that if I ever brought a boyfriend home, I'd be out on my ass so fast my head would spin, resonate in my mind. They reverberate eternally, into forever.

Amethyst pulls into my driveway and turns to me. "I'm sorry if I offended you earlier," she says.

"Huh?"

"What I said, thinking you were gay."

I shrug it off. "It's fine, but I'm not."

"Okay." She exhales a bilious cloud of cigarette smoke. "You were on fire tonight. You impressed the hell out of me."

I meet her gaze and smile. "Thanks."

"Vito was really impressed, too. If you keep that up, you'll be the manager in no time."

"Yeah, right." I yawn, exhaustion taking hold of my body.

"Go in and get some sleep. We're back at it again tomorrow."

I nod and open the door. "Thanks for the lift."

"Of course."

I trudge my way up to the house and through the door. I'm in the hall, and there's no sign of anyone. I force myself up the steps and into my room. I toss my jacket and messenger bag onto my chair and collapse face down onto the bed. I'm fast asleep before I can even feel Romana's sandpaper tongue licking my face.

I'm dreaming again. I don't know how I can tell for sure, but I can.

I look around me, and I'm in some kind of crypt. It's dark wherever I am and cold. I don't know why, but I'm scared, trembling. Why am I here? How did I get here?

A torch sputters to life on the wall, and I turn to see Erasmus standing before me. My breath catches in my throat as he slowly walks toward me. *Is he why I'm here? Did he kidnap me?*

Erasmus stops before me, and I can see that his eyes are no longer brown but a deep, violent blood red. "I've been waiting for you," he says, his voice barely more than a whisper.

My stomach aches with stress and a yearning at his voice, and a soft cry escapes my lips.

Erasmus leans in, and I can feel his hot breath on me. Goosebumps rise on my flesh, making me shiver. He reaches out and rips the collar of my hoodie away, revealing my pale neck. Before I can react, his lips are on my neck, caressing the skin and nibbling it with his sharp teeth.

I realize that my hands are chained above my head as I thrash in ecstasy.

He smiles and works his way down my body, making me arch my back in anticipation.

I cry out as pleasure alights throughout my entire body, taking hold and continuing relentlessly on. The pressure builds deep inside me until, with a triumphant cry of exultation, I burst.

I jolt awake, quivering. *Did I really just...* My hand moves down to the front of my pants and comes away wet and gooey. Disgusted, I yank the pants and my boxers down, letting them lie on the floor. *Why did I have that dream? Why was it Erasmus making me feel so... good?* My thoughts whirl in my foggy head, but before long, my eyelids grow heavy again, and against my will, I slip back into unconsciousness.

Chapter Five

I love weekends, mainly because I can sleep in as late as I want to. I have nowhere to be and nothing to do until three, so I'm free to exist only in my subconscious.

When I am pulled back to reality, I roll over and snatch up my phone. I am as blind as a bat without my glasses or contacts in. I hold the phone close enough to see more than a blur and squint.

8:39am. I was hoping that I'd sleep in later than that, but I can't complain too much. It's better than 5:45am, and I did get my required ten hours.

Romana jumps to her feet and squeaks as I sit up. She probably needs food or water. I reach out toward my nightstand and fumble around trying to find my glasses case, but then I remember, I passed out last night before taking my contacts out. I can't see because the contacts are slathered in eye boogers.

I get up and feel a breeze on my naked lower half. *Huh? Where are my pants?* I throw on a fresh pair of pajama pants – the fuzzy blue ones with polar bears that match my bathrobe – and stumble across the hall into the bathroom. I pull my contacts out, and the room gets noticeably fuzzier. I pull open the mirror and take down the two boxes containing my contacts. I definitely didn't win the genetic lottery when it comes to my eyesight. I'm near-sighted in one eye, far-sighted in the other, and I also have astigmatism in my left eye. Because of this, I have to have a special contact for my left eye that accommodates it.

After blindly scrabbling around, I put in a fresh pair of contacts, and the world is suddenly high-definition. I blink, and the excess solution runs down my cheeks like tears.

After using the toilet, I pad back into my room to discover that Romana is out of food. "Sorry, baby," I say as I cross to the closet. The purple bag of cat food is neatly nestled in the bottom next to my hamper. I fill her dish, and she hungrily pounces on it as soon as it hits the blue tray.

I yawn and stretch, and then the last twenty-four hours come flooding back to me like a tsunami wave. The new job went relatively well, but Erasmus… and the wet dream….

I spot my soiled jeans in a messy heap on the floor and quickly toss them into my hamper. For a split second, I feel like I'm in the clear, but then I remember that my mom will come in and empty my hamper. The thought of her finding my wet, cum-stained underwear and pants make me feel nauseous. *I'll just have to beat her to the punch.*

I heft the handled hamper and go downstairs. From the living room, I can hear the TV softly playing. It sounds like the news or some kind of talk show. *Grandma must be up.* I can also hear obnoxious noises coming from the family room, so Brent must be up watching *SpongeBob* or some equally annoying show.

I hope to sneak downstairs and throw my clothes in the washing machine without getting caught. If my mom catches me washing my own clothes, she'll know that something is up.

I tiptoe down the stairs, grateful they don't squeak in protest like they always do in the movies. *I might just stand a chance here.* I turn the corner and crash right into my mom. I drop the hamper, and the clothes scatter across the basement's cement floor.

"Sorry," I mutter, bending down and gathering the laundry as quickly as I can. I shovel it back inside, hoping and praying that my mom won't see the stains.

"What are you doing?" Mom asks, astonished.

"Laundry, what does it look like?" I say. It sounds harsher than I intended, and I can see the flames starting to burn inside my mother's head. *Oh shit, I've awoken the dragon.*

Her hand snakes out and latches onto my ear, her grip tight on the cartilage. It doesn't hurt too badly, but enough to make me gasp. "Don't you ever fucking talk to me like that!" she hisses, her voice low in her throat.

I shrug out of her grasp as soon as she loosens it and start filling the empty washing machine. Although I've never really done my own laundry, common sense takes over, and I soon have it filling with water.

I go back upstairs, feeling guilty. I lashed out at my mom because I was defensive and pissed off about Erasmus. She has a lot on her plate; I shouldn't be adding to her stress by taking my problems out on her.

I quickly do the dishes, clean the stove, and sweep the kitchen before moving to the bathrooms. Anything I can do to take some of the heat off of my mom.

I'm cleaning my toilet when Grandma walks by and stops. "Kids your age do housework?" she asks, aghast.

I can't help but smile. "Some of us do," I assure her.

"You're a good kid, you know that?"

I want to believe that, but I can't. If I was such a good kid, then Don wouldn't have disciplined me the way he did all those years.

My Grandma once again seems to read my mind and smiles warmly. "Don't let others' opinions of you define who you are, Graham. People see what they want to see and act how they want to act. That's nothing to do with you. Do you work?"

"Yes," I answer.

"Do you help take care of your brother?"

"Yes."

"Do you keep yourself out of trouble?"

"Yes."

"Do you do well at school?"

"Except for math, yeah."

"Then, see? You are a good kid." She strokes my head lovingly. "You're worth so much more than you know, bubala."

I feel my eyes start to sting with tears and turn to scrub the shower so that Grandma won't see the tears in my eyes. I focus on cleaning my shower. The disinfecting wipes do a good job of cleaning, but they go too quickly. I save one to use on the floor.

Grandma is still hovering in the doorway. "Tonight is Shabbat dinner. There'll be leftovers in the fridge when you get home. I need to go out, do you need me to pick you up some more of those when I'm at the store?" she asks.

"Yes, please. If you would." The thought of cleaning bathrooms without the wipes irks me. Before I knew that the wipes existed, I used one rag for the toilet – thrown away after each use – and one for the sink and shower. I think about people with poor hygiene reusing toilet rags, and my stomach groans in protest.

"Are you hungry?" Grandma inquires, hand on her hip.

"A little," I confess. "More nauseous than anything."

"You've got to start eating better, Graham. You don't want to end up in the hospital."

She's not wrong there. The last thing I want is to be stuck in a hospital bed with IVs in me while a nurse watches my every move. I shudder.

"What time do you work today?"

"Three."

"Well, at least you get *some* time to yourself," she notes.

I honestly don't mind. I'd rather be making money than being forced to look after Brent. Don always accused me of being jealous of him – the only thing I'm jealous of in regards to Brent is that Don and my mom always babied him. Even when he did something wrong, he barely got reprimanded. Once we got the diagnosis, it got worse. In a way, I get it. I'm not saying they should beat him, but I think they should've been stricter because he needs the structure more. He knew better than to disobey Don but knows he can pull shit on Mom because she feels guilty.

I finish the bathroom and go back to my room for a bit. I turn on Netflix to enjoy several episodes of *That '70s Show* and work on my reading. A few hours pass pleasantly until the doorbell rings. I don't think anything of it right away, but then I hear Mom sobbing and rush downstairs, my heart in my throat

At the front door, Mom is in tears, engulfed in Grandma's arms. *Oh, no. What happened!?*

Grandma turns and sees me, her face lined with sadness. Her eyes are red-rimmed, and her cheeks blaze with anger.

"What's going on?" I ask in a small voice.

"It's that bastard, Don," Grandma answers me. He's suing for custody of Brent."

Oh, no. Mom can barely make ends meet as it is. How is she going to pay for a lawyer? Once again, regret seeps in. *Did I really have to be such a jerk to her earlier?*

My mother is a mess, sobbing uncontrollably and clutching the papers like they're a lifeline.

"Go give your mom a hug," Grandma instructs as though I'm a child. "She needs you."

Dutifully, I cross to Mom and hug her. Despite her fierce temper right now, she looks and feels like nothing more than a scared little girl. She hugs me back, and I can tell that I've helped make her feel better, if even remotely.

****

A few hours later, Amethyst and I are cleaning shelves together. I started at the beginning of the new releases, and she started at the beginning of the old releases. We're across the store from each other, but thankfully we can still carry on a conversation.

"Dude, that's fucked up," Amethyst says as she wipes shelves and cases down.

"I don't know why I'm surprised. Don was always such a dick. If someone had asked me last night if it were possible for me to hate him any more than I already do, I'd have laughed in their face. That's life for you; it always keeps you on your toes."

"It just doesn't make sense. He doesn't care about anyone but himself. Why would he bother? To get back at your mom for leaving him?"

"If there's anyone that Don cares about besides himself, it's Brent. He was adopted when he was really young. His adoptive parents adopted another boy a year or two later. They are all dead now. He never wanted to look for his birth mother because he felt that because she gave him up, fuck her. Brent is all he has, I get that, but still..."

"Fuck it, we need to learn voodoo. We could make his hair fall out or something," Amethyst cackles.

How have I seriously not had a friend like this before? Having a friend who offers unwavering support is overwhelming. "Voodoo is for pussies," I joke. "I'd rather do real magic."

"We can do that, too," Amethyst shrugs.

I wish that magic was real and that we could do a spell on Don. Nothing too bad, we wouldn't kill him or anything drastic like that, just something to make him forget about us or maybe

---

Gabriel Mero

change his personality.

I'm so deep in thought that I don't hear the bell ring when the door opens. I can't see the lobby from my position around the corner, but neither can Amethyst. It's not until I hear the movie hit the counter that I become aware of the customer. I climb off my step stool and peer out, fixing a fake, friendly smile on my face.

I nearly choke when I see that Erasmus guy standing at the counter. I immediately feel myself grow hot and flushed. Memories of that bizarre dream rush back to me, making me lightheaded. A low moan escapes my lips. I can almost feel his mouth on me. *No. I will not make a fool of myself this time. Not again.*

"You can just leave it right there on the counter, and I'll check it in for you next time I'm up there," I choke out. *Why is it so hard to talk around him?*

"I think it might be late," Erasmus says, not moving an inch.

I want to ask Amethyst to handle him for me, but I know that I can't. I shoot a look over my shoulder at her, and she's staring. Apparently, she wants to see what I'll do with an unpleasant customer. Erasmus isn't really unpleasant, but he definitely irks me.

I walk around the corner and pass him on my way. He smells like lavender. *My favorite scent.*

I get behind the counter and punch the numbers in. As my fingers work the keyboard, I feel his eyes burning into me again, deeply. *What is this guy's problem!?*

The movie pops up and says that it's due today. "You're good," I say, looking up at him through my lashes. "It was due tonight."

"Great, thanks."

I watch Erasmus walk away, and I feel control slowly coming back to me like blood rushing back to a freed limb. I heave a sigh of relief. *Thank you, God!*

Erasmus opens the door and then turns back. Our eyes meet, and I feel tingly all over. He continues to stare as he walks until he's out of sight. *What the hell!?*

I walk back into the store, and Amethyst is staring at me. "What?" I ask defensively.

"What was all that about?" she quizzes intently.

"Your guess is as good as mine." I shrug and climb the step stool again. "The guy's a freak."

"He stares at you like you're a piece of meat or something. I think he likes you." I shoot her a dirty look, and she holds up her hands. "Tell him, not me."

"He makes me really uncomfortable." I start pulling movies down.

"He's really nice."

I pause. "Wait. What? You know him?" *This just keeps getting better and better.*

"Oh, yeah. A few years ago, we worked at Subway together. He actually trained me. He was dating this really skanky blonde chick. If he'd have been single, I'd have sucked his dick."

At the mention of said "skanky blonde bitch" I feel a stab of –what—jealousy?

"We stopped working together, though, because he would only work the night shift."

"That's weird," I comment, frowning. "How old is he?"

"I think he was like, twenty-six then, so he's around thirty."

"He looks about our age," I say.

"I know! He must take really good care of his skin."

I store all of this information into my memory banks for later dissection. "Well," I say, moving down a shelf, "if you know him and like him, then you can take care of him the next time he's in here. He gives me the heebie-jeebies."

"Oooh, my pleasure," she purrs. We both laugh.

When Amethyst drops me off that night, I walk in the front door and see Mom sitting at the dinner table with her head in her hands. She has copious amounts of bills splayed about her on the tabletop. At the sound of the door opening, she turns and peers at me. Even from here, I can see that she's been crying again. Her eyes are puffy and red.

I slip my shoes off and walk into the kitchen with my bag of Chinese food. Amethyst and I stopped on the way home because we were both starving, and it turns out that we also share an intense passion for Chinese food.

I grab a water bottle out of the fridge, and I'm about to head up to my room to give Mom privacy when she calls out my name. I turn toward her. "I'm sorry for lashing out at you earlier," she says, her voice husky.

I shake my head. "No, I'm sorry. I shouldn't have snarled at you like that. I was just grumpy, and I took it out on you."

"Well, you *are* barely out of your teens," she chuckles bitterly. "I wish that I could go back in time and just be twenty." She sighs and then, realizing how that sounds, continues, "not that I regret having you or Brent, it's just... hard."

"I know," I assure her. I don't know exactly how hard it is in her place, but I know that it isn't easy in the passenger seat, either.

"What am I going to do?" she croaks as fresh tears spring to her eyes. "I can barely pay my bills as it is. I can't afford a lawyer. I... I might have to just let Don take him. Maybe he'd be better off."

She completely breaks down, and my heart shatters. My poor mother. She never asked for any of this. All she wanted was a great man who would love and respect her. She never really wanted children. She'd honestly have been better off if she'd never had any.

I reach out and clasp her hand tightly in mine. "You can do this," I say firmly. "You're not alone. You've got Grandma and me. We'll help you as much as we can, you know that."

"I don't know where I went wrong in my life," Mom swallows. "I'm forty-one years old, and I can't even take care of myself."

"You've got this."

I hold her hand and eat my Chinese, and she continues to cry.

Chapter Six

As it always does, time marched unrelentingly on. August bled into September. The temperature started to drop, and the leaves began to turn orange and red as October began. October has always been my favorite month. Mainly because of Halloween, but also because my birthday is the twelfth.

My life fell into a comfortable school routine, helping out with Brent, and working. Being so anxiety-ridden, I have become comfortable with routine. There's less to be anxious about when things go according to plan.

I was relieved when Erasmus stopped coming into the video store. The last thing I need is more drama and complications in my life. Amethyst and I continued to get closer, to the point where I began to question how I had ever lived one day without such an amazing friend.

My grandmother took a sizable chunk of money out of her retirement to help pay for Mom's lawyer. Even that couldn't help, though. Don has more money than Grandma could ever dream of having. He's found himself a shark of a lawyer, and he is trying to paint my mother as an irresponsible, temperamental mess. Normally, the courts favor the mother, but money talks louder than a conscience.

Until matters can be settled with more finality, we have to surrender Brent to Don every other weekend, half the summer, and every other holiday. Every time she hands Brent over to Don, Mom cries like it is the first time. I deliberately avoid Don whenever he comes around. I lock myself in my room with Romana and read or watch TV.

I hate what this is doing to my mom, but a dark part of me delighted knowing that Don was spending a small fortune. A fool and his money are soon parted...

Amethyst has been asking me what I want to do for my birthday for the last month. The truth is, I have no clue. *Does sleeping through it count?*

This morning, she said she is taking me somewhere after class. I assume she's referring to the small bookstore that we frequent. I can't complain. I love bookstores.

When I get out of class, Amethyst is waiting for me. Now that it's getting colder, she's taken to wearing jeans and a faded green hoodie instead of her signature leggings.

"Ready, bitch?" she asks, practically jumping up and down with excitement.

"As ready as I'll ever be." I toss everything in my bag. I was able to do my French work at lunch, so I dodged the homework bullet once again. Who said that college is hard? I keep my messenger bag out of habit.

We're in the car and cruising across town before I know it. I lean back in the seat, watching the orange, yellow, and red leaves whir past. I hate winter, but I love the beauty of fall.

"So, where are we going?" I ask, trying to be sly.

"It's a surprise!" Amethyst cries, exhaling cigarette smoke.

"So?"

"You *do* know the meaning of the word, right?"

The truth is, I've never liked surprises. The unknown presents far too many variables to keep everything in order. I'm too much of a control freak.

I continue to watch out the window as we enter a part of town that I've not been to yet. I honestly didn't know that Willow's Crest had a "downtown." The trees fade away and are replaced by brick and mortar. Willow's Crest's downtown is in no way comparable to Detroit's downtown concrete jungle, but I am impressed.

Amethyst parks in the lot of a squat brick building with "Gypsies" stenciled lavishly in the large glass front.

"Gypsies'?" I ask, confused.

"It's an occult shop," Amethyst explains, grinding her cigarette out under the heel of her boot. "You said you'd never been to one, so I thought it would be fun for us to go together. They do Tarot cards, palm readings, and sell stuff here, too. I thought I'd get you one for your birthday."

I can't help but smile at Amethyst's genuine thoughtfulness. I'd be lying if I said that I had no curiosity whatsoever about occult shops. "Thanks," I say.

As we approach the storefront, I see an older black woman standing in the window watching us intently. "Is she staring at us?" I ask.

"Looks like it," Amethyst admits.

The woman has the door open before we even get to it. In her hand is a steaming cup. She's wearing a floor-length glittery purple robe. Around her neck are several silver necklaces. Her hair is tucked under a red turban.

"I've been expecting you," the woman says, handing me the cup. "It's Earl Grey, your favorite." She has an accent that I can't place. *Maybe the Caribbean?*

"Thank you," I say politely, shooting a look at Amethyst, who shakes her head. *Hmmm.* I glance down into the tea and notice that there is no tea bag, yet the amber-colored tea is there.

We enter the store, and immediately I can smell incense, a heavy amount of incense. I'm instantly reminded of summer trips to the Renaissance Festival. My eyes roam around at the schizophrenia of the room: shelves lined with books, counters displaying incense and oils, crystals, talismans, herbs, and spices, you name it.

"Drink," the woman commands, ushering me toward a plush red chair across from a round wooden table, complete with a crystal ball and several decks of Tarot cards. I sit down across from her. There's only one seat on this side of the table, so Amethyst stands there awkwardly. "This is a private reading," the woman says to Amethyst. "Feel free to browse."

Amethyst looks at me for confirmation. I nod, and she goes to look at crystals.

The woman sits down and watches me intently, hands steepled under her well-defined chin.

"So, uh, is your name Gypsy?" I ask, taking a sip of the tea. I'm astounded that it's just how I like it, complete with the honey.

"No, I'm Sioned," the woman replies, not smiling. The name sounds exotic, and I kind of like it. I've always liked exotic things. Years ago, I decided that if I ever have a daughter, I'll name her Annika. Of course, then I realized how much I loathe children.

"It was really nice of my friend, Amethyst, to call ahead and make this appointment for me."

"Your friend didn't make an appointment," Sioned informs me.

"Oh. How did you know that I'd be here today, then?"

"I saw it in my crystal ball." She's completely straight-faced as she says this. Either she is a good actress, or she truly believes this crap. "I saw that you'd come to me on the eve of your twenty-first birthday."

Despite the heat being on, a chill races up my spine, and all of the hairs on my body stand straight up. *This is freaky.* "What, did you check my Facebook or something?" I try to laugh it off. There are a few pictures of me drinking Earl Grey on my Facebook. That must be how she knew that it was my favorite, or she and Amethyst are conspiring together.

"I did not need to. I learned everything from the crystal ball." She looks at my teacup. "Leave a little at the bottom," she orders.

I take a deep gulp of the warm tea and hand her the cup. She shakes her head and instructs me on what to do. I shift the cup to my left hand and swish it three times left to right before placing the saucer on top and slowly turning it over so that the minute amount of tea drains out. Sioned lets it drain for a minute or so before motioning for me to turn the teacup upright again. She inspects it intently and then picks it up.

"I've never had my tea leaves read before," I confess as nervousness sets in. Sometimes when I'm nervous, I babble to compensate.

"Silence," Sioned barks. "I must concentrate." Chastised, I sit in silence, chewing my lip.

Sioned looks the cup over as if she is a detective searching for evidence of DNA. *At least she's thorough.* She turns the cup over and over, tutting to herself. I get impatient and look across the store to see Amethyst flipping through a musty old tome.

"It is as I feared," Sioned finally says.

"What? Feared?" I can feel myself beginning to panic.

"There is a serpent symbol near a leaf in the shape of a 'D.' Beware a man whose name begins with a 'D.'"

Don? I silently wonder. Why beware of him? He can't hurt me now. Maybe she saw the past?

"Here, we have a heart, which portends a lover. It is close to the handle, so they are very near." She stares at the cup a little longer, mumbling to herself. "I see… an anchor, meaning success in love or business. The palm tree predicts a good omen. Good things are coming your way."

So, I need to be wary of Don, but a great, successful love is on the horizon for me. Insightful.

She sets the cup down and laces her fingers on the tabletop. She regards me down her nose for several seconds. "Let me see your right hand," she commands eventually.

"I don't have much money," I caution her, keeping my hands in my lap. I am not about to waste money on some fake palm reading.

"No charge," she rasps.

That makes no sense. How does she expect to make money if she's giving out free tea leaf and palm readings? Nevertheless, I find myself extending my right hand. I feel her rough hands on mine, working it over like a sculptor with clay. I'm not used to this level of human contact, but I try to swallow my discomfort. She checks my left hand, too.

"I see a troubled past with much damage," she begins, "much pain and sadness. But on the right hand, your future, I see immense power and happiness. I see that you are an artistic person with a flair for writing. You care too much what people think of you, but you shouldn't. Your lifeline is rather long, so I expect you'll live well into your eighties. You'll be married once, and you'll meet your future spouse by the time you're thirty. I see..." she squints at my hand, pulling it closer to her eyes, "possibly two children for you."

"I don't like kids," I say unabashedly.

"You think of your cats as children," Sioned challenges, looking deep into my eyes. "A boy and a girl."

I go to pull my hand back, but she holds it more tightly. "You have what it takes to make it in whatever career you choose. You're a natural-born leader; you love bossing others around."

Okay, so a lot of what she said was spot-on, but, come on, me, a natural-born leader? I can barely lead myself, let alone others. And what immense power is she talking about? I can't even do pushups!

"You will gain self-confidence once you come into your powers."

"My... powers?" *This is a joke, right?*

"You'll find out tomorrow. On your birthday."

I shiver at that. *How the hell does this lady know that my birthday is tomorrow? Surely Amethyst wouldn't have gone to such an extent to freak me out for my birthday, would she?*

Sioned stands up and walks toward a bookshelf. She peruses the titles with a crooked, wizened finger and huffs when she can't find what she's looking for. "Wait here," she croaks and shambles off behind the counter.

Amethyst makes her way back to me, some crystals and a few vials in her hands. "Their prices are so cheap here!" she gushes. "I wish I'd come here sooner."

"You really gave Madame Sioned the dirt on me, didn't you?" I tease.

Amethyst looks at me, her brow knotted in confusion. "What are you talking about?"

"Come on, how else did she know that I'm turning twenty-one tomorrow, that I love cats, to avoid someone whose name begins with a 'D?'"

"I didn't tell her anything, I swear."

Amethyst is definitely a consummate actress. I believe her, even though common sense dictates the opposite. "How else would she know all that?" There's no way...Sioned comes back from behind the corner, hefting a musty tome, probably weighing more than she could safely carry.

I dart forward and grab the book before it can fall onto the floor. As soon as my hands make contact with the book, I feel a surge of electricity throughout my body, awakening me inside. I feel lightheaded and sway on my feet.

I can see shadowy figures knelt before the open book. A circle of candles burns around the figures, and I can faintly make out chanting, though the words are lost to me.

Amethyst steadies me and shoots Sioned an accusatory look. "What'd you give him?" she challenges.

"Tea and honey."

"I'm fine," I say, taking a deep breath. I feel like I'm high, or at least what I imagine being high feels like.

"I've been guarding this for you for a long, long time," Sioned says.

"What?" Despite my confusion, I can't help but feel like the book does belong to me, in some weird, cosmic destiny thing.

"It has been passed down in my family for generations, waiting for you."

"Are we family?" I ask stupidly.

"Not by blood, but by deed," Sioned replies mysteriously.

I struggle to find words as all of this eddies through my brain. Amethyst seems to sense my overload and takes the reigns. "Okay, well, thanks for that, but I think it's time to go." She sets her crystals and herbs on the counter.

Sioned stares at me the whole time she's ringing the items up. "$21.20," she says after a long, uncomfortable silence.

Amethyst hands her $25, and when Sioned hands her back her change, she grabs my hand and starts leading me toward the door.

"My door is always open to you," Sioned calls after us. "It is my privilege to assist you in any way possible."

"Yeah, right, psycho bitch," Amethyst mumbles, ushering me out of the door.

I am so in my head that I don't notice that the book is still in my hands, the car starting, or the drive back to my house. It isn't until Amethyst cuts the engine and taps my shoulder that I'm shaken from my stupor.

"Are you okay?" she asks, her features etched with concern.

"I'm fine," I say, forcing myself to smile. "That was just so weird."

"I'm so sorry, I never should have taken you there. I just thought it would be fun for us since you said you're interested in witchcraft and stuff."

"It was fun, really," I assure her. "I was fine until she handed me that weird old book, then I felt like I was in some kind of trance or something." *That vision I had, what was that? Was it a vision? A hallucination? Maybe the incense was laced with something?*

"Are you sure that you're okay?"

"I'll be fine," I promise. "I'm just tired and stressed out. I think a nap is in order."

"Okay, I can take a hint." Amethyst unlocks my door, and I get out, the heavy book still weighing down my arms. It's funny that as heavy as the book is, I simultaneously feel weightless, too.

"Thanks for the adventure." I hold the book close to my chest as if guarding it.

"Sure thing. Let me know if you want to do anything tomorrow for the big two one."

"Okay." I can feel my cheeks flushing with embarrassment. I hate it when people make a big deal out of my birthday. Well, not *hate*, but it embarrasses me a little.

Amethyst honks as she backs out of the driveway, and I wave before going into the house. As I shut the door behind me, I hurriedly rid myself of my shoes and scurry up the stairs. I don't want Mom or Grandma to see me with this book. My mom would roll her eyes and mock me for entertaining the idea of witchcraft. Grandma would probably have a conniption. She spends a lot of time at Temple, and I'm pretty sure witchcraft isn't part of the Jewish religion.

I make it to my room and feel the tension float out of my body as I close the door. I set the book down on the bed, and Romana sniffs it curiously, then she does that weird thing that cats do where they look up and hang their mouth open. It's a funny sight.

Suddenly, my door flies open, and I gasp as Grandma walks in a whirl with her colorful robes, completely unannounced. "There you are, bubala. I've been waiting ages for you to get home."

I want to move in front of the book, but I feel like I'm glued to the spot.

"Your birthday is tomorrow. I was wondering if you'd like anything special for supper."

"Uh…" I know I'm making myself sound like a dumbass, but for the life of me, I cannot think of a dish right now.

"Are you feeling all right?" Grandma asks, putting her hand on my forehead. She looks past me, and my heart drops when I see her eyes widen at the sight of the book. "What is that?" she asks, her voice barely more than a whisper.

"Uh, just a little something my friend Amethyst got me for my birthday," I lie. I realize too late that I am potentially throwing Amethyst under the bus for something she had nothing to do with.

She moves past me, eyes wide as she takes it all in. "*The Grimoire*," she gasps.

Huh?

Chapter Seven

What? Grandma knows what a Grimoire is? I don't even really know what a Grimoire is. The room spins a bit. What is going on today? I feel like I woke up in some freaking bizarre world that seems like mine but is monumentally more messed up. *Maybe I'm dreaming.*

"I can't believe it." Grandma's voice is barely more than a whisper. She's staring at the big black book in wonderment, eyes wide and mouth slightly ajar.

"I'll get rid of it," I say to try to assuage her before she goes off the rails. Worst case scenario, I can give it to Amethyst to hold it for me. She's a Pagan, or whatever, I'm sure she'd enjoy the hell out of it.

"Don't you dare!" My grandmother whirls on me, eyes ablaze. I shrink back in surprise. "I never thought I'd lay eyes on it!"

"I didn't buy it. The lady in the shop gave it..."

"What lady? What shop?"

"Her name was Madame Sioned or just Sioned, I'm not really sure. Amethyst took me to Gypsies for my birthday."

"It's been here, under my nose, for all these years!"

Grandma is talking more to herself than to me. It's weird. I'm waiting for her to freak out and say that no occult paraphernalia is allowed in her Jewish home. I mean, she's far from a Torah thumper, but I do know that she spends a lot of time at Temple and that her religion is very important to her.

She reaches out to touch the book and cries out in pain or surprise when a tiny bolt of lightning shoots from the book and strikes her hand.

"Are you okay?" I ask, grabbing her shoulders.

"I'm fine, bubala. The book won't open for me. I'm not its master." She turns to look me dead in the eye. "You are."

I can instantaneously feel my stomach scream in protest as it twists into knots. "What's going on?" I ask, swaying on my feet.

"Sit down. Sit down, dear." I feel my grandma's hands on my back, and they guide me down onto the bed. I take a few deep breaths to try to chase the gut cramps away.

"I don't feel well," I whimper.

"It's just nerves, dear. Breathe." Grandma demonstrates taking a deep breath in through her nose and out through her mouth. I mimic her and feel a little bit better.

"What is going on?" I demand, my eyes wide and pleading. This day has been nothing but a jumbled mess of confusion.

My grandmother frowns and adjusts her hair self-consciously, stalling. "Grandma?" I press.

"Well, I wasn't going to tell you this until tomorrow, but... Graham, my dear bubala, you're a..."

A what? A psycho? A paranoid schizophrenic? I'm dreaming, and this is all just a manifestation of some impurity in my psyche? "I'm a what?" I rasp.

"You're a witch."

As soon as her words hit me, I jerk with my bucking stomach, and I throw up all over the hardwood floor. I haven't had anything to eat today, so it's mainly yellow bile.

Grandma jumps to her feet and dashes across the hall. She comes back with a towel and starts soaking up the contents of my stomach.

"I'm sorry," I moan, fighting the urge to purge some more.

"It's quite all right, bubala. It's a perfectly natural response." *How can she say that so rationally?*

Through the pounding of blood through my ears, I hear the sound of approaching footsteps. My mom appears in the doorway, dressed in a pair of tight blue jeans and a cranberry-colored blouse. She's getting ready for work. "What the hell is going on in here?" she asks, looking between my grandma and me.

"It's happening, Beverly!" Grandma exclaims.

"What is?" Mom replies.

"His powers are awakening!"

My mom's face falls in shock, and the mug she has in her hand crashes to the floor, shattering into a million shards. "No..." she murmurs.

"Mom?"

She looks at me, her face still a mask of pure astonishment. "But how? I bound your powers as a baby..."

"You did what!?" This is all starting to seem like some elaborate scheme to mess with me. Would my mom and grandma really go so far as to recruit Amethyst and Sioned in this charade?

My mom shakes her head. "This can't be happening."

"Well, it *is* happening, dear, so shut your mouth and compose yourself. Your son needs you to be strong right now," Grandma ripostes.

My mom throws her hands into the air. "I can't deal with this right now," she says determinedly. "I have to go to work."

My mother turns on her heel and walks out of my room without another word. Silence falls upon us as Grandma and I stare at the space she had just occupied. That is my mother in a nutshell. Whenever something intense or emotional happens, my mom gets mad or panics and bails. No wonder I have so many issues.

"So… I'm a witch," I say slowly.

"Yes." Grandma rubs my shoulder comfortingly.

"How?"

"It's in our blood. All of the Imber women have been witches."

"But I'm not a woman," I point out.

"That is *strange*," she admits. "But maybe it's because you're, well, you know…"

I don't have enough fire in me to argue with her about my sexuality. All I do is frown. "Mom's not a witch." My grandma looks uncomfortable for a minute, avoiding my gaze. "Grandma?"

"Your mother *was* a witch," she confesses.

"Was?"

"When your mother was a teenager, she was training in the Craft… and there was… an *accident*…"

"And?"

"You'll have to ask your mum about that one. It's not my story to tell. But after the accident, she bound her powers. She gave up on the Craft. When you were young, she bound your powers, too."

"But how are my powers being awakened, then?" *None of this is making sense.*

Grandma sits down on the bed beside me. "I wish I could tell you, but that's one piece of the puzzle that perplexes me. Since the dawn of our kind, there have been whispers of an all-powerful witch who would sway the balance of the universe in favor of good or evil. When your powers started manifesting when you were still an infant, I hoped maybe the prophesied one would be you."

"I had powers?"

"After she bound your powers, your mother had me do a memory spell on you to protect you from your true identity."

"Holy shit..." I lick my suddenly dry lips.

"You had the power of resurrection. One day, you and I were walking out by the beach, and we found a dead butterfly on the side of the road. I picked it up, distressed. You know how much I love butterflies." She smiles sadly. "You wanted to hold it. I wasn't going to let you, but you were so insistent. I placed it in the palm of your hand. You closed your eyes tightly, kissed it, and the butterfly sprang to life! It circled around us a few times as if thanking you and then fluttered away. I was so proud of you!"

I honestly don't remember any of this, so either the spell worked, or my entire family is insane.

"And you're a witch?" I ask.

"Proudly!" My grandmother laughs. "How do you think I knew to have a mug of Earl Grey waiting for you on your first day of school? How do you think I know what you're thinking? I'm a telepath, dear."

"Oh, God." I quickly go back through my thoughts around her. Hopefully, I haven't had any inappropriate thoughts...

"Don't worry, dear. If I got to that, I'd just put you on silent."

Holy shit, she really can read my thoughts. Maybe I should...

"Can you be a witch and be Jewish? I mean, what do they think about that at Shul?" I can't help but wonder aloud.

"I am a Jew, but I don't follow the religion to the letter. I am a practitioner of Kabbalah, Jewish mysticism.

"How Madonna of you. So, how do your powers work?"

"Pick a random string of numbers, and I'll try to guess them."

"Okay." My mind scrambles to formulate a string of numbers. 2777015591809

"2777015591809," Grandma says without hesitating.

Holy shit….

"A witch's powers don't manifest until she turns eighteen. When yours didn't resurface, I accepted that you weren't going to get that back. It seems you're an exception to the rule in more ways than one."

"I've done spells," I confess. "Back in middle school. Simple stuff, really. Lost and found, make it rain, make it stop raining, warm myself…"

"And they worked?"

"Yes," I whisper, the gravity of the situation sinking in. *I'm a fucking witch!?*

Grandma gets to her feet and paces back and forth excitedly. "So, even after your powers were bound, they still bled through. Incredible…"

"What does that mean?"

"You are more powerful than any witch known to man!"

That makes my stomach spasm again. "Why, eighteen?" I ask.

"Well, you see, eighteen is the age at which a child is finally considered an adult. We don't want a bunch of immature amateurs running around witching everyone around them."

"And who decides? What, is there some sort of witch's council?" I gasp. "Is Hogwarts real?"

My grandma rolls her eyes. "Hogwarts is nothing but hogwash," she says disdainfully. "I wouldn't say that there's a witch's council per se, but we are an organization. It's called the Consortium of Magic."

I lie back on the bed and hold Romana tightly to my chest. This is all too much for me to process right now.

"I see you've already got yourself a Familiar," Grandma notes...

From my years of watching a lot of supernatural television shows and movies, especially pertaining to witches, I know that a Familiar is a witch's companion, usually in the shape of an animal. A Familiar assists the witch in her spells. *The Charmed Ones* had Kitt, Elphaba had Chistery, Willow, and Tara had Miss Kitty Fantastico.

"I guess," I murmur, looking at Romana as if for the very first time. If I actually *am* a witch, I won't find a better Familiar than Romana.

"Try one for me," Grandma says, eyes alight.

"Huh?"

"One of those spells you tried. You said they worked. Show me!"

I couldn't show her warming, and doing a lost and found spell wouldn't prove anything, either, since there's proof that I'd actually lost the item. That leaves weather manipulation. Outside, it's a chilly fall evening, a slight breeze scattering dead leaves everywhere.

I cross to the window and look out at the quiet darkness outside. It hasn't rained in a few days. Taking a deep breath, I open the window. I close my eyes and begin. Somehow, after all these years, the words still come to me easily.

Ancient Gods and Goddesses,

I invoke thee

Waters from the sky,

Let it be.

I command thee all,

To thee all

Listen to my desire,

Rainfall.

I do remember that the spell requires you to be outside, but considering that I'm kind of leaning out of the window, I hope that it will work.

A few seconds pass silently, and then I hear the sudden rumble of thunder and raindrops start pelting my face and hands. I lean back into my room and shut the window. The glass is immediately wet with rain. Grandma is grinning widely. *I did something, right? I actually did something right!*

"Oh, well done, Graham!" She hugs me tightly, and I can't help but laugh. "Make it stop now!" I feel a bit like a show pony, but I do as I'm told. I look back out the window and chant:

Gods of Power,

Gods of might,

I bid you now,

Stop this plight.

Stop the rain,

We need no more.

Let it fall,

Nevermore.

The rain continues to fall, but the intensity decreases. Slowly, it eases off until the rain ceases altogether. *Wow. I did that…*I beam at Grandma, feeling euphoric. I have never felt special in my life, not once. This is an entirely new feeling for me. I like it, but it's foreign to me.

Grandma hugs me again. "How do you feel?" she asks.

"Incredible," I admit. "Also, kind of tired and overwhelmed."

"I can only imagine. It's not every day that you find out that you're the most powerful witch on the Earth!"

"We don't know that," I remind her, trying to be logical.

"We'll have to start training you as soon as we can."

"Training?" I groan. Between school and my job, I really don't want to have to do more.

"We must hone your skills, darling. The sooner we get started, the sooner you can fulfill your destiny. And, once your powers are activated, you'll be the target for some nasty buggers."

"Wait, what!?"

"Both sides are going to try to win your favor and sway you their way. You'll have to be strong."

"I'm not strong." I sound like a little boy.

"Rubbish! You are the strongest person that I have ever met. Look at all you've overcome! You're so much stronger than you realize!"

"But I don't understand. If Mom bound my powers as a toddler and they didn't activate when I turned eighteen, why are they activating now?"

"That is a good question." She hums deep in her throat. "Perhaps the timing wasn't right. Perhaps you needed to be *here*, *now*, for them to take over."

Exhaustion sets in. This is all so overwhelming. How could my life have taken such a drastic turn in just a day?

"You look positively knackered, bubala," Grandma says as I lie back. She pulls the blankets up to my chin and kisses my cheek. "You should get some sleep."

"My mind is spinning," I yawn.

"Here, let me."

Grandma hovers a hand over me and chants quietly to herself. Despite how close we are, I can't make out what she is saying. Everything grows fuzzy around the edges, and I feel Grandma's weight lift off of my bed. Romana lies on my chest, purring.

Darkness takes over, and I am supplicant.

Chapter Eight

I open my eyes to pure blackness. My blackout curtains do a great job of keeping errant light out of my room. *What a crazy dream!* I think, stretching. In my dream, I had been a witch. The most powerful witch ever. My grandma had been a witch; my mom was a witch, too. I switch on my lamp and squint my eyes against the sudden onslaught of light. *Is this what a hangover feels like?* I wonder.

I pull on my glasses—I hate them, they make me feel trapped—and find my phone. I do a double-take when I see the time, 1:27 PM. I slept for over twelve hours! I know I've been burning the candle at both ends a bit, but not *that* badly! I can't believe that no one has come to wake me up yet. It is my birthday, after all. In fact, I turned twenty-one at 1:25PM.

Romana is curled up next to me, a ball of orange fluff. Maybe I've been spending too much time with her. Cats sleep an average of twelve to sixteen hours a day. Perhaps that bad habit is starting to wear off on me.

I can feel something hard digging into my leg. Did I fall asleep with a textbook or something in the bed with me? I can't remember bringing one home...I reach down and pull it up. As soon as my eyes brush the cover, anxiety shoots throughout my entire body, making me jump to my feet. The black book with the golden pentagram embossed on its cover lies beside where I had been. *So, it wasn't a dream. I am a witch.*

I swallow past the lump in my throat and open the book. I'd meant to last night, but there had been far too much going on. When I open it, the book groans in protest. I take in the weathered, yellowed pages that are creased with lines and age. Sioned hadn't been joking when she'd said that this book had been around for ages. Some of the writing has faded a bit, but I can still make out most of it. The handwriting is spidery and a kind of loopy cursive. I turn the page and cough as a cloud of dust invades my lungs. *Yep, definitely ancient!*

I skim through some of the pages. It's similar to the *Book of Shadows* from *Charmed* in terms of the spells and aged pages, but my *Grimoire* does not contain illustrations. Nor are there renderings of demons and warlocks. Maybe they aren't real.

As if guided by some unseen force, my fingers file through the musty pages and stop at one page toward the back of the book. It's entitled *Acquiring a Familiar*.

Acquiring a Familiar:

When you find an animal you would like to be your Familiar, simply approach it. Do so cautiously. Personalize the spell to fit the specific animal that you are asking. Ask its permission by chanting:

By the moon that shines at night,

And the sun so very bright.

I ask you once,

I ask you twice,

But more than twice

Would not be nice.

With a meow or a blink or a purr

Pray tell me now

What will you do?

Will you be my Familiar?

Give your answer unto me.

If the animal runs off, then it does not wish to be your Familiar. If it vocalizes or rubs upon you, then it has accepted your invitation.

As I read the words to the incantation, I can feel the power buried within them. I glance up at Romana, who has splayed herself across my lap, staring at me.

"Well, here goes," I mutter.

I meet Romana's gaze and repeat the words of the spell. I feel a crackle of energy with each line. It grows brighter the further I get. The words echo in my ear when I finish, and Romana slowly blinks her eyes at me. I have no idea whether this is a sign of kitty love or a sign that the spell worked.

Suddenly, Romana scrambles to her feet and leans up to rub her head on my face. *I'll take that as a yes.* I scratch her behind the ears, and she purrs loudly, sounding like an engine motor.

"I consent," a voice whispers, seeming to come from everywhere and nowhere simultaneously. "Who's there?" I ask, looking around. Save for Romana and me, the room is empty. I turn to the cat and narrow my eyes. "Was that you?" I feel stupid even asking her, but she answers me with a slow blink. "I'll have to see if there's a spell in here that'll let us communicate with each other," I say quietly. Once again, she blinks at me.

When I get to my feet, the wobble from yesterday is gone. I feel different, stronger. Maybe all I needed was a marathon sleep session to make me feel better.

After I use the bathroom and freshen up, I go downstairs. The sun is shining brightly through the stained glass windows, making me squint again. I find my grandmother in the kitchen, browning beef in a skillet. The smell of cooking meat makes my stomach grumble in protest. I didn't eat yesterday.

"Oh, Graham, there you are!" She kisses me on both cheeks. "How did you sleep, bubala?"

"Like a corpse," I reply with a wry smile. I've never understood why people say that they slept like a baby. Babies are constantly waking up, crying, and being obnoxious.

"Just a mild sleep spell."

It's weird hearing her talk about spells and magic. I know I never saw her much growing up, just one week a summer, but I feel as though I'm meeting her for the first time.

"I thought it was all a dream," I confess, sitting down at the small table.

"Why would you want it all to be a dream? With a little training, you will be *the most powerful witch* in the world! You should feel honored," she chirps.

"I do." *Do I, really? I don't know.*

"Have you done any looking around in the book?"

"A little," I admit. "I tried out a spell to make Romana my Familiar."

"Did it work?"

"I think so... she blinked at me and then started rubbing on me, then I heard a voice, it sounded like a woman. She said, 'I consent'."

Grandma whoops excitedly, beaming. "I always knew that you would be extraordinary!"

I duck my head in embarrassment. I know she means well, but it's still foreign to me. "What are you making?" I ask, trying to change the subject.

"Nacho Dip To Die For," Grandma replies.

"Sounds good."

"It's to die for," she cackles. "I thought for your special day, we could have a nice dinner. I invited your friend Amethyst."

"How did you get her number?"

"I went through your phone after you went to sleep last night." I open my mouth to chastise her, but she waves calmingly at me. "Don't worry, dear. I didn't snoop. I just went through your contacts."

"I appreciate the thought, Grandma, but next time maybe ask? Going through my phone is a huge invasion of privacy! What if I'd had... inappropriate pictures or something?"

"Do you?" she challenges, raising one perfectly manicured eyebrow.

"So not the point!"

She laughs and stirs the meat with her spatula. "Your mother isn't up yet. Would you go and check on Brent for me? He's in the living room, watching TV."

"Sure." I'm not really mad at her, but I am thanking my lucky stars that I don't have any nudes or anything on my phone. *I'm not making that mistake again.*

I pad into the living room and find Brent kneeling before the coffee table. He's meticulously arranging his tiny cars and trucks. After he adds one, he leans forward and closes one eye. He scrutinizes his creation with the other eye for any small imperfection. It doesn't make sense to me, it's just part of his affliction.

The truth of the matter is, I do feel bad for Brent. From what I understand, Autism is basically like being trapped inside your own mind and not knowing how to get out. He's highly intelligent–like his father–but he doesn't know how to harness it. He can walk through a parking lot and tell you the make and model of every vehicle there, but he can't do something as simple as use a toilet by himself. My mom and the schools have been working on potty training him for a while, to little success.

Brent sees me walk in and flaps his hands excitedly–another Autistic tic. "Happy birthday, Graham!" he squeals. Poor kid. His words–what few he has–come out garbled. He sounds like he has mush-mouth.

"Thanks, Brent." He gives me a hug and then takes my hand. "What's up?"

"Brent wants Graham to play *Jeep Off Road Racing.*"

I roll my eyes and groan dramatically. I hate that game. I grew up playing games, and in my time, I have mastered many gaming systems, but the Wii is one that just perplexes me. Every time I try to turn in the game, it over-corrects, and I end up hitting a rock wall or something. But, I can't say no to Brent.

"We need to check your diaper first," I say, feeling the diaper for moisture and the peering down the back. *Perfectly clean. Awesome.*

Brent turns the game on and hands me one of the Wii controllers. He picks his truck and then instructs me on which vehicle he wants me to drive, and then after he chooses the canyon level–his favorite–we begin.

As usual, he expertly navigates the serpentine course while I make it as far as the first turn and then collide with the rocky mountain. I lose myself in the game, forgetting about Don and the revelation that I'm supposedly a witch. I don't know how much time goes by, but eventually, Mom comes shuffling into the room, rubbing her eyes profusely.

I look at her, and our eyes meet awkwardly. I don't know what to do or say after her sporadic outburst last night. "How was work?" I ask.

"Shitty," she grumbles, sitting on the couch. After a few seconds, she crinkles her nose in disgust. "What is she cooking? It smells like barf."

"It's called Nacho Dip To Die For," I inform her.

My mom and grandma have always had a weird relationship. Grandma has always been good to me. She's never forgotten a birthday, Christmas, or Easter (since Don was Catholic), and every time I came to stay with her, she got me pizza and a gift.

Her relationship with her daughter, though, is immensely different. I don't know what exactly went down between them. I've tried asking Mom about it several times, but she always refuses to answer. All she will say is that Grandma was never a real mom to her. She pontificates that Grandma is selfish, childish, and annoying. I always assumed it had something to do with my mother turning her back on her Jewish roots and marrying a Gentile, but now I'm not so sure that's that main cause.

"Well, I'm going to go get showered. I don't know what time Amethyst is supposed to show up, but I haven't even brushed my teeth."

"What are you talking about?"

"Grandma's throwing me a birthday dinner."

Mom scowls. "Like I have nothing better to do than clean up after that." She shakes her head.

"I'll do the dishes," I assure her, trying to lull the dragon within back to sleep. She silently fumes.

Whatever. I have other things to do.

After showering and getting dressed, I come back downstairs. I can hear that my mom is in the other shower. I don't know what her problem is, but I get sick of her mood swings. She accuses everyone else of being selfish and yet, she's the one that throws a fit when things don't go her way. *How is my birthday dinner imposing upon her? All she has to do is eat!*

The doorbell rings, and I open the door to find Amethyst. She looks a lot different! Her dark hair is loose, spiraling down past her shoulders. Her glasses are gone, making her chocolate brown eyes really shine. "Happy birthday, dahhhling," she purrs, pulling me into a bear hug.

"Thanks," I manage, though my air is cut off. When she releases me, I smile. "You look really nice."

"Aw, thanks."

I lead her in. She kicks her boots off and stares in wonder at her surroundings. Grandma has eclectic taste. Her decorations range from statuettes of angels, to snowmen, to birds, to cats. "Such a cute house!" she gasps.

Before I can obligatorily thank her, Grandma comes out of the kitchen, skirts twirling with excitement. "Amethyst, I assume," she says with a warm smile.

"Yeah. Nice to meet you, Mrs...?" Amethyst shoots a pitiful look at me, but before I can answer, Grandma takes charge once again.

"Ginevra," she says, holding out a hand.

"Ginevra!" They shake hands, and Grandma leads us into the dining room. The table is immaculately set with a Halloween tablecloth and place settings for four. We all know that Brent won't eat anything we prepare at home anyway, so there's no place setting for him.

In the center of the table, the nacho dip simmers in a white cooking tray. It kind of smells like cat food, but it looks interesting. The main course looks to be a homemade Chinese buffet complete with fried chicken, sweet and sour sauce, egg rolls, white rice, and crab Rangoon. Grandma went all out!

My mouth waters as I take it all in. "Thanks, Grandma!" I exclaim.

"You're welcome, bubala. Enjoy." Grandma goes to get my mom and Brent, but Amethyst and I sit down.

"Are you having a good birthday?" Amethyst asks.

"It's definitely been… interesting," I allude. Amethyst frowns inquisitively, and I say, "later." The last thing I want today is to have the 'I'm a witch' discussion at dinner. I know she won't freak out and stop being my friend, but I still want one more day of relative normalcy.

Grandma comes back into the room, carrying Brent. Even though he's nine, he's still the size of a toddler. A few seconds later, my mom comes in. Her hair is neatly styled, and she's wearing makeup, complete with her signature blue eye shadow. *At least she's put forth some effort.*

They sit down, and I introduce Amethyst and my mother. Amethyst is delighted to meet her, but I can tell my mom is completely indifferent. I shoot her a warning look as if to say, *be nice!*

Brent sits in the corner at his small *Sponge Bob* table, eating chips. Meanwhile, we tuck into the Chinese. Chinese is my favorite cuisine, but I rarely eat it because Mom doesn't care for it too much. I drizzle my chicken with the sweet and sour sauce and moan appreciatively. This is some of the best Chinese food I've ever had! *Who knew that Grandma was such an amazing cook?* "This is incredible!" I extol, shoveling a forkful of white rice into my mouth.

"This is so good," Amethyst agrees, tearing into an egg roll. "You made this yourself, Ginevra?"

My mom scoffs, and Grandma shoots her a dirty look before pasting a smile back on her face. "Not entirely, my dear, but you could say that I *conjured* it up." Her eyes gleam mischievously.

I choke as the water I'd been trying to drink went down the wrong tube. *Grandma, stop!* Again, she smiles and winks at me. Amethyst seems to be unaware of the tension in the room, or she's politely ignoring it.

"Tell me more about yourself, dear," Grandma entreats Amethyst. "Graham speaks so highly of you."

"He does?" Amethyst blushes and shoots me a grateful smile. "There's not much to tell, really. I moved here from Detroit last year. In high school, my mom was in a car accident. She suffered some brain damage and can't be on her own, so she stays with my grandparents there. I needed to be on my own so I just...left."

"I'm dreadfully sorry to hear that," Grandma soothes. "What made you come here?"

"I don't know." Amethyst shrugs. "I just felt kind of *drawn* here, I guess. I've always been fascinated by New England. I'm a Pagan, so I'm into witches and all that. The goal was to check out Salem and New Orleans, but my car broke down here and I just...decided to stay. Something clicked in me."

"Really?" Grandma sips her wine. "We had family in Salem at the time of the witch hunts."

"That's cool... and sad," Amethyst replies nervously.

"It's dreadful what they did to our kind, isn't it?"

I bury my head in my hands. *Why is Grandma doing this? Surely we should keep the witch thing to ourselves...*

"Are you okay?" she looks at me.

"Enough," Mom says authoritatively. "We're here to celebrate Graham's birthday, not indulge some ridiculous fantasy!"

Grandma whirls on her. "Just because you've turned your back on our family responsibility–"

"Responsibility?" she scoffs. "It's a choice, Mom. Always has been."

"It's a choice for *some*."

I look at Amethyst, who smiles apologetically. This is about to get incredibly heated and awkward.

"Stop it," I plead. "Why can't we do anything normally in this family? Why does it always have to be passive-aggressiveness and fighting!? We're supposed to be a family. We're not. So let's just stop pretending." I look at my mom and then at my grandmother. "You two hate each other. Admit it." They both look down at the floor. "Whatever happened all those years ago, get over it! All you're doing is carrying this hatred and negativity inside of you and resurrecting it every day! I'm tired of tension. I'm tired of bitter silence and fighting. I'm tired of you!" I slam my hand on the table with fury, and the bulbs in the crystal chandelier above the table shatter. Grandma cries out in surprise, and at the exact same time, Mom jumps.

My anger swells, and a burst of bright orange flames shoots out of the fireplace in the corner. Brent starts crying hysterically, and Mom rushes to him. *Oh, sure. Be a mom to him, but fuck me, right?* I think bitterly.

I get up and storm out of the room, the photos on the walls slamming to the floor as I walk past. I am pissed, and it's like my anger has manifested itself through my newfound powers.

I feel a hand on my shoulder and turn to see Amethyst. Her kind features calm the storm inside, and my shoulders sag. "Want to go to my place for a bit?" she asks. "Just to calm down? I have tea."

I nod, wanting to go back and apologize for my outburst, but also knowing that I wasn't completely out of line.

Amethyst ushers me out the door and into her car.

Gabriel Mero

Chapter Nine

Amethyst sets a steaming mug of tea down on the coffee table and then sits down beside me on the shabby couch, tucking her feet underneath her.

"Sorry it's not Earl Grey," she says, lighting up a cigarette. The noxious odor of tobacco smoke turns my stomach, but I don't say anything. This is Amethyst's place, not mine. "All I have is green tea."

"Green tea is fine," I mutter.

Amethyst takes a drag on her cigarette and blows the smoke away from me. "We don't have to talk about–"

"It's fine," I intercede. *No point hiding anything now.*

"What was that?"

I sigh loudly. "That was my dysfunctional family proving once again that we cannot do anything normally." I sip the hot tea. It scalds my tongue a little but warms me up, too.

"I'm sorry. That was fucked up."

I laugh derisively. "Do normal families even exist?"

"Fuck if I know."

"I have so much going on right now. The last thing I need is more family drama."

"Yeah, what's up with your mom and grandma? There was some serious tension there."

"I don't know. Neither one will tell me what happened. All I know is that it was before I was born."

"It's been twenty years, at least, and they're still not over it?" She shakes her head in bafflement, exhaling smoke through her nose. "That's a serious grudge."

"That's my family for you." I swallow more of the tea. *How could I have been so stupid to think that dinner would go well?* Since we've moved to Willows Crest, my mom and grandma have avoided each other like the plague despite living in the same house. Mom has a raging temper, and Grandma knows just how to push her buttons. It's a sick game.

"And your grandma talking about witches, what the fuck was that? I kind of felt like I was on trial."

"In a way, you were," I confess. "She was testing you."

"Testing me for what?"

For a second, I contemplate just lying to her, but she has become a very good friend to me, and lying to her would be a violation of our bond. *Better to just tell her the truth.* I turn so that we're facing each other. "Remember how freaked out I was at Gypsies?" I begin.

"Yeah, that was just yesterday," she teases.

"What that old woman said was that there was immense power within me. She said other stuff, but it's the thing about power that struck a chord within me. Then, when she gave me that book, I just lost it."

"What was that book, anyway? It looked intense."

"It was a *Grimoire.*"

"Really?" Amethyst's eyes light up with excitement.

"My grandma saw it and dropped a major bomb on me." I swallow more tea as if it's liquid courage. "Apparently, my whole family are witches. I'm some rare male witch that was never supposed to happen, and it was predicted that I'd tip the scales between good and evil – one way or another – and that can't be undone. And I'm freaking out because I did a few spells and they worked! And then I lost my shit at the party, and all that weird stuff started happening..." I'm talking a mile a minute now. My face starts to turn purple from lack of oxygen.

"Breathe," Amethyst commands, patting me on the shoulder. I comply, and the pressure in my chest is relieved. "Are you okay?"

I nod my head in assent. *I'm majorly stressed out, and I feel like I just found out that my whole life has been a lie, but yes, I'm okay. Mostly.*

"Where is this all coming from?" she wonders.

"According to my grandma, a witch's powers are activated when she turns eighteen."

"That was the case for me," she frowns. "Wait, you said 'her.' There are male witches, too."

"That's not what my grandma said," Amethyst avoids my gaze.

"What?" I press.

"I don't want to say anything to upset you..."

"Just say it," I roll my eyes.

"It has to be because you're gay."

I feel like I was stabbed in the chest with a hot sword. "What are you talking about?" I challenge. "I-I'm not gay."

"Come on, Graham. It's 2011. Being gay isn't a huge deal anymore. No one will judge you."

I stare down at my hands in shame.

"It's not a bad thing. But you haven't shown any interest in a girl here, not even me, and I'm fucking hot!" She rubs my shoulder. "I'm not judging you, okay? I can't judge. I'm bi."

I always kind of suspected that, but never asked.

"On the bright side, Erasmus seems to be into you. Go take him for a test drive."

My chest feels tight again, but I force myself to breathe. This is the most awkward conversation I have ever had. But conversely, it also feels freeing. Don always said that if I came home with a boyfriend, that I was out. He always made a big production of how disgusting he finds gay people. *Am I really gay? I don't know. I've never done anything with a guy. I've never done anything with a girl either, to be fair, but still.*

"He's not into me," I finally say, meeting her brown eyes.

"Baby, he looks at you like you're his last meal on death row." That makes me blush, and I can't help the grin that tears at my mouth.

"Be proud of who you are," Amethyst says. "There's only one you in this world, so you have to own that shit."

I laugh, and the tension fades away. It wasn't like I'd imagined it being, my pseudo coming out. Amethyst didn't turn away in disgust. My reputation isn't forever tarnished. I guess part of what I was most afraid of was being labeled. I hate labels. I mean, I like designer labels, but not labeling people. I don't want my alleged sexuality to be what I'm defined by, and it seems like that's how most people define themselves, especially the gay people I've known. As far as I'm concerned, that only comes into play in the bedroom. There's no need for it to be on parade, no reason for *everyone* you meet to know that you're gay.

"Let me get you more tea," Amethyst offers, standing up.

"Thanks."

While she's in the kitchen topping our mugs, the white and orange cat sashays in from down the hall. He peers at me curiously.

"There's Sid Vicious," Amethyst says, returning with the tea. "Come here, Sid." She makes a kissy sound, and he lopes over toward us.

"Why do you call him Sid Vicious?" I ask.

"Watch." She waits until Sid is in her lap, and then she starts scratching one of his orange spots. "Mommy's going to get your spot!" she singsongs. Sid allows it for a few seconds, and then, with the trademark catlike agility, he bites her hand.

"He doesn't bite hard enough to hurt me," she explains. "He's such a little freak, but I love him."

I look around the apartment for the first time. It's tiny, but since Amethyst is the only one living here, that makes sense. There are two bookshelves behind us, full of paperbacks and decorated with Pop Vinyls. A few boxed action figures hang proudly on the wall. On the desk, several crystals lie in neat piles. I don't know much about crystals, but I do know that they somehow tie into the occult.

Gabriel Mero

"I use those to ward off bad juju," she explains, following my gaze. "There are so many types of crystals, though. I'll have to teach you." I nod. *Is that going to be part of the training that Grandma mentioned?*

Amethyst stands up again. "I haven't shown you the rest of the apartment," she continues. "My room is right over here."

She leads me down a hall to the first door on the left. Inside, the walls are painted gray with off-white trimming and are adorned with pirate ships, a pirate flag, and over the bed, a Marilyn Monroe print. *Nice touch.*

We sit down on the bed, and I'm impressed with how amazingly comfortable the mattress is. It's like lying on a squishy cloud. Amethyst leans down and comes back with a wooden box. "It's my witch box," she explains. "Normally, you keep that as close to you as you can."

"Okay." *It sounds like she knows her stuff.*

She opens the box and pulls out a few small notebooks, a deck of Tarot cards, and a few vials of herbs and spices–probably the ones from the store yesterday. "Oh, gosh, these stupid books," she says, covering her mouth.

"What are they?" I inquire.

"I was so angsty when I was in middle school. These are all stupid quotes and poems that I thought were very poignant. I also wrote spells in here."

"Oh?"

"Nothing too sophisticated. Just like good luck spells and purifying baths. Stuff like that."

I pick up her Tarot cards. "Do you know how to use these?"

"Of course. Want me to do a reading for you?"

"Sure," I shrug. I've never had my Tarot cards read before, not by someone who knows what they're doing. When I was in middle school, I was visiting my grandmother for a week one summer and found a deck of Tao Tarot cards. She noticed my interest and let me have them. I've used them several times in the years since then, but I never felt like I was doing it correctly.

Amethyst picks the cards up and shuffles them a few times. "Do you want to shuffle them again for good measure?"

"No," I say. "You're good."

"I need you to cut the deck for me."

"I don't know what that means..."

"Just divide it into two stacks," she explains. I take the deck from her and run my finger down the edges until a voice within me says to stop. "Ask it a question."

I hold the two piles close to me and whisper, "What will become of me?" I hand the decks back to Amethyst, and she nods at me and tells me to pick three cards.

I again listen to my intuition and stop when my inner voice tells me to. I lay the three cards face down on the bedspread and wait.

Amethyst flips the first card to reveal the High Priestess. The next card is the Magician. The final card is the Emperor. All three cards are upright.

"Is a life of power and luxury awaiting me?" I tease, lying back.

"You definitely deserve it," Amethyst replies. She's quiet for a moment and then begins. "The High Priestess card signifies spiritual enlightenment in your subconscious. You need to learn to embrace the femininity within and trust your intuition and psychic insight."

"Again, with the gay thing?" I moan dramatically.

Amethyst's lips quirk up into a smile, and she continues. "The Magician card is the first card in the deck. It portends a new beginning. If you dream it, you now have the tools at your disposal to make it happen; you just need to stay focused on your goals."

"Sioned did say that I have the power to make my dreams come true," I muse.

"See?" She shifts on the bed. "Now, the Emperor card is the father figure of the deck. Drawing this card means that you're about to step into that authoritative position. You will be powerful, respected, and wise."

"Wow!" I gasp.

"See? You let that asshole, Don, make you feel worthless, like you'd never amount to anything, and the truth is that you're bound for greatness. You're going to be a powerful witch, and everyone will respect you. You have to stop letting your self-worth be determined by other people's opinions of you – unless they are good opinions, like mine. Seriously, people will try to tear you down because they are insecure with themselves. It has nothing to do with you. And now that you know that you're this powerful, badass witch, you can be like, 'not today, bitches,' and put harmless little spells on them."

Hearing Amethyst go on and on about how wonderful I am, brings tears to my eyes. I am truly blessed to have such a devoted, genuine friend. "Thank you," I rasp, my voice choked with emotion.

"No, thank you. You make me feel valued and awesome. I fucking love you to death, and I hope you know you're not going anywhere. You're stuck with me."

We hug, and all the bad shit floats away.

Eventually, I have to go back home. Amethyst offers to let me crash at her place. The offer is tempting, but I can't help but think of poor Romana. She needs me there.

Amethyst offers to come in with me, but I tell her to go home. This cross is mine to bear, and mine alone.

I open the front door, and see Mom sitting at the foot of the stairs, tears staining her cheeks. She jumps to her feet and shoves me back against the door.

"Where the hell have you been?" she bellows, getting in my face.

"I was at Amethyst's," I reply.

"Why haven't you been answering your phone? We were worried sick!"

"I don't have my phone."

"Oh, bullshit. That phone is attached to you like your dick. What? You had to go whine to your little friend about how mean I am to you? How I make you take care of your brother? Well, boo-fucking-hoo. I was younger than you are and watching Julian so my mom could work."

Huh? Who? "Julian? Who's Julian?" I've never heard anything about Julian or any other siblings. My mom is an only child.

Panic glosses over her features momentarily before anger takes back over. "You need to stop being so self-centered. You ran out on your party and left us with all the cleanup. You upset your brother. And now I'm spending my day off worried that you'd gotten yourself killed or something."

I try to reign in my temper, but the more she yells at me, the harder it gets. The storm inside of me rages once again, and I clench my fists to keep it from exploding out of me.

"I'm self-centered? You're the one that makes everything about you. You're the one who can't make a good decision to save your life."

With each accusation, I step forward, and she starts to step back. "You're the one who married that sadistic fucker. You let him abuse me. Me. Your son. You never stepped in, never told him that he was going too far. Nothing."

"I never wanted to be a mother," she confesses, sniffling. "I knew I'd be bad at it."

"Then why did you have me?"

She's quiet for a few moments. "I wasn't going to. I'd scheduled an abortion, and the night before, I got really drunk so that I couldn't change my mind. Grandma kept telling me not to do it, and when it came down to it, I couldn't." She breaks down into sobs now. I pity her, but she needs to hear the truth.

"You ruined your marriage, Mom. You did it because you're selfish and cold, and you can't control your temper. He shouldn't have hit you. I wanted to kill him for that, but you pushed him too far. You've never known when enough is enough."

My hands shake as I struggle to contain the storm. My mother steps too far back and lands on her butt on the bottom stair.

"I'm sorry that your life didn't work out the way that you wanted it to. I really am. But I will not let you take your misery out of me anymore. You kept me, so live with your decision."

Grandma appears at the top of the stairs and hurries down. "Leave the boy alone, Beverly," she says. "You've done enough damage for one day, I think"

My mom crawls up the stairs, crying like a baby. I watch her go, feeling bad. *Maybe I was too harsh on her.*

"You weren't," Grandma says, reading my mind. "Your mother has always lashed out instead of looking in the mirror." She hesitates. "I overheard her telling you about the... abortion."

"Yeah," I nod.

"I'm sorry, Graham. I didn't want you to ever find out."

"It's okay. It doesn't hurt my feelings. She was young and scared and made a decision that felt right at the time. But thanks for fighting for me."

Grandma smiles and blinks back tears of her own. It's certainly an emotional day.

"I'm sorry that I freaked out and ruined dinner. And made a huge mess," I apologize.

"I'm sorry, too. I shouldn't have behaved like I did. I could read your friend's mind, and it hurt my feelings."

"What do you mean?"

"She was thinking about how much we all stress you out and how much she wanted to tell us off for it."

What little anger I have left melts away. "I owe you my life, Grandma. I think I can handle the occasional stress here and there."

She smiles warmly at me and blots her tears away. "Are you hungry? I could whip up some more of that Chinese food for you," she winks. "Oh, and you haven't tried your nacho dip."

"That sounds great, thanks."

Together, Grandma and I go into the kitchen to whip up some mischief.

Chapter Ten

When I wake up the next morning, I'm instantly overwhelmed with regret. Yes, my mother can be a cold, selfish bitch, but she's also my mom, and I love her more than words. *I shouldn't have exploded on her last night. She has enough misery in her life, I shouldn't be adding to it.*

Downstairs, I can hear the soft hum of Brent's television and Grandma singing softly to herself. She's in the choir at her Temple, one of the lead sopranos. I can't hear what she's singing but can hear her voice.

I have no motivation to get out of bed. I slept fairly well, but between the blow-up at dinner, being forced to come out to Amethyst, and the showdown with Mom, I am emotionally drained. I'm glad it's a Sunday, so I can just spend the day in bed, pondering.

Romana sees I'm awake and starts rubbing on my hand, begging me to pet her. Her purrs sound like a log splitter in action. *At least someone is happy,* I think, kissing the top her head where the orange pattern gets darker and forms an 'M'.

Maybe it's because she's never been outside, but she never smells bad.

I pull the *Grimoire* out from under my bed and flip through it while petting Romana. I still can't believe that all this stuff is real. It makes for great entertainment on TV but in real life... I don't know, it seems weird.

I was always raised to believe in God and try to do and be good. Despite Don being Catholic, we never really went to church except for when we lived in Port Huron, but the faith was still there. My secret Judaism lessons with Grandma were the only time I really felt it in my soul, though. I loved the connection to my roots and the grand affairs of the Jewish holidays. I never got to have a Bar Mitzvah, but I still feel like I've followed the faith closely. Wicca or Paganism, is considered a religion in its own right... *So by embracing this destiny or whatever, am I betraying my faith? Am I turning my back on the God who has looked after me, and provided for me, all my life? Am I damning my soul? In the Jewish faith, Hell doesn't exist, but there is an underworld called Sheol where souls go after death. It's a dark, cavernous terrain.*

I shut down these thoughts and focus on the worn pages before me. I see spells to bring good luck, spells to lose weight and gain weight, spells to summon money, and even spells to bring love. From what I've always seen on TV, the Wiccans believe in doing whatever you want as long as it doesn't harm others. The rule being that a spell should not be done for personal gain because it will come back to bite you on the ass threefold. At least, those were the rules on *Charmed*.

I stop at a page detailing how to learn telekinesis. I've always wished that I could move objects with my mind, mostly because I'm lazy, but also because I just think it would be awesome to be able to do so.

"What do you think, Romana? Should Daddy try it?" I ask her in a gentle tone. She yowls in response. I settle back against my pillows and read the page.

Learning Telekinesis

Some witches are born with the gift of telekinesis, while others must strive to learn the power. Learning to manifest telekinetic energy is not an easy task, nor is it a fast one. If you choose to learn it, you must be patient.

Sit down in a comfortable place. Focus on an object placed before you. In the beginning, it is best to start with something light such as a feather or a pen.

Focus on the object and breathe, clearing your mind and opening it to the energies that inhabit everything. When you feel those energies broadly, imagine the object slowly rising off of the bed or table. Do not strain, just simply let it be.

If you do not succeed at first, keep trying. Rome was not built in a day.

I can't help but laugh at the wry humor of the ancestral witch who had written down this lesson. You don't often think of people in the past as having a sense of humor, but they must have. Although, considering they were lucky to live past their mid-thirties... perhaps not.

I sit up cross-legged in bed, straightening my back. I can hear and feel the vertebrae snap into place at the movement. I take a fountain pen from my nightstand and place it on the cover of the *Grimoire*. I take a deep, calming breath and mutter, "Here we go, Romana. Help Daddy out."

I close my eyes briefly and then focus my gaze directly on the gray pen. It is immobile on the book, just as it should be. I squint my eyes at it and focus on it, imagining the weight of it and how easy it would be to lift it up with my hand.

I don't know how energy is supposed to feel. There is a tingling sensation within my body, and the air seems to warm noticeably. *Am I doing it right?* I wonder.

I squint harder and imagine the pen floating up off of the book. After a few seconds, I can feel myself straining and relax my muscles. When I do, I see the pen shift almost imperceptibly. No one would notice it if they weren't paying as close attention to it as I am. *Yes!* I exclaim mentally. *I did it!*

I try to quiet my mind again and repeat the effort, but the focus is tempered with my exuberance at having managed to move the pen – even just a little – on my first try.

Okay. I take another deep breath and close my eyes, calling back all the breathing techniques that I'd learned a few summers ago when I'd been super into yoga. I inhale through my nose, feeling my chest expand. I continue to inhale until I feel the need to exhale – and then I pause for a moment – before expelling the breath out through my mouth. I can hear the air rushing through my mouth as I do it. I repeat this several times until I feel my mind start to relax. *Maybe I should start doing yoga again*, I think. *It's so calming.*

I open my eyes and focus once more on the pen. I try not to strain and open myself up to the tingling and warmth. It washes over me, practically making me euphoric. I embrace it, feeling like I'm floating on a cloud.

The pen slowly shakes and then begins to rise, as if an invisible string or wire is pulling it up toward the ceiling. I gasp in wonder, and it starts a downward trajectory I regain my focus, and it rises until it's at my eye level. I exhale sharply and imagine it spinning. After a few hitches, it starts to spin.

My door opens, and I lose focus. The pen topples to the bed. It strikes the mattress and rolls across the wooden floor. Romana bolts and burrows under the bed in fright.

I look up to see my mother in the doorway, shuffling her feet nervously. "I knocked," she says quietly.

"I didn't hear. I was focusing on–on...."

"I saw." She chews her lip. "I never gave you your birthday present."

I blink a few times and then motion for her to come in. Slowly, she enters and comes to sit beside me on the bed. "I'm sorry about last night," she blurts, staring down at her hands, which are worrying each other nervously. "I'm sorry for everything."

I have never heard my mother apologize for anything, ever. *This is a first.* "I'm sorry, too," I say. "I shouldn't have said those things to you."

"You were right to." She nods her head. "I haven't been a good mother to you."

"Hey." I take her right hand and squeeze it. "It could have been a lot worse. I was never raped or beaten. I always had food and a roof over my head."

"But we didn't give you the things a parent should give their child. Self-confidence, love, support. The truth is, I don't know how to give those things or feel them myself. I never have." Her eyes glaze over, as if she's mentally reliving the memories of the past.

"Growing up, I was never close to my mom. She spent her days on the couch watching soap operas and putting curlers in her hair. She never hugged or kissed me. Never offered any kind of emotional support. My dad may have been drunk and lazy, but he was always good to me. I remember being a little girl and waiting excitedly for my dad to come home so that I could go in the bathroom with him and help him shave. I loved it." At the mention of this, her lips tug up into a smile and lines are gone from her face. Carefree, she is beautiful.

"But he started to get sick and stopped going to work. He started drinking more and more, and got mean."

As quickly as the smile had come, it vanished, bringing the worry lines back, adding years to her countenance. "We were already poor to begin with, but we really hit rock bottom. I remember only having one pair of purple pants to wear to school, and the crotch was ripped. I'd pray that no one saw. My mom had to go back to school and work two jobs to support us. After the house burned down and we built this place, their relationship got worse. She kicked him out. I get why she did it, but he was a sick man. It wasn't his fault. Mental illness runs in our family. My dad's mom was a paranoid schizophrenic. My dad had it, too. He managed it pretty well in the beginning, but in the end, it overtook him. The MS didn't help, either. He spent the last years of his life in a wheelchair, pissing and shitting his diaper." I notice that her eyes begin to glisten, but she continues her narrative.

"I started babysitting as soon as I could to earn money. I bought my own school clothes and supplies." She pauses. "I was molested a few times – by different guys. Family. I never told Grandma or anyone. There were a few times I considered suicide, but I didn't want to be a coward."

Tears spill down her cheeks, and I squeeze her hand harder to console her. Mom hasn't ever told me much about her childhood. Now I can see why. It sounds like something out of a Victor Hugo novel.

"Your dad and I weren't dating long before I got pregnant with you. He was irresponsible – pot, beer, and cigarettes were all he cared about. I knew marrying him would be a disaster, and I couldn't raise a baby on my own, and that's why I was going to abort you. It wasn't because I didn't want you or thought you would ruin my life. It was to save you from this mess that I am. But you saved me. In so many ways. You gave me something to fight for, something to live for. I know I don't always show it, but you're my best friend. I'd be lost without you.

"I'm sorry that I let Don hurt you like that. I should have stopped him; I should have left him. I was afraid of having to take care of myself. And I'm sorry that I've been so shitty since Brent was born. I just can't cope with this. He'll never grow up. He'll never learn to drive a car, or graduate high school, get a job. He'll never fall in love." Her voice breaks, and more tears wash down her face, like a river overcoming a dam. "And it's all my fault, I know it is."

I knew she blamed herself. "It is *not* your fault that Brent is Autistic." I stare into her eyes. "It's not."

"You don't know that."

"Don is the one who doesn't know his family history. Plus, he was older when Brent was conceived. Chances are he's to blame."

"But there's still a chance. You're not a parent, Graham, you don't understand how it feels."

I can't argue with that logic, but still. My poor mother should not have to go through the rest of her life thinking that she's to blame for Brent being Autistic. "There was always going to be something wrong with him," I remind her. "Remember? They thought he was going to have water on the brain?"

"Yeah." She nods her head. "They did an amniocentesis to rule it out. I'd decided that if it came back showing that he was going to be messed up…" she sighs. "I was going to terminate the pregnancy."

I hadn't known that part, but why would I? I was eleven at the time. "What did Don say?"

"There wasn't much to say. We both felt it wasn't right to bring a child into the world to go through that. That's not a life."

Some people would argue that, and accuse people, like my mother, of preferring death, over having one. But I'm not one of those misguided social warriors. I am a logical person who sees the daily struggle.

We are silent for a moment, gathering our thoughts. I was not prepared for such a bombshell from her, let alone the whole nuclear missile! She's basically laid everything bare before me. I'm not sure how to process it all.

"Why did you bind my powers when I was a boy?" I ask, picking up my next train of thought.

My mother sighs heavily as if the weight of the world is resting heavily upon her shoulders. "I didn't want this life for you, Graham," she confesses.

"Why not? It's pretty cool so far, if you ask me."

"Be careful, Graham, it's all fun and games in the beginning," she says ominously.

"What's that supposed to mean?"

"Just be careful. That's all I'm saying." And just like that, the wall that my mom has always maintained around herself is suddenly back up and intact.

"Why did you bind your powers?" I press.

"It wasn't for me." Her reply is short. She doesn't want to talk about it.

"Are you mad that I'm a witch?"

She stares at me for several long seconds before answering. "It's not the life I would have chosen for you, but if you like it and you're happy, then I won't say anything. How long have you been practicing telekinesis?"

"A half-hour, maybe."

She nods in approval. "I'm impressed. Back when I was trying to learn it, it took me almost a year to get my pencil to move, and even then, it was just barely. It wasn't until I figured out that my temper affected my powers."

"What were your powers?"

"*Power*," she corrects. "I really disappointed Grandma."

"I'm sure that's not true."

"My mother is this great, all-powerful witch. She's proud of her heritage. Proud of our destiny.

I'm the one who bound her powers and gave up because I couldn't hack it."

"She respects your choice," I assure her, as if I actually know. Maybe Grandma *is* disappointed in my mother for hanging up her broom and conical hat.

"I'll believe that when I see it."

"Could we unbind your power, if you changed your mind?"

My mom stares down at the *Grimoire* as if seeing it for the first time. Technically, she is. "I won't change my mind, but, yeah, I'm sure you could unbind them. My power was Thrall."

"You could impose your will on others?" I balk. She nods. "That's bad ass!"

"No, it is a dangerous power that should not be toyed with!" she exclaims, suddenly angry again.

"Okay..." I say with a small, defeated shrug.

Mom seems to regret her outburst and pats my knee. "Here." She hands me a parcel wrapped in Halloween wrapping paper. "Happy birthday."

Romana comes out from hiding and leap onto the bed. Surprisingly, Mom reaches out and pets her.

I smile and turn the package over to find the seam in the wrapping paper. I'm careful not to tear it. It's another of my weird quirks. I tear along the seam and pull off the paper to reveal a couple of the *Star Trek* books that I've been lusting after. *Survivors*, and *Imzadi I* and *II*. I beam. "Thanks, Mom!" I throw my arms around her, and for the first time in a long time, she hugs me back. It feels nice.

"You're welcome."

"Let's not fight anymore, okay?" I implore her. "Life is too short to always be fighting and hurting each other. I know you get mad and can't control your temper, but you need to learn to. You can't be psycho forever."

My mom laughs past her tears. "You think I'm a psycho?"

"Sometimes," I admit, chuckling. "You're a scary bitch when you get pissed off. You get all red in the face, and the fists go flying." I've been on the receiving end of her temper too many times, if anyone knows, it's me.

Mom pets Romana, scratching her soft, orange sherbet-colored belly. It's weird seeing my mom petting my cat. She doesn't like animals, and to the best of my knowledge, she never has. I wonder if this is an olive branch toward a newfound peace or just an effort not to be rude.

"She likes you," I say, smiling.

"Well, that's a first. Cats usually hate me. So do people."

"Only the stupid ones."

She smiles sadly at me. Her life has truly been plagued by so much disappointment, and loneliness, more than any one person should bear. *My poor mother.*

"You have to work things out with Grandma," I tell her. "Until you guys can work through all of that anger and hurt, you're going to be stuck in this rut of self-loathing."

"How did you end up being so smart?" my mother asks, swiping at her leaking nose. "You certainly didn't get that from me."

"You don't give yourself enough credit. I certainly didn't get it from my dad. At this point, I doubt he has any useful brain cells left."

"Probably not. Have you heard from him lately?"

"Not since I called him on his birthday back in April."

"Whoa."

"Yeah," I shrug. "It's okay, though. The last thing I need is more drama in my life. This whole finding out that I'm a witch thing has completely turned my world upside down."

"Graham, you're not just *a* witch," Mom says. "You're *the* witch. You're basically the Supreme." I love that she watches *American Horror Story* with me, so she can use the references.

"That makes it even more stressful!"

"You'll do great. I know you will. You've always been a good student when you apply yourself."

Wow. A compliment from my mother. It must be my lucky day. "Thanks, Mom," I say.

Mom stands up and pulls her bathrobe more tightly around herself. "Well, I should go check on Brent. I'm sure Grandma is ready to tear her hair out. He's a little shit when he wants to be."

"You're telling me."

"Are you coming down?" she asks.

"In a bit. I want to read the *Grimoire* some more."

"Okay. Happy hunting." She smiles and then opens the door, shutting it behind her. Romana looks after her, as if confused as to why her new friend was going away.

I get back under the covers. It's cooler than it should be in October, and despite my hoodie, sweatpants, and thick socks, I can still feel the chill. As soon as the blanket covers me, I'm basking in warmth again. *I'll have to try to find that spell to warm myself up again if it's already this cold.* I shudder to think what the winter will be like.

"Hey, Romana, do you want snuggles?" I ask her in my baby voice.

In response, she comes and nestles into the crook of my arm, purring contentedly. I kiss the 'M' on her brow again and crack open the *Grimoire*.

Chapter Eleven

By Halloween, it had become pretty chilly. Being the wuss that I am, I adopted a beanie and a scarf as my go-to fashion accessory. People look at me like I'm stark raving mad, but I can't help it. I've always been incredibly sensitive to the cold. Within seconds of taking my socks off, my feet turn to icicles. It comes in handy in the summer with no air conditioning, but it's a bitch in the wintertime.

Grandma is ecstatic for Samhain. I always thought that it was pronounced SAM-HAIN, but apparently, it's actually pronounced SOW'N. *Damned Gaelic or whatever language that is.*

Halloween is my absolute favorite holiday, but alas, I won't be able to properly enjoy it this year. Vito has decided to give me a test-run as the night manager. He gave me a key and printouts on how to run the end-of-day and balance the tills. I'm absolutely terrified of messing up, but I let the worry rage away inside. Outside, I am perfectly composed. If I want to be the manager, I have to learn how to reign in my emotions and get shit done.

I'm kind of bummed that Halloween/Samhain is on a Wednesday this year. To me, it should be a Friday or Saturday. I don't have to worry about deciding on a costume to wear today; we have the day off from classes, probably because Wicca has been recognized as a religion in recent years. As much as I enjoy college, I'm certainly not going to complain about getting to sleep in.

Amethyst wanted to hang out, so we made plans. She picked me up around noon, the ever-present cigarette burning away.

"So, where are we going?" I ask as we cruise down the streets in town. *I really hope she's not dragging me back to Gypsies'. I really can't handle another round of weirdness from Sioned.*

Her lips tug up into a mischievous grin, but her eyes don't leave the road. "I need to get some supplies," she says mysteriously.

"Amethyst, please tell me you're not taking me to *Gypsies'* again." We're driving slowly enough that I could probably jump, tuck, and roll and be mostly fine. Unfortunately, I haven't mastered levitation yet, but I also don't want to get too free with the magic. If the public saw that, I'd end up tied to a stake with flames licking hungrily at my feet. I shudder at the thought.

"No, dork," she cackles.

"Then what?"

"I'm taking you to my guy. We're going to get some weed, and then we'll get high at my place and watch TV or something. We can try some spells if you want."

Relief washes through my veins, only to be quickly replaced with trepidation. I can't smoke weed. I have to work in four hours and be a responsible, functioning almost-adult. "I can't get high," I tell her firmly. "Manager training day, remember?"

"It'll calm you down. You'll be nice and chill."

She's trying to tempt me like the serpent tempted Eve to eat the forbidden fruit. I hate to admit it, but I am tempted. I've never gotten high before. *No, I can't...*

"Not today. I have to be alert and professional."

"Okay," she sighs. "Well, I'm going to get high."

"Do whatever you have to."

It isn't a long drive. She parks near the high school and leads me off toward the woods. "Your drug dealer lives in the woods?" I query, my mind racing with possibilities. *Who lives in the woods? The Blair Witch lived in the woods... how did that work out for Heather, Mike, and Josh?*

"Yeah. He has a nice little cabin out there. He's not just a drug dealer, though. He and his boyfriend are members of the magic community, too."

"There's a magic community now, too?" *Jeez, there's a community for everything. I thought the LGBTQIA 'community' was bad enough. I've always hated that word and the idea that you're somehow bonded or connected just because you share a few traits with other people. If you ask me, it's incredibly elitist.*

"You know what I mean," Amethyst huffs, hugging her hoodie more tightly against the late autumn chill.

We enter the woods, and it makes me sad to see that the ground is already covered with a heavy layer of dried brown leaves. It's still technically October. *Does winter really need to sink its depressing, murderous claws in already?*

"How far in is he?" I don't like going too deep into the woods. Thanks to *the Blair Witch Project*, I have an intense irrational fear of going in and never coming back out again.

"It's just about a five-minute walk," she assures me.

"How did you meet him?"

"We used to go to school together. He's a few years older than I am, so he graduated when I was a freshman."

"So, he's a drug dealer and a witch?"

"I don't think he's a witch. I don't remember what he identifies as."

"I'm just curious because my grandma told me that male witches are rare."

"Yeah, you told me that. Weird."

We crunch our way through the dried leaves for several minutes before coming to a simple log cabin in a clearing. On the roof, the chimney spews a lilac-colored smoke out into the air. It smells like jasmine. *Just what does he cook up in there?*

As we approach the front door, it swings open, and a giant walks out. He's easily six foot four, and while not overweight, he's not a rail either. His light blond hair cascades down past his shoulders. Around his neck, he wears a triquetra necklace.

"I've been expecting you, bitch!" he calls. His voice is slightly higher than mine. Not the voice of a serial killer. I feel myself relax. He starts babbling in Spanish. I speak French and Welsh, so I tune it out. He turns and takes me in, scrutinizing me through slitted ice-blue eyes. "Is this the one you were telling me about?"

"Yeah," Amethyst replies, smiling at me. "Isn't he goddamned adorable?"

The blond giant shrugs. "He's okay, I guess. Not my type, but not totally disgusting."

"Excuse me?" I say before I think.

"I like bears, honey, not little twinks." *Bears? Twinks? What the hell is he talking about?*

"Be nice, Malachi," Amethyst intervenes.

"I'm sorry," he apologizes. "I'm just blunt. Don't take it personally."

"I... won't..." I drawl.

He examines me again for several seconds. "Yes, I can definitely sense a lot of power inside you. You need training, but you're definitely a natural."

"You practice magic?" I ask.

"Yes. I'm a Druid. A healing Druid, actually."

"Oh?" I didn't know that Druids were real, but I guess if witches are, so why not other far-fetched things?

"I've been practicing for years. I was into it before it was cool."

"I'm not into it because it's cool," I assure him. "Apparently, it's my destiny."

"It is extremely rare to encounter a male witch who hasn't crossed over."

"Crossed over?"

"Something about the testosterone or whatever, it blocks the magic out and makes men aggressive. Male witches almost always cross over to the dark side, the warlock side. Those who don't, well, they don't last too long." He pats me on the shoulder, providing little comfort.

Is he telling the truth? Why would Grandma lie to me? My head spins as I try to process this new information. For once in my life, I'd felt special, and now... I don't know exactly what I'm feeling right now.

Gabriel Mero

"Anyway, he hands Amethyst a little baggie full of pungent green leaves. "This is the prime stuff," he says.

"Right on." She hands him a roll of bills and pockets the baggie of marijuana.

"Do you guys want to come in for a bit, maybe smoke a joint?" Malachi offers.

Amethyst looks at me, and she must sense how uncomfortable that would make me because she shakes her head. "Not today. We have a movie we need to get to, just needed a little treat for after."

"Okay, well, you know where I am if you need anything." He stares into my eyes. "If you need any magical healing, feel free to stop by."

I nod, and he retreats into the cabin, belting out a Christina Aguilera song.

Amethyst and I head back to the car, and before I know it, we're safe in her tidy living room. She sits on the floor and rolls the leaves into papers. I've never watched anyone roll joints before.

"I wish you didn't have to work tonight," she says. "We could get high and talk to the dead."

"Talk to the dead?"

"Yeah. Ever since I was a little girl, I've been able to sense the energy and lingering spirits of the dead. At first, clairvoyance was a major letdown to me, but I've come to love it."

"You can speak with the dead?" I sit ramrod straight, amazed.

"I mean, I can mainly speak to them through a Ouija board, but today is Samhain. The veils between the world of the living and the dead are extra thin."

"Can we try summoning a ghost? A specific one?" My mind instantly goes to my dad's mom, my Grandma Marilyn. She and I were super close. My dad was her baby, and being his only offspring, I was practically royalty. She passed away unexpectedly when I was four. Even though my memories of her are misty, I can clearly remember the day I found out she died.

****

My mom and I had just returned to the duplex we shared with Don. My mother picked me up from daycare after work, and after some grocery shopping, we went home. As soon as we walked in the door, I noticed that the answering machine was blinking. I loved playing the messages, so I ran over and pressed play.

"Graham, hey, it's Grandma Ginevra... your Dad just called me. He asked me to tell you that... your Grandma Marilyn passed away."

If there was more to the message, I didn't hear it. Despite being only four and never having experienced death of any kind before, I knew what the message meant. No more Grandma Marilyn. I didn't even know that she was ill.

Though my vision was blurred with tears, I made my way up the stairs to my room and sobbed in my bed.

I was desperate to see her just one last time at her funeral. I went up to the casket and tried to peer inside. Thankfully, Grandma Ginevra stopped me.

After losing his mother, my dad was never the same, and I saw him less and less, and then we moved downstate.

****

Thinking about it now, I tear up. All I remember about Grandma Marilyn is that she was sweet. She never yelled at me, never hit me. She was always warm and loving. She always had sweets for me, and she simply adored me.

"Are you okay?" Amethyst asks, seeing the tears in my eyes.

"Yeah." I refuse to let them fall. "Can you contact my Grandma Marilyn for me?"

"I can try."

She gets up and walks down the hall. She returns with her arms full of white candles a few moments later. She arranges the candles in a circle big enough to surround us, plus some. Then she comes back with more candles and places them at the five points of a pentagram. Amethyst does not mess around when it comes to witchcraft!

"Sit here with me," she orders, sitting cross-legged on the hardwood floor. I sit, and she takes my hands. "Just close your eyes and think of who you want to contact. All I need is her name."

"Marilyn Norris," I say without hesitation. I close my eyes and think of her, doing my best to remember her smile, her voice.

Amethyst starts the incantation.

Spirit show yourself,

Spirit reveal,

Spirit come to me

So I know you are real!

As the powerful words leave her mouth, a chill creeps into the air, and I crack open an eye to see the flames of the candles flickering from an unseen, magical wind. The room grows dark, and then a spot of light appears. It grows larger, taking on the shape of a woman. The light gets so bright I have to close my eyes—it's like staring into the sun—and when I open them after a minute, my grandma stands before me.

She's bathed in light and is translucent, but it's her. She's dressed in a simple white floor-length gown. Her dark hair is close-cropped, just like I remember it. Her glasses reflect Amethyst, and me sitting on the floor. Her smile makes me choke out a sob, and I stand, reaching out for her.

"Grandma?" I rasp, incredulous. *This is amazing.*

"Hello, Graham."

"I can't believe it worked. I can't believe you're here!" I stand up—careful not to knock over any candles or break the circle—and touch my hand against hers. Of course, my hand goes through hers, and there's a sensation of coldness... kind of like sticking your hand into a bucket of dough. "I've missed you."

"Oh, my baby boy," Grandma Marilyn says. "You always were such a sweetheart."

"Are you okay? Are you... are you happy?" It sounds lame, but I need to know.

"I loved my life. I loved being a mother, a wife, and a grandmother. I loved you all so very, very much."

The tears flow and I feel absolutely no shame. "Why did you go?" My voice is so heavy with emotion that it comes out as barely more than a whisper.

"I didn't want to, my love, but it was my time. The Lord was calling me home."

"But I never got to say goodbye. Never got to tell you I love you or hug you one last time."

She smiles sadly. "And I regret that. I wish we could have said goodbye. You were so young. You couldn't possibly have understood what was going on."

"Are you in Heaven?" I sound like the little boy I was when she was alive.

"Yes. I am at peace. I watch over all of you! I am so proud of the young man you've become, Graham." That breaks the dam, and I sob. No one has ever told me that they were proud of me before. It feels good.

"We all miss you."

"I am alive in all of your hearts and memories," she says warmly. "Just do me one favor?"

"What? Anything!"

"Forgive your father, Graham. I know he's hurt you a lot, but you just can't ignore him. He's not as strong as you are. I babied him. I turned him into a codependent brat. When I passed on, he just couldn't cope. He numbed the pain with drugs and alcohol. But he does love you."

"I don't know if I can," I admit. "I don't need more pain in my life."

"Please try, for me."

I can't deny her request. "I'll try."

"Good boy."

"How long can you stay?"

Grandma Marilyn looks over at Amethyst, who is grunting a little in her effort to maintain the connection. "I don't know how much longer she'll last. It's hard work building a bridge between the two worlds."

"I don't want you to go!"

"I must, my love. I don't belong here anymore. If you ever miss me, just remember my love for you."

"Can we summon you again sometime?"

"I look forward to it."

"All you have to do to break the connection is sever the circle. Move one of the candles." Amethyst's voice is heavy, as if she, too, is crying.

My vision blurry with tears, I step to the side and nudge one of the candles out of alignment. I watch through a wave of tears as my Grandma fades into nothingness.

I stare into the space she occupied and suddenly feel Amethyst's strong arms around me, rubbing my back. The tears continue to fall, harder than ever before.

I pull myself together just in time for us to go to work. She had to take a quick nap to recharge after the séance, but now she looks better than ever.

****

Vito welcomes us and hands us a giant orange bowl full to the brim with an assortment of candy bars. Reese's, Kit Kat, Milky Way, Clark bars, Smarties, you name it. My mouth waters a bit as I take in the plethora of delicious sugary sweetness. "These are for the trick or treaters," he explains. "We normally have a decent turnout, so use them sparingly. When you run out, you're out." He takes in my quiet demeanor. "Are you okay?"

I nod. I am okay. I'm sad that Grandma Marilyn had to go again, but I am incredibly grateful that I got to see and talk to her again. I'm still processing it.

"You weren't smoking the ganja with this one?" He nods toward Amethyst, who sticks her tongue out.

"No, I tried to get him to, but he wouldn't. He's too professional."

"Excellent!" He claps me on the back. "You've got manager written all over your face."

I smile. "Thanks."

Vito leaves soon after. I set about washing and arranging shelves. Amethyst offers to be on trick or treat duty since she's more outgoing. I don't fight her for the "coveted' task. I hate kids.

I shut down and focus entirely on my task. I barely hear the ding of the door opening or the shrill children's voices. I only stop once I reach the last shelf and realize that I've done the whole store! Apparently, when I put my mind to it, I can be extremely productive.

I sweep and mop the store, and when I finally look up, it is eight o'clock. Time to send Amethyst home. The trick or treaters have died out, and a peaceful quiet has settled in. I can spend the last hour reading my *Star Trek* book.

Amethyst clocks out and rifles through her purse for a cigarette. "Are you sure you don't want me to hang? I'll give you a ride home."

Gabriel Mero

"No, thanks," I reply. "Go home and snuggle with Sid Vicious. I can walk home. It's only a few blocks."

"Are you sure? It's pretty cold out there."

"Yeah. The walk will do me some good."

"Okay."

"Thanks for what you did today. I owe you one."

"Don't mention it. Text me."

"Okay."

I watch her leave and then take a seat on the stool behind the counter. Vito said he doesn't mind if we take it easy as long as we work the majority of the shift. Considering I did everything that needed to be done, he'll be okay with me relaxing with my new book. I crack it open and lose myself.

I only get through a few pages before the sound of the bell above the door brings me away from the gut-wrenching poverty, rape, and gutting of a poor ginger cat that I can't help but picture as Romana.

I look up to see Erasmus walking toward me. *Okay,* I decide. *No more letting him make you into a freak.*

"Hi," I say, forcing myself to remain calm.

"Hi." He smiles wide, and my heart skips a beat. Yeah, he's definitely attractive.

He strides past me into the store, his hair coiffed up in a stylish pompadour, as always. I watch him for a few seconds and then stare down at the book. It's riveting. I don't recall ever reading a book that has engrossed me so deeply within the first few pages. It is a little dark for a *Star Trek* book, but considering Tasha Yar and Data are the main characters, I assume that the beginning is a flashback to Tasha's tragic childhood.

"Have there been any good horror movies out lately?" Erasmus asks, making me jump.

"Um... I don't know. Let's look." I sound dumb, but he regards me with a kind smile, so chances are he doesn't notice how awkward I'm feeling. I walk around the counter and into the store, my eyes scanning the shelves. "*Megan Is Missing* was good, but kind of out there," I say over my shoulder. "*Cabin In The Woods* sucked. I was disappointed in *The Caller.*"

"It doesn't even have to be a new one," Erasmus continues. "I'm a fan of the older stuff like *Halloween* and *Friday the 13th.*"

"Me, too," I admit with a shy smile. *Oh, my God! We have something in common!*

"I see that you guys have the newer *Halloween* movies, but not the old ones."

"Yeah, if they don't rent after a year, we pull them for sale."

"Shit."

"Yeah, sorry." I almost tell him that I own them all, but that isn't pertinent to the conversation. I highly doubt that Erasmus Mayfair and I will spend any time together outside the store.

"The *Texas Chainsaw Massacre* remake from the early 2000s is really good," I say, pointing to it. On the opposite shelf, I find *The Last Exorcism*. "This one was pretty good. It's one of the better contemporary horror movies, in my opinion. It's found footage."

Erasmus looks at me, and his grin makes me tingly all over. *Fuck, he's hot.* "You and I have the same taste," he says. I smile secretly. *We may have the same taste in horror movies, but I highly doubt that he's mentally undressing me right now like I am him. Where is this aggressiveness coming from? I'm not even sure I am gay…*

I suddenly remember a good one and lead him to the 'W's. "The first one was really good." I point to *Wrong Turn*. "After that, they kinda sucked."

His brown eyes scan the back cover, and he grabs the rental cases. "I'll trust you."

"Awesome." Trust me with your sex? I pull up his account and start punching in the ID numbers on the cases.

"Why haven't I seen you before?" he asks. "Before August."

"I'd just moved here."

"From where?"

Is he really that interested in me, or is he just being polite? "Michigan," I answer, popping the tabs out of the cases.

"That's quite a drive. What brings you to Willows Crest?"

"Divorce."

"Oh, I'm sorry."

"Don't be. My stepdad is a total douche, so..."

"My dad wasn't the greatest either." He hands me a $5 bill. All of the movies he grabbed are old releases, so they're only $1 a piece, definitely a bargain.

"Why haven't I seen you in here for a while?" I ask, turning the tables on him.

"Oh, uh," he stammers, "I had some business out of town."

I nod and hand him his change. "Those'll be due back on Monday."

"Thanks. Have a good one."

"You, too, thanks."

He shoots me that delicious grin one last time and leaves. As soon as he's gone, I exhale loudly. *I cannot believe how well I handled that!*

I glance at the clock and am surprised to see that it's 8:59 PM. *Time flies when you're mentally devouring Erasmus Mayfair.*

When the clock switches to nine, I lock the front door before switching off the open sign, and then I grab the key from the cash drawer. I walk out into the club room. It is an adjacent room to the video store that we rent out for movies, parties, and stuff like that. It's cold and dark out here. I walk over to the drop box, remove the lock and take out a few movies before shutting it and locking it back up. As I turn, I can see through the glass door. There is a man standing on the sidewalk across the road. He's standing perfectly still, staring at me.

"That's fucking scary," I mutter, hurrying back into the video store. All of the doors are locked, so if the weirdo wants to hurt me, he'll have to break in to get at me.

I check the movies in and put them away while the end-of-day program runs. When the printer spews out the papers I need, I circle the total sales with tax and then remove that amount from the till, placing it in a bank bag along with the papers. I slip it into the safe in Vito's office and then switch the light off.

I tug on my coat and turn the lights off. At the door, I peer out, trying to spot the creepy guy. I scan the street, but see nothing more than a gray cat strutting down the sidewalk and a few leaves blowing along the road.

Taking a deep breath, I unlock the door and slip out into the cold air before locking the door again behind me. I slip the key into my right coat pocket and put my gloves on. My hands are extremely sensitive to the cold, too, so I try to keep gloves within reach once summer is over.

I shiver against the autumn chill and pop my earbuds in. Whenever I walk anywhere, I like to listen to *Out Tonight* from the *Rent* soundtrack and pretend that I am Mimi. *Yeah... definitely gay.* I walk down the sidewalk, moving a little to the music. This is probably my favorite song in the whole world.

I cross behind the alley and just turn onto Meyette Street when I am knocked to the ground from behind. I hit the cement hard, the air rushing from me. My lungs burn, and I use all my will to roll over to face my attacker. Even though it's dark and the streetlights are all mysteriously out, I can ascertain that my attacker is the guy that was standing outside the shop. *Why didn't I get a ride home?*

"Stay down, witch," he hisses, his voice is deep and rumbling.

"What?" I gasp. How does this guy know I'm a witch? I've been very careful not to perform magic out in the open.

"Adrammelech sends his regards." His face is bathed in light, and a ball of fire ignites and hovers in his palm. I gasp as I take in his appearance. His eyes are slitted like a goat's. Horns protrude from skin as black as the darkest night. His lips peel back in an evil sneer to reveal a row of razor-sharp canines.

Before throwing the fireball at me, he's suddenly tackled to the ground. The fireball goes wild, shooting past me and striking a dumpster across the road.

I get up and see the weird guy in a wrestling match with my savior. I squint. *It looks like… no, it can't be… can it?*

Erasmus grits his teeth, trying to crush the guy's windpipe.

"What's going on?" I demand, panicking.

"Quiet!" Erasmus growls, straining. The guy underneath him kicks and bucks, but suddenly there's a loud, wet *snap!* and he grows still.

Erasmus rolls to the side as the guy's body starts to convulse as if having a seizure, and then it bursts into bright green flames. My nostrils are assaulted with the smell of sulfur.

"Come on," Erasmus grabs my hand tightly and starts running, pulling me away.

"Wait!" I turn back to gaze at the burning body behind us. The flames lick at the body and then instantly fade out. "Tell me what's going on!"

"When we're safe."

We race through backyards and, in minutes, are standing in my driveway. *How does Erasmus know where I live?*

I go to open the front door but find it locked. My hands shaking, I fumble for my keys. Erasmus snatches them from my shaking hands and unlocks the door. I open it and rush inside. He stays put.

"Are you waiting for an invitation?" I snap sarcastically.

"Actually..." he shrugs.

"Come in."

He steps into the house and pulls me upstairs to my room. *He knows where my room is, too? This is too creepy!*

He shuts the door behind us and locks it. I sit down on my bed, watching him. Erasmus is in my room. *Holy shit!* "What's going on?" I ask, regaining my composure.

"You were attacked. I saved you."

"Thanks for the newsflash, Captain Obvious," I bite at him. "I appreciate you helping me out back there, but why were you there? How did you know I'd need help? Who was that guy? What was with the green fire?" The questions rattle out of my mouth like bullets from a machine gun.

Erasmus patiently waits for me to stop talking. "I don't know where to start," he confesses, pacing. "I was hoping I'd never have to tell you the truth."

"What?"

Erasmus stops his pacing and looks into my eyes. "Graham, I'm not what you think I am."

"Hmmm?"

He sighs. "I'm a vampire."

I stare at him, aghast.

Chapter Twelve

"I'm sorry," I say with a sarcastic chuckle. "Could you run that by me one more time?"

"I'm a vampire," Erasmus repeats, rolling his eyes.

A vampire? Seriously? I'm starting to feel like I'm being *Punk'd* or something. Is Ashton Kutcher hiding in my closet with a camera crew, waiting to rush me and reveal that the last month of my life has all been a joke? I mean, come on. The whole witch thing is farfetched enough; now add Druids and vampires into the mix... I feel like I'm in a Charlaine Harris or Kim Harrison novel. What would Sookie and Rachel do?

For a second, I feel like I'm going to throw up—from stress or the fact that I haven't eaten all day, I'm not sure—but the feeling passes when I feel Erasmus' strong hands on me. Even though I'm not cold anymore, I feel a chill creep up my spine, and goosebumps rise all over my body. Under my shirt, my nipples harden.

"You're joking, right?" I ask, sliding my coat off and tossing it over the back of my chair. *Where's Romana?* I wonder, noticing that she's nowhere to be seen. I remove my gloves, exposing my red palms.

"You're hurt," Erasmus gasps.

"The gloves took the brunt of it." I hold my hands out in front of me. The top layer of skin is gone, it stings a little, but I'll be fine. "It's no biggie." I let Erasmus scrutinize them, relishing the feel of his hands on mine. Hopefully, he can't read my mind…

Erasmus guides me over to the bed and eases me down, sitting beside me. He sits so close that our knees are touching, and I hear my heart racing in excitement. "I am dead serious," he says with a straight face.

I burst out laughing, clutching my sides. He eyes me curiously at first but then gives in and smiles. I decide that I'd love to see that smile every day for the rest of my life. "Can I ask you some questions?"

"Of course."

"Do you sparkle in the sunlight?"

"God, no," he rolls his eyes in disgust. "I turn to ash in the sunlight."

"Do you have a soul?"

"That's a theological question that I cannot answer."

"Okay," I nod, "but you're obviously a good vampire, right? Like Angel?" Leave it to me to make *Buffy the Vampire Slayer* references at an important time like this. *God, I'm such a nerd!*

"I don't feed off of humans," he clarifies.

"What about animals?" My blood starts to boil in anger as I anticipate his answer. I'd honestly rather he feed on humans than animals. At least humans can defend themselves.

"Indirectly."

"Meaning?"

"I get blood from a butcher." I relax. Crisis averted.

"So, you *are* like Angel?"

"In that regard, yes."

"Can you turn into a bat?"

"No."

"What about flying. Can you fly?"

"No more than you can."

"Pyrokinesis? Transmogrification?"

"No, and no."

"Telepathy?"

"Not that I've noticed."

"Garlic?"

"I'm partial to it, but it's not a necessity."

"What about the mirror thing?"

"That's a plot device conjured up by Bram Stoker or whomever to make us seem scarier."

"Do you have superhuman strength?"

"Not even close. Though I am relatively fit."

He's not lying there. I sneak a glance at his chest. He's very thin, but who knows what he's hiding under his sweater?

"How often do you feed?"

"At least once a day. See, vampires need blood in order to keep their bodies from decomposing. We're essentially better preserved, sentient zombies."

I wrinkle my nose in distaste at that image. "Can beheading kill you?"

"Yes."

"Holy water?"

"Another fallacy."

"Stake through the heart?"

"Bullshit. Vampires don't have hearts."

"Why are you warm? When your hand touched mine earlier, I noticed that you're warm, at least warmer than I am."

"I had just fed before I came to the store. We heat the blood, and it warms us."

I nod. That makes sense; as much as I hate I admit it. "But Amethyst said she used to work with you at Subway."

"I insisted on only working the night shift," Erasmus extrapolated. "Haven't you noticed that I only come into the video store after dark?"

I shrug. "I just assumed you got out of work late," I confess.

"I don't work. I don't have to. As long as I've been around, I've amassed substantial wealth."

Hot and rich? Who is this guy, a vampiric Christian Grey? "How old are you?"

Erasmus sighs. "Millennia. I was born long ago in the days before Christ. Before God. When I was growing up, we worshipped the Greek gods. Zeus, Hera, Athena, Ares, Aphrodite..." A sad smile alights his face. I imagine he's recalling his childhood.

"How were you... turned?"

"That's one bit that the movies and books get right. A bite on the neck, being drained almost to the point of death, and then ingesting the infected blood."

"Is it as painful as it looks in the movies?"

"It's ten times more painful."

"Oh." I frown. "I'm sorry if that was a personal question."

"Not at all. It's been so long since I've been close with someone outside of my kind. It's refreshing."

"We're close?" I didn't mean for it to come out as rudely as it does. "Sorry."

Erasmus smiles. "You must be totally blind."

"What do you mean?"

"Well," he scoots closer to me, and my heart beats faster. It feels like it's about to thump right out of my chest. "I have been flirting with you every time I've seen you."

"You have?" My voice is breathy, quiet. *That explains it. I'm dreaming. This is another twisted Erasmus dream that will haunt me.*

"Are you not used to guys courting you?"

"No," I confess. "I'm not used to anyone 'courting' me."

"You're joking."

"Nope. When you look like I do, you tend to spend your life in the corner."

"I think you are the most beautiful man I have ever seen," Erasmus whispers. He's so close now that his words sound loud in my ears, and I can smell the peppermint on his breath.

I blush at his words. "I've got nothing on you," I rasp.

"Please," he scoffs.

I feel his hand twining the hairs at the nape of my neck. His face is less than an inch away from mine. I close my eyes, and his lips find mine. In that instant, it's as though I have finally found the missing piece of myself. Every question I've ever had suddenly has its answer. I feel whole, complete.

I break the kiss unexpectedly.

"I'm sorry," Erasmus says, fingers at his lips. "I shouldn't have done that."

"No, it's okay; I'm just... kind of unsure right now. It's all so confusing."

"I understand." He leans back a bit to give me space.

"It's not you," I assure him. "It's me."

"Such a cliché," he jests.

"I've got a lot going on right now. I'm really just discovering myself and sorting everything out."

"I understand."

"That was my first kiss," I admit.

"Shut up! Are you serious?" I nod, my cheeks burning. "Well, you, Sir, are a natural."

"You're no newbie yourself," I assure him. He grins proudly, and I have to resist the urge to grab him and kiss him again. This is all way too fast.

"Who was that guy who attacked me?"

Erasmus grimaces. "That was a demon."

"A demon?" Witches, Vampires, Druids, and now Demons!?

"Sent by Adrammelech."

"Adre-who-lech?"

"He is one of Lucifer's fallen angels."

"Lucifer is real? I'm Jewish, we don't believe in a physcal manifestation of evil."

"That doesn't make him any less real."

"I'll give you that one."

"Adrammelech is the President of the Senate of Demons."

"Demons have a Senate?"

"You have a judicial system; why shouldn't demons?"

Fair point. "Why was he trying to kill me?"

"I don't think he was trying to kill you."

"He was about to incinerate me with a fireball," I protest. "If you hadn't jumped in…"

"Chances are he was just trying to scare you. You're worth way more alive than dead."

"What do you mean?"

"Well, given your *unique* standing in the magical community—"

"You know about that?"

"Every supernatural creature knows about it."

"How? I've only told Amethyst."

"We can sense it. There have been whispers for years that the prophecy wasn't true. Yet, here you are."

"I might as well get a tattoo on my forehead. 'Witch bitch,'" I groan.

"You don't have to worry. I'll keep you safe." *Ugh. Why is he so damned charming?*

"What's your interest in all of this?"

"I want you safe," he says simply.

"But you hardly know me..."

"That's true, but I feel as though I do. I feel... drawn to you."

Much in the same way that I've felt drawn to him? "You can't be with me twenty-four-seven," I point out.

"True. But now that your powers are activated, you're going to be the subject of many more attacks. I think that demon earlier was planning to bring you to the underworld to give to Adrammelech."

"For what?"

"It's no secret that he's vying for Lucifer's throne. If he can corrupt you and let evil overtake the world, he'll have proven himself worthy of that position."

"So, it all comes down to politics." I groan. I loathe politics

"They're everywhere," he agrees.

"I'm not going to have to lock myself away in this house, am I?"

"You're no safer here than anywhere else."

"I have college. I can't just stop going."

"We'll figure it out."

Wow. He said we. I want to scream out ecstatically, but propriety stops me. "You can't go to my classes with me."

"If I go through the sewers—"

"Oh, no. You're not following me around stinking like raw sewage!"

"I'm going to keep you safe!"

I see the intense fire burning in his eyes and back off. Except for Amethyst, I haven't had anyone so willing to protect me before. Honestly, I like it. I like it a lot. "How long before Adra-whoosit sends someone else after me?" I ask, hugging myself.

"I honestly don't know," Erasmus confesses. "All I know is that it's all over if anything bad happens to you." I nod, and he catches himself. "Not that that's the only reason I'm here. I like you."

"Is that a vampire thing?"

"What?"

"Falling in love with total strangers? Does that come from the eternal life full of solitude?"

Erasmus cocks his head at me. "I'm not in love with you. Yet."

"Ha!" I laugh sarcastically.

"Let's consider this our first date."

"Dates usually consist of dinner, a movie, skating, walks in the park, a concert... not saving wimpy little novice witches from demons," I remind him gently.

"You are not wimpy. You're just untrained. Starting tomorrow, I'm going to teach you how to fight. Your magic is strong, but sometimes a well-placed fist in the face gets the message across more clearly."

I picture myself fighting and shake my head. I'm so uncoordinated that if I ever got into a fight and tried to kick my attacker, I'd fall on my ass. Don was fond of calling me "Grace" because I always fell and tripped. Just call me Bella Swan.

"Maybe a protection spell," I suggest, the cogs in my head were turning. "Or a protection amulet..."

"Both couldn't hurt, but they're not guaranteed. You're going to need all the protection you can get." He tosses me a baggie filled with what looks like black pepper.

"Pepper? Are you planning on seasoning me up before you take a bite?"

Erasmus laughs, and it makes my stomach do a cartwheel. "No, it's black salt. It's for protection. You can either keep it on you or cast a ring around the house with it. I've got plenty more for you."

"So, no getting rid of you, huh?"

"Over my undead body," he quips.

I laugh, and our eyes meet again. I wish I had the courage to kiss him again. I yawn, the day's events finally hitting me. "I should get to bed."

"Good idea. Which side of the bed is yours?"

"Excuse me?"

"You heard me."

"You're staying the night!?"

"Graham, I can't protect you if I'm at my place."

I'll admit he has a point, but still... "I can't let you stay here. What if my mom or my grandma comes in?"

"You're not allowed to have friends over?"

"They know that the only friend I have here is Amethyst."

"Wrong. I'm your friend... for now. Hopefully, soon I'll be your boyfriend."

His words cause a wave of desire to wash over me. "I need to go brush my teeth. We'll settle this when I get back."

"Sure."

I give him a dirty look and head to the bathroom. I floss, brush, then use the mouthwash before washing my face. The charcoal cleanser will sure have its work cut out for it tonight. As I finish rubbing my moisturizer in my phone rings. I hurriedly answer it, not checking to see who is calling.

"Hello?"

"Hey, bitch, how'd it go?" Amethyst asks.

"Oh, hey. It was fine. Maybe you're right. Maybe I do need to give myself more credit."

"Abso-fucking-lutely." I hear her exhale, but I can only guess whether she's exhaling cigarette or marijuana smoke. "What are you doing?"

"Just finished washing my face. I'm taking my contacts out now. You?" I pluck the contacts out and slide on my glasses. *Wait, I don't want Erasmus to see me in these… it's sure to send him flying out the window.* I'll never be drop-dead gorgeous, but at least with contacts, I look passably better. If I keep my contacts in, though, I'll have to throw them away in the morning; if I sleep in them, they get dried out and gooey.

"Just smoking a joint."

"Seems like kind of a waste before bed, to me," I say, stretching.

"Dude, this shit calms me right down. I sleep so much better when I smoke a little before bed."

"That makes sense." I want to tell her everything, but I don't. I'm sure Erasmus doesn't want it getting around that he's a vampire. "I have Erasmus in my room," I blurt.

"What!?"

"I know."

"How did that happen?"

"He came in around close, we talked about scary movies. We bonded. He offered to walk me home and... yeah."

"That's fucking awesome! See? I told you he's into you."

"Mhm." I wince. "He wants to stay the night. What do I do?"

"You say yes and get your ass into bed with that sexy man!"

"I am not having sex with him," I inform her sternly as I strip out of my work clothes. "I'm not that easy."

"Good, you're better than that. Just cuddle the shit out of him."

"I've never done that." I pull on my blue flannel pajamas.

"It's amazing. Trust me, you'll love it."

"We kissed."

"How was it?"

"It was... amazing!" I giggle. Who knew that I was capable of such giddiness?

"Damn, that's so cool. I'm happy for you."

"Thanks. He says he wants to be, like, a thing."

"Get itttttt," she trills.

"We'll see. I have enough on my plate—"

"Oh, no!!" Amethyst interrupts. "If a guy like Erasmus Mayfair wants to date you, you say yes! You're a queen, baby; he can take very good care of you."

"I know..."

"Now, hang up and get that sexy ass into bed with your man."

"He's not—"

"Ah! Love you, bye."

"Love you, bye." I hang up and shake my head, chuckling to myself.

I walk back into my room and stop in the doorway when I see Erasmus—shirtless—waiting for me in bed, Romana purring away beside him. Is this guy freakin' perfect!?

"How'd you get her to do that?" I ask, shutting and locking the door behind me. Just in case.

"She just came to me." Erasmus grins. "Just like you're about to."

The sight of him with Romana melts away the last of my resolve. "All right, you can stay," I announce. "But no funny business."

"I wouldn't dream of trying anything untoward with you until you're ready," Erasmus replies sincerely.

"Okay." I plug my phone in and set it on the bedside stand. Erasmus pulls the blankets back, and I slide in. As soon as I'm in bed, he replaces the covers and secures them around me with his arm. I almost swoon.

I go to switch out the light, but he stops me. "Wait."

"What?" I ask, hand poised over the switch.

"Let me look at you again." Slowly, I turn so that he can take in my nerd glasses. I won't meet his gaze. "Goddamn, you're gorgeous," he says. *Yeah... he's perfect.*

I switch out the light and put my glasses into their case. I settle back against Erasmus, his arm draped protectively over me. I've never felt safer. Romana moves so that she's on my other side. I'm in the middle of a cuddle sandwich.

"Goodnight," I whisper.

He kisses my cheek. "Goodnight."

I close my eyes, and despite the excitement of it all, I am asleep within seconds.

Chapter Thirteen

My alarm goes off on time, jarring me into wakefulness. I crack open an eye, and although I can't see anyway, I note that my room is still pitch black. *Damned daylight savings time!*

I switch on my lamp, and the sudden light stings my eyes. I slowly open them again and make out the black blob of my glasses case. Sitting up, I put my glasses on.

Romana bolts from her perch on my legs and looks up at me, her topaz eyes wide and pleading. That's the look that she knows makes me want to fake sickness and lie back down so we can spend the day in bed, cuddling. She is a terrible enabler! I can't skip class, though. Amethyst would kill me, and besides, I have an exam in anthropology.

The previous day's events rush back to me as my body starts to ache. I remember the jarring fall to the pavement, the creepy goat-eyed guy with the fireball, and... Erasmus...?

"Erasmus?" I call, whirling around. I wince as pain lances through me. The other side of the bed is tidy, as if no one had slept there. Did I dream it?

Brow knit, I grab my phone, slowly stand up and shuffle toward the door like a zombie. Mornings are the bane of my existence.

As soon as I switch the light on in my bathroom, I see an envelope on the counter. *A note?* I sit down on the closed toilet and break the seal on the envelope, pulling out the neatly folded paper inside. It's handwriting that I'm unfamiliar with. *Maybe last night wasn't a dream, then. But that would mean that Erasmus and I had made out and cuddled... and I enjoyed it.* I shake my head. No, it's too early to be trying to understand and reconcile my elusive sexuality.

Graham,

You're even more gorgeous while you sleep. You look like an innocent child as soon as sleep takes you. It warms my (lack of a) heart.

I wanted to spend the night holding you, content knowing that you were safe in my arms, but, unfortunately, being that close to you for so long... well, it spiked my hunger. I'm sorry that you'll wake up without me, but I didn't want you to see me when the bloodlust takes over. You'd change your mind about me and tell me to go to Hell.

I want you to know that this night has been the best of my very long, very interesting life. Before you say it, no, that isn't just a line to get you into bed. I have you there right now, and it's pretty amazing. I wouldn't be opposed to a rain check on the all-night cuddles.

I went to go get some "food." By the time you shower and get ready for class, I'll be back. We won't have long—sunrise always comes—but we need to discuss your schedule and how I AM going to be keeping an eye on you. I know it feels stifling for you, but if anything bad were to happen to you, the world itself would be in danger. I can't let that happen. So, whether you want to think I'm altruistic or just a bossy, overprotective (potential!) boyfriend, that choice is yours, but it is not negotiable. Stop fighting me; it just turns me on even more. ;)

Make sure you run the water extra hot in the shower. You took quite a fall last night, and you'll be pretty sore when you get up.

Sleep well, and think fondly of me when you awake

Love,

Erasmus

I set the note aside and frown. I'm still so confused and conflicted about my sexuality, and Erasmus is not helping at all. On the one hand, I find him attractive, and kissing him was... pleasant, but does that mean I want to have sex with him? I certainly don't want anything going in my back door. On the other hand, he's incredibly bossy and clingy, and most of the time, he drives me crazy.

I sigh and start brushing my teeth. *When did life have to become so complicated?* As a kid, all I had to worry about was catching the bus to and from school. Aside from Don's abuse, my childhood was pretty stress-free. But now... Now I'm attracted to a vampire older than Judaism and, conversely, want him out of my life. *Being an adult-ish is so much fun! Not.*

Post-shower, I open the door and start when I see Erasmus sitting on the bed, Romana curled up in his lap, her belly exposed and purring. "Jesus Christ, Erasmus!" I hiss, stalking toward him. "You can't just sneak in here like that! I almost had a heart attack!"

His lips tug up into a smirk. "Sorry. I thought this was better than surprising you at your front door."

"Barely!" I shoot him a dirty look.

"I'm sorry," he says, the smile vanishing. "I forget what it's like to be human."

"Apparently." I unbutton the top of my pajamas. "How did you get in here, anyway?"

"I climbed the trellis," he replies simply.

"Remind me to have that taken down." His face tightens in pain or sadness for the briefest of moments, and I regret snapping at him. "Sorry. I'm cranky in the morning."

"I can tell."

I open my closet and pull out my blue and white plaid shirt and ripped jeans. I pull the plaid on over a t-shirt, grateful that the neck is big enough to fit my head without crushing my hair. I roll on some deodorant and pull a pair of boxers and black socks from my dresser. "I need you to turn around for a minute," I say, tugging the socks up.

"What for?" he asks.

"Because I'm about to be naked from the waist down, and having you there staring at me makes me uncomfortable."

"I'll see it eventually," he says. When I don't move, he rolls his chocolate brown eyes and turns his back to me.

I quickly pull my boxers and jeans on and then slide into my black pea coat. Erasmus stands and helps me with my scarf. "Thanks," I say.

"My pleasure." He smiles, and I melt a little inside. It should be illegal for someone to be as attractive as Erasmus is. *No wonder I'm confused.*

I sling my messenger bag over my shoulder. "Down the trellis, vampire boy," I say.

"Again? I can't just walk down with you?" He pouts his lips, and I ache to kiss him again. *No. Fight it.*

"Are you going to explain to my mom and grandma that you stayed the night and that you're 'courting me?" I riposte.

"Fair enough," he grumbles, opening the window. "Hopefully, your neighbors aren't watching."

"I'll meet you in the driveway."

"You'd better." He winks at me, and I can't help the grin that washes over my face. *He's so intoxicating!*

I kiss Romana goodbye and hurry downstairs. I rush past Grandma in the hall and shut the front door behind me. Once I round the walkway to the garage, there's Erasmus in all his glory. The gentle breeze toys with his black pompadour.

"Ready to go?" he asks.

"I am. But again, you really don't need to come with me," I insist. "I'm a big boy."

"Like I told you last night, you aren't safe. You're untrained in your craft and in self-defense."

I stop walking and turn to him. "Is the magical community out?"

"What?" A confused frown mars his wrinkle-free face.

"Are they out? The whole world knows about them?"

"No. We like it that way."

"Then why would these demonic forces or whatever attack me at college or work? Aren't those public places?"

"Yes..."

"And wouldn't that be outing themselves in a *huge* way?"

"Yes." He's gritting his teeth in irritation, which means I'm making sense to him.

"So, in your *expert opinion*, should I not be safe to go to school and work unaccompanied?"

Erasmus taps his feet in frustration, and a self-satisfied grin lights up my face. "At least let me drive you." It's not a question. Honestly, that appeals to me more than standing out here in the chilly morning breeze, cursing the cold.

"You have a car?" I ask.

"Graham, just because I'm older than time itself doesn't mean I'm not modernized. I have a car."

He waves to a fancy black Cadillac parked at the curb. *Nice wheels!* "Okay," I say, hoping for casual. He opens my door for me, and for a second, I feel like Mariah Carey.

The car roars to life, and I take in the black leather upholstery and breathe in the citrusy scent of leather cleaner. I fasten my seat belt as Erasmus pulls away from the curb. "I really wish you'd just let me go with you," he says, glancing at me through his dark lashes.

"Would you want a babysitter?"

"I can take care of myself."

I snort. "No offense, Erasmus, but you're hardly intimidating. You're shorter than I am and probably weigh about the same. You just look like a skinny emo pop-rock singer."

He glares at me and then smiles. "I tell you what. I'll make you a deal."

"What kind of deal?" My stomach starts to twist into knots. *This can't be good.*

"I'll drop the bodyguard routine."

"If?" I press.

"If you let me take you out on a date."

I roll my eyes. *Here we go again with that nonsense.* "We already discussed this…"

"We'll do dinner and a movie," he entices. "The standard date."

I hate to admit it, but it does sound kind of appealing. I'm not overly whelmed at the idea of people seeing us and assuming that we're a couple, but if it gets him to loosen the chains, just a smidge…

"When?" I ask, defeated.

His grin is smug and oh, so delightfully sexy. "Tomorrow night?"

"Fine. I pick the movie."

"Deal." He holds out his hand, and I put mine in his to shake it. However instead of shaking my hand, he lifts it to his lips and teases my knuckles with his soft, pink lips. I moan and feel a tingle below my waist.

Erasmus rounds the corner and parks in front of the college. "I won't be able to pick you up." He glances out at the sky, which is starting to turn a pinkish-orange color as the sun rises.

"Erasmus, hurry!" I exclaim, heart pounding. I don't want him to burn for me. I open my door and jump out. He rolls down my window.

"Meet me at my place after class?"

"Where do you live?" I lean in to hear him better.

"A couple blocks away. I have a mansion set on the cliff overlooking the beach." *Wow, sounds perfect!* "I'll text you the address."

"Okay. Go!"

Erasmus leans over quickly and kisses me. I forget everything except the feel of his lips and find my fingers burrowing in his hair. *God, I want him so badly.*

"I have to go," he pants, pulling away.

"Then go." My voice is soft, like a child's. I want to kiss more. His kiss is like heroin. I feel weightless and tingly all over.

"See you soon," he says.

"Bye."

With one last seductive smoldering look, Erasmus peels away, burning rubber as he goes. I watch his car until it fades from sight. *Damn, he's such a good kisser!* My fingers brush my lips as I walk toward the front door.

A couple of hours later, at lunch, Amethyst is grilling me on what happened between Erasmus and me last night and this morning. "So, he spent the night?" she asks.

"Yeah." My thoughts go back to the elation I felt when he held me in his arms. *I want more of that.*

"Did it go okay?"

"It went fine. Even Romana liked him."

"You know that animals can sense evil."

"Yeah. Definitely." Subconsciously, I'm sketching Erasmus on the back of my Remedial Math notebook.

"Are you okay?"

"I'm just... confused," I admit.

"I get that."

"He's a good kisser. No, a *great* kisser. And the cuddling was good, as well."

"So, what's the problem?"

"Well, I mean, this isn't a life that I want..."

"Sexuality isn't a choice, Graham. It's just who you are."

She has a point, but what if I don't want to be into guys? I don't want to spend the rest of my life drenched in self-loathing. "How do you sort it out?" I question.

"You know that I don't waste time giving a fuck what anyone else thinks. If I see a guy I think is hot, I go after him. If I see a girl I think is hot, I go after her. It isn't all that complicated."

"It wasn't ever confusing for you?"

"No." Amethyst shrugs. "It sounds like you've just been programmed to think that being gay is bad, so you don't want to identify as gay."

"Could be." *She does have a point there.*

"So, when are you seeing him again?"

"Later today." She squeals in delight. "He wants me to come over for a little bit."

"Hot! You should get him all hot and sweaty and then take that dick for a test drive."

My face suddenly feels like it's a million degrees. "I'm not ready for that."

"I'm just giving you shit. You go at your own pace. Don't let him force you into something you don't want to do."

"He wants to go out on a date tomorrow night."

"What did you say?" Her brown eyes are wide behind her glasses.

"I said yes."

"I am so excited for you!" She claps her hands excitedly, and I smile.

"I'm nervous as fuck," I confess.

"Don't be. He really is a great guy. You honestly have nothing to worry about with him. He's a perfect gentleman, very old school."

Yeah, because he's thousands of years old, I say silently.

After dumping my juice box in the trash, I gather up my binder and books and go to Remedial Math.

"Do you want me to give you a ride over to his place?" Amethyst asks as she tosses her empty food wrappers into the nearest trashcan.

"If you want to."

"Anything for you, baby."

We put our arms around each other affectionately and head back in.

Chapter Fourteen

I meet Amethyst by the clock tower; it's in the middle of the campus and a convenient spot for us to rendezvous. It's been a long day. I'm excited and nervous about going to Erasmus' house for obvious reasons. Things tend to get blurry around him. Then there's the prospect of sparring with him. I've never been in a fight in my life. My fighting experience is through *Buffy* and *Xena*.

I have a paper to write when I get home. Maybe I'll be knocked out or get a concussion. I won't have to do my homework if I'm in the hospital, right?

"Where does Erasmus live?" Amethyst asks as I tighten the laces of my shoes.

"One sec." I fish my phone out of my pocket and feel a little ping of excitement when I see that I have a text from Erasmus. *But, wait, I never gave him my phone number, and I never got his… he must've done it last night while I was asleep. Sneaky bastard.* I open the text, and an ear-to-ear grin lights up my face.

29053 Merrimade Lane. Have a great day, gorgeous. Xoxo

My fingers fly over the keyboard as I type out a reply with more elation than I intend.

OMW. Hope you had a nice sleep and enjoyed your blood. See you soon. Just to be naughty, I include the kissy emoji. *That's sure to perplex him.*

"He's on Merrimade Lane," I tell Amethyst. "Wherever that is."

"That's the rich people part of town." She sounds impressed.

"He did mention having money."

"Why was he working at Subway, then?"

That is a very good question. "Boredom?" I suggest. I can't tell her the truth until I know it's okay with Erasmus that anyone besides the two of us knows he's a vampire.

We walk out, and the chill wind hits me in the face. I glance up and see that the sky is a dark, maudlin gray. We duck our heads and run across the parking lot. Amethyst fumbles with the key and opens her door. I duck in as soon as mine is unlocked, desperate to get away from the maelstrom outside.

"Fuck, it's cold!" I cry, shivering. I'd forgotten that it's officially November now. That means it's only a matter of weeks before my least favorite thing starts: snow. *Fuck.*

"It wasn't that cold earlier," she says, cranking the heat up as high as possible.

"I hope there's not a storm coming."

"Those do look like snow clouds..."

"FML."

"Amen."

My phone vibrates, and I see that it's from Erasmus.

Front door is open. See you soon.

He used the wink face emoji, too, and heat grips my body. Is it lust?

Within five minutes, the car is sufficiently warmed up, and we're on our way. Sure enough, snow starts to fall from the sky, sparsely at first but then building momentum to a nice steady downfall. I silently pray that it doesn't stick.

"Not too much further," Amethyst narrates, lighting a cigarette. She cracks her window enough to let the smoke wisp out.

"I'm nervous," I confess.

"Why? This is a good thing. I know it's overwhelming, but it'll be worth it, trust me."

"He wants to teach me how to fight."

"Erasmus does?" Her voice is tinged with surprise.

"That's what I said."

"He's smaller than you are, if that's possible."

"I know. It's ludicrous."

"Is he trying to butch you up?"

"If I tell you something, you have to promise not to freak out, okay?"

"Okay..."

"Erasmus didn't really walk me home from work last night. I was alone. This thing attacked me, and it would've killed me if he hadn't come out of nowhere and killed it."

"What was it?"

"He said it was a demon. Apparently, some big wig demon named Adrammelech down in the Underworld wants to usurp Lucifer, and getting me would help him do that. I'm basically a walking target."

"Shitttt."

"My grandma said that this would happen once my powers were activated. My powers are supposed to tip the scale of good and evil indefinitely." I shoot her a look. "But don't worry. Demons don't want their presence blasted all over Facebook and Twitter, so they won't try to get me in broad daylight. I'm safe until I'm alone at night."

"No more walking home for you," Amethyst says with finality. "Give me your necklace."

"My necklace?" Instinctively, my hand goes to my gold Star of David. I had to wear it hidden inside my shirt back home, but subconsciously I've started wearing it free so that it's visible.

"Yes. Give it." She holds her hand out expectantly.

"Why?" I ask as I pull it up over my head and set it in her extended hand.

"I'm going to bless this for you and make it into a protection charm."

I quirk an eyebrow. "Isn't that a little sacrilegious?"

Amethyst rolls her eyes and slips my necklace into her purse. "It'll be fine."

"Will it work? Don't you need an actual amulet or something?"

"Usually, yes, but this is personal to you. It has some of your energy stored in it. It'll be specifically charged to protect you."

"Oh."

We pull up outside of a brick house. It's a bi-level that sits at the precipice of a cliff face, towering above the beach down below. Bay windows overlook the driveway, blending in with the cream-colored brick.

Amethyst brakes and stares at the house and grounds, eyes wide in stupefaction. "Holy hell," she gasps.

"That ain't no shit," I shoot back.

"You didn't mention that he was loaded!"

"I kind of thought that he was kidding," I admit.

"Well, fuck, do you need a third? I'll blow both of you if I get to stay in this big ass house!"

"I tell you what, if we get married or whatever, you can come stay with us," I tease. In no way do I think that Erasmus and I will get married. Even if lust did turn to love, innocent romance hardly lasts beyond your twenties.

I open the car door and sling my messenger bag over my shoulder.

"Be safe, okay? I mean it," Amethyst orders.

"Always. Thanks for the ride."

"Anytime."

I turn and walk up the steps to the concrete porch. Erasmus' text had said that the door was open, *so am I supposed to just walk in?* I don't feel comfortable just walking into someone's house, but it's too cold to stay out here and wait for him to answer the door.

I open the door and walk in, shutting the door behind me. When I turn back to the inside of the house, a gasp of wonderment escapes my lips. The inside of the house is decorated like a designer from *Architectural Digest* had been there. The floors were genuine hardwood, meticulously polished. The walls are brick, too, but a red brick instead of the pale stuff outside. All of the light fixtures are opulent glass and crystal. *This must have cost a fortune.*

I kick my shoes off and lay them neatly by the door. Through the frosted glass of the windows on either side, I see Amethyst back out of the driveway and head back the way she'd come.

"Erasmus," I call, "I'm here."

"Coming," he calls back. It sounds like he's in the kitchen, maybe?

He rounds the corner, and my heart leaps into my throat. His signature pompadour is messy from sleep. He's naked except for a pair of tight black boxers that perfectly accentuate his package, which bounces with each step. As he reaches up to itch the back of his head, I note that his body is hairless except for tufts of black hair under his armpits. His skin is pale, and although he does have some muscle definition, I can't tell if he's actually muscular or just so thin that he looks muscular. His arm tattoos are colored, and although I'm not really a tattoo guy, I find his sexy as fuck, even though I can't tell what they are.

Erasmus sees me ogling his body, and he grins proudly. "Sorry, I just got up," he says.

"Don't be sorry." I subconsciously wipe my mouth for stray drool. *Man, he is hot!*

"I look better with the boxers off." His brown eyes shine mischievously, and for a second, I'm tempted to say fuck the rules and have my first gay experience, but common sense stops me. He's hot, sure, but I barely know him. I don't want him to think that I'm a whore.

"Trying to get me into bed already?" I come back. "We haven't even had our date yet."

"Can't blame a guy for trying." He wags his eyebrows at me seductively, and I chew my lip to keep myself grounded.

"You have a nice place," I say, changing the subject.

"Thank you. I like nice things."

"I can tell."

He leads me down the hall into the kitchen, and I can't help but steal glances at his mouthwatering bubble butt, straining against his black Calvin Kleins.

The kitchen is as ornate as the hall, with stainless steel countertops and appliances. The light fixtures look foreign and expensive. His kitchen is bigger than my bedroom!

"Are you hungry?" he asks, pulling a bottle of what looks like wine out of the fridge.

I am hungry, starving, in fact, but not for food. I'm hungering for Erasmus' body. "No," I force myself to say, trying as hard as I can to keep my voice steady.

"You're going to want to change before we spar," he says, taking a sip of what I assume is cold blood.

"I didn't bring any spare clothes."

"I have stuff you can wear."

He disappears again and, within a minute, is back, carrying gray sweatpants and a tank top.

"Thanks." I take the clothes and set my messenger bag down on one of his fancy white leather chairs.

"You can change in the bathroom. It's just around the corner. First door on the right."

I nod and follow the hall until I come to the bathroom. I quickly strip out of my clothes and change into his. As soon as I slip the tank top over my head, I'm intoxicated with the scent of Erasmus. Lavender mixed with laundry detergent. I fold my clothes neatly and place them on the counter.

When I get back to the kitchen, Erasmus has changed, too. He's still shirtless, but now he has on a pair of tight black sweats. *God, even in sweatpants, he's amazingly sexy!*

"Ready?" he asks, setting his glass down.

"As ready as I'll ever be," I reply.

"Come on."

Erasmus leads the way down a flight of stairs. About midway down, there is a very noticeable temperature change. I shiver at the sudden cold.

We come out into the basement, which is dark and gloomy. In the scant light, I can see workout equipment: a treadmill, medicine balls, a yoga mat, and a bench press. *It looks like Erasmus tries to keep his body up.*

The floor is covered with the padded mats that we used in gym class. For a second, I feel that sense of trepidation I always felt in high school gym class when I knew I was about to embarrass myself.

Erasmus faces me, his eyes gleaming darkly. "You need to learn how to protect yourself. Adrammelech's foot soldiers will attack, and they're going to fight dirty, so don't worry about fighting fair. You do whatever you need to do to survive. Bite, scratch, go for the nuts, whatever."

"I've never been in a fight," I admit, hunching my shoulders in shame. "And do demons have nuts?"

"I wish you'd never have to fight," he says, "but, unfortunately, this is the hand you've been dealt." He comes up behind me and throws his bicep against my throat. My air supply is cut off, and my eyes bulge in fear. "If someone comes up behind you and tries to choke you, you're most likely going to be surprised and go into panic mode." I try to tug out of his vice grip, but he holds me firmly in place. "I recommend going for the instep."

My lungs start to burn from a lack of oxygen, and I cough through my constricted throat. "Instep! Instep!" I grunt and lift my leg up a bit before slamming it down on the inside of Erasmus' foot. He cries out and releases me before hopping up and down with his wounded foot up in his hand.

"I'm sorry!" I gasp, stepping toward him. *Shit, I didn't want to actually hurt him!*

"Never stop to talk to your assailant!" he growls, lunging at me. Time seems to slow down, and I duck, so that he sails right over me and skids across the mat. I assume the fighting stance that I learned from watching *Buffy*: feet firmly planted, hip cocked, and fists up.

Erasmus gets to his feet and lunges at me again. I feel myself go down, and I instinctively bury my foot in his stomach as I use his momentum to push him past me.

"Good!" he boasts. "For a beginner, you're not bad. You have good instincts." He stands up and comes over to face me again. "Do you know how to punch?"

"No," I say, shaking my head.

"Punch me."

"What? No, I am not going to punch you!"

"Why not? Are you afraid? Are you a little wimp? Can't even defend himself? You make me sick. Get out."

His words make my blood boil, and with an angry cry, I ball my hand into a fist and swing. My fist connects with his arm, but then my wrist rolls, and a loud, wet *snap!* pops out.

"Fuck!" I cry, dropping to my knees. My wrist burns with pain. "I broke it. I think I broke my wrist."

Erasmus drops the tough guy act and kneels down beside me, his brows furrowed in concern. "You didn't lock your wrist," he says, taking my hand in his.

"How the fuck do I do that!?" I grit my teeth against the pain. It's not as intense as when my mom accidentally broke my finger, but it's more than I care to feel.

"You just do." He grips my wrist. "Can you move it?"

"I don't know," I grunt and move my wrist. "It hurts a little, but I can do it."

"It's not broken," he sighs, relieved. "Probably just sprained."

"I tried to tell you that this wasn't a good idea," I moan.

"It's necessary," he argues.

"I'm such a loser."

"No, you aren't." His dark eyes meet mine. "You are incredible."

"Yeah, right. I threw one punch and hurt myself."

"You're learning," he soothes, massaging my shoulders. *Oh, my God, it feels amazing!*

"Maybe I'm not cut out for this," I protest.

"I wish you could see yourself the way I see you." I can see in his eyes that he's being truthful, and I soften toward him a little more. *Maybe I should give him a chance and take the date seriously.*

I shove him playfully, but he isn't braced. He tumbles backward and pulls me with him. We roll across the mats and stop with me on top of him. He sputters with laughter, and I join in, mirth overcoming us. It feels so good to just… be.

Suddenly, he flips us so that he's on top. His head is inches from mine, and our eyes dance together. I pull him down closer, meeting his lips with mine. Initially, he is stunned into immobility, but then I feel his tongue pushing against my lips. I part them, and he slides inside my mouth, his tongue finding mine as they begin a passionate, complex tango.

I lose myself within Erasmus. I forget my anxieties, I forget my pain, and I forget my inhibitions.

Chapter Fifteen

The following night, Amethyst and I were in my room. Outside, the sun was starting to set in the west. As soon as night falls, Erasmus will be on his way to take me out on our first date. *Wow. I honestly never thought I'd have a date, let alone a first date.*

I pace back and forth, my fingers rifling through my damp hair. I was able to get a trim this afternoon after class. It looks nice, but it's at the itchy stage that drives me insane. Rollers adorn my head, fresh from being blowdryed. Of all the hairstyles I've tried over the years, I've never tried curly, and I decided that tonight was the night for me to try it. I'm wearing nothing but a towel, and water from the shower still wets my back and pools down. Romana lays on my pillow, watching me with interest. Amethyst is lying on her stomach on my bed, her eyes glued to the TV. I made the mistake of introducing her to *Sex and the City,* and now she's hooked.

I open my closet and assess my options. Immediately, my eyes fall on the clothing bag that houses my one and only suit. Mom bought it for a wedding back home, a cousin that I don't even know. Wearing the suit tonight is pointless, though. Erasmus said we're doing dinner and a movie, so it would be overkill, times a thousand. I need something more casual. Considering the weather, though, I can forget about t-shirts.

"What do you think about this?" I ask Amethyst, holding a black *St. John's Bay* sweater up against my torso.

"You wear too much black," Amethyst says, biting off a piece of licorice. "And too much plaid."

"Black is my favorite color. It's pretty much all I own." I take a red Stafford dress shirt out of the closet and set them together. "I could pair these together. Black and red go good together."

"Next," she vetoes.

I groan and replace both items. Unfortunately for me, my taste in clothing is pretty limited. I like graphic tees, sweaters, dress shirts, plaid, and hoodies. I enjoy dressing well, but I also enjoy wearing dark clothes.

My eyes catch on a nice blue/gray hoodie that one of my friends back home got me as a birthday gift last year. It fits me perfectly. "How about this?" I ask, showing it to Amethyst.

"It's still too dark," she chastises.

Next, I try a sweater that I don't often wear. It's wool, with green, brown, and blue diamond patterns.

"Not bad, but you can do better."

"I'm telling you, Amethyst, I don't have anything that isn't black or dark gray." I put the sweater and hoodie back and pull out my light gray sweater and lavender-colored dress shirt. She's going to veto it, but it's worth a shot.

Amethyst looks at it, and suddenly I have her full attention. "That's the one!" she insists.

"Okay." I work both items off the plastic hanger and undo the buttons on the dress shirt. I slide it on my bare skin and quickly do three spritzes of my cologne before rolling on some deodorant. I button the shirt up most of the way, leaving the last two buttons undone, and then tug the light gray sweater on.

"Looks good, but no dark pants. Brighten it up." Amethyst throws a few pieces of popcorn into her mouth. I'm far too nervous to eat anything before dinner.

The top shelf of my closet houses my jeans. I have a few pairs of jeans ranging from light blue to indigo and dark grey, black with ripped knees, and regular black skinny jeans. I also find a pair of blue jeans that are quite stylish. They're ripped, but the designer applied an under-layer of denim to the rips. The dark blue of the denim contrasts nicely with the lighter blue of the jeans.

I drop my towel and Amethyst whistles at my tight baby blue boxers. Not that it matters. Erasmus won't be getting in my pants tonight anyway. Truthfully, I'm wearing them for me. They make me feel sexy.

I pull on the jeans and let her scrutinize me. "Well?" I prompt after several seconds of silence.

"You're hot, holy fuck!" She fans herself as if she's on fire or having a hot flash. Another perk of having an awesome best friend is that they constantly build you up. I don't know what I'd do without Amethyst, and I don't want to know, either.

"Thanks," I say with an uncomfortable laugh. I still don't know how to take compliments very well. "I'm going to go do my hair. I'll be right back."

"Hurry up," she points out the window where the sky has turned black. "He'll be here soon."

Shit! My pulse quickens, and I rush into the bathroom. I turn on *Panic! At the Disco* as loud as it will go as I methodically get ready, making sure that I look as good as possible.

I go back into my room and start to peruse my shoe collection. I have the nasty ones I wear to work, a nice pair of leather black and white kicks, my gossamer green high-tops, and a pair of black and white tennis shoes. The Vans are the most expensive pair, and considering it's snowy out, I really don't want to chance staining them. The work shoes are obviously out, too. So, that leaves the leather kicks or Nikes.

"What shoes should I wear?" I ask Amethyst, desperate.

She laughs. "Oh, my God. You're totally Carrie. And I'm Samantha."

"I have the nose for it," I agree, trying on both pairs of shoes and checking myself out.

"I like the kicks," Amethyst says.

"Me, too. Okay." I pop the tennis shoes back into their shoebox and replace them on the shelf. "How do I look?" I ask, spinning around so she can see the whole ensemble.

"For the millionth time, you look hot! I really like the curls by the way, very Carrie." Amethyst pauses my *Sex and the City* DVD and comes to stand before me, hands on my shoulders. "Erasmus totally digs you. You've already won him over, so relax."

"Just because we've made out a few times doesn't mean that I've won him over." She shoots me a *come on,* look. I sigh. "I don't even know how dates work!"

"He picks you up; you go have dinner and talk. After dinner, you go to the movie. After that, you either go home, or you go get coffee or something. If you really, *really* like him, you go back to his place and fuck all night."

"You really *are* Samantha," I note.

"And Samantha is always right, isn't she?"

"Almost always."

"Good enough."

My phone starts to ring, and ERASMUS flashes across my screen.

"Hello," I gulp, sounding like I swallowed a frog.

"Hey, Sexy. I'm almost to the rendezvous point," he says, his voice sounding hotter than ever.

"Okay. We're leaving now. See you in a few."

"Bye."

"Bye."

I hang up. I'm not quite ready to do the whole I'm-going-on-a-date-with-a-guy conversation tonight, so I told my mom I'd be out with Amethyst. Grandma agreed to put Brent to bed.

"He's there," I relay, pulling my faux fur coat on. It's probably a little extra, but I want to feel like a glamourous star tonight, not the loser I usually feel like.

"All right, let's go." Amethyst shuts off the TV and shoulders her purse. "Bye, Romana. It was nice to meet you finally." Romana blinks at her.

"Bye, baby," I whisper, kissing the top of her head. "Wish Daddy good luck tonight." She rubs her face on mine and licks my nose. *Okay, good luck, it is.* Amethyst opens the door, and I follow her out, turning out the light.

Forty-five minutes later, Erasmus and I sit in a posh, dimly lit restaurant. The only illumination comes from a surfeit of candles burning scantly everywhere.

Erasmus looks drop-dead gorgeous in skinny black jeans with the knees cut out, black combat boots, a white t-shirt, and a fancy leather jacket. I want to reach across our small, intimate table and run my fingers through his black hair.

"I love the coat by the way," he says.

I can't tell if he's kidding or not.

"Amethyst and I were watching *Sex and the City* earlier and I decided to channel my inner Carrie tonight."

"You definitely have the nose for it."

"So, you've been alive, like a *long* time," I say quietly, so that no one can overhear. "It must get lonely."

"I *have* been on my own for quite some time," he agrees, spearing a piece of bloody steak with his fork and popping it into his mouth.

"Didn't you have a girlfriend a few years ago? Amethyst told me that you were dating a woman when you were working at Subway. Melania or something?"

Erasmus takes a sip of his wine and slowly swallows before replying. "She was a... momentary distraction," he says carefully. "She needed help getting on her feet, and I needed to look like a normal human."

"But you slept with her?"

"Yes." I feel a cold stab of jealousy in my gut. "Is that a problem?"

I want to say yes, but I have no right to be upset about something that happened before we met... do I? "No, I mean..." I sigh. "I don't know. So you're not..." I look around to make sure that our server isn't within earshot. "Gay?"

Erasmus laughs heartily, and it sounds like heavenly music to my ears. "You *can* say the word gay in public, Graham. We're out on a date. In public."

For the first time, I realize this and look around, searching for looks of disgust or disagreement. No one is paying attention to us.

"And, for the record, no, I'm not gay. If I had to label myself, I'd say I'm pansexual."

"Okay..." At least it's a sexuality that I'm aware of. Nowadays, there are so many genders and sexual identities that it's mind-blowing.

He reaches across the table and squeezes my hand. "I really like you," he says with that heart-melting smile.

"I like you, too," I say before I can stop myself. I realize then and there that it's true. I do like Erasmus.

"Does that mean we can do this again?" He makes a ridiculous face with his mouth and eyes open wide in excitement. He looks like a little boy who just opened his Christmas present to see that he got exactly what he wanted.

I can't help myself; I burst out into laughter. "I don't want to count my chickens before they hatch, but... yeah, I think it's safe to say that we can go out again."

"One more date after that, and you know what that means…" He wags his eyebrows suggestively.

I roll my eyes. "Just for that, you won't get laid on the third date." I cross my arms over my chest and set my chin determinedly.

"Actually, what I was *going* to say is that after the third date, we'll officially be boyfriends." He shoots me that grin again, and I can't help but smile.

"I want to go slow," I say, sipping my water. "My life runs smoothly because it's a routine. College, work, helping with Brent… I don't want to rush into something just because it feels good. The magic stuff is so new, and I really need to focus on that."

"I understand completely." He swallows more wine. "I mean, you're not even out yet."

"That's true." I take a bite of my pasta. "It's all so confusing."

"I'm here for you, whenever, wherever."

"Thanks. I'm just not sure… I mean, obviously, I'm attracted to you; I mean, I'm here. I do think women are pretty…"

"Are you a virgin?"

My cheeks glow red with shame. "Yes."

"I think that's so awesome," he says, smiling.

"You do?" I find it hard to believe that a sex god like Erasmus Mayfair is delighted that I'm a virgin and don't want to put out right away.

"Yeah. The kids of your generation are having sex in middle school. I think it shows that you have a lot of integrity and that you haven't just slept your way through your classmates."

"I can't say that I've done that."

"I meant what I said that first night about being patient. I'm not going to pressure you. I'll wait as long as it takes for you to trust me. I'll wait forever if I have to. It's just time."

I don't quite know why I believe him. He's not just feeding me a line to convince me to give it up to him in the backseat of his nice Cadillac.

"How is everything?" our server asks. She's a pretty girl around my age with piercing blue eyes. Her blonde hair has pink and purple streaks, and she has it clipped back, up out of her way.

"Great, thank you," I say, smiling.

"Are you ready for boxes?"

"Yes, please," Erasmus answers.

"Is this going to be on the same check or separate?"

I feel a cold sweat start to build on my lower back, but Erasmus steps in and saves the day. Well, kind of. "Same check, please."

"Perfect. I'm sorry I have to ask that. We're not supposed to assume." She shrugs. "You guys are really cute together, by the way."

"Thanks." Erasmus reaches out for my hand, which has grown ice cold.

"How long have you two been together?" she asks.

"This is actually our first date."

"Get outta here!" Our server looks amazed. "You guys have such great chemistry. I just kind of assumed you have been together for a while."

"Well, I'm hoping that this is the start of our forever." Erasmus squeezes my hand.

"Well, you've certainly got the right attitude." She looks around to make sure that no one else needs her assistance. "I'll be right back with your check and those boxes."

"Thank you," I murmur.

She leaves, and Erasmus kisses my hand. "See? We have great chemistry."

"I won't argue with that." I finish my water. "So, what are we seeing at the theater?"

"I thought I'd let you pick the movie since I picked the restaurant."

"Okay, well, how about the new *Footloose* movie?" I suggest.

"Perfect!"

Our server comes back with our takeout boxes and the bill. Erasmus snatches it and leaves a $100 bill on the table. He stands up. I follow suit, shrugging my coat back on. "Have a good night," I say to the girl.

"Thanks; you, too."

We walk out into the brisk cold, and Erasmus puts his arm around me. It gives me a little extra warmth, but not much. Still, it's the thought that counts.

Within minutes we're at the movie theater, and conveniently there is a showing of *Footloose* that is just about to start. "Did you plan this?" I ask, arching a suspicious eyebrow.

"Maybe." He tries to keep a straight face but ends up guffawing. I like that about him. Despite his advanced age, Erasmus is still young at heart. I find it endearing. "Do you want any popcorn?"

"If you do. "

"Always!"

A few minutes later, we enter the dark theater and score the seats perfectly in the center. Erasmus holds the bucket of popcorn between his legs.

I glance over and entertain the idea of reaching over and rubbing him a little. I may want to take things slowly, but I have a seventeen-year-old's libido. *Not on the first date*, I decide.

It's cold in our theater, and as the movie starts, I snuggle up against Erasmus. He holds me tightly, and I think I might fall in love with him.

After the movie, we head back toward my house. "Well, how was your first date?" Erasmus asks, glancing over at me.

"It was perfect. Thank you," I gush.

"My pleasure, *mon amour*." *My love!* My heart trills.

Too soon, we're parked in my driveway. I unbuckle my seat belt and turn to face Erasmus. "I had a really nice time tonight."

"So did I," he assures me. "When can I see you again?"

"When do you want to see me again?"

"I want to take you home with me and never be apart from you again, but considering we just met, and this is our first date..."

"Well, you're welcome to climb in through my window anytime."

"Oh, really?" He cocks an eyebrow.

"I quite enjoyed sleeping with you."

"So did I."

"Maybe we can do that again soon," I suggest.

"Right on. I'd like that."

"Just don't get us caught. I don't want to try to explain all of this to my mother just yet."

"You think she'll care that you're dating a dude?"

"I honestly don't know, but she is going to freak when she finds out that you're a vampire."

"We'll wait to tell her then."

"Good idea." I lean over and kiss him, relishing his lips. "Thanks again," I whisper, pulling away.

"You're welcome."

I grab my takeout box and get out of the car. "Goodnight."

"Goodnight."

I rush to the door, desperate to escape the cold. Inside I turn back long enough to steal one last glance at Erasmus. He's staring at me intently. I wave, and he nods, reversing out of the driveway. I force myself to go inside and shut the door behind me.

Who knew that a night could be so perfect and magical? My lips still tingle from that last kiss, and I grin. *There's much more to come. Much, much more.*

Chapter Sixteen

With the fall term over and a break until the winter term begins in January, I decide it's time to really crack down on my Craft studies.

As much as I'm creeped out by Sioned's bizarre behavior, Gyspies' is the only magic shop in town. I need supplies, and I don't see the point in doing it all online; I can face Sioned, really.

"Do you want me to go in with you?" Erasmus asks, puffing on his cigarette. I've never thought of smoking as sexy, but goddess, does it look sexy when Erasmus does it, and not just because I'm dying to experience what his mouth can do.

"No, I need to do this alone. I'll be safe," I promise before he can protest. "Besides, the sun is out for another half hour at least. Unless you're trying to immolate yourself, I don't think going outside is the best course of action."

"I can throw a blanket on."

"Yeah, 'cause that won't rouse suspicion," I say sarcastically. "Stay here. I'll be right back."

I shut the car door and hug my arms around myself as I scurry through the biting cold wind. *Why did I decide that this was a good idea again?* I wonder as the frosty air penetrates my gloves and makes my cold fingers even colder.

I push the door open and see Sioned regarding me with her cold dark eyes.

"Tea?" She holds out a mug. The smell wafts toward me, and my mouth starts to water.

"I guess I don't need to ask how you knew I was coming. I slide out of my coat and hang it and my scarf on the stand by the door.

"I have the gift of prophecy," she replies, confirming my suspicions.

"Doesn't it get old knowing everything?"

Sioned regards me steel-faced for several seconds before her lips tug up into a smile. This act removes years from her face. "I do not know everything, though I wish that I did."

"I suppose you know why I'm here, too?"

Sioned nods. "You wish to know more about your destiny. You're concerned with the attempts on your life."

"Sioned, two, Graham, zero." I clap my hands on my thighs loudly. "Look, I'm sorry if I was rude the last time I was here."

"Think nothing of it. I dumped a lot on you all at once."

"I just never thought that any of this," I gesture around the shop, "could actually be real."

"You weren't raised in this world like I was; it's only natural that it would take you some time to adjust. How does it feel?"

"Finding out that witches are real?" I shrug. "Kind of like a dream come true for me."

"No, I mean finding out how special you are."

I sigh, trying to find the right words to describe it. "It still doesn't feel real. I mean, I have never been special in my life, not once. And to find out now that I am, it's overwhelming. It's like finding out you were adopted as a teenager. Your whole world just gets turned on its head."

"Have you been practicing?" Sioned hands me the warm mug of tea, and I take a grateful sip.

"Not as much as I should be," I admit. "Between work, and college, and everything, I'm pretty ragged. But I practiced telekinesis, and I moved the pencil a little on my first try."

"How long ago was that?"

"My birthday." I can feel her judging me as I say it.

"It's been two months!" Sioned cannot hide her disappointment. "I know how important education is, but your powers, Graham, they are who you are! They're a gift!"

"I know. That's part of the reason I'm here. My friend Amethyst made me a protection amulet, but I want more. I have some black salt that I've been using, but I want to stock up. I need to know that I'm safe when I leave my house."

Sioned nods and walks over to the shelves. She mutters under her breath, perhaps thinking aloud. I watch as she gathers some crystals and a bag of something purple.

"Peonies," she explains in her thick accent, "are good for protection spells and rituals. Smokey Quartz and Tourmaline for protection, Carnelian for stabilization, Clear Quartz for cleansing, healing, and concentration, Amethyst for strength, and Sodalite for mental stabilization."

I watch as she hands me the baggie of peonies and the crystals. Their colors range from black to yellow, to red, to pink, to clear. I know next to nothing about crystals.

"You'll need to charge them before using them," she informs me. I'm about to open my mouth to protest when she holds up a quieting hand. "Simply run them under clear water, and that will suffice. Though, I highly recommend using moonlight."

"You can charge crystals with moonlight?" Wow, I sound like the world's worst witch right now.

"Yes. Place the crystals under the moonlight and leave them for seven hours to charge."

"Is this a no more, no less situation?"

"Perhaps if you spent less time being witty and more time practicing your Craft—"

"You're right; I'm sorry." I shake my head in disappointment.

Sioned rings up the items and then fixes me with her dark gaze. "Go ahead and ask me."

I want to protest, but I know it's no use. "It's just…you can see the future. I can't help but wonder if…am I going to pull it off? Am I going to be able to fulfill my duty?"

"I cannot tell you that," Sioned answers glumly. "You must walk that path alone."

"Of course." I smile tightly. "Can you at least tell me if Erasmus is right for me?" Sioned arches an eyebrow at me and like a chastised child. I bow my head and start to walk away.

"Graham?" Sioned calls after me. I turn to face her, my brows knit in confusion. "He will do everything he can to make you happy. You could do a lot worse."

My heart skips a beat, and I laugh in astonishment. "I'll let him know, thanks."

"Blessed be."

"Blessed be."

The door eases closed behind me as I slip back into my jacket and scarf. Erasmus sees me and pulls the car up to the edge of the sidewalk, ever the gentlemen. "You look cold," he says as I open the door and get in. Of course, he has the heat blasting, so I relax into the seat, fastening my seatbelt.

"Should I take you home now, or do you want to grab a bite?"

"You don't eat," I remind him gently.

"I do for you."

He waggles his eyebrows, and I can't stifle a giggle. "Sioned says you'll do everything you can to make me happy."

"It's true." His face lights up. "Wait, does this mean that you're *actually* taking us seriously?" A twinkle in his dark eyes makes me feel giddy inside; I hate it.

"There is no *us*," I remind him. "We went on two dates."

"Two amazing dates," he corrects me with an impish grin that makes me want to kiss him until our lips fuse together forever.

"Look, Erasmus, I had a really great time with you the last few weeks; I really did. You're so sweet, and you're gorgeous…"

"But…?" he prompts.

"I need to focus on my Craft. I have enough distractions in my every day life without adding you to it."

"So, I'm a distraction?" That light in his eyes dims, and I hate myself a little for hurting him.

"You're not a distraction, per se, but if I have to worry about your needs, too…" I sigh, at a loss for words. "I just don't know how to juggle all of this. I've never had a boyfriend before."

"Do you like me?" He asks, and it's like someone punched me in the stomach, knocking the air from my lungs.

"Yes." It comes out as barely more than a whisper.

"Then, how about this? Let me take you on another date. Let's pursue this, Graham, and see where it goes. I promise I won't be too much of a distraction for you."

I want to shut him down and get as far from him as I can because I'm scared of getting hurt at the root of it, but Sioned's words whisper in my ear. What if I turn him down and miss my chance? It's not like I have a slew of other options, and certainly none as kind or as good-looking as Erasmus. Plus, he's a vampire, so I don't have the added stress of trying to hide my secret from him.

"Do you promise not to hurt me?" I ask him in my weak, little boy's voice.

"Oh, Graham." His face softens into one of pity, and he squeezes my hand. "Hurting you is the last thing I would ever want to do. I know we haven't known each other that long, but I feel a connection with you that I have never felt before.

"Okay," I say, nodding. "We can go on another date."

"Yeah?" His face lights up again, and I laugh.

"Yeah."

Erasmus whoops triumphantly and starts the car. "Let's get you home so you can practice your magic before our next date."

Before long, we're parked in my driveway. Grandma is at Temple today, but Mom is home; she works a lot around the winter holidays, so she's most likely sleeping. I won't have to explain to her who dropped me off in the fancy black Cadillac.

My fingers hover on the latch. "I'd invite you inside but…"

"I get it." He smiles warmly at me. "When the time is right, I'll meet your family. I don't take it personally."

"Good. It's definitely not personal." I clear my throat. "Thanks for the ride. I'll, uh, be in touch."

Erasmus grabs me and pulls me into his arms. Instinctively, my lips find his, and I moan as we kiss. His lips are cold, but they're soft and feel great on mine, almost like they belong.

I let it go on for a minute, and then I force myself to pull away. "I'll see you soon." My voice is husky, heavy with lust.

"I'll be here."

I grin at him and then open the door. The cold air grips me, and I rush into the house, waving at him before I close the door behind me

The house is silent, so I hurry upstairs into my room. I hang my coat and scarf and place my shoes on the rack before sitting on my bed, cross-legged in the center. I set a pencil down before me, close my eyes, and take several deep, steadying breaths, trying to rid my mind of thoughts of Erasmus' lips and the stresses of life. I shift my thoughts to the pencil, how light it is, how easily it will respond to my powers.

As my power starts to ignite, I feel pressure in my head, like a headache beginning to build. If I try too hard, no doubt I'll end up with one of the optical migraines I used to get in high school. I'll have to tread lightly.

I imagine the pencil floating off the bed slowly, light as a feather. I open my right eye a crack and see that it's working. I imagine it starting to spin now, slowly, at first, but gradually building momentum. This takes more concentration, and the pressure in my head builds.

Once more, I open my eyes and see the pencil spinning in the air. It grows faster, a flurry of movement. "I'm doing it!" I gasp. Last time, I'd barely been able to get it airborne!

Romana suddenly stalks over, batting at the pencil curiously. I narrow my eyes and move it up out of her reach. Before I can stop her, she spring-loads herself into the air after it. My right hand flies out, and she stops mid-air. I widen my eyes, realizing that I am simultaneously levitating the pencil and holding Romana in place. My powers are growing!

I lower my hand down to the bed and watch as Romana slowly follows suit, her already big eyes almost bulging out of her head. "It's okay, baby," I assure her, petting her back, "Daddy just doesn't want to risk you getting hurt." She mewls loudly at me, and I release her. Blinding pain sears through my head, making me cry out.

I'd known that learning telekinesis would be hard and might physically exhaust me; but I hadn't even thought about it giving me a migraine. My head starts to throb, and I release the pencil. It drops onto the bed and then rolls across the floor where Romana quickly pounces on it.

My hand goes to my forehead as if the mere act of rubbing it can alleviate the pain within. It hurts more with my eyes open, but as I go to close them, I see a spot of blood on the back of my right hand. I swipe at my nose and see more blood.

I've never had a nosebleed in my life, and I am not prepared for the amount of blood gushing from my nostrils. Panicked, I spring to my feet and dash across the hall to the bathroom, careful not to bleed on the carpet. I grab a wad of toilet paper, stick it in one nostril, and then fill the other. The migraine quickly drains me, and I feel my knees getting wobbly. Grabbing the roll of toilet paper, I crawl back to my room and drop into the bed. At this angle, I can feel the blood start to flow more slowly as my eyelids grow heavy.

I'm ecstatic that my powers have grown already and that I am capable of such feats; but this migraine sucks. At least it's not so bad that I can't see, and my face is going numb.

I pull the blankets up over my head to block the sunlight streaming in through the windows. The darkness helps with the pain a little, but not enough. Through the pain, my mind drifts back to Erasmus and how it would feel if he were here right now. *I'd have my head on his chest, he'd be holding me tightly, and It would be amazing...*

I lose myself in these thoughts and slowly drift off to sleep.

Chapter Seventeen

On our third date, Erasmus and I saw William Shatner on tour. We watched *Star Trek II: The Wrath of Khan*, then Mr. Shatner came on stage and talked about his recollections of working on the show and the subsequent films. After that, we got to take a picture with him. It was phenomenal!

For our fourth date, we had a home-cooked meal at Erasmus' place. I guess being immortal lends itself to myriad skills. His chicken parmesan was resplendent and succulent. He insisted that I wash it down with this amazing fruity wine called Pink Moscato. I did get a little drunk from it, but he made sure that I didn't get too bad and that I got into bed safely.

Outside, the ground froze as the temperatures continued to dip, and winter started to take hold of Willows Crest. November bled into December, and the impending doom of Hanukkah began to set in. I've never been a fan of Christmas. I hate the cold, and I hate the forced festiveness of it all. This would be my first year actually celebrating Hanukkah and not being forced into Christmas.

The attempts on my life have not continued since that one night, which has kept me on edge, waiting for the next scare. I've continued to practice with Erasmus. I learned how to throw a punch—without hurting my wrist—and several defensive maneuvers. I'll never be Mike Tyson, but I'd like to think I can hold my own now.

Amethyst turned my Star of David necklace into a pretty badass protection amulet. If I'm in danger, it glows a bright purple. There's definitely no missing it. We tested it out with Amethyst coming at me with a knife.

My powers have continued to grow and develop. I haven't tried Thrall yet, but I've gotten better with telekinesis. I can close doors and windows now and bring objects to myself. I don't want to be a jack of all trades, master of none, so I've focused on telekinesis. Grandma wants me to try Resurrection again soon. I don't quite know how we're going to study that one. It honestly freaks me out. I don't want to unleash a horde of zombies on the town.

The whole time that I've been going on dates with Erasmus, my mom has completely ignored it. I don't know if she thinks that Amethyst and I are dating or if I'm just very proficient at hiding things. Regardless, sooner rather than later, I will have to tell her the truth, and I'm not looking forward to it. I don't know how she'll react. She's worked with gay guys and seems okay with the abstract idea, but I've also heard her use gay slurs.

****

Erasmus and I are snuggled up on his white leather couch, a fire burning brightly in the fireplace. I'm laying on him, my head nestled into his bony chest. Despite his analogy of vampires as better-maintained zombies, I've never noticed him rotting or anything. On the contrary, his teeth are perfect and white, and he always smells pleasant. He must keep up with his blood intake.

His hand is stroking my hair lovingly, and I hate that I'll have to get home soon. I wish that I didn't have responsibilities there. Erasmus and I have been spending a lot of time together recently, and it's getting to the point where I don't want to say goodbye to him at the end of the night. Sure, he sneaks into my window, and we sleep together, but we haven't had sex yet. I don't feel comfortable doing it in my grandmother's house, and all I can think of is my mom walking in on us. A part of me wishes that I could just come and stay here in Erasmus' palace, but I know I can't. Responsibility sucks!

"It's getting late," Erasmus says, noting the time in the corner of his flat-screen TV.

"Five more minutes?" I beg, nuzzling his neck.

He smiles and kisses the top of my head. "I don't want you to get into trouble. If I make a bad impression, your mom might forbid us from seeing each other."

I lift my head and meet his brown eyes with my blue ones. "I would *never* let her do that, okay?"

"I know you wouldn't, not by choice."

"Even against my will."

"She's still your mom, Graham. It might be an adjustment for her, but from everything you've said, it sounds like she loves you a lot."

"She does," I agree. "It's weird, though. Most of the time, it's like we're friends instead of mother-son, which is fine, but then she randomly tries to pull a parental trip on me and doesn't understand why I can't take it."

"Oh, to be young again."

"What does that mean?" I lift myself up onto my forearms like I'm planking above him.

"It's nothing against you," he assures me, "but young people always think they know everything. Your parents are always trying to be controlling and pulling on your dick. A few years from now, you'll have matured a bit and see that your mom just wants what's best for you."

"I know she does," I sigh. "She wants me to get a degree in graphic design or animation or something."

"And you don't want to?"

"No. I didn't even want to go to college. I think it's just that they make being an adult so fucking elitist. Plus the fact that college is so damned expensive! Who in their right mind wants to willingly put themselves into hundreds of thousands of dollars into debt for a piece of paper that no longer guarantees you a job? Sounds stupid to me."

"What do you want to do?"

"I've always liked acting. Ever since I was little, I'd find a movie I liked, and I'd watch it over and over again, memorizing the dialogue and acting it out. I can make myself cry."

"Let's see it," Erasmus chuckles.

"Just give me a second." I exhale and close my eyes. I recall a nightmare I had months ago of Romana being torn away from me. It wouldn't be that big of a deal to most people, but to me, it is as monumental as the scene in *Sophie's Choice* where Meryl Streep's character is forced to choose which of her children will live.

I widen my eyes, and my vision blurs. I make my bottom lip tremble, and crocodile tears rain down my cheeks.

"Not bad!" Erasmus claps ebulliently. "That was so good!"

"Thanks." I wipe the tears away and sit down as he pulls his legs up out of my way. "I don't know. Don wasn't very supportive of that as a vocation, either."

"Why not?"

"He said it wasn't 'logical.'" I make air quotes. "He thought I should do something related to business, which of course, I detest."

"You'd look good in a suit, though," Erasmus contradicts.

"I thought about being a teacher for a while, but there isn't much of a market for that, and I realized that I hate kids. Plus, my anxiety... my students won't respect me if I'm in the corner having panic attacks all the time.

"I went through a phase when I was watching *Scrubs* and *ER* for the first time that I entertained the idea of being a doctor. I knew that wasn't a good match, though."

"Why not?"

"Because I am terrible in a crisis. It wouldn't be fair for me to go into medicine and put people's lives in danger just so that I can make money."

"That's decent of you."

"Besides," I say with a shrug, "I like my sleep way too much. I can't function properly on a doctor's sleep."

"You'll figure it out," Erasmus assures me.

"Speaking of Don..." I pinch the bridge of my nose in frustration. "He's coming over tomorrow to pick Brent up for the week."

"Do you have to see him?"

"I've been avoiding him this whole time. I'd like to hide in my room tomorrow, but Hanukkah is kind of a big deal for my grandma. She isn't going to let me entomb myself in my room."

"I'm sorry that you have to see him. Would it make it better if I was there for moral support?"

"It would make it a lot easier, but I can't just bring you over on a family holiday. I haven't even come out to my mom yet."

"You could talk to her tonight," he suggests softly.

"I could." I hug my knees. "I'm scared too, though."

"Why?"

"What if she—?" my voice cuts out as emotion chokes me. "What if she doesn't take it well?"

"She will. She's your mother. A mother's love knows no end."

"I guess."

"I'll help you tell her, if you want."

"No," I decide. "I need to do this on my own. I've just been burying my head in the sand about it."

"I get that, but I *am* coming over tomorrow. I'm not going to let you face that prick by yourself."

"Oh, Erasmus!" I throw my arms around his neck and squeeze him tightly. I don't know if I properly love him yet, it has only been a month, but he has greatly enriched my life. I don't want to picture a life without him now.

"I'll always be here," he whispers, and I kiss him, holding his face in my hands.

"How did I ever get so lucky?" I ask rhetorically.

"I'm the lucky one," he insists. I kiss him again. "We really should get you home, though."

"Okay," I relent. "If you insist."

Erasmus shuts the TV off and closes the glass on the fireplace as I put on my coat, hat, gloves, and scarf. We walk out to the car, and he starts it, the engine roaring to life.

"You know," I say, shivering, "my mom is a car chick; she'll drool over this car when she sees it."

"See? I'm winning her over already." He shoots me a grin.

The drive back to my house doesn't take nearly long enough. In the blink of an eye, we're pulling into the driveway, and Erasmus is throwing the car into park. "What time is Don coming over?" he asks.

"Probably around eleven, noon," I estimate. "At least he's giving us enough time to do Christmas morning with Brent. Brent was raised on Christmas, so we're not going to change up his routine now and switch to Hanukkah only."

"The man is a saint!" Erasmus' voice is dripping with sarcasm. "I should probably just stay the night, then."

"Probably, but how are we going to explain how you're already here?"

"We'll just be honest. We're not doing anything inappropriate, just cuddling."

"True…" I slap my thighs. "Okay, well, I guess I'll see you later tonight."

"It's a date." He pulls me in for a kiss, and I lose myself in his lips. "Good luck with your mom," he says when he finally breaks the kiss.

"Thanks," I mutter.

I force my legs to propel me away from Erasmus, away from love, comfort, and peace; and step into the house. I make a pit stop to dump my coat, gloves, and scarf in my room. Romana perks up at the sight of me. "Wish Daddy luck," I say, scratching her cheeks. She closes her eyes and tilts her head back in exaltation.

When I get back downstairs, my mom is in the kitchen, making herself a salad to take with her. At the sound of my feet, she looks up and smiles grimly. I can tell she's devastated about spending Christmas away from Brent; it's the first Christmas they've spent apart since he was born. "What's up?" she asks, grating a block of cheese into the plastic dish.

"Do you have a second?" I sit down at the island, fidgeting nervously. My heart is beating so loudly that I can hear it in my ears. I feel short of breath but force myself to think of Erasmus, and I find an inner strength.

"A few, yeah." She sets the cheese down and gives me her full attention.

"There's, uh, something I need to tell you," I begin.

"Okay…"

"I haven't been completely honest with you the last month or so when I said I was hanging out with Amethyst."

"What were you doing that you couldn't just tell me?" Her forehead wrinkles in confusion. "If it's drugs, well, I'm not mad. I smoked my fair share of pot at your age. As long as you're not failing your classes, I don't really care."

"Thanks for the permission, but it's not drugs, Mom."

"What, then? Not alcohol!" She sighs and puts her hand on her forehead as she begins to pace. "You know alcoholism runs on both sides of your family."

"I have had a glass or two of wine," I confess, "but what I mean to say is…" My throat feels tight, but I force myself to keep talking. "I've been seeing someone."

"Why were you afraid to tell me?" She folds her arms across her ample bosom. "Well, who is she?"

"He," I blurt before I can convince myself not to.

My mom is silent. I look up and see her looking at me, her face unreadable. "You're gay," she says.

"Yeah."

She nods. "I can't say that I haven't been expecting this," she admits.

"What?"

"Well, honey, you like Mariah Carey more than I do. You were obsessed with Madonna for, like, a decade." She smiles. "Do you remember back when we lived in Bay City, and we had that fight?"

"No."

"We had a big fight, and you said you were moving out, going to live with your dad." *Back when I thought that Dad hung the moon,* I think. "You went into your room and then my closet. You came out with your *Goosebumps* beanbag chair and my gold pumps. I asked you if the pumps were for you or your dad."

Despite my tension, I burst out into laughter. Mom joins in, reaching out and squeezing my hand.

"Honey, I want you to know that this doesn't change anything. You're still my boy. I love you."

That does me in, and I burst into tears. My mother doesn't say the "L" word often. I can't remember the last time she told me she loved me.

I feel her arms encompass me, and I cry into her chest. "Shhh, it's okay," she soothes, stroking my head.

"I was so afraid to tell you," I croak.

"Why? You had to have known that I wouldn't stop loving you."

"All those things that Don said..."

"Fuck, Don. He's not here. What he thinks doesn't matter."

"Erasmus wants to meet you," I say, swiping at my eyes.

"Of course, when?"

"He was thinking of coming over tomorrow."

"I can't guarantee that I won't look like an old handbag, but he's more than welcome to come over."

"Thanks."

My mom stands up and looks at her watch. "Shit! I have to get going. Can we talk more about this later?"

"Sure."

"Okay." She puts the lid on her Tupperware salad and dons her orange puffer coat. "This doesn't change anything," she reiterates.

"Okay."

She gives me a quick hug and rushes out the door. I stare after her for a few minutes before standing up. I microwave a Lean Cuisine and head up to my room.

I devour my meal and get lost in *Sabrina the Teenage Witch*. It feels like minutes have passed, but it was actually hours. A soft knocking on my window brings me back to reality. I pause the show and bolt to the window, pulling it up. Erasmus' beaming face greets me. He climbs through the window and shuts it behind him, locking out the bitter cold.

"Hey, babe." He brushes his lips against mine. "How'd it go?"

"It went well," I laugh. "She can't wait to meet you."

"I'm great with moms," he assures me.

"I guess we'll find out tomorrow."

"Definitely." He removes his leather jacket and tosses it across the back of my computer chair. "I'm so proud of you," he whispers into my hair as he embraces me.

"I couldn't have done it if it weren't for you," I tell him.

"That's not true. You're a badass!"

"Hardly." I blow air out of my cheeks.

"The Powers That Be didn't choose you for this life by chance."

"Didn't they?"

"No, they chose you because you are intelligent and strong."

"I'm definitely not strong," I argue, moving away from him.

"You are the strongest person I know."

I scoff. "You have to say that. You're my boyfriend."

"My being in love with you has nothing to do with it."

I turn back to face him, shocked. He *loves* me? He's never said that out loud before. "You love me?"

"Isn't that obvious?"

"I thought you were just with me for my sparkling wit," I tease.

"There is that." Erasmus comes to stand close to me once more. "Graham, I've been alive for centuries. I've known *a lot* of people. I've loved a lot of people, but no one has meant nearly as much to me as you do. I haven't loved anyone else the way I love you."

Wow! Two I love yous in the same day. I must have done something right for once!

"I love you, too, Erasmus." The words leave my lips tingling, as if I've used that peppermint chapstick that Amethyst insists makes my lips plumper.

He wraps his lithe arms around me, and we move toward the bed. Romana runs over to us and butts us both with her head. Apparently, she wants in on the love, too.

"What were you watching?" Erasmus asks as we lie down together in the spoon position.

"*Sabrina the Teenage Witch*," I answer. "It's hilarious."

"Life almost imitates art. Well, hit play!"

I laugh and do as I'm told. *Yes, I decide; this is happiness. This is perfection: cuddled up in bed with my boyfriend, Romana, and good TV.*

With Erasmus' arms around me, I feel like I can do anything. Maybe I can stand up to Don tomorrow and show him how far I've come since I escaped his clutches. With a good support system, I can do anything.

Chapter Eighteen

Consciousness comes to me slowly, in stages. First, I become aware of the feel of Erasmus' arms around me—holding me tightly. In those first precious few moments, I feel pure bliss, but then my mind starts to boot up, like a computer that's just updated. I remember what today is and how much strength I will need to make it through.

My stomach acid turns sour, burning in my intestines as the nerves burst to life in spastic hyperactivity. *I can't do this! Why did I ever think that I could face Don?*

Somehow, Erasmus senses that I'm awake, and he kisses my neck, his lips soft and ticklish. "Good morning, my love," he rasps.

"Good morning," I reply emotionlessly as I put my glasses on.

"How did you sleep?"

"Fine until now."

"What's wrong?" he presses me more tightly against him, as if the mere presence of his body can somehow imbue strength inside of me.

"I don't think I can do this," I confess, closing my eyes in shame.

"See your stepdad?"

"Yeah."

"If it's making you that anxious, then we don't have to. You can say goodbye to your brother before he gets here, and we can stay up here until he's gone."

"You won't think that I'm a coward?" *There's the little boy's voice again.*

"I could never think that you are a coward. You are the bravest person that I have ever met."

I roll over so that we're lying face to face. Erasmus' usual immaculate pompadour is messy with sleep. The bangs hang in strings over his dark eyes, and tufts stand up here and there. Somehow, despite this, he is still the hottest thing I have ever seen, but not in a lascivious way. His is a natural beauty that cannot be diminished. I wish I could be that attractive.

He smiles at me, and I feel a warm sensation in my chest. Did my heart skip a beat? I reach out and brush his cheek lovingly. He closes his eyes in exaltation and kisses my hand tenderly.

"I'm not brave," I negate, smiling sadly.

"Of course you are! Look at all you've overcome, and still, you've maintained your kindness and purity of heart."

"I don't think that that qualifies as bravery."

"What is it then?"

"Maturity? Part of being a human being? I don't know."

"You don't give yourself enough credit."

"That's what Amethyst says."

"Amethyst is right."

I notice that my bladder is full and aching to be emptied. I force myself to sit up and then swing my feet to the floor. Even through my socks, I feel the hardwood is cold as ice. I shiver and quick-step as Romana brushes past my feet, squeaking at me.

"Daddy has to pee real quick. I'll fill your dish when I'm done, okay?" I say in my baby voice. In response, Romana cries again, her topaz eyes wide. "Daddy will be right back."

"I can feed her for you," Erasmus offers, throwing the covers back to expose his white t-shirt and gray sweatpants.

"Could you?"

"Consider it done."

"I'd kiss you… but morning breath." I widen my eyes dramatically.

"I happen to love your morning breath, but if you're more comfortable brushing your teeth first, I can wait."

"You're the best boyfriend ever," I call over my shoulder as I open my door and cross the hall to my tiny bathroom.

I brush my teeth and put my contacts in, my stomach a broiling mess. *Maybe I'll ask Grandma for a Xanax*, I think, spitting toothpaste down the drain. *Anything to calm me down.*

I pour a shot of mouthwash into my mouth and swish it furiously, willing it to freshen my breath substantially and strip any surface stains that may exist from my heavy tea intake.

My mind drifts back to Erasmus and how important to me he's become in such a short amount of time. I had a whole life without him, just fine, and now, the thought of going just one day without him feels like a punch to my stomach. *Is this how love is supposed to feel?* I wonder, cracking my neck.

I spit the mouthwash out and rinse it down the drain before baring my teeth to my reflection in the mirror. They look fairly good to me, save the crooked canine on the left side. It wouldn't be too noticeable, considering I have a tiny mouth, but for the fact that all four of my canines are big and sharp, like vampire fangs. *How ironic. Erasmus and I will have to compare fangs sometime.*

There's a knock at the door, and I open it to see my mom looking exhausted despite her perfectly coiffed hair and makeup. I don't know what time it is. She should be in bed, but I know she won't sleep until after Don comes to get Brent.

"Hey," I say, casting a nervous glance past her to my bedroom door. I hope she didn't try to go in there. I really don't want to face the explosion that will ensue if she knows that Erasmus spent the night. *What was I thinking?*

"Hey. We'll be opening presents soon," she replies, her voice laden with exhaustion.

"What time is it?"

"A little after ten."

"Wow! I slept… quite a while." *Who can blame me?* Of course, I slept with Erasmus holding me and making me feel safe and loved for the first time in my life.

My mom nods and yawns. "Honey, I wanted to talk more about last night."

"Okay."

"Not in the bathroom, though. Let's go to your room."

Sweat starts to form all over my body. "My room is cold. Let's just talk on the stairs or in the living room."

"Okay…" she frowns in consternation.

I go and sit at the top of the stairs, my feet on the first step. My mom follows suit. "I'm sorry that I had to rush out last night," she begins. "I don't want you to think that I was running from you or anything."

"No," I shrug. "You said everything was cool, so I believed you."

"This isn't the life that I would choose for you. I know that it isn't a choice; it's just that... being gay is not an easy life. It isn't as big of a deal as it was when I was young, but still, people are cruel."

"I know." I've been bullied for as long as I can remember. *Believe me, I know.*

"But I will support you because it's who you are, and I'm your mother. I just want you to be happy."

"Thanks, Mom. I want that for you, too."

She scoffs. "I'm as happy as I can be, I guess. I've made so many mistakes in my life. I wish I'd gone to college, I wish I'd never started smoking... I could go on for hours."

"I just don't want you to feel bad or blame yourself," I say.

"For what?"

"Well, deep down, my greatest fear is that you'll think that all of this is something that you did. One son is a queer, and the other is special needs..."

She gasps and takes both of my hands in hers. "Graham, no! I do *not* think of it that way. I'll admit that I do worry that something in me made Brent the way he is. I know that you just are who you are. I don't think that it reflects at all on my parenting. I'm proud of you, and of Brent."

"Beverly, Graham!" my grandma's voice dances up the stairs. "It's time to open presents!"

"We'll be right down," my mom calls back, rolling her eyes. We stand up and step back up onto the second floor.

"I'm just going to run to my room for a sec. I'm a little cold. I need my bathrobe."

"Okay. I'll meet you downstairs."

"Okay."

I go back down the hall and slip into my room. Erasmus is lying in bed, scrolling through his phone like a typical millennial.

"Sorry, my mom caught me and wanted to talk some more," I say as I pull on my blue fuzzy bathrobe with polar bears on it.

"You look so cute in that." I can't tell if he's being facetious or not, but I don't really care. It's warm and comfy.

"I have to go open presents with my family. Are you okay up here by yourself?"

"I'll be fine," he assures me, "but I'm still waiting on that kiss."

I roll my eyes as if in frustration, but the truth is that making out with Erasmus is hardly a chore. I cross to him and onto the bed, kissing him softly.

"Better?" I ask, quirking an eyebrow.

"I can think of some things that would be even better, but, yeah, that'll do."

I shake my head. "So sexual," I tease.

"You love it."

"I love *you*."

"I love you, too."

He pulls me into another kiss, and I forget all about my duties as passion grips me tightly. I slide my hands underneath his t-shirt and run them up and down his smooth chest. His flesh isn't as warm as I'd like, but it's not too cold, either. My breath quickens as our kiss deepens, and his hands start to skim over my body. A moan escapes my lips, and I throw my head back. Erasmus' lips start caressing my throat and neck. I bite my lip to keep another moan from sneaking out.

I hear Brent squeal from downstairs and come back to myself. "Sorry," I say, my voice raspy with lust.

"Don't be." Erasmus smiles. "I got a little carried away."

"I like it when you get carried away." I wink.

"Don't tempt me," he growls.

"I'll be back." I kiss him quickly on the lips. "You might want to shower and change while everyone is distracted."

"Good idea."

I smile and go back out of the room, my heart pounding with excitement. I don't know how much longer I can fight the urge to have sex with Erasmus. He's so intoxicating and sweet and understanding. He's literally perfect.

I take steadying breaths as I descend the stairs, trying to smooth my hair and erase any sign that I did anything unseemly. I pad into the living room to see Brent sitting on the floor by the Christmas tree, his arms flapping excitedly. My mom kneels beside him, and Grandma sits on the love seat, watching him happily. Beside her, the menorah sits on the mantle, six burnt candles in the holders, just awaiting the seventh candle. I love that Judaism is more grandiose than Christianity; Christian holidays are a day long, while Jewish holidays last up to eight days, like Hanukkah.

Everyone looks up at my approach, and my mother does a double-take. "What were you doing up there?" she asks.

"Nothing. Why?" I try to sound as innocent as possible.

"You're all flushed," she says.

I nod. "I've started doing push-ups, and I did a couple extra today." They seem to buy the lie because they turn back to the presents. Grateful, I drop into the chair.

Brent tears the wrapping paper off of the box and shrieks, "Lofty!" when he sees that it's a *Lofty* toy from *Bob, the Builder*.

"Say 'thanks, Grandma,'" my mom coaches him.

"Thanks, Grandma," Brent slurs. *Poor kid.*

My mom slides me a gift. I pick it up and start to open it. I've never really liked opening gifts in front of anyone. It's a lot of stress to be under, having everyone watching you and waiting for an appropriate reaction. At least we're poor this year, so I won't be getting much.

I remove the wrapping paper to find a copy of Anne Rice's *Interview with the Vampire*. I shoot my mom a questioning look. *Does she know? How could she know?*

"You watched the movie not too long ago," she clarifies. "I know how you are. If you like a movie like that, you have to read the book it's based on."

"That's awesome, Mom, thank you." I heave an inaudible sigh.

My mom hands Grandma a gift that I know is from me. It feels nice to be able to actually buy presents for people this year. That's a first for me. Grandma is delighted when she unwraps the newest James Patterson novel. He's one of her favorite novelists.

"Whoo-hoo! James Patterson! I love him! Thanks, bubala."

"You're welcome." I blush.

This goes on for some time. I end up with a few more books and a gift card to *Barnes and Noble*. I'm content. Grandma gets an ornate Kiddush cup that will come in handy for Shabbat dinners. Mom gets a pair of diamond earrings that I went in on with Grandma. Brent gets a few toys and some new DVDs.

As we're wrapping it up, I hear footsteps and look up to see Erasmus standing in the doorway. His hair is back to its standard perfection. He's dressed a little less like a bad boy today; he's wearing a baby blue sweater and skinny gray jeans that cling to his hips.

My mom and Grandma exchange confused looks, and I jump to my feet, walking over to Erasmus and widening my eyes at him. "Erasmus, you're here early," I say with a faux surprised laugh.

"I just felt like you needed me now," he replies cryptically.

I shoot him a, *huh?* Look, but turn back to face my mom and grandmother. They're staring at us expectantly.

"Mom, Grandma," I say with forced fearfulness. "This is Erasmus."

"The boyfriend?" Grandma hisses to my mom, who nods.

"It's great to meet you," Erasmus enthuses, shaking my mom's hand and then Grandma's. Grandma regards him with a knit brow but then smiles.

"This is my brother, Brent." I take Brent's hand and lead him over to Erasmus. Brent keeps his eyes downcast.

"Nice to meet you, buddy." Erasmus sounds genuinely enthusiastic.

"Can you say hi to Erasmus, Brent?" I coax.

"Hi," Brent says after a long silence, then he goes back to play with his *Lofty* toy.

"He's not much of a conversationalist." I shrug.

"How did you get in here?" Grandma asks Erasmus.

"I left the side door open for him," I answer without missing a beat.

"I'm sorry if I'm too early. I was just so excited to meet you all," Erasmus continues.

"Not all, dear," Grandma assures him. "We're so pleased to have you. Dinner won't be until around four o'clock."

"Perfect. I'd be more than happy to help out with anything you need."

I like him, Grandma mouths to me. I grin. *One down, one to go.*

"Sorry, I look like such a mess," my mother apologizes. "I worked all night and haven't gotten to sleep yet."

"You look beautiful, Mrs. Norris."

"Oh, it's Beverly," Mom corrects. "I haven't been Mrs. Norris since I divorced Graham's dad."

"Oh, I'm sorry," Erasmus says penitently.

"Don't be." My mom waves it off. "So, how did you two meet?"

"Erasmus is one of my customers at the video store," I cut in.

"Ooh, scandalous!" Grandma jests.

"You don't go to school?" my mom asks.

"No, I graduated last spring, so now I'm in the work force."

"What do you do?"

"I work in security. Well, computers. Cyber security."

"How old are you?" Mom continues her polite inquisition.

"How old do I look?" Erasmus asks.

My mom shrugs. "Late twenties," she guesses.

"I'm twenty-nine."

"Ah, to be that young again."

Before Erasmus can reply, there's an impatient knocking at the front door. We all exchange nonplussed looks.

"Are any more of your friends dropping in?" Grandma remarks, looking at me.

"No." I frown. "Unless Amethyst is trying to surprise me, which, honestly, is something she'd do." The knocking comes again. "I'll go get it."

I rush down the hall to the front door and tug it open excitedly. The smile vanishes from my face, and bile rises in my throat. Don stands before me, scrutinizing me with his froggy face and reptilian brown eyes. "Don," I gasp.

"Graham," he says, smiling. "How are you, bud?"

His question completely catches me off guard, and I struggle to find my way back on course. "Never better," I manage.

"Good. I'm glad." *Why is he being so nice?* Usually, kindness from Don is the proverbial calm before the storm.

"Uh, Brent is in the living room. We just finished opening presents." I open the door wider to permit Don entry.

"Brent," he calls with childlike excitement.

"Hi, Dad!" Brent yells back, rushing into the foyer. He giggles and splays his hands in front of his mouth; it's another one of his tics. "Dad, look what Brent got for Christmas!" He runs into the living room and is back in seconds, holding his *Lofty* figure.

"Lofty!" Don exclaims. "Wow! Wait until you get back to my house. Santa brought you a lot of toys!"

Brent laughs again, and I notice in Don's eyes a deep sadness. Maybe a part of his cruelty stems from his inability to cope with emotions. It has to be hard not knowing where you come from and then having your only blood relative be moderately cognitively impaired. *Maybe I haven't been strong enough when it comes to Don. Maybe I was too eager to play the victim and make it all about me instead of considering his feelings.*

My musing is brought to an abrupt halt when Erasmus rounds the corner, his face etched with concern. Any other time, I'd be relieved and delighted to see him; this time, I want to murder him. "Is everything okay?" he asks, eyeing Don warily.

"Yes," I hiss, widening my eyes at him, hoping he'll get the hint and go back to the living room.

"Who's this?" Don demands, crossing his arms over his chest.

"Uh, this is Erasmus," I stutter.

"I'm Graham's boyfriend," Erasmus extrapolates, squaring his shoulders and puffing his chest out.

"Boyfriend?" Don whirls to look at me, his face a visage of pure disgust. "You really are a fag!"

I want to put Don in his place, or better yet, use the self-defense techniques that Erasmus has taught me and punch Don, but instead, I freeze up like the pathetic loser I am and lower my head.

"What did you call him?" Erasmus growls, getting in Don's face.

"Back the fuck up, faggot!" Don's words are dripping with venom.

"You can call me whatever you want to," Erasmus articulates, "I really don't care, but you will not insult and demean him anymore. You've already hurt him enough for one lifetime."

Don sneers and is about to say something else when Mom and Grandma come around the corner, fire in both of their eyes.

"What did you call my son?" Mom enjoins. Her voice wavers, anger trembling within her.

Don seems to remember where he is and clamps his mouth shut. His face reddens with fury, and I sink into myself, waiting for the volcanic eruption.

"Get out of my house." Grandma's words are measured but laden with authority. "I will not tolerate abuse in my house."

"Say bye to your mom, Brent," Don says shortly.

"Bye, Mummy." He turns to me, "Bye, Gayam." He never could say my name correctly.

"Bye, honey." Mom kneels down and gives Brent a hug.

"Bye," I mumble, and push past Don to the stairs. I hurry up them, the hot sting of tears fueling my trajectory. I hear footsteps behind me; Erasmus is saying my name, but I continue on, stopping only to open my bedroom door.

"Graham, I'm sorry," Erasmus apologizes. "I wasn't thinking."

Gabriel Mero

"That's pretty fucking obvious." I snort. "If you'd have just kept your mouth shut…"

"I'm sorry," he repeats, putting his hands on my shoulders to cajole me. I shrug them off, my body a maelstrom of anger, sadness, and disappointment. "I was worried about you being alone with him. I was just trying to protect you."

"I don't need you to protect me!" I exclaim. "Everyone treats me like just this fragile Fabergé egg."

"Because we care about you. We don't want to see you get hurt by someone."

I throw myself down onto the bed and start burrowing under the covers. Romana is nestled up by the pillow, and I bury my face in her golden fur. I want it all to stop: the pain, the feelings of inadequacy, the confusion. Life is always so hard for me, even the simplest task seems herculean to me. Everything is so much harder for me than it is for anyone else, and I want to know why. I want it to stop. I need it to stop. If this portends the rest of my life, there's no way I'm going to live to middle age. Existing like this isn't living; it's suffering.

Erasmus takes my silence as being directed toward him, and he sighs. "Maybe coming here today was a mistake," he says. "I'm sorry that I caused you more pain. I'll leave."

"No!" I cry out instinctively.

He stops and turns back to me. "You want me to stay?"

"Yes. Please stay with me. Hold me."

He crosses to the other side of the bed and lays down. I feel his body against mine, and then his arms are around me like a shield. "I'm sorry," he says again, more softly this time.

"It's not your fault." I blink tears away. Stubbornly, they refuse to dissolve. "I'm not mad at you. I'm not even mad at Don. I'm mad at myself."

"Why?"

"In the four months that I've been here, I have worked so hard to overcome the tragedies and scars of living with him. I made a friend, I got a job, came out, and started seeing you. I've even managed to quell my anxiety a bit and regain some of my self-confidence. But when it really mattered, when I was face to face with him, I let all of that fall by the wayside, and I reverted to that needy, pathetic child. I didn't even have the strength to stand up to him myself."

"You choked, so what? That doesn't mean that you haven't made progress. I've noticed such a change in you since that night I first met you."

"You have?"

"You were a nervous wreck that night. You couldn't look me in the eye, stuttering and stammering. Look at you now; you're growing into your powers. You've been able to overcome that. You're in college and work part-time while helping with your brother. You somehow found the strength to come out to your mom."

"I did that for you," I confess.

"You still did it. You're going to have setbacks once in a while, Graham, but that doesn't mean that you should beat yourself up over it when you do. You're human. Give yourself some credit."

"You know, you're pretty wise for a glorified zombie," I say, a smile tugging at my lips.

"There's my boy." I can hear the smile in Erasmus' voice, the smile that I've come to adore more than I ever thought possible.

"How did I ever get by without you?" I ask rhetorically.

"You didn't. And I didn't without you."

I roll over and move my head to his chest. "Can we just cuddle for a while?"

"Anything you want."

I close my eyes and bask in this newfound Nirvana I've discovered in his arms.

"For the record," Erasmus broaches, "what that narrow-minded pissant thinks about you is irrelevant. You are so much better than he is. Never forget that."

"You're going to have to keep reminding me."

"I've got eternity."

I'm so content with Erasmus that I drift off to sleep. I hear Erasmus' soft voice, and I open my eyes to darkness.

"Hmmm?" I grumble, rolling over to see him standing before me.

"You must've been over-tired. You slept all afternoon," he says.

"What time is it?" I ask, sitting up and taking the blankets with me.

"It's almost five. Your grandmother sent me up here to tell you that dinner is ready."

I slept for almost six hours! "I was supposed to help with dinner."

"Shhh." Erasmus puts a forceful hand on my chest. "I helped out. I think your family likes me."

"I love you, so they love you," I assure him, slipping back the covers.

My bones and joints creak to life as I stand, popping and cracking like a morbid bowl of *Rice Krispies. God, when did I get so old?*

I follow Erasmus along the hall and down the stairs. Grandma has once again made the table up opulently with an array of scented candles in the dining room. A veritable buffet is displayed along the long wooden table. The succulent aroma of kugel, latkes, brisket, Challah, and Sufganiyot makes my mouth water. I realize just how hungry I truly am. It's kind of scary how I'm able to ignore hunger.

"It smells amazing!" I compliment, taking a seat to the right of my grandmother.

"Are you all right, bubala?" Her voice is tinged with sadness.

"It's whatever." I shrug. "It's not like verbal assaults from Don are hardly a new thing."

"Well, I told him off," she says proudly.

"You sure did." I shoot her an appreciative grin.

My mom comes into the room wearing halter top and tight jeans. She looks beautiful. "I told him he is to stay in his car from now on," she adds.

"How long is this custody battle going to go on?" I query.

"We have a court date set for March, but it's difficult to get us both in the same state."

"Enough depressing talk," Grandma cuts in. "We've got two more nights of Hanukkah. We're all here together; we're all well."

After Grandma begins the meal with a quick blessing in Hebrew, we're allowed to begin eating. Normally, we'd do the whole affair, but since we have a guest tonight and Brent's absence has us all feeling a little down, none of us cares about being totally correct about it.

We start eating, and I try to act like Erasmus eating food isn't weird. Sure, he ate when we were out on our dates, but that was always bloody steak, so he was at least getting some actual food from it. Nothing here is going to sate his hunger.

"This is delicious, Mrs. Imber," he compliments, swallowing a mouthful of moist turkey.

"Why, thank you, dear," Grandma beams. "And it's Ginevra, please."

"I'm old school," Erasmus explains with a shrug.

"Your parents must be so proud. It's refreshing to see a kid your age with proper manners."

"Your parents were okay with you spending the holiday with us?" Mom asks him.

Erasmus swallows some water. "My parents passed away a long time ago," he informs us. "I'm on my own now."

My mom winces in embarrassment. "Sorry."

"I'm so sorry, dear!" Grandma frowns in commiseration.

"Don't be. It was a long time ago. I barely even remember them. Fortunately, they left me with a considerable amount of money, so I can take care of myself."

I want to ask him more about his parents, but I don't want to out him to my family. That's his decision to make, not mine. I make a mental note to ask him about them later, in private. He hasn't told me much about his human life. I don't even know how and when he became a vampire. *Is that personal information that I shouldn't ask about? I don't want to pry.*

A comfortable – or is it uncomfortable? – silence settles over us. Things still aren't great between Mom and Grandma. Their frigidness has abated minutely, but they're not even remotely friends. Mom is upset about being away from Brent, Grandma is wistful, why I don't quite know, I'm still smarting from Don's assault, although I'm trying to play it off like I don't care, and Erasmus is the poor, uncomfortable monkey in the middle.

"How are you doing?" I ask him.

"Never better." He shoots me that smile that I've come to love so much in such a short amount of time.

When we've finished eating, Grandma stands up and starts clearing plates. We all chip in and help. I run a sink full of dishwater and start washing dishes, with Erasmus drying and Mom and Grandma moving the leftovers to Tupperware. There are a lot of dishes, but within an hour, we have them all done. *Now I remember why I hate holidays…*

I catch Erasmus' eye and pull him over into a private corner. "Thank you for being so awesome today," I say, my arms instinctively snaking over his shoulders.

"Thank you for including me in your family. It's been so long since I've felt a part of anything besides loneliness."

"I won't ever let you feel lonely again," I promise him. I lean in to kiss him.

"Graham," my mom calls, stopping me short of reaching my desired destination.

"Yeah?" I try so hard to keep the frustration out of my voice.

"Can you give me a hand for a second?"

"Yeah." I roll my eyes but smile. Erasmus and I file out into the hallway, where my mom is standing on her tiptoes, trying to reach the top of the China cabinet.

"I can't reach the good platter. I thought I'd make that chocolate and peanut butter cake you like."

I haven't had that in years. It is to die for. Literally. I've never watched her make it, but it's a cake made out of chocolate and peanut butter that gets frozen until it hardens. It's basically a frozen Reese's. I reach up and grab the platter easily. "Here."

"Thanks." Suddenly, her eyes widen. "Graham, your necklace is glowing," she says.

I glance down and see that it is. But that means...

I push Mom out of the way as a clear ball flies at us. I squint my eyes and extend my hand, stopping the energy ball before it can hit me. "Go!" I yell at Mom. Without powers, she's defenseless. Erasmus grabs her and pulls her from the room. I turn and see the culprit: a black woman with pale white eyes. *Is she blind?*

She hisses at me and prepares to throw another energy ball. I quickly use my telekinesis to lob the one in my grasp at her. She tries to duck, but it strikes her in the side. A painful scream escapes her lips, and she dives behind the table.

Grandma comes rushing in with Erasmus hot on her heels. Mom watches from the doorway. Grandma closes her eyes briefly and holds her hands together as if in prayer. When she pulls them apart, an energy ball quivers.

The demon looks between the two of us, trapped in the middle. "This isn't over, witch!"

She fades in a wisp of smoke, and I drop my defenses. Suddenly, I feel a force hit me, and I fly through the air, crashing into the wall. I slide to the floor, groaning as I try to get up. "What the fuck?" I groan as pain lances through my sore muscles.

"You got hit," Erasmus says, helping me up.

"No shit," I say a little too harshly.

"Are you all right?" Grandma is rushing toward me.

"I'm fine." I hear a gasp from Erasmus and look at him, frowning. "Erasmus?"

"Run," he whimpers. I put a hand on him, and for the first time, I see that I'm bleeding from my hand. It isn't too bad, but it must be baiting him.

He lunges at me, his eyes blood red and his teeth sharp and gnashing. My eyes widen as his hands tighten on my throat, cutting off the flow of oxygen. "Erasmus!" I sputter.

He growls, and his teeth move closer to my neck. I try to wriggle out of his viselike grip, but I'm not strong enough.

"Get off of him!" Grandma cries, unleashing her energy ball at him. Erasmus is too preoccupied with ripping my throat open to notice. When the energy ball hits him, he smashes into the china cabinet, shattering the display's glass.

I cough as my bruised throat allows air through it. "Get behind me, Graham!" Grandma exclaims.

"Give him a chance," I urge.

Erasmus stands up, and his eyes are a little less red. He looks me dead in the eye. "I'm sorry," he says.

"Go!" my Mom yells, grabbing him by the collar and yanking him to his feet. "Get out and don't come back!"

Erasmus eyes me sadly and then bolts out the door and into the dark night.

"Erasmus," I whisper, taking a step toward the door.

"Did you know?" Mom asks, looking me over for more serious wounds.

"Yes," I confess.

"A vampire!?" she exclaims. "Really, Graham!?"

"It's not his fault!" I insist. "He's not like that. Maybe he-he forgot to eat or something last night. He needs to eat."

"He needs to be decapitated," she says in disgust.

"No, he needs to eat," I say forcefully.

"Everyone needs to calm down," Grandma mediates. "I think we've all had enough excitement for one night."

"I have to see him."

"Fuck, no!" Mom grabs me by the shoulders and shakes me. "Do you have brain damage? That is not boyfriend material. He is a monster, a monster who will *rip* your throat out and leave you to die on the floor."

"He is my boyfriend! I can't just leave him!" I shrug out of her grip.

"Graham, you're gay. I support that. That's who you are. But I will not support this..." she waves her hands drastically, "...shit show. A vampire is not a boyfriend."

"I won't stop seeing him. I'm all he has."

"He's a monster!"

My blood begins to boil. "*You're* going to judge *me* on my taste in men?" I balk, whirling on her. "That's rich. Your first husband was an alcoholic pothead, and your second was an abusive asshole. You can really pick them, Mom."

"I am your mother!" she shrieks, balling her hands into fists. "Don't talk to me like that."

I laugh dryly. "You don't get to pick and choose when you're a mom and when you're a friend," I snap. "I'm going to see him whether you like it or not. I'm old enough to decide." *Does she really think she can pull a parental trip on me now? Sorry, it doesn't work like that. Any other time she wants to be a friend instead of a parent.*

"Go to your room," she screams.

"Fuck you. Don isn't the only one who's damaged me. You've done your fair share too, Mom. And now you want to make it worse? You want to deny me the one thing that I have? The one person that I love, and who loves me back? Fuck you. I won't turn into the miserable bitch that you are."

She lunges at me, but Grandma stops her. "No, Beverly," she says. "You still haven't learned that violence isn't the answer?"

My mom storms out of the room, and I follow suit, stomping up the steps. I go into the bathroom and wash the blood from my hands. Fortunately, the bleeding has stopped. The wound is minor.

I go into my room and yank my coat on. Romana eyes me from her perch on my desk. "Sorry about the noise, Baby. Things got a little crazy down there. Daddy has to go for a little bit. I'll be back." I kiss her head and tug on my shoes before going back downstairs.

As I pull the door open, Mom comes down the hall. "If you walk out that door, don't even *think* of coming back," she says, her tone full of ire.

I turn back to face her. "This isn't your house," I tell her. "Maybe you should leave." Before she can hit me, I'm out the door and down the driveway.

Erasmus doesn't live too far from me, but the walk to his place is more miserable because of the bitter cold. I keep my hands buried deep in my pockets, lowering my face with each gust of winter wind. *I fucking hate winter.*

The first few miles aren't too bad, but I start to question my intelligence by the time I get about halfway there. It is too cold for me to be walking like this. Why didn't I ask Grandma if I could borrow her car? Why didn't I call Amethyst?

The walk seems to take years, though it probably takes about half an hour. By the time I walk up his driveway, I'm shivering uncontrollably, my teeth chattering.

I knock on his door, ready to rush in as soon as he opens it. Seconds tick by, becoming a minute before I try again. Still nothing. I twist the handle, but it's locked. *Fuck!* Desperate, I wave at the door, and it creaks open.

I step into blessed warmth and close the door behind me. "Erasmus?" I walk into the living room, where there's a fire burning. Erasmus is huddled on the sofa, a coffee mug before him.

He looks up and scowls. "What are you doing here?" He sounds pissed. *Why? What did I do?*

"I came to make sure that you're okay."

"No. I was okay before you came along and complicated my life." His words sting like a slap across the face, and I feel my eyes burn as tears well.

"I know that what happened wasn't ideal," I say, stepping closer to him, "but it's okay. I'm okay. My mom will get over it."

"No, it's not okay!" I can see tears in his eyes. "I could've hurt you, Graham. I could have—" His voice breaks, and he cuts off.

"But, you didn't." I sit on the couch next to him. The heat from the fire is so intense that I take my coat off to keep from sweating. "I'm okay."

Our eyes meet, and I can see the turmoil inside of him. He's mad at himself for what happened. He thinks he could have killed me. "I thought I'd eaten enough..."

"You'll do better next time."

"There isn't going to be a next time."

"What do you mean?"

He meets my gaze. "I mean, it's over. I don't want to see you anymore."

"But... but you said you loved me..." I say in a tiny voice.

"I do."

"Then… why?" The tears spill down my face and are quickly replaced by more. *This can't be happening. Erasmus can't be breaking up with me. We've just found each other! For the first time in my life, I feel safe, sexy, and confident; and most importantly, happy.*

"Because I can't risk losing control again," he says. "It was foolish of me to think that this could ever work in the first place."

"You won't!" I insist. "Everyone makes mistakes!"

"Not everyone loses control and almost kills the person they love," he growls.

"You are the only reason I'm still alive. If you hadn't been in that alley that night, that demon would've killed me or dragged me to Hell. I owe you my life."

"So, I deserve to succumb to blood lust and hurt you?"

"No, but I'm not mad. That's what matters. I still want to be with you, Erasmus."

"I want to be with you, I do, but I can't put your life in jeopardy every time we're together."

"You don't. How many times have we been together, and nothing like that has happened? You didn't drink enough blood; that's all it is. It's an easy mistake."

"Why are you trying so hard to change my mind?"

"Because I love you, and I don't want to spend the rest of my life missing the way you make me feel. I don't want to live another day without you."

"Then you're an idiot. How could you love me? I'm a monster! I'm not worthy of your love."

"Don't I get to decide who is and who isn't worthy of my love?" I put both hands on his shoulders. "It's you, Erasmus. It has always been you."

He blinks tears back, and I kiss his warm cheek. Apparently, he's fed since leaving my house. I quickly glance down at this coffee mug and see that the contents are red. *Oh...*

"You need to leave," he says, turning away from me.

My heart feels like a knife has been driven through it, cleaving it. "Erasmus," I choke out.

"Don't come back."

I sit and stare at him for a minute before realizing that he isn't going to budge. There's nothing I can do. He's made up his mind. I've lost.

Slowly, I gather my coat and stand up. I slide my arms into the coat and start walking out pausing in the doorway. I turn back to him. "If tonight really is our last night together, will you at least do me one favor?"

Erasmus grudgingly looks at me, and I can see that his cheeks are wet with silent tears. "Anything," he murmurs.

"I didn't want to say anything to you, but lately, I've been daydreaming about what it would have been like to go to my prom with you. I've never slow danced with a guy to a romantic song. I've never danced with a guy that…" I gulp. "A guy that I love."

Erasmus eyes me sadly and then stands up. "All you want is one dance?" he asks.

"Not just *one* dance," I clarify. "I want to make the most of our last night together. If I'm never going to see you again, then I want to have memories to cherish for the rest of my life. You know what they say; your first love is something you never forget."

"I don't know if that's such a good idea…"

"Please," I beg. "If you're going to break my heart, please, at least give me this. It's the least you can do."

"Fine," he relents. "But there's no music."

"One sec." I pull my phone out of my pocket and take it over to his stereo system. I plug the aux cord into my phone. I open my music library and select one of the most romantic songs I can think of, *So Blessed* by Mariah Carey.

The song begins with soft instrumentation, and Erasmus comes to me. "Who leads?" he asks.

"I'll let you."

He takes my right hand in his left, and his right hand goes to my hip. We move in closer, and I can smell the freshness of his breath. He must have had a mint or something before I barged in.

Mariah begins to sing, and we start to sway to the slow beat. "I've been listening to this song a lot lately," I confess.

"You have?"

I nod. "I listen to it and think of you. Of how blessed I am to have you." Brown eyes meet blue. "I know it doesn't change anything," I amend. "I just wanted you to know. You have made me so very, very happy."

"You made me happy, too," he confesses.

"I'm going to miss this feeling. I'm going to miss you more than I've ever missed anything. You've brought so much joy into my life."

Erasmus opens his mouth to say something but closes it again before nuzzling my neck. I stare at him, trying to burn the image of him tonight into my memory forever. I've never seen a more handsome man.

"Do you promise never to forget me?" I ask.

He smiles and nods. "I could never forget you."

"Me neither." I inhale his intoxicating scent. "I guess I'll have to learn how to perform that protection spell. That's two attempts now. I guess they really aren't going to stop until they have me."

"Are you trying to use reverse psychology on me?" he queries, raising an eyebrow.

"Maybe," I laugh.

The song ends and turns into another, *I Surrender* by Céline Dion. Erasmus and I turn our heads at the same time, and our mouths brush past each other. Our eyes find one another and combat indecisiveness weakly before our lips find their way back together.

If this is the last time I'll ever get to kiss him, I will make it memorable. I kiss him deeply, my fingers finding the stubble at the back of his head. He grips me more tightly, and he moves his lips to my neck again, making me shiver in delight.

I find my hands under his shirt, caressing his bare flesh. I want to remember every inch of him. No one else will ever be able to compare to his easy perfection. Without realizing it, I pull his shirt over his head, dropping it onto the floor at our feet. He does the same to me. His bare chest is flush against mine, and I cry out in ecstasy as his lips find my nipples.

I feel an aching need for him deep in my bones. I want to give myself to him. I need to experience him in every way that I can.

My fingers go farther down than they have before, exploring his stomach and the waist of his skinny jeans. I look into his eyes to see if he's okay with me going further or not. I'm surprised that his eyes are glowing with something that I've only ever seen on TV: pure, unadulterated lust.

I unbutton his jeans and ease the zipper down. Underneath, he's wearing black boxers. Apparently, I'm not the only one whose signature color is black. I tug his pants down until they pool at his feet.

We start kiss passionately, and our feet move of their own volition. I don't even notice that we're no longer in the living room but in Erasmus' dark bedroom. One second, I'm standing, kissing him, and the next, I'm on my back on his bed. His hands are working at removing my jeans.

It's funny. I always assumed that when the time came when I'd finally lose my virginity, I would feel nervous and back out, but here, now, with Erasmus, it just feels right.

I hear Whitney Houston's I Will Always Love You playing through the surround sound outside the bedroom. *How ironic.*

Before I know it, we are both naked, and Erasmus is on top of me once more, kissing me. I can feel his erection poking my thigh. I cast a glance down at it and grin when I see that he's also gifted in that department.

I roll over and straddle him. My breathing accelerates. "What makes you think that I'm on the bottom?" I ask. *Yes, after meeting Malachi that day, I did some research.*

Erasmus grins. "Lucky for you, I'm versatile," he says.

We start to kiss again, and I seem to float out of my body. I can feel myself sliding into him, the initial resistance, and then the all-encompassing warmth and pleasure, but it isn't my focus. My entire focus is on savoring Erasmus as much as humanly possible.

It stretches out into an infinitesimal cloud of euphoria as our bodies move together. Our lips continuously find each other as if drawn by magnets. I lose myself in his body, experiencing it bit by bit.

Long after we've both finished, we kiss each other, tangled in each other's arms. I pray that this night will never end. I'm not ready for the cold reality of tomorrow.

Chapter Nineteen

When I awake, I'm surrounded by total darkness again. The air is chilly, and I shiver, my bare skin rising in goose pimples. I reach over to Erasmus, but my hand finds only cold sheets. "Erasmus?" I whisper. I get no reply.

I tug the blanket with me and tentatively get down on the floor, rummaging around in the dark for my clothes. As I recall, I had my underwear and jeans still on when Erasmus and I moved our passion into the bedroom.

I find my underwear and then, nearby, my jeans. I pull them on by touch, hoping I don't have them inside out or backward.

I crawl toward where I think the door is, and when I feel the wall, I slowly rise and thumb around for a light switch. It takes a few tries, but I finally find it and close my eyes before flipping it. I wait a few seconds and slowly open my eyes against the sudden light. It's still bright, and my eyes water, but it's manageable.

The illuminated room is a shambles. The bed is torn apart, blankets and sheets ripped off the mattress. The bedside stand is littered with shards of broken lamps, and there's a dent or two along the walls. *Wow. Just how into it did Erasmus and I get? And where is Erasmus?*

I find my socks and tug them on, my cold feet thanking me. I walk out of the room and shuffle down the hall to the living room. I peak in, but it's uninhabited. *That's strange. Erasmus is almost always in the living room.* I realize that there's so much of this house that I haven't explored. I find my shirt on the floor, cast aside in a lustful haste. When I put it on, I shiver at its coldness. I'm so used to a fire burning in the fireplace. I'm not used to this chill in here.

I smell the stomach-rumbling scent of frying eggs and follow it into the kitchen. I see Erasmus at the stove, a towel over his shoulder as he stirs and flips eggs in a cast-iron skillet. He hears my soft steps on the floor and smiles at me. "Good morning," he says.

"Is it morning?" I can see through the windows that it's dark outside.

"For us." He flips the eggs again.

"What time is it?" I sit down at the island, hugging my arms around myself for warmth.

"Almost seven."

"At night!?"

"Oh, yeah."

"How many times did we...?" I pause, considering it. *What did we do last night? Fuck? Make love? Have sex? What do people call it?*

"I lost count," he says with a smirk. "Who knew you were such an animal?"

I feel myself blushing and bite my lip. "You were quite insatiable yourself."

"It has been a while." He flips the eggs again. He looks so docile and domestic in the kitchen. It's hard to believe that he has a dark side, a dark side that almost ripped my throat out last night.

"I was worried when I woke up, and you weren't there," I confess.

"I'm sorry. I figured you'd be hungry after last night."

"I am." As if on cue, my stomach grumbles loudly.

"Here." He shovels some eggs onto a plate and sets it before me. The delicious aroma of the eggs makes my stomach growl again.

"Thanks." I tuck right in, eating a whole egg in the blink of an eye. I don't think I've ever been so ravenous in my life!

Erasmus sets the dishes in the sink and sits down across from me, staring. "Are you going to watch me eat?" I ask, covering my mouth self-consciously.

"No." He chuckles. "I just wanted to apologize for last night."

"For what? Attacking me? For breaking up with me? For keeping me up all night having sex?"

"Well, the first two, absolutely. The last one, even if I live for eternity, I will never regret that."

I beam. "I'm glad you enjoyed yourself. But what does this mean for us now? Are we still broken up?"

Erasmus sighs. "I thought I was strong enough to stay away, but you've witched me. I'm completely under your spell, Graham."

"I feel the same way. I can't explain it... it's like you're an extension of me. Not like in a creepy, narcissistic way, but it's like... like you're my heart, or my lungs, or something... even though I lived years without you, I don't think I could do it now. You're a part of me."

"Can I tell you something?" He's suddenly serious.

"You can tell me anything."

"But you have to promise not to freak out. Before we go any further with this relationship, I have to unburden my load. I've been carrying these secrets for so long."

"Well, I can't promise not to freak out, but I promise not to hold it against you. Probably."

"I'm afraid that it'll change how you think of me." He stares down at his hands. *What could possibly be so bad?* Erasmus isn't given to hysteria or melodrama, so it must be very serious.

"Nothing could change my feelings for you, I promise. Just tell me."

He takes a deep, courageous breath. "Do you remember last night at dinner when I told your mother that I've been on my own for a while?"

"Yeah. I just assumed that you were sparing her the whole I-like-boys-and-girls schtick."

"Well, that, too." He shakes his head in disgust. "I haven't been entirely honest with you about my relationship with Melania. We were lovers, yes, but it was more than that. She wanted to become like me. She wanted me to turn her. I refused. I wouldn't wish this life on anyone. One night when we were... being intimate... I gave in to temptation, and I fed off of her. Only a little. She found the experience to be..." he searches the air for the perfect words, "celestial. She really enjoyed it.

"I was desperate to do anything to keep her alive, so I would routinely feed off of her, just enough to make her lightheaded. I'm not proud of it; I'm not. In hindsight, I can see how sick and twisted it was. I knew that if I didn't do it, someone else would. I wasn't in love with her; to be quite honest, I pitied her. How empty and shallow a life it must be to yearn for this eternal, solitary existence."

"What happened to her?" I ask, on the edge of my seat in anticipation.

His features go dark once more. "We had a fight one night. She was becoming more insistent that I turn her. She said this mortal existence held nothing for her but heartache and pain. She longed to be free of the shackles of humanity. I tried to convince her that her life was worth living, that the life of a vampire is not as romantic and exciting as the media portrays it.

"She threatened to do whatever was necessary to get me to turn her. I told her that the last thing I'd ever do is curse her like I'd been cursed. She stormed off for a while to cool down, I thought. Eventually, she came back, calmer but with an air of mystery about her. She said that she was going to take a bath and invited me to join her.

"I gave her a little while to herself before going in to check on her. At first, what alarmed me was the water washing out of the bathroom and soaking into the carpet. I tried the door, but she had locked it. I used all of my might to kick the door down, and there she was, in the tub, the water up around her neck. Her head was leaning back against the wall. Her chest barely rose and fell. There was an empty pill bottle on the ledge, something she'd bought from some thug.

"I pulled her up and checked for a pulse; it was faint, but there. I tried to do CPR, but I don't breathe. I couldn't do it. I tried a finger down her throat, hoping she'd puke, but she didn't react. I was left with an impossible decision: to let her die or do whatever I could to save her...

"I knew I'd regret it, but I did the only thing I could. I drained her almost to the point of death, and then I opened my wrist, draining my cursed blood down her throat. I've never made another like me before, so I didn't know how much blood it would take. Once I started to feel weak, I hurried into the other room. I drank enough to heal the wound, and then I went back to check on her."

"Did it work?" I demand, chewing my nails.

"The Melania that I had known and come to care for was gone. What was left in her place was a wicked creature with a lust for destruction and an unquenchable thirst for blood. At first, I didn't see it because I didn't want to. I wanted to feel like I'd done the right thing, giving her a chance to make amends for the trespasses she had inflicted in life.

"I was wrong. She killed indiscriminately: men, women, and children of all colors and creeds. Her malice knew no bounds. It was all a game to her. She loved to torture her victims, to make the parents watch as she drained their beloved children dry, the sound of their cries fueling her maliciousness.

"I didn't like it, even though it was practically staring me in the face. It wasn't until she brought her sick games back here that I realized I'd made an error that night. I should have let her die. She played me like a fiddle from the first day we met. She may have been beautiful on the outside, but inside, she was so hideous, so grotesquely wrong, that she was beyond help.

"I refused to partake in her murderous rampage, and she turned on me. We fought, but being younger, she was stronger. She made me watch as she…" His voice breaks, and he sobs, biting his hand. "She made me watch as she murdered half a newborn nursery ward."

"Oh, my God!" I gasp, sniffling past my own tears. I may not like children, but I definitely don't want to think about defenseless newborn infants being killed by a psychotic vampire bitch.

"I tried to get out of my restraints, and I eventually did, but I was too late. I couldn't save even one baby. I wanted to kill her. I found myself more furious than I'd ever been before. It was a tough fight, but in the end, I bested her. I stood over her, sword arced back, ready to behead her and end her reign of terror, but before I could, I saw something in her eyes, fear, maybe, or remorse, I don't know. I hesitated, and she kicked me in the balls. While I was down, she took off. I haven't seen her since."

"So, she's still out there?" I shiver at the prospect of my boyfriend's sadistic ex lurking around, on the loose. *Will she come back to exact her revenge one day? Am I a target?* I don't care about her hurting me, only about what my death at her hands would do to Erasmus.

"Somewhere." He sighs and rubs his forehead as if staving off a headache. *Do vampires get headaches?*

"I'm glad that you told me," I say, rising to my feet. I walk around to the other side of the island and enfold him in my arms. "This doesn't change anything," I whisper

"You don't know all of it," he continues, rubbing my shoulder.

"What else?" I inquire, pulling back so that I can see his eyes.

"I carried that guilt with me for a long time. Or, at least, it felt like a long time to me. Time is still as relevant to me as it is to you mortals, despite being immortal. Melania was supposed to be my saving grace, the long-awaited arrival of my destiny. It turns out she was nothing more than another disappointment among an eternity of disappointments.

"I became very depressed. I stopped eating, and my body began to decompose. One night, I decided to end it. I didn't want to live in this exile anymore. I didn't want to be weighed down with the guilt anymore. I just wanted it all to stop. So, I went and stood on the highest cliff in town, and I watched as the moon started to fade as the sky grew from black to a brilliant pink.

"I stood there, awaiting my blessed release. I made my peace with the gods of my time and the ones of today."

"What changed your mind?"

"I felt something, a presence. I can't exactly explain it because I still don't understand it. It was like I suddenly had a purpose again, a new beginning."

"When was this?" I ask, my mind racing.

"August nineteenth," he answers, his tone matter of fact.

"Wow," I gasp, pacing. I've never believed in fate or destiny. I've always believed that life happens to you, and you're powerless to do anything about it.

"What?" He stands up and faces me.

"That's the day I got to town," I say. I shake my head in disbelief. "Could it be that we're somehow... *fated* to have found each other?"

"I don't much believe in that nonsense," he muses, "but I think if I was ever to believe that something was written in the stars, it's us."

I smile. "That's the sweetest thing anyone has ever said to me."

"So," he sniffs, "has my story changed your feelings toward me?"

"Erasmus," I walk over to him and grip his shoulders, "nothing you say could *ever* make me love you any less. I mean that."

"You're a fool," he chuckles.

"I should probably tell you something, too." I worry my bottom lip with my front teeth.

"Tell me," he urges.

"Over the summer after graduation, I was going through a rough patch. My mom and Don were fighting a lot more than usual, and I was left in charge of Brent more and more. Don started being even more cruel and controlling. My friends stopped talking to me because I could never hang out with them. I was isolated. I felt like I had no one on my side. I tried to shake it off by burying myself in work: taking care of Brent, doing my share to keep the house up. I even started learning Welsh on this app on my phone.

"For a while, it helped. I began to see the light at the end of the tunnel. This guy from school—he was absolutely gorgeous—his name was Jordan, he started texting me. I thought it was weird at first because even though we'd gone to school together for years, we'd never really talked. He was popular, a typical jock, and I was, well, me.

"He said he got my number through a mutual friend. Believe it or not, I was more sociable back home. Sure, my anxiety was still overpowering, but it was manageable. So, we started talking. At first, it was the usual 'Hey, how's your summer? Why didn't you start college yet?' kind of thing. I assumed he was just trying to get me to help him with his work. That happened a lot.

"Gradually, the conversations got more involved, more personal. He confided in me that he didn't really love his girlfriend. He said that she felt safe and familiar, but he really wanted something entirely different. He told me that he was gay, or at least he suspected that he was. He confessed to having a crush on me.

"I was overwhelmed at the idea of him liking me like that. Truth be told, I'd always admired him from afar but knew that as long as I was living in Don's prison, that would never be possible for me. I convinced myself that it wasn't who I really was; it was just the power of suggestion. I've been teased about being gay for as long as I can remember, since long before I even really knew what being gay was.

"I told him that I was flattered but I was just interested in being his friend. He was persistent, though, he would message me all day, and he started sending slightly inappropriate pictures. At first, it was just shirtless pics, then it turned into pictures of him in his underwear. I wanted to be strong, but I'm human. I sent him some back, against my better judgment. Nothing too bad, but enough to do damage.

"The next day, it was all over our class page on Facebook. He posted my pics and twisted the whole thing to look like I'd chased him. Because he was popular and good-looking, everyone believed him. I became a laughing stock. It hurt because, after weeks of talking, I started to think that maybe—impossibly—he actually liked me. I was crushed. The thought of all of those assholes who'd bullied me in school being proven right made me sick. If I thought that it was bad before, that would be nothing compared to what I would be subject to now. And, you know, the thing that hurt the most was that none of my so-called 'friends' even contacted me to offer their support. Some even commented on the photos, saying that they'd always known that I was a 'fag.'

"I had a complete breakdown. I could barely get out of bed, but I couldn't tell my mom why. I felt... lost at sea. I decided that there was one solution, it would be messy, but it wouldn't hurt

Gabriel Mero

anymore. I wouldn't feel lonely anymore.

"I went downstairs and rooted around in the closet. I finally found my mom's old apron from when she used to work at Lowe's. Sure enough, there was still a box cutter in it. I tested the blade; it wasn't very sharp, but it would do.

"I went to my room and put on my favorite clothes. I didn't care that they were about to be ruined. I just wanted to leave behind a well-dressed corpse. I got into bed and buried myself beneath the covers—Don kept the house like a meat cooler—and played Mariah Carey's *Emotions* album. When the final song ended, I took a deep breath and picked up my mom's box cutter. I extended the blade and then held it just above my wrist, preparing to make the cut.

"But just as I was about to do it, Romana came and rubbed on me, pushing the blade away. In my selfishness, I'd forgotten all about her. What would happen to her if I killed myself? That simple act of love was enough for me to see that I did have something to live for, even if it wasn't society's view of importance."

I was so engrossed in my story that I don't even realize that I was crying until the tears hit my hands, jolting me back to the moment. Guilty, I look at Erasmus, and I see his clenched chin. He wants to yell at me for being so stupid, for thinking that the world would be a better place without me in it; that the lives of those I would've left behind would not be irreparably scarred. But he doesn't yell. He just holds me close.

"What a pair we make," I joke. "We're like the poster boys for mental illness."

"We both had the courage to not go through with it," he reminds me.

"So, you don't feel different about me?" I ask.

"None one bit."

Erasmus moves in to kiss me, and I pull back. "I haven't brushed my teeth," I protest, turning my head away from him.

"I don't care." He puts a hand under my chin and gently guides it back toward him. "If we're going to be boyfriends, then we have to be realistic about this. We can't be perfect all the time. We're going to see each other's imperfections."

"I can handle your imperfections if you can handle mine." I brush my lips against his. His lips hungrily invading mine gives me all the answers I'll ever need.

Chapter Twenty

A couple of days later, Erasmus and I lie side by side in his bed. I haven't been home since the Hanukkah fiasco, and I haven't told him why. Despite my elation at getting Erasmus to myself with no interruptions and the sudden lack of responsibility, deep down, I do miss home. Well, I miss Romana. The poor thing would be a total wreck without me... and here I am, being a selfish prick and choosing my hot, undead boyfriend over her. I'm a terrible father.

As if he can read my mind, Erasmus rolls onto his side to face me. "I need to ask you something," he broaches.

"Okay..." My defenses immediately stand to attention.

"You know that I love having you here and being with you..."

"I guess..." *Oh, no. Is this it? Is he going to tell me that we've gotten too close too soon and now he's bored with me? I knew I shouldn't have slept with him so soon! Slut! Whore!*

My face must betray my inner turmoil because he lovingly puts a hand on my cheek. "Don't worry, I'm not breaking up with you."

"Phew!" I feign relief. *Just get to the crux of the matter!*

"I love having you here, but why haven't you gone home? Is everything okay?"

I sigh and stare up at the grey ceiling. I don't want to lie to him—lies are like cancer to a relationship—but I don't want to tell him the truth and hurt his feelings. If he knows the truth, he'll try to break up with me again, and we'll be stuck in this melodramatic rut of make up and break up. But I can't lie to him…

"If I tell you the truth, do you promise that it won't change anything between us?" I lay down the challenge gauntlet.

"I promise." His chocolate brown eyes are so intoxicating that I can't help but give in.

"After you left that night, Mom and I had a fight," I confess. "She doesn't want me seeing you, but I told her that it isn't her choice; it's mine."

"You stood up to your mom for me?" His voice is incredulous.

"Of course!" I kiss his hand. "I'll always choose you."

"That's the nicest thing that anyone has ever done for me." His lips tug up into a smile, and my heart skips a beat. I never in a million years ever thought that I would be so enraptured by someone. Seeing him so happy makes me elated.

"She told me that if I left the house, I wasn't to come back."

"And you still came to me."

"Without hesitation."

"What about Romana? You must miss her."

"More than words." I rub his chest. "I'll figure it out. My mom can be a royal bitch, but she needs me there. And, really, it's Grandma's house; she would never kick me out. I just have to let everything blow over for a few days." As I say it, my mind drifts to the idea of those two in the house without me there to mediate. *Fuck.* "If they're still alive," I add.

"Do they at least know that you're here?"

"I told my mom I was going after you."

"I don't want her to be upset."

"I don't either, but she needs to lay off. I'm an adult. I can decide whom I date."

"I guess."

He grows quiet, and I decide to try to lighten the mood. "I thought you were going to tell me that you've grown bored with me. That I gave up the 'V' card too soon or too easily."

"No." He laughs. "I told you I'd wait as long as it took for you to be ready."

"You don't think I'm a slut for sleeping with you in the first month?"

"As long as it was because you wanted to and not because you felt you had to, I don't care. I'm not going to lie and say I haven't enjoyed it."

"Oh, trust me, I *know* how much you've enjoyed it," I tease.

"Am I that translucent?" he asks with pretend shock.

"The moaning and multiple orgasms kind of gave it away."

"Fair point," he laughs.

I suddenly notice a stiffening below my waist. All of this sex talk is getting me aroused. While we've had our fair share of sex over the last few days, today, we haven't. *Time to change that.*

I reach over and start rubbing his chest. Erasmus quirks an eyebrow at me, smirking. He knows what's up. My fingers work down to the hem of his shirt then my hand slips under it, caressing his smooth, silky skin. He looks over at me with dark, lustful eyes. He's like a drug to me. I am completely and totally addicted to this gorgeous undead man.

I sit up and start pulling his shirt up over his head. He lifts himself to help, and once I free the shirt, I toss it on the floor before descending upon his lips. His lips are still well maintained for a dead guy, and they feel amazing pressing against mine. I don't think I'll ever get my fill of his touch and his body.

Our kissing becomes more passionate as my hormones race into overdrive, and my lust is unleashed into my veins, searing my synapses. A guttural moan escapes me as he moves his lips down to my most prominent erogenous zone: the left side of my long neck. The brush of his lips there makes me shiver and tingle with delight.

Erasmus moves so that he's on top of me, holding himself up above me. His eyes glow with a devilish glint, and I can't help but giggle.

"What's on your mind?" I ask.

"I was just thinking that we could try something new," he responds.

"Has our sex become routine already?"

"Not even close," he assures me, "but I'd like a turn."

A turn? A turn at what? Being on top? I do seem to recall being on top every time we've had sex, well, on top and behind... "A turn?" I ask, my voice husky with desire.

"Don't freak out, but I thought it might be nice if we switched roles."

"You want to be on top? Sure. I'll lie here and let you do all the work."

"I want *to* top," he specifies, assessing my face for a reaction.

Oh. He wants to top me. He wants to be the guy this time. As realization sets in, my stomach cramps as it worries itself into knots.

"You've been doing a great job," he assures me, "I'd just like to be inside you for a change."

Honestly, in a gay relationship, I believe that it should be fair. I understand that each partner has his own sexual position preferences. But I believe that it should be shared equally. At least that way, it's fair.

"Graham?" he presses, snapping me out of my thoughts.

"I'm going to be totally honest with you," I say, looking him in the eyes. "I am absolutely terrified of bottoming."

"I get it," he nods. "It's quite a harrowing experience, especially your first time." He tries hard to mask his disappointment, and guilt nibbles at me. He doesn't want to bottom every time, so if this relationship is going to work, then I have to be willing to try it for him. *Oh, boy...*

"Does it hurt?" I ask, teasing the backs of his shoulders with my fingertips

"At first, yeah," he replies, "but once you get into it, it feels great, if your partner knows what he's doing."

"And you do? Know what you're doing?"

"I *have* been around for millennia." I know he means it to be all in good fun, but I think of him having sex with other people—men and women— and I feel the cold stab of jealousy in my chest.

"Will you go slow?" I ask.

"Of course," he promises, kissing my neck again. Despite my nerves, it feels good. "But are you sure? I don't want to force you into doing it."

Oh, Erasmus, ever the gentlemen. "I'm willing to try," I say calmly

"I'll stop if you tell me to," he promises.

"You'd better."

We kiss again as our hands work on each other's pants. Before I know it, we're both naked, and his impressive erection is poking my stomach.

"We should probably prep—"

"Just go slow," I interrupt.

Erasmus nods, and as he starts to get into position, my heart threatens to hammer through my ribcage and out of my chest. I don't think that I have ever been so nervous in my life. He gently lifts my hips so that my butt rests on his thighs, and then he drapes my legs over his shoulders. I can't help but feel self-conscious and wholly exposed.

"Are you sure you want to do this?" he asks, kissing my throat again to get me revved up.

"I want you to be happy," I reply.

"I promise it isn't as bad as you imagine it is."

"Okay."

He's quiet for a few moments as he adds lube to his cock. *I can't believe that that huge flesh appendage is going inside me. Holy fuck!*

He lowers himself back into position, and I struggle to swallow past a severely dry throat. *Any second now...*

"Just breathe," he advises. "Deep breaths."

I take a few deep breaths to appease him and quiet my nerves. *People have been receiving anal sex for a long time, so why is this such a big deal for me?*

Erasmus kisses my neck, and I feel him move closer. I bite my lip to stifle a whimper. I can feel his penis against me, and as he flexes his hip to coerce it in, I feel myself start to stretch and a lance of pain. Panic sets in immediately.

"Stop!" I cry, wiggling away from him as best I can. "Please."

"Graham, are you okay?" he asks, letting me up.

I sit against the headboard, my knees to my chest. "Please don't hate me," I whisper, too embarrassed to look at him.

"Hey," he kneels before me, frowning in concern. "It's okay." His hand rests on my knee.

I shake his hand free and stand up, tugging on my pants. My cheeks feel like they're on fire with shame. *Now I've gone and messed it all up. Erasmus isn't going to want me now, not a wimp like me.*

Erasmus leaps to his feet and seizes me. "Graham, look at me," he coaxes me. I don't want to, but I feel my eyes lift of their own volition. He doesn't look disappointed nor mad. He just looks like caring, sweet Erasmus.

"I'm sorry," I say, putting my head on his shoulder.

"It's okay," he soothes, stroking my head.

"I wanted to do it for you." I really did, despite my fears.

"You're not ready," he iterates. "It's a big step."

"Not for you."

"My first time, it was. I thought my heart was going to beat right out of my chest."

"That's how I felt!"

"My first time was hardly a pleasant experience."

"What do you mean?"

"I had it forced on me." His face goes dark. "Back in my human days, sexuality was fluid. It was nothing more than pleasure and the occasional political ploy. My parents were wealthy Greek consuls. Well, my father was. As the Empire began to fall, my father needed to curry favor from someone with power. My virtue got thrown to the wayside for familial duty."

"Oh, my God!" I gasp. "That's terrible. Erasmus, I'm sorry!"

"It was a long time ago," he says, coming back to me.

"Still. How could your parents do that to you?"

"Like I said, it wasn't a big deal back then."

My heart breaks for him. How could anyone hurt this beautiful, kindhearted man? Despite his maturity, he has somehow managed to maintain a childlike spirit. I hope that whoever had done that horrible thing to him had paid dearly.

"Is that why you're pan?" I can't help but ask.

"No," he shakes his head. "For as long as I can remember, I've been attracted to beauty, non-discriminant beauty." He smiles sadly. "We don't have to talk about all this."

"I want to," I say firmly. "I want to know everything about you."

"Not today. I'm not in a mood to drudge up the past."

"I understand."

He shoots me a grateful smile. "Eventually, I'll be ready to tell you my tale."

"Eventually, I'll be ready to let you in," I reply.

"How about this," he proposes, "I'll tell you what you want to know the day you're ready to let me top."

"Deal."

"You trust me, right?" Erasmus asks.

"I trust you, implicitly," I assure him. "I'm just afraid."

"Okay." He nods in acceptance. "I'd never hurt you."

"I know."

"You're the first person I've told about my rape," he admits.

"I am honored that you trust me." I envelop his slim body in my arms. I want so badly to comfort him, to assuage his pain. My poor, poor Erasmus.

"I'm honored, too."

"About what?"

"That you even gave me the time of day."

"What?" I splutter. "Erasmus, you're hot. You do know that, right? Like, you're so hot that you can have any man or woman you want. I should be honored that you even gave *me* the time of day."

"I see my reflection in the mirror," he says, "but all I see is a thing, a dead creature that's only half here."

"You seriously don't see what I see?" He shakes his head slowly. "Well, then, you're crazy. I'm not going to lie, your good looks initially drew me to you, but you're so much more than that. You're so much more than you know."

"How can you do that for me but not for yourself?" He quirks an eyebrow challengingly.

"I guess we're all tainted by our own shit," I muse. "Only a narcissist obsesses over his own vanity."

"I just wish that you wouldn't always be so hard on yourself."

"I'm trying. I have a long way to go, but I'm trying. It's a work in progress."

"I'm going to do everything I can to build you up," he promises.

"I look forward to it." I suddenly shiver as I realize that with my embarrassment dissolved, the air is cold against my naked torso. "But in the meantime, can we get back into bed and warm up?"

"Oh, you want me in bed, huh?" His grin exposes his straight, white teeth.

"Is that a problem?" I play along.

"Never."

Before I know it, we're back in bed, and the world around us is irrelevant.

Chapter Twenty-One

When I go back to work the next day, I'm excited to see Amethyst. I haven't seen or spoken to her since our last day of classes a week ago. Like with Romana, I've neglected to check up on my friend and make sure that she's okay.

Amethyst sees me walk in the front door, and I can tell she wants to smile, but instead, she fixes me with a pointed look. *Oh, no, I'm in for it now.*

"Hey," I say tentatively as I unbutton my pea coat and shrug out of it.

"Where have you been?" she demands, hand on her hip.

"I've been with Erasmus the last few days—"

"Of course." She scoffs and rolls her eyes. "I should've known that you'd be one of those people."

"One of *what* people?" I tuck my coat under the counter.

"One of those people that gets a boyfriend and then suddenly disappears off the face of the Earth. You revolve your whole world around who you're dating, and the rest of us become inconsequential."

Her words hurt, but only because they're true. I have been up Erasmus' ass—literally and figuratively—lately. Of course, it wasn't my intention to become negligent of my other relationships. It's just all been so crazy. It's all happened so fast.

"You know what hurts the most?" she asks. "I actually thought that we were friends. Real friends. But, no, you just used me to get rides and a job."

"No! That's not true!" I protest.

"Have I even crossed your mind since last term?"

"Yes! I was going to call and wish you a Happy Yule, but then things got really intense and..." I don't finish and shake my head.

"And you couldn't have answered your phone? I've been texting, calling, Facebooking you. I haven't gotten even one response. No, 'Hey, sorry, I'm super busy right now, I'll call later,' or 'Fuck you, bitch,' nothing. Like, I don't even matter to you. And you're ignoring your Craft. Do you know how lucky you are to be blessed with this immense power? You're just wasting it. Boyfriends come and go, dude."

I can see tears welling in her eyes, and I put a comforting hand on her shoulder. She shrugs it off and launches into another tirade.

"Your mom and grandma have been calling me nonstop. Apparently, they haven't heard anything from you, either. We've all been so afraid that you were dead in a ditch somewhere or off in some psycho's slut dungeon."

"Slut dungeon?" I ask, stifling laughter. *What the hell is a slut dungeon?*

Amethyst glares at me for a few seconds, and then a smile starts to creep over her lips. She tries to fight it, but we break at the same time and erupt into laughter. It feels so good to have the tension loosen a little. The stress of the last few days washes away, and I almost feel like a normal person again.

A customer comes in, and we struggle to compose ourselves. It's an older lady with a sourpuss face. *Great.* She shoots us both a dirty look and then scrunches up her face at Amethyst. She sticks her nose in the air as she struts past us.

We walk over to the sale bins and talk quietly. "What's a slut dungeon?" I ask, chuckling.

"You know, like that pit thing in *The Silence of the Lambs*. 'It rubs the lotion on the skin, or else it gets the hose again,'" she explains.

"The likeliest of scenarios," I snort.

"Ahem," the snobby old lady clears her throat loudly, as if we weren't like ten feet away from the counter.

"I know someone in *desperate* need of a slut dungeon," I mutter, walking over to her. "Sorry for your wait," I say without any sarcasm.

"Johnson," the old lady barks. *Jesus, what a fucking old bitch!*

"First name." I don't ask.

"Roe."

I quickly ring up her movies. I tell her the total, and she proves herself to be the stupid bitch that I suspect her to be when instead of handing me her card, she tosses it on the counter. *Wow!* I swipe the card, and as I hand her her card back, I 'accidentally' hit the computer monitor, and the card slips out of my hand.

"Sorry," I say as genuinely as I can muster without making myself puke.

She rolls her eyes again and picks the card up. "Do you throw credit cards at all of your customers?" she bitches.

"Just the special ones," I mutter.

She huffs. "I don't appreciate your tone, young man."

"I don't appreciate you coming in here and sticking your nose up at my friend and me," I challenge.

She balks and gathers up her purse. "I want to speak to your manager," she declares.

I grin and cross my arms over my chest. "You are."

She gets flustered and tries to form words, but a jumbled mess of sounds comes out instead. She stomps out, slamming the door behind her.

Amethyst comes around the corner, eyes wide. "Dude, you are my hero!" she exclaims.

"I didn't like the way she was treating us. Especially you. No one looks at my friend like that." Amethyst smiles but then punches me in the arm. "Ow!" I gasp. "What was that for?"

"For being a shitty friend."

I rub the tender spot on my bicep. "Feel better?"

"A little," she sniffs.

"So, are you done being mad at me? Are we friends again; because I have a lot to tell you."

"I guess." She tries not to smile, but she can't resist me.

"So, a few nights ago, I came out to my mom, and she was totally okay with it," I begin.

"Good!"

"Christmas day, Don showed up and was being nice until Erasmus told him we were dating."

"I'm sure that made him *very* happy."

"Oh, yeah. He was screaming homophobic slurs. Grandma booted his ass out. Oh, then after dinner, a demon attacked, and I fought her off but got a little wound. I was knocked into the wall and sliced my hand open. Erasmus smelled my blood and went crazy, and tried to kill me. My mom freaked out and told me that I couldn't see him anymore. She did the whole 'Vampires do not make good boyfriends,' talk"

"Wait!" Amethyst holds up a hand to halt my diatribe. "Erasmus is a *vampire*!?"

Oops. Shit. Fuck. Shit motherfucker fuck shit! I forgot that I'd decided not to tell her that pertinent little piece of information. "Uh-huh," I whine, knowing that I've really dug myself a deep hole now.

"You're dating a vampire, and you didn't tell me, your best friend!?" She smacks my arm. "How could you not tell me that vampires are real!?"

"I wanted to!" I exclaim. "The only reason that I didn't was out of respect for Erasmus. I wasn't sure if he was okay with me telling anyone or not. Not that I don't trust you because I do."

She tries to say something but only gets a syllable or two out before stopping and repeating. She does this several times before lapsing into silence for several minutes. "I get it," she says finally. "So, your mom didn't take it well."

"No. She doesn't get that vampires aren't like they're traditionally portrayed in books and stuff. They're normal people who have to drink blood to stay alive. Erasmus says that if you're a good person in life, you're a good vampire. All that stuff about no reflection and stakes through the heart isn't real."

Gabriel Mero

"Good to know, in case he ever hurts you for real, and I need to kill his ass."

I laugh. "So, we had this huge fight, and I stormed out. She told me not to come back. I walked to Erasmus', and he broke up with me, but I convinced him to dance with me. That led to sex, and, yeah, we're still together."

"Oh, my God!" she cries. "*You* had sex!?"

"Several times." I grin devilishly.

"How was it? Is he as hot without clothes as he is with clothes?"

"It was amazing. And, yes, he's perfect!"

"I'm so happy for you!"

"Thanks." I frown. "He wants to top me."

"Ouch," she groans. "Anal sex hurts like a bitch."

"You've tried it?"

"Once. But he was really rough."

"We tried, but I freaked out before he could get it in."

"Is he okay with it?"

"He's being patient. He made me a deal that when I let him in, he'll tell me his story."

"An ultimatum, I love it!"

"But what if I can't do it? What if I never get up the courage?"

"You will. You love him. When you love someone, you do things for them more than for you."

"I just don't want him to be unhappy."

"He's dating you; how could he be anything but happy?"

I give her a side hug. "I'm sorry I've been so selfish lately. I didn't mean it, I swear."

"Eh." Amethyst shrugs it off. "I'm a needy bitch sometimes."

"Never."

She laughs. "You really should check in with your mom. She and your grandma are apoplectic."

"I should," I agree. I don't really want to go home and face my mother. I'm still miffed at her for being so cruel and narrow-minded about Erasmus, but Grandma doesn't deserve to be put under this stress. Plus, I need to go back for Romana. I miss my beautiful girl. "All right, I'll do it, but I'm not backing down if my mom starts anything."

****

Erasmus shows up at close. In the dim lobby, he's still beguiling. *How does he manage to look amazing all the time? Is it a vampire thing?*

"Did you have a good day?" he asks, kissing me over the counter.

"It was okay. Amethyst was mad at me at first, but we worked through it. She had some good points."

"Oh?"

"I've been so wrapped up in you that I've been neglecting everything else in my life. I love you, but I can't revolve my life around you."

"I'd never ask you to. I just ask for you to be faithful."

"I won't cheat on you," I assure him.

"So, you're going to want to go home tonight, I take it," he says as we rush from the store out to the car. The wind is biting, and my pale susceptible flesh quickly turns red.

"Probably for the best," I answer.

Erasmus starts the car, and the warmth embraces me. It is heavenly. *I cannot wait for spring! Only three more months.* I watch him as he stares out the window, waiting for me to get warm, and I blurt out a question. "Are you happy?"

He turns to look at me. "You make me very happy," he says.

"I'm flattered, but I mean, in general, like, do you like being a vampire? Were you ever happy with your undead life?"

"Vampirism isn't all it's cracked up to be. It's not the romantic interlude it seems."

"No worries." I hold up a placating hand. "I don't want to be a vampire. This isn't *Twilight*. I'm happy being me. And I want you to know that if anything ever happens to me... no matter how badly it hurts you, I do not want you to turn me, okay?"

His dark eyes stare into mine for several seconds before he softly says, "I promise."

"Good." I nod with finality. "Now, answer my question."

Erasmus throws the car into drive and peels out of the parking lot. "At first, it seemed amazing to me. Never being able to die, never aging. But as the years crept by, loneliness set in. Unless I choose a partner of my own kind, I'll outlive any lover I have."

"We'll cross that bridge when we get to it," I assure him.

"I miss so much about being human," he confesses, his eyes not leaving the road.

"Like what?"

"Being able to enjoy the sun. Until you, sunrises were the most beautiful thing I've ever seen. I'll never see another one, not really. I would love to sit out with you and watch the sun rise. I'd love to walk through the park with you when it's not dark. Nothing is ever as beautiful in darkness as it is in the light."

My poor Erasmus. He's such a dark, conflicted man. He is destined to spend an eternity in the darkness, knowing that the thing for which he yearns the most will kill him and leave nothing but ash in its wake.

"And I miss food. Even now, when I eat normal food, I don't taste it. All I can taste is blood. I miss the comforting feeling of my heartbeat." His hand rests on his hollow chest.

"Maybe I can help you," I say without thinking.

"How?"

"Well, I *am* a witch," I ponder. "I won't be able to restore your humanity, but maybe I can find a way to let you see the sun again."

"I appreciate the thought, Graham, but magic can't help me. This is my life now."

I vow to consult the *Grimoire* later. "Sorry I brought it up."

"Don't ever apologize for trying to bring joy to me. I'd give anything to be able to live your life with you. I know how it feels."

He pulls into my driveway, and I hear the click as my door unlocks itself. "I'm scared," I confess.

"Don't be. They're your family. It's their job to love you, no matter what."

"What if it gets ugly?" I grimace as I feel cramps in my gut.

"I'm only one call away," he says, and it's the sexiest, most romantic thing I've heard.

"I love you." I give him a quick kiss and get out. "Maybe you can sneak in my window later."

"As tempting as that thought is, I don't want to disrespect your mother."

"You're, like, the perfect guy, you know that?"

"I try."

Palms sweating, I make my way into the house. At the sound of the door, my grandma pokes her head out of the living room. "Bubala!" She engulfs me in a bear hug. "Where were you? Your mother and I were worried sick!"

"I know, I'm sorry. I stayed at Erasmus', giving Mom a few days to cool down."

"Oh, she's nuclear by now!"

"Shit. Well, I need to grab some things, then." I start to go up the stairs.

"Oh, no. You're staying here," Grandma says.

"But... she told me not to come back."

"Like you said, this is my house, not hers. I would never kick you out."

"I need to go see Romana," I say, taking another step up.

"Yes, go, go. I'll bring you up some tea."

"Thanks."

When I open my bedroom door, I see that Romana is curled up on my pillow, an orange, striped ball of fur. She pops her head up at the sound of the door opening, and when she sees me, she vocalizes and jumps off of the bed, scurrying over to me. I pick her up and rain kisses down on her head.

"I'm so sorry I left you," I whisper as tears pool down my cheeks. "Daddy missed you so much! I promise I won't ever leave you like that again. Never."

Romana starts to purr and licks my nose. Her sandpaper kitty tongue is rough, and it hurts a little. "Looks like you missed Daddy, too," I coo, holding her tightly in my arms.

I've been so wrapped up with Erasmus that I forgot that while he is great and makes me happy, I have other good things in my life that make me happy, too. Never again. I can't hurt the ones I love again, not through selfishness.

I carry Romana over to the bed and peel the covers back. We slide in, and a sigh of contentment escapes my lips. It feels good to be home.

Chapter Twenty-Two

The next morning, I found Grandma in the kitchen baking banana and zucchini bread. She seriously never stops moving. It's a wonder that she finds time to sleep.

"Good morning, bubala," she says as she places two bread pans into the oven.

"Morning," I reply. My voice is raspy from dehydration and lack of usage. I go to the fridge and grab one of my water bottles—açai and grape flavored. The icy coldness of the water feels good on my parched throat, and I can feel it slide down my esophagus and work its down to my stomach.

"Are you hungry?" she asks, eying me disapprovingly.

"A little."

"It doesn't look like you've eaten a crumb while you were gone."

"I got lots of protein," I say, snickering behind my water bottle.

"Your health is not a joke, Graham. Starving yourself is not healthy. Do you want to end up in the hospital? That's where you're headed. You're messing with your metabolism and your blood sugars."

"Erasmus made sure I ate," I assure her. "I just wasn't that hungry. I was stressed out."

"Well, that's understandable. You have undergone quite a few changes in the last few months."

"You're telling me. I wake up every day and have to convince myself that it hasn't all been a dream."

"How dreadful! Your life was droll before. Now it's... magical!" Her eyes twinkle joyously.

"I could do without the random attacks," I say, taking another gulp of water.

"Attacks? There's been more than one?" She widens her eyes in worry.

I really need to get better at communicating things with people. I'm literally the worst friend and relative ever. I have so much going on in my brain all the time that I forget to tell people things, and I forget whether or not I've already told them things.

"Yes," I admit, sitting down.

"What? When?" In a swirl of robes, my grandmother sits down next to me, her gaze fixed intently.

"Halloween night was the first one. I was attacked on my way home from work. That's when Erasmus and I... clicked."

"Why didn't you tell me!? You've been walking around unprotected for over a month!"

"I didn't want to scare you. You have enough on your plate without worrying about me being attacked by demons."

"I could've handled it!" she chastises. I feel like a little boy again, and I hang my head.

"I'm not unprotected, though," I allay. "Erasmus has been teaching me how to fight. Amethyst turned my Star of David into a protection amulet—it glows purple when I'm in danger. I have protective crystals in my room and black salt. I've been practicing my telekinesis religiously."

"Some protection amulet," she grumbles. "It didn't stop you from destroying my china cabinet."

"Sorry about that."

"It's not your fault," she says with a sigh. "I just wish you'd *told* me. I can't help you if I don't know what's going on."

"I'll tell you from now on," I promise.

"Do you know which demon, specifically, is after you?"

"Adrammelech," I reply. My grandma goes pale, and her hand flies to her mouth.
"Grandma?" *Why does she look like she's seen a ghost?*

"Are you sure?" Her voice is a barely audible whisper.

"Yes. The demon that attacked me said, 'Adrammelech sends his regards', before Erasmus snapped his neck."

"Oh, bubala, this is much, much worse than I imagined." She stands up and starts pacing the kitchen.

"Why? We've handled it pretty well so far."

"Adrammelech is the vilest demon known to man. He will stop at nothing to get his claws on you. Unless you can kill him, he will keep coming for you until he gets what he wants."

"He wants Lucifer's throne," I say. "He wants to influence me to use my powers for evil, then he can stage a *coup d'état*. Erasmus already filled in the blanks for me."

"Adrammelech won't stop at seducing you to the dark side. He needs you out of the picture altogether."

"Why doesn't he just come up here and kill me himself, then?"

"He's trapped in the Sitra Achra, the realm of evil. He's sending his foot soldiers to get you. Once he gets you to pledge yourself to darkness, he'll kill you and harness your powers to return to the Earth, where he'll wreak insurmountable turmoil upon us all."

"You're forgetting one vital piece of information," I remind her. "I won't pledge myself to darkness."

"He has his ways of seducing you," she cautions.

"He's not going to get his hands on me."

"Oh, the arrogance of youth."

"Not you, too," I groan, rolling my eyes

"What do you mean?" Grandma presses.

"Erasmus is all freaked out about this, too. He was going to shadow me to class and work so that he could keep an eye on me."

"That's a brilliant idea!" she gasps.

"Are you forgetting the whole vampire thing? He'd be a pile of dust by lunchtime. It's not like I can get him some potent sunscreen."

"But there is *something* you can do."

"Which is...?"

"Go get *the Grimoire*!" she orders.

I don't have the energy to fight her, so I go upstairs to my room. I find Romana once again curled up into a ball but on the book this time. *Is she... protecting it?*

"I need you to get up," I whisper, grabbing the book. Romana opens an eye and regards me before jumping to her feet and sauntering away to lie on my pillow. "Sorry, baby." She blinks at me slowly in response.

When I return to the kitchen, Grandma is once again seated at the small table. I set the tome down on the table before her and sit down. Instinctively, she reaches for the book but stops, remembering the jolt she'd received last time she'd tried to touch it.

I flip it open and start scanning the pages for anything useful. "What am I looking for exactly?" I query.

"Anything about invoking a sun deity," she answers.

"Invoking a sun deity?" I parrot skeptically.

"If you find the right spell, you can enchant a piece of jewelry to protect Erasmus from the sun—as long as he wears it."

"Like the Gem of Amara."

"What's that?"

"Sorry, *Buffy* reference," I say, turning my attention back to the book. "Erasmus did tell me last night that he misses the sun."

"See? If we can sort this out, you can give him something that will make him very happy, and then he can keep you safe."

"But I am safe at college," I point out. "I told Erasmus the same thing. Demons aren't going to attack me in public. They don't want to make themselves known to the general public."

"No, but they're watching your every move, Graham. For example, if you pop into the bathroom quickly, it only takes a second to grab you and teleport out."

"So far, they've done nothing but try to kill me," I point out.

"They aren't trying to *kill* you. They're trying to render you unconscious so they can grab you and drag you down to Sitra Achra."

"Delightful."

My eyes continue to scan the book. I see spells for good health, to change eye and hair color, cleaning spells, love spells, getting over an ex spells... the list goes on. I spot one about communicating with a Familiar. I tuck an envelope into the page to mark it for now and continue my search.

"If it *does* happen," Grandma continues, "if they manage to abduct you, it is important that you remember one thing."

"Hmm?" I don't even look up, lest I miss something useful.

"You mustn't eat the food. They'll anticipate your resistance to their treachery. They'll try to seduce you through food, drink, and sex."

I glance at her under an arched eyebrow. "Can't they force me to eat or drink or... whatever?"

"No. The choice *must* be yours. It must be done of your own volition. They'll try to trick you with hallucinations. They'll make you see, smell, taste whatever your heart wants or your body needs."

"I'll keep that in mind." My heart skips a beat when I alight upon a spell that is conveniently just what I'm looking for.

Protection from the Sun

Perform this spell during the daylight, as the sun's light must touch the piece of jewelry in order to charge it.

You must center yourself and focus on the spell, lest it goes awry

Once you've centered yourself, sit on the floor, place the item in the sunlight, and chant:

Atum, Horus, Sekhmet,

Ra and Sopdu,

Hear my plea.

I call upon thee

To enchant this ring

To protect me from the sun

As long as I wear it.

Nevermore shall the sun harm me

So mote it be.

I flip the book so that Grandma can see it and push the book closer to her. I watch as her eyes scan the page with interest.

"You've found it," she says. "Of course, you'll need to personalize it. You won't be wearing the ring, Erasmus will… and of course, you'll have to find a ring…"

"He has one," I blurt. "He has a silver band he wears on his right hand."

"Excellent! You'll need to get that from him and purify it."

"Just run it under water or let it charge by moonlight?"

"You *have* been neglecting your studies," she tuts.

"Anyway…" I droll sarcastically.

"Purification or cleansing is when a witch removes unwanted energies from their tools. Since the ring is not yours, you'll have to imprint your energy upon it so your spell will work."

"Sounds easy enough. I'll get on that the next time I see Erasmus."

The oven timer rings and Grandma checks her bread before removing them and putting another three into the oven.

"Where do witches come from?" I ask. I've meant to ask her, but there's been so much going on lately that I haven't wanted to delve too deeply into it.

"Well, bubala, when God created man eons ago, he made Adam out of the clay of the Earth."

"And he made Eve from Adam's rib," I intercede. I went to Bible study for a while with a neighbor in Port Huron. I know the stories.

"Eve wasn't the first woman."

"What? Genesis says—"

"The *Old Testament* has been butchered almost as much as the New Testament by misogynistic men since the dawn of time to amend the words of God to suit themselves. God made a woman out of the same clay as Adam. She was called Lilith. She wasn't docile and submissive like Eve, though. She would not submit to Adam. She fought off his advances, instead, giving herself to the Archangel Samael. They fell in love, and Lilith refused to join Adam in the Garden of Eden. Lilith was cast out and denounced as a demon.

"As the world's population grew, Lilith was labeled a child stealer, and like all empowered women, she was thought of as a witch. Her children were raised in secret; no one knew they existed. But being part human, part Angel, they possessed qualities that humans do not. Magic! All witches are direct descendants of the children of Lilith and Samael."

"What happened to her?" I ask.

"No one knows. There's only one mention of her in Genesis, but it doesn't say much. Most Jews revile her as a demon and mother of all monsters. It's believed that she resides in the Underworld with the others of her kind."

"But she wasn't evil!" I protest, flabbergasted.

"Neither was Joan of Arc. That didn't stop them from burning her at the stake. Throughout history, empowered women have been silenced and oppressed by the patriarchy."

"I'm all for female empowerment," I remind her.

"Of course, you are, dear. You were borne of a family of strong women."

"So, if you don't believe the Torah, then why do you go to Temple? Isn't being a witch against all of Judaism?"

"The traditional Judaism, yes. But knowing the truth, I overlook it. As for being sacrilegious, there are many words for God since the dawn of time and many incarnations. Who's to say which one is right? I was raised a good little Jewish girl, but then I found the Kabbalah, and everything changed.

"That makes sense."

"Do you have any more questions for me?"

"So many," I admit, "but I don't want to overload my brain. You just blew my mind with the whole Lilith thing."

"Most men are dumbfounded by her," she says with a chuckle.

"I just can't believe that something as major as that was just… omitted from history. From religion."

"You'd be on your ass if you knew *everything* that's been omitted over the years," Grandma taunts.

"Okay, no more confusion for today. What's our next step with Adrammelech?"

Grandma grins. "When I'm finished here, I will perform a protection spell around the house. No demons shall be able to penetrate it, but first!" she reaches into a drawer and hands me a phallic bundle of what looks like leaves.

"What is this?" I ask, turning it over in my hands.

"Sage, my dear. You burn it, and it cleanses the energies in the house. Trust me, we need it."

I laugh and accept the lighter she offers me. I light the tip of the bundle and wave it around as the smell of the sage pervades the air. "Grandma?" I ask, suddenly serious again.

"Hmmm?"

"Do you like him? Erasmus? You don't care that he's a vampire right?"

"I would prefer you didn't date one of the Undead, but I get that love is love. I think he's a mensch."

"Thanks." I smile, glad that she thinks he's a good guy. "Go now," Grandma urges. "Get every room!"

Holding my hand below the slowly burning bundle to keep from getting ash anywhere, I start making my way through the old house. It's definitely more interesting than making banana bread.

Chapter Twenty-Three

Erasmus stretches languorously like a cat and catches my eye. "Are you sure you wouldn't rather stay in tonight?" he asks. "Amethyst's party does sound pretty rad, but not as much fun as you and me in bed."

"I already told you," I chide, rolling my eyes dramatically, "we need to get out and do things with other people."

"Is the vampire boring you already?" he jokes, standing up. His sweatpants hang off of his hips deliciously. His bare chest gleams under the dim overhead lights. He slides his ring off and sets it on the bedside stand. I pretend not to notice.

"It's not that," I say, pulling the blankets more tightly around myself to stave off the winter chill. Erasmus may be undead and immune to the temperatures, but I'm still highly sensitive to the cold. "We have to do other things besides just hangout together, just the two of us. I have to keep studying my Craft. I've got a destiny to fulfill, and as much as I love you, I need more in my life; I need friends. Amethyst was really hurt that I ignored her last week."

"I understand." His lips tug up into a smile. "I wouldn't dream of monopolizing you or keeping you from your friends."

"Good."

"Well, if you insist on going to her New Year's party, then I need to go shower. Can't show up smelling of rot."

"Good plan," I laugh.

He starts to walk out of the room but turns and shoots me a look that tingles below my waist. "Care to join me?"

I do, I really, *really* do, but if I'm going to surprise him with the sun protection spell, I need to get his ring without him noticing. He only takes it off when he's in the shower.

"In a few," I reply lackadaisically. "The bed is too comfy."

"Suit yourself." He smirks and saunters out the door. I stay in bed until I hear the sound of the water turning on in the shower, and then I roll over and snatch his ring off the bedside table. It's cold in my palm, driving me to complete my task.

After my conversation with Grandma yesterday, I delved into the *Grimoire* and brushed up on cleansing. I had no idea that it was so involved. Through my studies, I learned several ways to cleanse an object, and each object requires its own method. For instance, using water to cleanse a crystal could potentially damage the crystal. Who'd have thought? I learned about recaning; using smoke to cleanse an object or room. That's what the sage burning was for. I also learned about charging with sunlight, salt, earth, crystals, and sound.

I also learned about the elements. Being born on the twelfth of October, I am a Libra, an air sign. However, of the four elements, the one that I've always felt the most drawn to is water. I've always loved the rain. Summoning rain was the first spell I'd ever cast, and it worked. I've always found the feeling of warm water soothing, which is maybe part of the reason that I like tea so much.

Given my affinity for water, I decided to use water to cleanse the ring. I would have thought that just washing the object in water would suffice, but the book surprised me. Like everything else with the Craft, there are a myriad ways to do something. I can boil the ring, wash it, or spray it with charged water. Considering my limited time, I decided to just give it a quick wash.

I take the ring and tiptoe into the kitchen. I turn the faucet on and run the ring under the stream of warm water, closing my eyes and focusing on neutralizing the energy it bears. Maybe it's the power of suggestion, or maybe it's actually working, but I can feel a clearness.

I turn the faucet off and hurry back to the room. I grab my messenger bag, head into the foyer, and out onto the front porch. The sun is still out, but not for long. *I hope there's enough sunlight left to sufficiently charge the ring.* It's freezing cold out, and I shiver, praying that this spell won't take long.

I sit cross-legged on the porch and place the ring on the pavement, directly in the sun's dwindling rays. I open my messenger bag and take out a few candles. I've also done my research there, and am pleased to discover that gold candles are good for spells dealing with male and solar energies. There are quite a few pages dedicated to candles in the book, but I'd skimmed instead of actually reading. *How hard can it honestly be?*

I close my eyes again and focus on harnessing the sun's power, channeling it into the silver band.

Atum, Horus, Sekhmet,

Ra and Sopdu,

Hear my plea.

I call upon thee

To enchant this ring

To protect Erasmus from the sun

As long as he wears it.

Nevermore shall the sun harm him

So mote it be.

As I chant, I can feel energies crackling all around me, making the hairs on the back of my neck stand straight up. I imagine the hair on top of my head standing to attention, too, and I stifle a giggle.

I don't know how long I'm supposed to stay like this, but in the back of my mind is the anxious ticking of the clock, reminding me that Erasmus won't be too long in the shower. I don't know how he would react to me trying this. I don't want to get his hopes up in case it doesn't work for some reason.

The energies start to dissipate, and I open my eyes. The ring doesn't look any different—not at all. *Should it?* I'd imagined that it would take on a golden hue or something. I blow the candles out and pour the wax into the grass before tucking them back into my bag and hurrying into the house. I heave a sigh of relief when I hear the shower still running.

I rush into the bedroom, tossing my messenger bag under my side of the bed and set the ring down where he'd left it. Okay. Now to distract him...

I go into the bathroom and squint through the steam pervading the air. Over the rush of the shower, I can hear Erasmus singing quietly. *His voice is amazing!* He starts out low and hits a few high notes. *Damn!*

I shake off my entrancement and strip out of my clothes. Barefooted, I pad to the shower door and knock. Erasmus stops singing and uses his hand to make eye holes through the steam on the glass. *What a dork!* "Can I come in?" I ask. He stares at me for several seconds before using his index finger to draw a big 'U' under the eyes, making a smiley face. I laugh and open the door.

The hot air rushes to embrace me. It feels amazing after the cold outside. "I was starting to wonder what you were up to," he says, pulling me close. He kisses me deeply and then furrows his brow. *Oh, no! What? Does my breath stink? I haven't brushed my teeth since I got up this morning, but I had a mint not too long ago, and I've been staying hydrated.*

"What's wrong?" I ask, shuffling my feet self-consciously.

"You taste different," he muses. "Did you do a spell?"

Shit. Busted. "Um, yes," I confess. How was I to know that he could taste magic? "I did a spell to... cover a pimple."

He regards me coolly for a second. "Well, it seems to have worked. Your complexion is crystal clear."

"Thanks." I heave an inward sigh of relief. *I just want to surprise my boyfriend. Is that too much to ask?* "I really taste differently?"

"Not in a bad way," he assures me. "You just taste..." he searched for the right adjective. "Earthy."

"I'm sorry. I'll go brush my teeth—" I start to turn away, but he grabs me.

"Stay," he says, his voice heavy.

I decide to change the subject. "Why didn't you tell me that you can sing?" I ask.

"I don't like to brag," he jests.

"No, seriously. You have an incredible voice. You could be a singer."

"Well, thank you. I was for a while, many, many years ago."

"I bet you were very popular."

"Popular-ish." He lathers his hands up with soap and massages my back. His hands on my knotted back and shoulder muscles feel amazing. I close my eyes in ecstasy. We need to be at the party at six, but he's making me feel so good... *oh, fuck it, Amethyst won't care if we're a little bit late, and, besides, being fashionably late is en vogue.*

****

We get to Amethyst's apartment a little after six-thirty. The night is dark, and a cold rain falls on the streets. It's supposed to turn to snow later. *I just hope it doesn't freeze.*

"Happy New Year!" Amethyst exclaims when she sees us.

"Happy New Year," Erasmus and I say in unison, meeting each other's eyes and blushing.

"Christ, you two are so goddamned adorable. You're already talking in unison," she says with a proud smile. She steps aside to let us in. The apartment is quiet, and the only person there is a pretty blonde girl looking at Amethyst's bookshelf.

"Are we early?" I ask. "I thought you said six."

"I did. You know I hate everyone. I only invited you two and Alisha over there." Alisha turns at the mention of her name and waves shyly at us. I wave back. She is short, with white-blonde hair, big blue eyes, and a thin frame. "I met her at the record store. Hot as fuck, but so shy."

"She looks... nice," I supply.

Amethyst turns to Erasmus. "I know about you being a vampire," she says quietly. "Don't worry, your secret is safe with me."

"I appreciate that," Erasmus says. "You have a nice place."

"Thanks, it's home. I'm just glad I *finally* got you over here. I've been trying to get you to hang out with me for years."

"Well, now you know why I never took you up on your offer," he replies with a wink.

"The gay thing or the vampire thing?"

"I'm not gay; I'm pansexual," he corrects gently, "but mostly the latter."

"Oh, I'm sorry."

"Don't be," he smiles assuringly.

"So, what's the plan for tonight?" I ask, playing peacemaker.

"I got a few joints rolled, some tea waiting to be made, and video games," she replies. "I wanted this to be a cool, adult party, but then I remembered that I can't hold my alcohol, and you don't drink, so…"

"A night with friends is always a good night," Erasmus says. "It's been so long since I've been around people or even *had* friends."

"I am offended!" Amethyst exclaims. "All this time, I thought you and I were friends."

"We are, but not the hanging out type, at least, not until tonight."

Amethyst beams and loops her arms around both of us, steering us into the living room. "I've got pizza and junk food for days, so help yourselves."

Erasmus sits on the couch and extracts a slice of pizza from the box. It's gooey with melted cheese, and I lick my lips. I am starving, and pizza is my second-favorite food. I take a slice, too, and sit beside him. I know he's eating for show, but I am eating for enjoyment. *God, this pizza is so good!*

Amethyst lights up a joint, and she and Alisha sit on the other couch. "If you guys don't want to game, I've got Netflix. We can watch movies, whatever you guys want to do."

"I'm pretty easy going," Erasmus declares, "I'm just happy to have company."

"Same," I say.

We decide to start with something on Netflix. Nothing too heavy, so we can talk and come and go as we please and not be robbed of great entertainment. I cuddle up with Erasmus and stuff myself full of delicious pizza.

By the end of the movie, we're all realizing how lame this night is actually turning out to be. Great friends are good and all, but this is New Year's Eve; we should be partying, not sitting here watching Netflix and drinking tea.

"This night is a total bust," Amethyst groans. She and I are in the kitchen alone. "I'm sorry."

"Don't be," I say, shrugging. "We can fix this."

"How? Alisha looks bored to death. This was supposed to be a low-key double date thing."

"Oh. You actually like her?" I ask.

"I think so; we've been talking for a week or so now."

"We need to liven this party up, then."

"But how?"

I think for a second. We can get alcohol—I wouldn't imbibe—but I don't want to be the only sober one, and I imagine the club scene here is tired. We'll just have to bring the party to us. "We need music," I say. "Dancing."

"I do have a pretty good surround sound system."

"I'm a terrible dancer, but I will embarrass myself if it helps you get Alisha."

"I am so damn happy I met you," Amethyst says, her eyes misty.

"Me, too."

We head back into the main room, and Amethyst puts on YouTube, playing some *Insane Clown Posse*. I grab Erasmus and start dancing. I see Amethyst shyly asking Alisha to dance. Alisha looks furtively at me, and I give her a thumbs up. I can tell she's a nervous wreck like I am, but if I can come out of my shell, so can she. She nods, and they start dancing too.

With each song, it gets easier. You don't have to worry about being judged when you're in a safe space. You can just be yourself. It's incredible.

We dance and dance as the hours tick by, approaching midnight. Of course, Erasmus is a wonderful dancer. *Is there anything that he can't do?* Being with him like this, I almost feel like a normal person with his boyfriend. I forget the impending doom hanging over my head and the fact that my mom is not speaking to me.

We stop our dance party around 11:30 PM so that we can watch the ball drop on TV. Personally, I think it's a dumb tradition, but everyone else is into it, and I refuse to be the party pooper.

Before we know it, the year is taking its last breaths.

****

It's weird how attached we get to years. We know they're not going to last forever, and yet we pin so much hope on each one. We think of each new year as a clean slate. We think that our lives will magically get better, but they won't. If we want our lives to get better, we have to make that change ourselves.

If you had asked me a year ago where I saw myself on New Year's Eve, I'd have said back home in the basement playing my PS2 or watching *Rent* or something, still in the closet, still oppressed by Don. Never in a million years could I have imagined being here, in a wonderful friend's apartment, with my vampire boyfriend. I never imagined I'd be able to be myself, free from Don, or that I'd become a very powerful witch. Maybe I don't give things enough credit. Maybe I'm too busy being a curmudgeon to stop and smell the roses. My life has really come together in the last few months, and I have to believe it will continue to get better into the new year.

****

I'm so lost in my reflection that I almost miss the ball drop. Amethyst and Alisha count down excitedly, and I feel Erasmus snake his arm around my waist.

The New Year begins, and I pull Erasmus into a deep kiss, trying to convey all of the things that I can't find the words to say. I'm so grateful for him and how he has enriched my life. I'm hoping beyond hope that my spell worked and that he'll be safe to walk in the sun again. It breaks my heart to think of him depressed and alone during the day, trapped in the darkness eternally.

"I love you so much," I say, holding him tightly.

"I love you more," he replies.

"If you say so."

"I do. I really do."

I believe his words. He has never lied to me and has proven time and again how loving and devoted he is. This new year will be full of so many blessings; I can already feel it.

Chapter Twenty-Four

Classes start back up a few weeks later. Since elementary school, I've always dreaded the first day of a new semester. New teachers, new schedules, new classmates... too much change. College is no different. There has always been comfort in structure and routine. I can't help but wonder if I'm not slightly autistic, too. Or was it simply the result of living with a tyrannical control freak?

Amethyst texted me while I was in the shower this morning to let me know that she wouldn't be on campus today. She says she's feeling sickly, but I suspect it has more to do with the fact that she and Alisha have been fucking like rabbits since New Year's. I'm happy that she's happy, but I am dreading facing this day without her. After four months at Burnham University, I have only made one friend: Amethyst. My profs all like me because I'm always prepared for class, and I excel in them, but professors aren't really your friends.

On autopilot, I once again find myself outside Lilja's office. I haven't seen her since that first day, and she looks very different now. Her curls are gone, her brown hair cascading in waves down past her shoulders. Her glasses are missing today, and I can see that her eyes are emerald green, not brown.

"Do you like it here at Burnham University?" she asks when I step up to the table.

"It's a lot smaller than my high school," I say. "Less running around for sure."

"Wonderful! I haven't seen your name on any disciplinary reports, so you've obviously been keeping yourself out of trouble."

"I'm here to learn, not cause trouble."

"What extracurricular activities are you involved in, Graham?"

"None," I respond. "I'd like to be part of the Theater Wing, but I have a lot on my plate already."

"Why, yes, of course," she purrs, as if she knows the truth. "Our Wiccan group is starting up soon...if you're interested. "

Her green eyes bore into me, and I flinch. *Does she know!?* "Wiccan group? Why would I be interested in that?" I hope I manage to sound convincing.

"Just a hunch." Her fingers toy with her necklace. "Anyway, off you pop."

I dart through the crowd and out into the hallway. Instinctively, I know to make my way to Professor Perrou's study hall. In high school, we always went to homeroom on the first day of a new semester. I'm not sure why. I mean, why not just send us to our first period class?

Professor Perrou smiles politely at me. I smile back and take a seat in seat in the back of the room. As I sit down, I realize what I'm doing. *Why am I sitting in the back?* I've always been a front of the room, prefer to go unnoticed kind of guy... and yet... this seat appeals to me. Could everything that's happened recently changed me?

The room quickly fills up with the other students, the peaceful serenity disrupted with the shuffle of feet and loud conversations. Without Amethyst, I feel naked and exposed, wholly alone. Thankfully I had time to stop at a local café for an Earl Grey and vanilla drink called a London Fog. I pull out my planner and glance over the syllabus and reading lists for the semester.

I have French II with Madame Colbert. She is a quirky, artistic woman with infectious energy. My French teacher in high school, Madame Benedic was very much like that. There is a comforting sense of the familiar when I'm in her presence.

Next on the list is Computer Information Systems II. Unfortunately, comfort goes out the window, as I have a new professor for this course. I've grown quite fond of Professor Mittelstadt and his dorkiness, but now I have Professor Maries. I've never met her, but I have seen her around the lab wing. She reminds me a lot of Patti LuPone.

Next on the list for this semester is Intro to Geometry. This is a repeat for me. I didn't do so great, and my guidance counselor suggested that I retake the course to improve my GPA. I'm not looking forward to the experience, again with Dr. Payne—trust me, the class *is* a pain.

Finally, I've got British Literature II with the exotic Professor Lenhausen three times a week. All in all, not a bad schedule. *I wonder if I'll have any classes with Amethyst. I hope so because this semester on campus will otherwise be extremely lonely.*

After finishing my tea, I collect my things and make my way to the Foreign language wing. When I get to the lecture hall, I catch Madame Colbert tap dancing in the. The hall is the same size as the others, but hers seems so much bigger. She's taken a lot of care to decorate the room and make it inviting: masks, the French flag, and pictures of famous French people. There's even a mural recreation of Van Gogh's *Starry Night* on the back wall.

Madame Colbert sees me and bows. *"Bon matin-* good morning , *Guy-François,"* she says. Earlier in the year, she had us pick French names to help immerse us in the culture I'd chosen Guy-François for its flair.

"Bon matin à vous, Madame. Comment ça va – good morning to you, Madame. How are you?" I know it isn't properly formal, but Madame and I are like friends, so it's not a huge deal.

"Très bien, merçi, et toi – very well, thanks, and you?"

"Bien! Je suis bon, aussi, merçi – okay! I am well also, thank you."

French had always come to me easily. I like to think it's because of my French heritage on my father's side, but realistically, it's probably just a natural affinity for languages. I've always had a good grasp of grammar, too.

After French, I go to my computer class and face Patti LuPone. Professor Maries is average height, with short brown hair and a very intense face. She seems nice enough, but all I can think of is Patti. As long as she doesn't stop her lecture to have a diva fit because someone's on their phone, I think this class will be okay.

The next day, I find Intro to Geometry dreadfully dull, as always. I have no idea what's even going on. I never have when it comes to math. No amount of extra help or tutoring has ever been able to help me. I just do my best and skate by in the 'C' range.

In the student union, at mid-day, I'm sitting alone at the end of a table in the corner, and I become hyper aware of how I must look to everyone else; the emo kid sitting alone, reading. I wish I could say that I've evolved past caring what anyone thinks of me, but sadly I haven't. I'm so used to not fitting in and being bullied that I've just come to expect it from everyone. I'd like to make friends here besides Amethyst, but I don't know how to.

I watch the people around me, see their effortless smiles and easy confidence. No one even notices me watching them, too busy living their lives. *It must be so nice to be normal.* I decide to go for a walk to clear my head and ease my anxiety.

My feet do all the thinking and carry me down the halls, desperate to escape everyone else. I really thought that I was doing better. I thought that with all the new positive relationships in my life and the immense power that courses through my veins, that I'd be able to overcome my anxiety. Yet here I am, feeling like a freak because I don't know how to connect with other people.

As I blink, my contact detaches from my eye a little, agitating it and making it water. I swipe furiously at it and bump into someone. I'm off balance and topple to the floor. I look over and see the waitress from the fancy restaurant smiling down at me. Her blonde hair is loose today, and I can see her pink and purple streaks. "I'm so sorry! Are you okay?"

"No, it was my fault. I wasn't watching where I was going." I get to my feet. "I'm okay. You?"

"Great." She smiles, and I see a gap between her two front teeth. I find small flaws like that endearing.

"We haven't officially met, but I'm Deanna." She extends her hand expectantly.

Gabriel Mero

"Graham." I shake her proffered hand. It's warm against my ice-cold flesh.

"So fancy!" she laughs. "Where were you going in such a hurry?"

"I was just clearing my head. Sometimes my anxiety gets too much and I have to move around to make it go away."

"Right on. When I have anxiety I just smoke a bowl and watch a movie with my cats, but everyone has their coping mechanisms."

"I'll have to try that sometime." I smile, feeling semi at ease around her.

"How have you been? Are you still seeing that guy?" My cheeks burn.

"Erasmus? Yes. Can you not… mention him to anyone? I'm not ashamed or anything. I'm just a really private person, and I don't want people knowing my business."

"Of course. Sorry."

"Don't be. So, uh, where were you headed?"

"The Wicca meeting."

"Huh?"

"We finally got enough members to warrant an on-campus Wiccan group; I'm so excited. I've wanted to be part of a coven for years, but I have yet to find my tribe."

"That's awesome," I say, brushing myself off self-consciously.

"Do you want to come?" Deanna asks.

"To the Wicca meeting?"

"No, to the moon." She punches my arm lightly. "Yes, to the Wicca group."

I hesitate. I do think it would be interesting to be around other witches outside of my family, but I don't want to out myself either. I don't know who I can trust. And yet, I must admit that I'm tempted.

"Okay," I relent, falling into step beside her.

"Awesome! Are you Wiccan?"

"Not exactly," I confess, "but I respect it."

We enter a classroom, and I see the expected attendees: a couple of Goth girls and guys with black hair and lips, eyes darkened by serval layers of eyeliner. There are also a few nerdy girls who look desperate for any sort of validation and company. There's also a girl with a Latina skin tone, her hair back in a braid. She's wearing a black leather duster that reminds me of Spike from *Buffy*. She eyes me with disinterest.

"I brought a guest," Deanna announces, motioning toward me.

One Goth girl, with major resting bitch face – RBF—shoots to her feet and stalks toward me. "What is he doing here?" she demands, her voice husky

"This group is welcome to all, Sabrielle," Deanna reminds her patiently. She shoots me an apologetic look.

"Apparently," the Goth guy scoffs. He looks almost identical to Sabrielle. *Twins, maybe?*

"Enough, Sabriel." Deanna's voice is losing its trademark cheer. Sabriel and Sabrielle... yeah, definitely siblings.

"He doesn't belong here!" Sabrielle growls.

"What is your problem with me?" I demand, squaring off against her.

"Oh, I don't know, maybe the fact that you're stuck up snob, who sits in the back on his elitist ass and thinks he's better than everyone else."

What? That's not true! I'm not a snob, I'm not an elitist, and I certainly don't think that I'm better than anyone. Is this how my peers see me?

"You couldn't be more wrong about me, Sabrielle," I say, my voice steady. "I don't think I'm better than anyone. I'm sorry if that's the impression that I have given you. The truth is, I have pretty bad anxiety. There's a little voice in the back of my head constantly telling me that I'm not good enough, that no one could *possibly* like me. So, believe me. I do not think that I'm *better* than you. I think *you're* better than me."

She stares at me for a long time, blinking slowly. "Likely story. We all have anxiety. Get over it."

"Back off, bitch!" a voice bellows. I turn to see the Latina girl—Marina, I think her name is—shoot to her feet.

"Oh, stuff it, Marina."

"This is a group for Wiccans. Who are you to decide anything? I've never seen you so much as look at a spellbook. If anyone doesn't belong here, it's you with your boring-ass Goth makeup. You're a poser. I mean, could you *be* any more of a stereotype?"

Sabrielle's mouth quivers, and ducking her head, she hurries to her brother in the back of the room. I go and sit next to Marina. "Thanks," I mutter shyly.

"Don't mention it. I've been looking for an excuse to tell that bitch off for years."

I laugh. "Well, you sure told her."

"I can't stand hypocrites."

"Is that really how people see me?" I ask. I don't know why I'm clinging to Marina like she's a friend, but I'm vulnerable right now, and Amethyst isn't here to calm me down.

Marina sucks air through her teeth. "You do come across as very holier than thou," she admits. "Personally, I never thought you actually were, but you don't talk to anyone except Amethyst. I can see why people think that."

Shit. Here I thought that everyone hated me because of my nervousness. How ironic.

Deanna sits down next to me. "I'm sorry about her," she says. "Sabrielle is a bitch."

"It's fine," I assure her. "Just please don't ever leave me alone with her. Something tells me she'd stab me rather than look at me."

"You're probably right."

The faculty adviser comes in and my jaw drops. It's Lilja. It all makes sense now. She's a witch. She did some kind of magic mumbo jumbo to look younger, probably a glamour, and the jar she wears around her neck is a spell jar.

"Blessed be," she intones, holding out her hands in supplication.

"Blessed be," the students reply. I quickly return the greeting.

"At long last, we have enough members to warrant the first Wicca group in Willows Crest history. I've called our inaugural meeting because I am so excited to be sharing this experience with all of you. There was a time when we'd have all been burned at the stake for our beliefs, but now we're free to practice our religion out in the open. It is a wonderful experience!

"Before we get too involved, I must inform you that this is a bully-free group. I know this campus is technically a bully-free zone, but that doesn't stop people from causing each other psychological damage. However, this group is small, and I'll be better able to monitor you. If I witness any bullying in this safe haven, you will be immediately dismissed from the group and will not be allowed to come back. Is that clear?"

Great. Where this lady was five minutes ago?

"For those who don't know me, I am Lilja Edwards, the Dean of Admissions. I've never been married and have no children except for my cat, Cersei. I've been a practitioner since my teen years, back when it was uncool to be a witch. I've mastered the art of potions, a rare commodity these days. For you guys, it's all about the powers and spellcasting. Those are great and all, but there is so much more to the Craft than that.

"In this group, we encourage spells that do not garner personal gain. That means no love spells, no weight loss spells, no money spells, no glamour spells, and certainly no spells that harm others. Wicca isn't about that. If that's what you came here for, please leave now."

The other Goth girl stands up and leaves, along with a couple of the nerdy girls. Lilja watches them go without reacting.

"Now that we've thinned the herd, I've only got a minute or two, she says, glancing at her watch. Our first official meeting will be next Wednesday at four, right here. I hope that you all can make it. If we don't have an adequate turnout, the fascists will disband us, so please, please come."

She stands signaling the end of the meeting, and people start filing out. As Marina, Deanna, and I leave, I see Lilja regarding me with an arched eyebrow and a wry smile

"Will you be coming next Wednesday?" Deanna asks.

"I'll try," I say. Not having a car kind of hinders spontaneity. Plus, there's still Brent to watch.

"You should come," Marina interjects.

"What kind of witch are you? I'm primarily a Green Witch." Deanna can't keep the pride out of her voice. "I focus on the powers of Nature and its energies.

"There are different types of witches?" I balk. *How do I seriously not know this? So much for that destiny.*

Marina snorts. "There are *many* different kinds of witches. I'm a Celestial Witch."

"And that means…?"

She grins. "I incorporate the moon, the planets, stars, and celestial energies into my magic."

"That sounds cool. I think I'm…I don't know a Loner Witch? Is that a thing?"

"A Solitary Witch?" Deanna interjects. "Sure. You strike me as a lone practitioner. "

"I *do* get Natural Witch vibes from him, too, though," Marina adds.

"Can I be both?"

They look at each other and laugh. "Sure, why not?"

I part from my new—friends? Coven members?—whatever they are, and make my way to the Humanities wing.

I am absolutely jubilant when class lets out at 3:30 PM. Today is the day I will try out my spell on Erasmus. The sun is still high in the sky, and he should be asleep; if I can get to his house, I can try to figure out a way to test it without spoiling the surprise.

Last night, I lay in bed and scoured the book for a solution to my transportation problem. In the eleventh hour, I'd found a teleportation spell. I'm not sure it will work—I could end up scattered into billions of atoms or in Persia—but it's worth a shot.

I work against the tide of bodies spilling out the front door and go into the men's restroom. I quickly make sure that no one is in the room with me and then enter one of the stalls. I pull the *Grimoire* out of my messenger bag and open it to the page I'd saved with a letter. I scan the page to ensure I've memorized the incarnation correctly. Then I close my eyes, think of Erasmus' living room, and begin chanting.

There is a place I want to go

I want to teleport there now

Please bring me to

My desired place

To Erasmus' house

Let me travel now.

Over land and sea

So mote it be.

I repeat the spell five times and feel a tingling sensation wash over my body. It's like I'm floating. I think of the living room with its lush leather sofas and roomy atmosphere, and the lavender smell that entices me so.

I'm standing in Erasmus' living room when I open my eyes. *I did it! My spell worked!*

I set my messenger bag on the sofa and go down the hall to the bedroom. I put my ear to the door and hear nothing. *Duh. Erasmus doesn't breathe, so he's not going to snore or anything.*

Pulse hammering, I open the door a crack, and through the crypt-like darkness, I can make out Erasmus' motionless form. In sleep, he looks dead. I cringe at the thought but open the door wider to allow myself entry. The door creaks, and Erasmus rolls over. I pause, waiting for him to wake up and recognize me. He doesn't. He simply rolled over and resumed his corpse-like stature.

I creep past the bed to the window. Through the thick black curtains, I know that the sun is shining oddly bright for a January day. I don't want to surprise Erasmus like this, but there's no way that I can trick him into going outside. If I want to do this and be sure without dashing his hopes, then I have to be a little underhanded.

I stand with my hand poised over the curtain. *Please work,* I pray. *Please don't hate me!*

I tug the curtain aside, and sunlight immediately spills into the room. It lights up the bare, pale flesh of the back of Erasmus' shoulder. Nothing happens for a few seconds, but then, my stomach drops, and I gag as smoke starts to rise off of him, and the air is tinged with burnt flesh. I panic and slap the curtain back down at the same time that Erasmus stirs and flies to his feet.

"Graham? What the fuck!?" he growls low in his throat. He switches on a lamp and comes at me.

My eyes widen instinctively. "Erasmus, I'm so sorry! I forgot! I—"

"You *forgot!?*" My heart breaks at the hurt, anger, and disappointment laden in his voice.

The tears come—tears of failure, tears of regret, and tears of frustration. *Why didn't my spell work? I'd done exactly what the book had told me to do, and I'd even added the candles as an extra bit of pizazz. What the hell!?*

I weep uncontrollably and feel the comfort of Erasmus' cool arms around me. "I'm so sorry," I sob. "I'm so, so sorry."

"Shhh." He strokes the back of my head soothingly. "It's okay."

"No, it's not!" I pull out of his embrace. Through my watery eyes, I can see his beautiful face. "I could have *killed* you!"

"There's no other way I'd rather go."

Gabriel Mero

"Don't joke about it." I sniffle. "I could have lost you!"

"But, you didn't."

"I can't be reckless like that again."

"Just stay away from my curtains."

"I'm sorry." I throw my arms around his neck and hug him again. His solid chest is comforting, even if it is chilly with a lack of blood.

"It's okay," he repeats. "What's going on? You seem emotional today."

"I had a rough day," I confess. "Amethyst bailed again, so I was all alone.

"I'm sorry."

"And then I went to this Wicca meeting, and this Goth girl attacked me. She said I don't belong there. Did you know that everyone thinks I'm a stuck-up, elitist snob?"

"Why do you care so much what everyone else thinks about you?" he asks gently.

"Because! I don't want people to think of me like that!"

"It doesn't matter what they think. Fuck those people. I love you, Amethyst loves you, your mom and grandma love you... you have people who see you for who you really are. That's what matters, not what a bunch of strangers think about you. They probably hate themselves more than they could ever hate you."

I look into his dark eyes and fall more in love with him. "I love you," I croak.

"I love you, too, my beautiful boy."

Despite my tears, I smile. "Can you just, like, tell me that all the time?"

"Whenever you want."

"Good."

He frowns as if just realizing something. "How did you get here?"

"Teleportation spell," I answer proudly.

"Graham," he chastises. "Those are dangerous!"

"It worked, didn't it?"

"*This* time."

"I'll use them sparingly," I promise.

Erasmus yawns, and I remember that he'd been asleep when I'd arrived. "I should let you get back to bed,"

"Stay."

I stop at the door and turn back to face him, well, what I could see of him through the scant light. "I am kind of tired," I admit.

"Come here." He lies down and motions for me to crawl in with him. I should get home and figure out why my spell didn't work, but I can't resist cuddles with my sexy vampire.

I kick off my shoes and lie down beside him. He pulls the blankets over us and kisses my neck before lying back on his pillow. Having him so close calms down my irrational emotions, and I start to feel my eyelids grow heavy. My contacts will be fine if I take a quick nap with them still in.

I surrender to the darkness and let sleep take me, wrapped in Erasmus' loving arms.

Gabriel Mero

Chapter Twenty-Five

I can't exactly say that I was surprised when I was called into Lilja's office on Thursday. I was just leaving Intro to Geometry when my phone pinged. It was an email from Lilja asking me to report to her office ASAP. I consider running out to the car to drop off my messenger bag, but I'd rather get this over and done with. I'd taken the *Grimoire* out of my bag last night, so at least I had a lighter load to carry around. And, if anyone was to go through it, all they'd find is school-related accoutrements. *Scandalous*!

It's a short walk down the hall to the administrative offices, but it feels like it takes forever. I know that I'm not in trouble. I mean, I am pretty much *the most* boring adult alive, except for maybe an Amish elder. I knew she wanted to speak to me at the meeting, but I'd fled the scene like a criminal. The last thing that I want to do is draw any attention to my powers. Unless she's telepathic, I can just play dumb and get this over with.

Her office is right outside the main office. I pause before her door and take a deep, calming breath before raising my right hand to knock. However, before I make contact with the door, she wrenches it open and is regarding me with oddly shaped eyes. I hadn't noticed it yesterday, but her eyes have a very feline shape.

"Uh, hi," I say awkwardly.

"I've been expecting you," she purrs.

"Yeah... I got an email..." I remind her. I try not to come off as bitchy, but she's being majorly weird.

"Please come in, Graham." She opens the door wider and steps aside to allow me entry. I follow her lead and step into the office, crossing my arms over my chest.

"What's up?" I take in her office as she walks past me and around the great wooden desk to the comfortable chair behind it. On the wall is a diploma from some college I've never heard of, as well as pictures of Lilja with a pretty calico cat; Cersei, presumably. On a small table, a stick of incense burns slowly, dousing the air with a flowery scent that reminds me of a meadow in late spring.

"Have a seat." She gestures grandly toward the vacant seat across the desk from her. I notice that in contrast to the voluminous waves she sported the other day, her hair is now curly again and red-gold in color. I've never been a huge fan of curly hair on women, but I have to admit that she pulls it off well. It adds to her eccentric persona. She also ditched the thick glasses again, making her jade green eyes more visible. "Tea?" she offers me a cup on a saucer, and I instinctively take it and sip. It's not Earl Grey, that's for sure.

"I'm sorry," I say haltingly, "why, exactly, am I here? I mean, I'm not complaining. I have a few hours before I have to be at work, but uh, I've never been called to your office before."

"Why do you think you're here?" She uses her therapist's voice, and calmly folds her hands on the desktop.

"I have no idea," I bluff, shrugging and inverting my lips.

"Come now, Graham, surely you don't think that I'm *that* stupid." She arches an eyebrow challengingly.

"I don't think that you're stupid at all, Ms. Edwards—"

"You may address me by my first name, Lilja." Her tone is weary.

"Lilja...Is that Swedish?"

"It's Icelandic," she clarifies.

"Is that where you're from?" I realize that I've never met or seen anyone native to Iceland, except for Björk, so I don't really know how Icelandic people are supposed to look. I guess it explains her unique features.

"I was born in the United States," she answers acrimoniously.

"But you have a British accent."

"My parents were English. Now, how's about we cut the unnecessary conversation, and you tell me the truth."

"I don't know why I'm here!" It's not a *total* lie. Technically I *don't* know why I'm in Lilja's office.

She scrunches her mouth up almost imperceptibly and then smiles, trying a new tack. "I saw you at the Wicca group meeting."

"Okay… and…?" I drawl. My antagonistic side is coming out, and, quite frankly, I'm loving it.

"Why were you there?"

"I'm sorry, Ms… Lilja, but you called me in here to ask me why I went to the Wicca meeting? I mean, is it a crime or something?"

"Hardly." She smiles wryly, and I can feel my irritation start to fester.

"So, if I'm not in trouble, then can I go? I have to get my brother off the bus at 3:45."

"Not until you tell me why you were there."

I sigh and tap my feet impatiently. "I had no intention of going to the meeting, and I didn't know there was a Wicca group until you mentioned it. My friend has been out sick all week, so I was all alone. I was in the Union and started feeling anxious, so I went for a walk around the campus, and bumped into Deanna. She invited me. I had nothing better to do, so I joined her."

I once read somewhere that when lying, the best thing to do is to stick as closely to the truth as possible. I'm also mindful of the body language of a liar: avoiding eye contact, fidgeting, slouching. I look Lilja dead in her green eyes.

"Look, Graham, I appreciate your dedication to protecting your secret, but the cat is out of the bag."

"Your cat? Cersei?"

Lilja scowls. "I'm not your enemy, Graham. Trust me. I sensed your immense power yesterday. I could sense it since the first day we met. I've never felt that much power in one witch before I'm… intrigued." *What is it with these freaking witches and their ability to sense power in others? Did I miss that memo?*

I must have grown pale or something because she laughs low in her throat and continues. "You're a consummate actor, I almost believed you."

"What gave me away?" I reply sarcastically. If I can keep up the ruse of ignorance, perhaps she'll drop it.

"You have a tell," she says, "but I'm not going to tell you what it is. I like having an advantage over you."

"Whatever." I feel irrationally angry. *How am I ever going to learn how to protect my secret if I have a tell? Thank God I've never taken up poker. I'd be the laughing stock of the card table.*

Lilja leans forward, licking her lips. "I don't think that I need to tell you that you're one of the only ones in the group who actually possesses any real power."

"I didn't get the whole sensing power in others gift, so, no."

"It will come to you in time."

"So, if the others are just hacks, then why are you allowing them to stay?" Surely I can let my guard down a little? I mean, yes, I literally *just* met Lilja and the Wiccan group, but I should be safe with my sisters in the Craft.

"Like I said yesterday, I need a certain number of members to keep the group up and running. Just because most of the others don't have powers, does not mean that they can't be Wiccans. Any person off the street can cast a spell successfully if it's done correctly. And I can always train the most talentless ones the art of potion-making."

"Well, you've thought of everything, haven't you?" I ask. Honestly, I'm impressed. I see no apparent fault in her reasoning or course of action. I decide to play along, see what I can glean from her. She can know I'm a witch; she doesn't need to know that I'm the Chosen One.

"I try. Our kind have been persecuted since the dawn of time, and our numbers have suffered greatly. I'm doing my part to rebuild the sisterhood." I raise my eyebrows warily at her choice of words. "Sorry."

"Okay, so you 'know' that I'm a powerful witch or whatever. Why did you call me here?"

"I thought it best to approach you privately as opposed to outing to you to the whole group. I think we know there would be more than a little dissension amongst the ranks if I did that."

"Probably."

"Who's been instructing you in the ways of the Craft?"

I suddenly feel a compulsion to come clean and tell her everything. I know I shouldn't trust her, but it's as if I can't control myself. "No one, really," I admit. "I mean, my Grandma is a witch, too, but she says that I have to do all of the legwork myself. She doesn't want me to become dependent on other people."

"Your grandmother is smart woman."

"She is."

"How have you been learning, then? If I may ask."

"I have the *Grimoire*," I answer simply. "It tells me what I need to know."

"Excellent! No wonder you're so far advanced. You really are the Chosen One! The *Grimoire* has been kept safe for millennia, waiting for your arrival." She claps her hands excitedly. "I saw it once a long, long time ago. I'd love to see it again. Perhaps you could oblige me?"

"Uh maybe." I don't really feel comfortable sharing my book with her yet, so I change the subject. "Advanced?"

"Well, when I was your age, I could barely make a pencil float, let alone harness the amount of power that you obviously have."

"See," I lean in closely, "everyone keeps saying that I'm supposed to be this almighty powerful witch to end all witches, blah blah. I just don't *feel* all that powerful. I mean, I'll admit it's crazy that I was still able to cast minute spells despite my powers being bound, but I've been working with active powers for months. I still haven't done anything… remarkable."

"How many spells have you cast?"

I consider this for a second. "Half a dozen, a dozen, I don't know."

"And how many have failed?"

"One, that I know of."

"See? That's pretty remarkable. What kind of spell was it? Teleportation?"

"Nope. That one was easy."

"I'm impressed!" Lilja claps her hands.

"I was trying to invoke a sun deity, well, several. I found a ring to channel the energy into, I cleansed it, charged it in the sun. I personalized the spell and added some gold candles for extra magic."

"That *is* a pretty big spell for a new witch to attempt. You're lucky it didn't backfire and incinerate you."

"I guess," I sigh. "I want to know why it didn't work. I did everything right! I know I did!"

"Did you make an offering to the Gods?"

"An offering to the Gods?" *The book didn't say anything about making an offering to the Gods.*

"It isn't always necessary, but invoking Gods for a spell of that magnitude usually calls for some kind of offering."

That makes a lot of sense, actually. Back in the olden days, people were constantly making sacrifices and offerings to their Gods to win their favor or appease them. I should have known.

"What kind of offering? Not, like, a goat or a sacrificed virgin or anything, right?"

Lilja guffaws. "That sort of offering is usually saved for black magic."

"Then...?"

"Which Gods were you invoking?"

"Ancient Egyptian."

"Ah, a classic! I imagine a sufficient offering would be some wine, perhaps, or grapes?"

"The *Grimoire* didn't mention that part," I say. *I feel so stupid! I really wish that Grandma would be more proactive in helping me with this endeavor. I could use the guardianship.*

"You're still learning." Lilja reaches across the table and takes my cold hand in her warm one. "I might be a little bit presumptuous here, but I would be honored if I could be your instructor in this mysterious new world." I open my mouth to speak, but she holds up a silencing hand. "You don't have to answer right away, just know that I'm offering. It would be a privilege to herald in a witch of your prowess."

"Thanks. Look, I appreciate the offer, but I'm not sure all of this is what I'm looking for. I'm kind of a no-strings kind of guy." I feel high. *Is that really incense? Or a strain of marijuana that I'm not familiar with?*

"I know this is a lot to take in," she commiserates.

"I thought it was a lot *before* you came into the picture. Now, it's like the past few months have been nothing but bombshell after bombshell."

"I understand. Will you be attending the next meeting?"

"I'm not sure," I confess. "I have responsibilities at home, and I don't have a car."

"There's always a teleportation spell," Lilja says with an exaggerated wink.

"I don't want to become dependent upon them," I insist. "I understand that they're pretty dangerous."

"They can be if performed by an amateur. You're hardly an amateur."

"As flattering as that is, I am." I stand up to go. "Thanks for the, uh, pep talk."

"By the way, I hope you liked the tea. It's a special herbal blend created to extract the truth."

"You drugged me with a truth potion!?" I exclaim.

"Oh, do calm down. You wouldn't cooperate, so I had to…force the issue."

"You want me to trust you? How can I trust you when you use magic on me to get information?"

Lilja sighs. "All right, *fine,* it probably wasn't my *proudest* moment, but I had to know the truth. Try the spell again and if it works, maybe you'll reconsider trusting me? If I promise to never use magic on you again?"

"Swear on the Goddess Hecate," I say.

"I swear on the Mother Goddess, Hecate."

"I'll get back to you." I'm furious with her, but a small part of me is impressed that she is so crafty.

"Keep studying your book," she calls after me. "I think the truth will surprise you."

What is that supposed to mean? I nod at her and then push the door open and tread the hallway as my mind reels. *So, not only is the Dean of Admissions a Wiccan, and the faculty adviser of the school Wicca group, she's also incredibly perceptive and cryptic. Great. Yet another mystery.*

In the car, Amethyst and I catch up over the phone. "It was so weird," I say, recounting my meeting with Lilja. "Somehow, she just *knew* everything about me. She wants to instruct me now, and see the book. You haven't even really seen the book! I can't trust a woman I've just met! Plus, she drugged me with a truth potion."

"That *is* pretty creepy," Amethyst agrees. "We should do some reconnaissance."

"I don't want to spy on her." My tone is firm. "No secret squirrel shit."

"Not, like, stalking her at home or anything, but what if we joined the Wicca group and scoped her out that way?"

"I'd have to check with my mom..."

"Considering the fact that she hasn't spoken to you since last month, I'd say fuck her, do your own thing. It's nice of you to watch your brother for her, but that's her problem, not yours. He's not your kid."

"You *do* have a point," I muse. "I don't know what to do. We need to patch things up, but I don't know how to. It seems like ever since we've moved here, it's been nothing but fighting and drama between us. It's exhausting."

"Most of it is on her end, too." Amethyst coughs loudly a few times. "I get that she's your mom, and she wants you safe, but she's wrong about Erasmus, and giving you that ultimatum was childish and way out of line. She's being petty now."

"Oh, my God!" I laugh a deep, rolling belly laugh. "That is so terrible!"

"Just saying."

"I just wish that things could be easier between us like they were before. Sure, we had our occasional little riffs, but nothing major."

"It's because you're an adult now, and becoming more independent. All moms go crazy when their kids get to that age where they do their own thing and don't need them anymore."

"It could be." I give up and change the subject. "Here I am whining about my day, and we haven't even discussed Alisha. How is that going?"

She sighs wistfully *Obviously, things are going well.* "I stayed home the last few days, but I wasn't sick," she confesses, sounding jubilant.

"I figured."

"I needed a day to recharge. We fucked like rabbits."

I've seen *The L Word*, so I know that lesbians are capable of a lot more than I ever would have given them credit for otherwise. Kind of like how a friend back home once told me that she didn't think that gay guys could have sex in the missionary position. She said the anus isn't located in the same spot as the vagina. I chuckle at that memory. *Oh, so, so wrong.* Erasmus and I have had sex in numerous positions, missionary being one of them, and my personal favorite. I love being able to see his face and to kiss him when I finish.

"I had a little magical help if you know what I mean," Amethyst continues.

"What do you mean? Like a spell to make you last longer or something?"

"No. I wrote a spell to grow a dick. Alisha loved it. It did wonders to calm her down and ease her confusion."

"Wait, what? You grew a penis?" I hiss.

"Yeah."

"What... is it still there?"

"No, I undid the spell after we finished. Orgasms are so much more intense with a dick!"

"Is it?" *I've never had an orgasm without my penis, so I'm clueless.*

"Yeah, you should try it sometime. Maybe you can spell up a vagina and let Erasmus have sex with that. Less painful than anal."

"I'll... keep that in mind." *No way would I actually do that.* "So, are you and Alisha, like, a thing now? Are you dating?"

"No." She shakes her head. "I don't think I'd ever date a chick. Ideally, I want to date a hot guy who makes enough money that I don't have to work, and then have a live-in girlfriend that I can go down on and then go shopping with. My husband and I can share her, or she can just be mine."

"Well, aren't we greedy," I riposte.

"Bitch, you know it. What about you? Would you ever do a chick?"

"I don't think so." I *have* thought about it in the past, just to try it. "I don't know, Erasmus is what does it for me."

"See, I've always been bi, so I can't imagine being that limited, only being attracted to one gender. It has to suck."

"Not really. It doesn't bother me so much anymore"

"You wouldn't do it even if it was for Erasmus?"

"Absolutely not," I blurt instantly. "I am all for being free with your sexuality if that makes you happy, but no way am I okay with sharing Erasmus. As long as we're dating, he will be having sex with me and *only* me."

"Too jealous?"

"Absolutely, and to be perfectly honest, I don't see the point in being in an open relationship." She clears her throat, pointedly. "No offense," I add.

"It's all good." I glance at the time, 3:33 PM. "Shit! I should go, Brent will be home soon and I have to get him off the bus I hate not having any classes with you!"

"Me, too."

"See you at work?"

"Definitely. And we can make plans to meet on campus during the week."

"Duh. I'll meet you at our spot after my Biology lecture."

"All right. See you then."

The ride home is filled with thoughts. *I have to get some wine so I can try the spell again, but I can't risk burning Erasmus a second time. I'd feel awful if he got hurt because of my inadequacy. I could just tell him the truth, but if the spell doesn't work again I'd feel terrible about getting his hopes up for nothing.*

I'm surprised when I find myself in the driveway, the car idling. Thankfully I didn't cause any accidents on the way home. Before I lose track of time again, I head into the house. I open the door quietly and freeze in my tracks when I hear the sound of a raised voice. *Oh, God. What now?* I close the door behind me and hold my breath, listening.

"You need to tell him the truth, Beverly!" Grandma says sternly.

"I am not telling him anything. Drop it!" Mom sounds livid.

"He *deserves* to know the truth!"

"Haven't you interfered enough? If you would've minded your own business, we wouldn't be in this situation right now. You had to go and give him the idea that he could keep seeing that filthy bloodsucker."

"If he's old enough to embrace his powers, then he's old enough to choose whom he dates!"

"That is *not* your choice, Mom! None of this is your choice! You did something to him, didn't you?"

"Beverly! How could you think that I'd—"

"Well, *something* happened! I bound his powers, they didn't just magically unbind themselves!"

"Why is it so hard for you to think that he's special? That his powers are stronger than any of us could ever have imagined?"

"Why is it so hard for you to allow me to raise my son the way that I want to raise him? He is *my* son, Mom, not yours, and thank God for that. You and Dad did a bang-up job on me, I won't let you do it to my son, too."

"Beverly, you are letting your own fears and guilt rule you. What happened… what you did—"

"I'm not talking about that. That was a long time ago."

"You aren't the only one that got their heart broken that day."

What are they talking about? What happened a long time ago? Is it the thing that made Mom turn her back on magic forever? What was it? How bad could it possibly be? Is that the reason for the constant tension between the two of them? Was Grandma really a bad mom? Her disappointment is obvious. My mom turned her back on magic and our Jewish faith, an unforgivable act in Grandma's eyes, but Grandma seems to care very deeply for us. I know Grandma isn't perfect, but who is?

"You're going to quit filling his head with this nonsense, or I'll take the boys, and I will leave."

"And where will you go, Beverly, hmm? You can barely pay your bills as it is. How are you going to afford an adequate house for you and the boys? The most you can afford is a shitty apartment, and you do that, the social worker will take one look at it and decide that Brent belongs with Don. At least Don can afford a house."

I hear the scuffle of feet and dart into the kitchen. Mom is standing before Grandmother, screaming in her face. Grandma is shrunken in upon herself, tears streaming down her cheeks.

"Enough!" I howl, my voice deep and authoritative. Both Mom and Grandma turn to see me, surprise on their faces. "I don't know what you two are fighting about, and I really don't care. But you're going to stop your incessant quarreling! This is... this is so ridiculous! We're supposed to be a *family,* and yet you two are as cruel to each other as strangers. It's sick!

"I'm tired of hearing you two fight, and I'm tired of having to play the mediator. You're both adults, damn it! So, grow up and leave the past in the past!" I turn to my mother. "And *I* will decide my own life, not you. I *choose* to embrace being a witch. It is the only thing, the *only thing* that I have *ever* excelled at. I'm not giving that up! And I'm not giving Erasmus up, either!"

My mom is clenching her jaw as each word hits her like shrapnel. I can see the fury burning in her eyes. She's barely containing her fiery temper. *Well, let her try me. I'm done cow-towing to her and her tyrannical ways.* "Go to your room," she seethes.

"No. You subjected me to enough fighting as a child. I had to sit there, helpless, and wait it out. Not anymore. Do you want me to move out? Because I will, and if I do, you won't be hearing from me again. I will wash my hands you and all of your toxicity. For good."

"Graham," Grandma cautions, putting a hand on my shoulder to quieten me.

"Well, Mom?" I press, squaring my shoulders.

"You two deserve each other." She's blinking back tears of her own, but I don't care. She stomps out of the kitchen and down the hall. I hear the front door open and then slam shut hard enough to shatter glass.

"I'm so sorry, bubala," Grandma says, dabbing at her eyes. "You're right. We shouldn't have been fighting."

"I appreciate you letting us come stay with you, but you two are like oil and water. You shouldn't cohabitate. You're poison to each other."

"We could try counseling, maybe..."

"It's too late for that." I laugh bitterly. "You should have tried that years ago."

"You're right," she concedes.

"I won't live like this anymore. I *can't*. Maybe I should just go stay with Erasmus or Amethyst."

"No, Graham, please…" Her lips tremble. "Please don't leave me."

"Make amends, then. Both of you. Work it out somehow, I don't care how. Just do it."

"I'll try. You know how stubborn your mother is."

"Do I ever," I mumble. "What did she do, anyway? What happened all those years ago that destroyed your relationship?"

Grandma's face darkens, and fresh tears spring to her eyes. "I can't," she whispers.

"Someone has to tell me the truth!"

"That's your mother's story to tell, my dear. She told me to quit interfering, so I shall. She'll have to tell you."

Grandma sniffs and sets about cooking, it's what she does when she's flustered or upset.

So, she won't tell me. Mom won't tell me. How am I ever going to find out the truth of what happened? The only way I'm going to be able to help save their relationship is if I know the whole story.

I'll consult the book. If worse comes to worst, I'll cast a truth spell. Even if it's the last thing I do, I will find out the truth.

Chapter Twenty-Six

By the following week, things have not calmed down in the house. Mom took a lease on a small apartment. Grandma has tried to reason with her. My mom, of course, isn't having any of it.

She's been working on moving her things, and today is the last day. She didn't even ask me if I want to go with her, she knows that she's in the wrong with this one. I just don't want her to uproot Brent again. Kids with Autism do not handle change well, and the move here was disastrous enough, not to mention going back to spend time with Don frequently. The poor kid is a nervous wreck. He's barely eating, and he's even more pale than usual. Grandma has been begging my mother to take him to see a doctor, but she will not listen.

I skipped the Wicca meeting to try to quell the issue here, to no affect. I'm sure that Lilja is irate with me, but family has to come first. *What good is my power if I can't live even a fraction of a normal life?* I wish that there was a spell to just make all this drama go away. Actually, there is. I could try my hand at a memory cleansing spell and erase all this from our memories, but I refuse to invade my mom and grandmother's brains like that. That is a total invasion of privacy, and who am I to decide what people should and shouldn't remember?

****

I sit at the bottom of the stairs, watching my mom carry the last few boxes out to the Lincoln. It's a wonder that the car is still running. It's been on quite a few road trips, and it's almost twenty years old. Don bought it for her last year, after her prized Cadillac started to go to shit. She loved that car more than anything—more than she loves me, I suspect—and cried the day it was towed away. I still can't fathom being attached to something like that, although, few people understand my attachment to Romana. But at least she has a soul.

Brent is playing with a few of his toy cars, oblivious to the events going on around him. I won't admit it out loud, but sometimes I envy him. I know that sounds bad, but it would be fantastic to not be aware, to live stress-free. Sometimes I fear that I'm going to drive myself insane. Between that, and bottling up my emotions, I'm either going to end up crazy or a sociopath. Maybe I'll turn evil like Faith on *Buffy the Vampire Slayer*.

Grandma comes into the room, wringing her hands fretfully. She doesn't want my mom to go, she's worried—rightfully—about Brent and what will happen if they can't hack it on their own. *Why does Mom have to be so damned stubborn? Can't she see that she's not only hurting herself but the rest of us, too? Does she even care?*

"Beverly, come on," she implores, her eyes wide. "Stop this."

"Nope," Mom says simply, shoving past Grandma with Brent's TV in her arms. Normally, I'd have helped her, but I don't condone what she's doing and won't play a role in it. If she wants to abandon this family, then she's going to do it on her own. She'll have to get used to it, anyway.

"You're being irrational!" Grandma exclaims, throwing her hands up and stamping her feet

"That's me. I'm always the irrational one, right?" Mom throws a trash bag over her shoulder before going out the front door.

Grandma turns to me. "I don't know what to do, bubala," she says, her shoulders sagging in defeat.

"She won't listen, you're wasting your breath," I say emotionlessly. I know that I should be more upset about this whole thing than I am, but I am so tired of the constant drama, the incessant fighting. If Mom leaving will stop it, then fine. I don't hate her or anything, but the old saying, 'absence makes the heart grow fonder' could turn out to be true. I just hope that things don't blow up in her face, and Brent gets taken away. If she loses him, it will absolutely destroy her. I don't want that to happen.

She comes back in and grabs another box— the last one. She carries it out to the car and then crosses her arms over her chest. "Come on, Brent, it's time to go."

Brent looks up at her, his icy blue eyes analyzing her as if he can see something that the rest of us aren't privy to.

"Come on!" she grunts, pulling him to his feet, impatiently. "We're leaving."

"No!" Brent cries, throwing his cars. They scatter all over the room. "No!" His face burns red as his temper flares, and tears pour from his eyes.

"I am *not* doing this," Mom hisses, hefting him up into her arms. Brent starts thrashing and bucking like a wild horse in her arms. Lucky for her, she's strong and is able to keep hold of him.

"Beverly, he doesn't want to go," Grandma points out.

"Too bad. The world doesn't revolve around what he wants."

"You're upsetting him! Can't you see you're distressing the poor child?"

"Don't *you* tell me how to parent my child." Her words drip with venom and unspecified accusations.

"Fine, Beverly. If you want to go, then go. You've always done what you wanted in life. Why should this be any different?"

"Don't patronize me, Mother. You and I can't live together. We don't even like each other. You can't forgive me for what happened that day. I can't forgive myself for what happened that day. We're at an impasse."

Another mention of the mysterious happening from when my mom was still a practicing witch. *Come on*, I urge silently, *spill the beans!*

Grandma stares down at her slippered feet. She can't deny it. She hasn't forgiven Mom for what happened. It must be pretty bad, then.

"At least you have the courtesy not to pretend," Mom says, her voice quaking with emotion. She turns on her heel and walks out the door. I hear the Lincoln roar to life and then silence all over again. Just like that, she's gone.

I hear Grandma sniffle, the tears are coming. She scurries out of the room. I'm alone. *God, isn't that the fucking story of my life?* I get to my feet and bend down to pick up Brent's toy cars. I tuck them into my hoodie pocket. I'll give them back to him the next time I see him, whenever that is. If Grandma is public enemy number one, then I'm definitely public enemy number two.

I can hear Grandma crying in the other room, but I don't go to her. I've never been able to handle emotions well. I don't really understand them. Most of the time, I don't even feel human. Human workings and emotions are a mystery to me. I feel like Seven of Nine from *Star Trek: Voyager*: human-like in appearance, but alien on the inside.

Erasmus has been the perfect supportive boyfriend through all this, but I don't want to lean on him too much. I love him, I know that for certain, but I don't want to come to rely upon him too much. I know that nothing lasts forever. We're happy, and things are going great, but they won't always. Chances are, we won't be a lifelong thing. We can't be. I'm mortal. I certainly want to remain that way, but I don't want to spend my life with him and then die and devastate him.

I want to call him, ask him to come get me, but I don't. The sun will be out for another few hours. I've put off trying the sun protection spell again because of all the shit going on at home. Maybe I should try it again soon—but not today. I feel empty, hollow on the inside. I'm not sad, I'm not angry, I'm just void.

I should go back up to my room and immerse myself in the *Grimoire*, but I have no desire today. I kind of want to just take a melatonin and sleep it off, but that's a waste of a day, and I know that if I do that, I'll be up at two in the morning, wide awake.

My phone vibrates in my pocket, and a second later, the chorus of *Lying is the Most Fun a Girl Can Have Without Taking Her Clothes Off* by *Panic! At the Disco* starts to play. I pull my phone out and see that Amethyst is calling.

"What's up?" I answer.

"How are you doing?" I told her about my mom moving out today. *She's a good friend to check up on me.*

"I'm fine, it's cool," I assure her. "Do you want to go do something? I'm getting stir crazy over here."

"Are you feeling okay? You're the biggest hermit I have ever met."

"Yeah, well, I feel like a new person."

"It sounds like it. I can come get you in, like ten minutes. We can go get a movie from work, hang out at my place, have some tea..."

"Sounds great."

I hang up and go upstairs to my room. Romana is not in her usual spot on the bed, but curled up on my chair, on top of my coat. I don't want to wake her, and it's unseasonably warm today, so instead, I open my closet and pull out my black leather jacket. It's a bit beat up. It was a Christmas present seven years ago. Being the clutz that I am, it had been pristine for a week or so, until I tripped over a pipe, falling onto the pavement and scraping up the arm. Don was furious, of course, but it wasn't my fault. Who has a tiny pipe-thing sticking up in their yard?

I slide the jacket on, and for an instant, I am thirteen again: chubby, hideous, and friendless. I have come so far from that disgraceful loser, and I'm thankful for that.

I sneak out of the room, mindful not to wake Romana, and spot my mom's open bedroom door. I don't know why, but I find my feet dragging me into her empty room. The bed is made, and the room looks uninhabited. If it weren't for the wisps of her *Victoria's Secret* perfume, I wouldn't even have known that she was here. I feel a weird sensation inside—sadness? Remorse? I quickly quell it, burying it deep down inside. I sit down on the bed and notice a packet on the floor between the bed and the nightstand. I pick it up. It's a pack of Marlboro Menthol Lights—Mom's cigarettes. It must have fallen out of her purse or something. My mother is not a messy person, nor is she disrespectful. Grandma abhors smoking and wants it nowhere near her house, so Mom always did it outside and kept the cigarette butts in an empty coffee can.

I stare at the mint green package. I've never understood the draw to cigarettes. The smell of tobacco smoke is gross, and it's been proven that smoking can cause cancer. My high school psychology teacher told us one day that only depressed people smoke. Maybe he was right. Calling my mother depressed is the understatement of a lifetime. My dad smokes, too, always has. I've always had the impression that he is still very much in love with Mom. She tolerates him for my sake. If my assumption is correct, the core of my father's absence is losing both my mother and his mother. Watching me be raised by a more financially stable man couldn't have helped either. Still, that doesn't make it okay. Part of parenting is sucking up your own shit and making sure your kids are well. He has never been able to do that.

My fingers open the pack and see that there's at least a dozen cigarettes inside, as well as an orange lighter. My curiosity is piqued. No better time to experiment than the present. I spend so much time hating myself for being so boring and perfect. Everyone thinks that I'm a goody-two-shoes—I do well in college, I work, I help with Brent, I don't smoke, drink, or do drugs. There's always been a rebellious streak inside of me, but I ignored it because of Don. The last thing I ever wanted to do was give him a real reason to be a bigger dick to me, and I didn't want to cause my mom any more grief.

I pocket the cigarettes and head downstairs. Amethyst should be here any minute, and I don't want to be rude and keep her waiting. I open the front door and then sit down on the edge of the porch, putting my legs on the first step. I pull the cigarettes out of my pocket, fish one out, and flick the lighter to life.

I inhale the smoke and erupt into a fit of coughs. My pristine lungs struggle to adapt to the sudden onslaught of carbon monoxide, tar, and the pharmacy of chemicals. I should throw the cigarette away and admit defeat, but as the coughing ceases, I feel a sense of triumph coursing throughout my veins. I am doing something bad, and if this is how bad feels, then I bloody love it! I take another—small—drag and cough less. *I bet that by the end of this cigarette, I'll be good on the coughing.*

A couple of puffs later, Amethyst pulls up. Grinning, I get in, and she eyes me with shock. "What?" I ask, playing dumb.

"Uh, who are you, and what have you done with Graham?" she queries.

"Whatever do you mean?" I bat my eyelashes dramatically.

"You're smoking!"

"Oh, this?" I drag on the cigarette and blow the smoke out the window.

"Graham, you don't smoke."

"I didn't smoke *before*," I correct her. "Now, I do."

"Are you having, like, a midlife crisis or something?"

"Look, I'm tired of being so... *good* all the time. I am so repressed! I'm trying on the bad boy pants."

"Well, you look hot in them," she admits.

"Thanks."

By the time we get to the video store, I'm practically smoking the filter. I drop the cigarette onto the asphalt and grind it out under my boot. I start to bend down to pick it up but stop myself. The old, boring Graham would have picked the cigarette butt up, but the new and improved, naughtier Graham says rules be damned!

I'm feeling elated when we walk into the store but stop dead in my tracks when I see Vito behind the counter. He sees me and the smile evaporates from his face, to be replaced by a deep frown. *Uh oh. This isn't looking good.*

Amethyst says "Hi" to him and starts perusing shelves. Vito narrows his eyes, regarding me coolly.

"Can I speak to you in the office for a minute?" He says it so that it's not a question.

"Sure. Amethyst, I'll be right back," I call. Normally, I'd be freaking out right about now, but screw it. It's not worth it.

"Sure thing," Amethyst calls.

Vito shuts the door behind us and sits behind his desk, folding his arms across his chest. "How are you finding the job?" he asks.

"Fine."

"Good. How do you think you're doing? Manager appropriate?"

Oh, I know what this is about. That old bitch must've complained about me. Fuck her. I'm not apologizing.

"Mostly," I answer simply.

Vito smiles, but it isn't a genuine smile, it's intimidating. "I spoke to a lady this afternoon who had a lot of things to say about your performance, when she was in here not too long ago."

"Oh?"

"None of them were good. What were you thinking going off on her like that, Graham?"

"She was being rude. Not only to me but to Amethyst, too," I defend myself. "She was looking at her like she was trash!"

"I know how nasty the customers can be, believe me. But you've got to keep your shit together. You can't be going off on my customers. I don't know if you've noticed, but the movie store business is hardly thriving. Okay? With streaming services, we're lucky to still be open. The bills are barely getting met. I cannot afford for you to cost us customers because you can't rein in your temper."

"My *temper* isn't the issue, here. People like that are. They come in here and treat us like we're beneath them. They don't treat you like that because you're the boss. So, don't tell me you know we feel, because you don't. You get respect automatically."

Vito blinks, shocked. I don't think that he was expecting me to stand up for myself. After a few seconds, he regains his composure. "Sometimes, you have to deal with assholes."

"No shit." I quirk an eyebrow. I definitely know that.

"Well, I should fire you. If it was anyone else, I would, but you're a good kid, so I'm not going to, but I am extremely disappointed in you, Graham."

"Join the club," I mutter.

"I can't have a manager behaving like that, so, I'm sorry, but you're not in line for that promotion."

"It's whatever," I shrug. "It's not like I have a lot of time to devote to this job, anyway."

"You and Amethyst are the only employees, so I'll still need you to close on your shifts…"

"Okay."

"I know you have a lot going on at home, but you have to find a way to get rid of your pent up aggression. Otherwise, you're going to go nuclear and do something you'll regret."

"Thanks for the heads up, chief." I stand up. "Are we done here?"

"Yes." He sighs, pinching the bridge of his nose.

"Awesome." I turn on my heel and walk back out into the store. I can feel my temper simmering within me, but I try to ignore it. I'm not going to make matters any better if I get myself fired from my job.

"What was that about?" Amethyst asks, eying me curiously.

"That old bitch told on me."

"After this long? Bitch."

"I know. Vito isn't going to fire me, but I'm not going to be manager now."

"I'm sorry."

"I'm not," I crack my neck. "That bitch had it coming."

"Maybe if I talk to Vito, explain to him that you were just protecting me—"

"Don't bother. He's not interested in our side of the story. All he cares about is that he lost a customer. Typical businessman. The customer's always right, right?"

"Horse shit."

Laughing, we get our movie and head out. As soon as we're outside, I light up another cigarette. Everything around me is crumbling down, and the truth of the matter is, I couldn't care less. I'm so used to chaos that I'm numb to it now. *Bring it on.*

Chapter Twenty-Seven

The next day, I enter the building to see Lilja waiting at her office door. She spots me and crooks her finger, summoning me. *Great. Now I'm going to get a lecture about skipping the Wicca group.* I groan but follow her into the office.

She shuts the door and narrows her eyes at me, as if trying to read me from a great distance. *I hope she isn't a telepath, too.* It's awkward enough living with one and constantly being afraid that I'm going to think the wrong thing. It's a wonder that I was able to keep Erasmus' true nature a secret for so long, actually. Maybe I'm better at masking my thoughts than I'm aware of.

Lilja puts a hand on her jutted hip. *Here it comes...* "You missed the Wicca meeting the other day," she says, her tone accusatory.

"I know. I had... *stuff* going on at home."

"Was this *stuff* more important than learning your Craft and embracing your destiny?"

"Look, lady, I appreciate your interest in me, but I never agreed to join your cult—sorry, coven. I said I'd think about it and I did. Something more important came up. Besides, I don't really see how a hobby Wicca group is going to help me much. You said it yourself, there are only a few people in the group that are even legit."

Lilja grits her teeth, and I'm reminded of my mom when she's about to lose her shit. Apparently, I just know how to push everyone's buttons. I like to think of it as a natural, God-given talent.

"Besides," I continue, "I'm not really one for groups. I work alone, I thrive alone. I'm like a lone wolf."

"The solitary witch," Lilja mutters.

"Exactly. It's nothing personal. I've been on my own my whole life. It would be kind of hard to change that now."

"Aren't you curious about other witches?" she presses.

I consider that. It would be interesting to be around other witches and get their firsthand knowledge, but I'm not going to go out of my way to get it. "I am," I admit. "It would be cool to get tips on mastering my powers, but, again, I've never been a team player."

"When did your powers manifest themselves?"

"Back in October."

"Have you mastered any yet? You don't seem too dedicated to your Craft."

I want to be insulted, but I really can't be. Since Erasmus came into the picture, I have put the whole witchcraft thing on the back burner. I've been working my ass off in the self-defense department, though. When Erasmus and I spar now, I actually give him a run for his money.

"I mastered telekinesis quite early on," I allay. "My grandma told me that when I was little, I had the power of Resurrection."

"Resurrection? There hasn't been a witch with that power for centuries!" Lilja exclaims. "Have you tried it since your powers came to fruition?"

"No. I've been afraid to."

"Why afraid?"

"Because... what if this is all a misunderstanding and I'm not the witch Messiah? What if it's all a fluke? I don't know if I could handle that kind of disappointment. All my life, I've wanted to be special, and so far, it hasn't happened. I've been nothing but extraordinarily ordinary... until this whole witchcraft stuff. A small part of my thinks it's too good to be true."

Lilja crosses to me and takes both of my hands in hers. "It is not a fluke!" she says firmly. "There is no such thing as a fluke when it comes to magic. If there was any chance that you aren't who you're portended to be, you wouldn't be where you are now. You know how rare the male witch is."

"Yeah, first I heard it was impossible, and then I heard that it's rare because they either die or turn evil. So, which is it?"

Lilja frowns, her creased mouth loosening wrinkles upon her alabaster skin. "Who told you it's impossible?"

"My grandma."

"I believe that she was just trying to protect you."

"From what?"

"The truth."

"Which is...?" *Why is everything like pulling teeth when it comes to witchcraft? Why can't there just be an awesome witchcraft Google that I can easily consult for no-hassle answers?*

"Male witches *aren't* impossible, but they *are* rare because testosterone tends to lend itself to the seductiveness of evil. I can't tell you how many of our ranks we have lost over the years to darkness. That's why witches are so few in number. We try our best to keep the males in the dark about powerful magics. If...when they turn, they're giving a leg up to the dark witches. Why give our enemies all of our trade secrets?

"Some witches choose to bind their son's powers when they're young to nip the problem in the proverbial bud, and it almost always works. But in your case, your powers are so brobdingnagian that nothing short of death could stifle them."

"What did you just say?" Brod-what?

Lilja winces. "I'm sorry. I was an English major in college. Brobdingnagian is a fancy 18th Century word meaning 'big.'"

"Hmmm," I muse. "I like it."

"I wish you'd reconsider your stance on the group. It could help you greatly to know more about your roots and learn with others who are just starting out themselves. Witchcraft has a lot of nuances to it. I'm sure that book of yours doesn't hold *all* of the answers."

"Probably not," I agree. "Why are you pushing so hard for me to join, anyway?"

Lilja sighs dramatically. "Your grandmother asked me to. She says you've been neglecting your studies, focusing on your paramour. She thought maybe getting you into a group setting would help you out of your shell a little, encourage you to learn more."

"I appreciate the thought, but I'm fine for now. I have to do this at my own pace. All my life I wanted to be special, to stand out for being excellent at something, but now... I just want to be normal."

"Being normal isn't all it's cracked up to be. And why would you want to be normal when you can be exceptional?"

"I wish I knew," I say sadly.

"Well, if you change your mind, you know where to find us. I'd still love to help you learn more about the Craft. It would be the greatest honor for me."

I glance at my watch. I've got two minutes to get to French. If I leave now, I should *just* make it. *I hate flying by the seat of my pants!*

"Maybe I'll surprise you," I say, before ducking out of her office. I'm not about to run down the hallway like a spaz, so instead, I power walk. I haven't been tardy since sixth grade, and that was only because I was trying to master opening my locker, and my nerves kept getting in the way. I was late by seconds. Not that it matters now, even if I am late, Madame loves me and would never be angry.

I get to class right as it starts. The room is filled with students and I feel my anxiety grow as they watch me.

"It's not like you to cut it so close, *Monsieur* Norris, is everything okay?" she queries.

"Oh, yeah. Ms. Edwards caught me coming in, and our session ran over a bit. No big deal," I brush it off.

"All right. I'm glad everything is okay."

"A-okay."

I cross the threshold into the classroom and scurry to my seat. Class is officially in session, and I am not late. *Score!*

****

I space out through the next few hours. *Was Lilja right? Was I doing more harm than good by refusing to open up to others?* Being part of a group, a community makes me roll my eyes subconsciously. The idea of togetherness and community irritates me. My mother raised me to be self-sufficient. I'd say that mindset hasn't exactly steered me wrong.

And yet, maybe being a part of a coven wouldn't be *such* a terrible thing. It would be nice to be able to share this experience with someone besides Grandma and Amethyst. Erasmus is incredibly supportive and all, but he's walking a different path. In the old days, I'd have talked to my mom about all of this, but she has been so against the whole witchcraft thing that I haven't even bothered.

I'm usually immune to loneliness, but when it comes to this, I have to admit that I do feel it immensely. *How am I supposed to learn and advance with this new identity if I have no direction?* Up until now Grandma has just wanted me to read the book and learn from that, but the book is gargantuan, and I do not have the attention span to read it cover to cover.

Would joining the Wicca group really be so bad? Amethyst has agreed to join it if I do, so there wouldn't be that intense awkwardness of not really knowing anyone there. I know Deanna a little, but we're hardly friends. Marina stood up for me, but that was more about telling Sabrielle off than anything to do with me personally.

****

I'm trying to enjoy some tea in the union when I glance up and spot Sabrielle and Sabriel glaring at me from their darkly made-up eyes. The hatred is palpable. Their mouths move silently, threateningly. I try to ignore it, but now I can feel it, as if burning into my flesh. I stand up, storm across the room and stop before the twins. "What is your problem with me?" I demand, challenging them.

They exchange sullen looks, and then Sabriel speaks up. He has a high, reedy voice that grates on my nerves. "You try too hard," he says.

"I *try* too hard?" I am aghast. "How do I try too hard?"

"You try too hard to appear perfect," Sabrielle extrapolates.

"I don't try to be perfect *at all*," I argue. "I don't try to be *anything*. All I want is to be left alone and for you two to stop glaring at me. I don't like you, you don't like me. We can agree on that, yes?"

"Yes," Sabrielle mumbles.

"So, can we end this?"

"Just stay away from the Wicca group, if you know what's good for you."

I balk. "Are you *threatening* me?" I ball my hands into fists.

"Think of it as a promise," Sabriel says.

"I'm not afraid of you. Either of you. I have more power in me than both of you combined. So *you're* going to back the fuck off, or you two will spend the rest of your college careers in the special education class because your tongues will be removed, *capisce?"*

They both widen their eyes and then try to right themselves. "See you around, Graham," Sabrielle purrs, pronouncing it *Gram*. Chuckling cruelly, they saunter out of the union.

My temper is burning, whistling like a boiling teapot. I need to take a quick minute to myself to calm down before I go postal. I can see lunch trays wobbling a little, my temper igniting my telekinesis.

I spot a restroom down the hall and go in. There's a nerdy student with glasses and pit stains drying his hands. "Out!" I bark. He shrinks back like an abused dog and scurries out. *It's nice to know that some people fear me, at least.*

I turn the faucet on cold and splash water on my face, trying to cool myself off. I have *got* to learn how to manage my temper. The last thing I want to do is have a temper tantrum and get some innocent bystander hurt.

I take deep, shaky breaths, feeling my pulse hammer away inside my chest cavity. *Why do I let Sabrielle and her brother get to me?* I don't care what either one of them thinks. The whole Goth thing was cool in the early 2000s, but it's definitely had its day. 2003 called, it wants its eyeliner back.

The more I breathe, the more I can feel myself start to relax a little. I can only hope that I don't ever get seriously ill from skyrocketing blood pressure.

The sound of a shoe scuffing the tile floor makes me whirl around. I start at the sight of five men standing before me, their faces blurred as if they had moved at the exact moment that a picture was taken. Through the blur, I can make out goat eyes. Their dirty clothes reek of sulfur. *Oh, no, here we go again...*

I really wish these demon things would attack me on some kind of schedule instead of just randomly appearing. Do they have some kind of monitor on me that alerts them when I've been lulled into complacency? Are they stalking me?

I swallow past a dry throat. I'm not going to lie, I'm a little bit scared. I've battled a few demons since my birthday, but only one at a time, not five. And I've never been alone, either. *You've got this*, I tell myself silently.

I lean back on the sink casually, as if completely unfazed by the sudden appearance of five blood-thirsty demons hell-bent on kidnapping me and dragging me to back to their master, Adrammelech.

"I was wondering where you guys have been," I say. "I was starting to think you'd given up. It's been almost a month." They start to move forward, and I laugh. "Come on, this is hardly a fair fight, is it? Five against one? Is there no honor amongst demons?" I crack my knuckles and start rolling my shoulders, warming up. "How about this: you come at me one and a time and do this the right way. I mean, think of it like this: if one of you gets me, are all of you going to get rewarded? Or just the one who succeeds?" I see them turn and eye each other. Just a little reverse psychology. I crouch down and pull a blade from my messenger bag. I'd found it at a knife show back home. It has a black handle and a wicked, jagged blade. Pretty easy to fuck someone up with this bad boy.

The first demon rushes me. Instinctively, I kick out, my booted foot hitting him square in the throat. He drops to his knees, and I waste no time driving the sharp blade down into his skull. As I yank the blade free, smoke rolls out from the wound instead of blood. "Next?" I quip.

Two of the shadow men exchange looks and disappear into puffy cloud of acrid smoke. *One killed, two bailed, that leaves two left!*

The next one throws a fireball at me, and I dive out of the way. The flames connect with the trash can, and it goes up. Pretty soon, the fire alarms will go off, and the building will be evacuated. *At least I won't have to worry about casualties.*

I use the sink as leverage and propel myself into a flying kick that snaps the demon's neck immediately. His body drops to the floor, and starts burning.

I turn to the remaining assailant, and he just stands there. Suddenly, something flies over my head and bites into my throat. *A chain?* My throat tightens, and I gag as air tries to enter my lungs. I'd forgotten the number one rule: always know who and what is behind you. One of the scaredy-cat demons must have psyched me into thinking that he'd bailed. My eyes widen in alarm. This was not part of Erasmus' training... or was it? I scramble to remember. *If you're being attacked from behind, the instep of your assailant's foot is an easy point of access,* Erasmus' voice sounds in my head.

I lift my foot and slam it down as hard as I can on what I think is the demon's instep. I feel his grip loosen just enough to allow precious air in, and then I use my feet to propel me up a stall door, and then I'm sailing through the air. I land behind the demon, and before he can try anything else, I drag the blade across his throat, terminating him.

"You may kill us, witch," the remaining demon hisses. "But we will not stop until you've joined our ranks. We are infinite. We never tire. You are mortal. Not even you can be on guard every second." He laughs deep inside his chest.

"Blah, blah, blah," I groan, rolling my eyes. "I've heard the spiel before, and I gotta tell you, you don't make it sound any better than the last two meatheads. I'm not interested in what you're selling. Go back and tell your master that he's wasting his time. I'm not joining him. Not now, not ever. Amscray."

He regards me coolly for a few seconds and then charges me. I duck under his punch and drive my fist hard into his gut, knocking the wind out of him. I prepare to end his miserable existence, but then think better of it. *He's way more valuable to me as a hostage. If I can somehow get him and I back to the house, we can interrogate him and find out their plans for me.*

I flip the blade around and crack him on the head with the handle. He slouches down, and I put my arm around him, gagging as the sulfur smell invades my nose. I close my eyes, and think of our kitchen before incanting:

There is a place I want to go

I want to teleport there now

Please bring us to

My desired place

To our kitchen

Let me travel now.

Over land and sea

So mote it be.

The tingling sensation starts in again, and then there's the feeling of being reduced to nothing but atoms. I'm weightless. I clamp my eyes shut against the uncomfortable feeling and only open them when I feel whole again and smell the familiar scent of my grandmother's baking.

I look down and see that the smelly demon is still unconscious in my arms. *I am on a roll today!* I push him off of me and then stand up. "Grandma?" I holler.

"Graham?" Within seconds, she is in the kitchen, frowning in confusion. "What are you doing here? It's not even noon yet."

"Five demons bum-rushed me in the bathroom. I took out three and captured this one."

I kick his leg to exaggerate my point.

"You brought a *demon* into this house!?" Grandma shrieks, growing pale.

"I figured we could interrogate him or something."

"Sound reasoning, but must you drag him in here? I've just had the furniture steam cleaned!"

"We'll leave him on the ground. Do we have any rope or anything to bind him? I don't want him getting aggressive."

"I might have some in the garage. Let me check."

She disappears in a flurry of skirts, and I hold my hand over my unconscious quarry. Just because he can't move doesn't mean he can't shimmer or teleport away. *Try a binding spell*, I think. *I've not had much practice with personal spells, but I can't risk leaving him alone to go get the book.*

I look up as my grandmother comes back in with a length of rope in her arms. "Is this enough?" she asks.

"Perfect." I flick my hand, and the rope coils around him like a boa constrictor to its prey. His arms and feet are rendered immobile. "Can you watch him for a second?"

"Why? Where are you going?" Grandma is flushed in the face with excitement... or aggravation... maybe both?

"I need to find a binding spell and I've got demon all over, and I reek. I just need to run upstairs."

"You do reek." She sniffs distastefully. "Well, go on then! Hurry!"

I take the steps two at a time and throw the door open so quickly that I startle Romana. She launches to her feet and eyes me.

"Sorry, baby," I murmur, tugging my shirt over my head. My necklace smacks my chest with the movement. No wonder *I had no warning about the attacks. The necklace was under my shirt.* Kicking off my boots, I wiggle out of my skinny jeans and toss both my sweater and jeans into my hamper. I pull on a pair of gray skinny jeans, a black tank top, and a white sweater. I really want a shower, but there's no time for that right now.

I grab the *Grimoire* from its home underneath my bed and hurriedly flip through the pages, looking for anything that might help me. As my eyes scan the pages, I spot a Truth Spell that might come in handy, so I slide a bookmark into that page for later. If I can just find a binding spell, the demon won't be able to leave, he'll be rendered powerless.

I suck in a breath as I come across a yellowed page with *Strip A Magical Being Of Its Powers* written in fancy handwriting.

Strip A Magical Being Of Its Powers

If ever you should need to temporarily strip a magical being of his or her power, look no further than this spell. As a precaution, this spell is not recommended for a novice witch, for too much could go awry if the magic isn't balanced. Either have an elder witch assist you, or wait until you've mastered at least three powers before attempting.

First, bind your prey and draw a pentagram with salt to hold them in a circle. Once the circle is complete, recite the following spell. Its effects should last about three hours.

Bind this demon

Strip his powers herewith

Strand him here

Until I'm done

Let him cause us no more harm

Let no one detect him.

So mote it be.

"Daddy's found a spell!" I exclaim to Romana, using my finger to keep my place in the book. She stares blankly at me, but I know she's proud of me. *Is this similar to the spell that Mom placed on me?* I can't help but wonder. While this one has a time limit, the one she used was more long-term. Had Mom performed it alone, or had she guilted Grandma into helping her, desperate to remove the magic from my blood like a cancer?

I rush back downstairs to see that Grandma is standing sentinel over the fallen demon. He doesn't appear to have roused yet, so at least luck appears to be on our side.

"Did you find anything?" Grandma inquires, bouncing with nervous energy. Apparently while vampires may be welcome in her home, demons are most certainly not. *You have to draw the line somewhere.*

"Yeah, I found a spell to temporarily strip his powers, but I need your help."

"What do you mean?"

"It says you need a lot of experience to make this one work, and let's face it, I don't have that yet."

"We can hold hands and I can channel some of my magic into yours, it should be strong enough to make it work."

"Great." I reach into the pantry and pull out the bag of salt; I can't help but notice that it's Kosher. I open it and pour it on the floor, making a sloppy pentagram around the demon. As soon as the last grains hit the floor and complete the circle, it glows a bright gold color, and the air inside the circle glimmers.

I grab Grandma's hand and open the book to the page the spell is on. "Ready?" I ask, licking my dry lips as nerves start to kick in.

"Oh, yes," Grandma exclaims, a wicked gleam in her eyes. I think she's over the moon to be performing a spell with me.

We start reciting the spell, our voices blending together, sounding much louder than they should. The air around the demon swirls and lashes against the protective circle, as if fighting to get out.

As we finish, there's a bright burst of light and then a calmness grips the kitchen again.

"Did it work?" Grandma asks, worrying her bottom lip with her teeth.

"One way to find out," I say, turning to her. "Can you sense anything from him?"

She squints, focusing hard on the task, but then shakes her head. "Nothing. I could feel him before, but now...nothing."

"Great." I heave a sigh of relief. This will buy me time to figure out my next move. I can perform the Truth Spell on him and make him tell me everything he knows so that I can be prepared for the next barrage. I doubt it'll be too long from now, considering I captured a member of their dark legion.

Romana makes a sound behind me. I turn around, and panic takes hold of me when I see the final demon from earlier with a blade poised above her. He's got her in a tight grip so that she can't move.

"Let her go!" I scream, my hands unconsciously worrying my hair.

"Without your Familiar, you'll be vulnerable to a lot more, witch. Consider this payback for my fallen comrades."

He drives the blade between her shoulder blades, and Romana cries out, hurting my ears. With a wicked laugh, the demon fades away. I fly over to Romana, who lies prone in my arm. "I'm so sorry!" I whimper. "Stay with me, Romana! Please!"

Blood is draining from the wound, but instead of crimson, it's an inky black. "No!" I scream. *What the hell did he do to her!?*

Chapter Twenty-Eight

My pulse thunders in my ears as I struggle to forge a coherent thought. Romana is in my arms, oozing black blood, staining my white sweater, bringing her close to the precipice of death. The demon had stabbed her with a knife, but since when can knives do *this*!?

I look down into her topaz eyes, and they're wide with fear and probably immense pain. *Pull yourself together*, I tell myself. *Romana needs you, don't shut down!*

"Okay," I mutter, pacing. "There's a veterinarian's office not too far from the house. Will she make it that long? How long does she have? Oh, God!"

I yank my soiled sweater off and swathe Romana in it, holding it tightly to try to stanch the bleeding. *Common sense. Yes. Breathe. Think. Act, don't react.*

"Demon knives are deadly. Once they break the skin, they release a neoplasm that acidifies and eats you from the inside out,"

Grandma explains solemnly.

"Why can't anything ever be easy for me? Just once! We just need to heal her."

"I don't know of any spells strong enough to help, bubala. She hasn't got long." She reaches out and strokes Romana's pink nose. Romana starts to convulse in my arms. "Oh, no, it's started! Graham, you shouldn't see this! Say your goodbyes and give her to me."

"No!" I hug her more tightly to my chest. She isn't going to die. I'll… I'll figure this out. Give me your keys. I'll run her to the vet—"

"That won't help! This isn't a natural affliction. This is dark, demon magic. No one outside of the magical community can even begin to comprehend the complexities of it."

"I'll take my chances," I say with finality. I hold my hand out expectantly. My grandmother stares at me for several seconds before crossing to her purse on the counter and removing her keys. She tosses them to me. I catch them one-handed.

"Be careful," she cautions.

"Always." I nod my chin toward the captive demon. "Don't let him go anywhere. When all of this is over, I intend to make him pay for his partner's mistake."

"I do not fear you, witch!" the demon says, suddenly conscious again.

"Big mistake. Big. Huge." I go to stand before him. "You and your gang of smelly dumbasses have messed with the wrong witch."

"You've gotten lucky, that's all. We have not sent the Berserker."

"You say luck, I say super powerful witch."

I throw a jacket over my tank top and run out to the garage. I unlock the door, climb into the seat, snap my seatbelt on—with Romana tight to my chest—and turn the key. The engine roars to life, and as soon as the garage door is up, I throw the Buick into reverse and floor it.

I rocket out of the driveway and onto the road. I brake and shift into drive before burning rubber.

This time of day, there aren't many people on the roads. I'd left campus shortly after lunchtime, so I won't have to contend with too much traffic for a while. In my pocket, I feel my phone vibrate and then it starts to ring. I have both hands clamped around the wheel, my white knuckles screaming in protest, so I ignore it. Taking my eyes off the road now would almost certainly get us in an accident. I glance down at the speedometer and see that I'm pushing seventy-five miles per hour. I say a quick prayer that there aren't any cops out right now.

I come up to a stoplight. It's yellow. As I press my foot more firmly against the pedal, the car lurches as gas floods the fuel pump. The light turns red, and I whip the wheel, jerking the car into a right turn. The car going through the intersection swerves to avoid colliding with me. *Sorry!*

I right the car and floor it again. I only have a few blocks to go. "How are you doing, baby?" I ask, glancing down. Romana meows weakly. *Shit! Time is running out.*

I blow another red light and see the vet's office up ahead on the left side. I have no time for traffic etiquette or turn signals. I merge into oncoming traffic and sail into the parking lot. I slam on the brakes as the curb looms, and kill the engine. I whip the seatbelt off and rush out of the car, leaving the door ajar. Right now, the only thing that matters is saving Romana's life. She is the most important thing in my life. If I lose her... I don't know what I'll do.

I push the door open and stagger up to the front counter. The gentleman behind the counter eyes me warily over his stylish glasses. I imagine I must look quite a sight with a blood-stained jacket, all wild-eyed.

"Can I help you?" he asks, his voice small.

"I need to see the vet, like, right now!" I say.

"What's the problem?"

"My cat, Romana... she-she was stabbed or something, and she's lost a lot of blood! She needs help. Now! Right now!"

The man purses his lips. "Dr. Zorn is on lunch right now. This facility is by appointment only unless it's a dire emergency."

"You're not listening to me. This *is* a dire emergency. She's losing blood and was convulsing!"

"I can get you some gauze to help with the bleeding, but—"

"I don't need any goddamn gauze!" I roar. "I need to see the vet. Right. Now."

"As I said, Dr. Zorn—"

"Go fuck yourself." I open the nearest door and lie Romana down on the examination table. I round the corner, but Dr. Zorn isn't there. *Fuck! Where could she be?* I hear water running, and then a door opens, and a chubby middle-aged woman with graying black hair and glasses comes out.

She sees me and halts. "I'm sorry," she says, "did we have an appointment?"

"No! But I need your help! My cat got stabbed by a—something, and she's dying. I need your help."

The woman—Dr. Zorn, presumably, nods. "Is that blood on your shirt?"

"Yes. Her blood is coming out black, and she's seizing."

The door opens, and the guy from the counter comes in. "I'm so sorry, Dr. Zorn, he wouldn't listen—"

"It's fine. We're here to help," she replies. "Come on, Romana, let's get a look at your wound." She uses a soft, calming voice. This woman knows how to handle animals. She lifts Romana up and peels off my sweater swaddle. Romana's golden fur is spoiled with black, as if an ink quill has upended on her. Romana whimpers and looks for me. I try to smile encouragingly despite the dire circumstances.

By this point, I am sweaty and out of breath. The adrenaline that coursed through my veins has set me on overdrive. I'm like a crack addict who's just done a line of premium cocaine.

"What stabbed her?" Dr. Zorn asks, probing the wound site with a rubber-gloved hand.

"I don't know," I lie. I can hardly tell my veterinarian that a demon materialized in my house and stabbed my Familiar with a demon knife that is causing her body to eat itself from the inside out. "I came in from the other room, and the window was broken. She was on the floor, lying there, looking dead."

"The flesh around the wound seems to be receding." She knits her brow in confusion and gets a little bit of the blood onto her glove. She gasps and runs to the washing sink, tearing the glove off and putting her finger under the stream of water. "The blood ate through my glove!"

"What?" I play dumb.

"Something in her blood is burning my skin." Dr. Zorn washes her hands, furiously to get any remainder off her flesh.

"What can you do to help her?" I ask. "Like, dialysis or something?"

"I'm afraid that's impossible. The only thing I can recommend is the humane thing."

My heart drops when I catch her drift. "Put her down?" I guess.

"I've been a vet for almost thirty years, and I have *never* seen anything like this before. She's in excruciating pain. It's like her insides are eating themselves slowly, working their way out. I don't expect her to make it too much longer. She's a thin cat, so there isn't much to her."

"I can't..." I sob. "It's not her time! She's not even that old!"

"I'm sorry I can't do anything more. But if we do it now, at least she won't have to suffer anymore."

Dr. Zorn has a point, but how can this be happening? Romana can't die.

My phone rings again, jarring me. I pull it from my pocket and see that it's Amethyst. "Hello," I mumble.

"Where the hell did you go? You didn't meet me at the clock tower!" she exclaims.

"Something came up."

"Are you okay? You sound upset."

"It's Romana. She's dying."

"What!?"

"The vet can't heal what's wrong with her. She says it's best to just euthanize her now. She won't make it to tomorrow."

"What about Malachi?"

"What about Malachi?" I shoot back.

"He's a healing Druid, or whatever. He can probably help you."

I'd forgotten all about her drug dealer friend in the woods. He had been a little... much for me, but cool enough. I don't know anything about Druids, but he had said that he practiced healing magic. Perhaps he could help me out...

"I have to let you go," I say. "Talk later."

I hang up and gather Romana up into my arms. "Where are you going?" Dr. Zorn asks.

"I can't do it," I tell her. "She needs to be at home, where she feels safe. Thanks for your help, I really appreciate it."

Without another word, I hurry back out to Grandma's car.

****

The short drive to the woods behind the high school seems to take forever. Romana's breathing is growing shallower, I can feel it against my chest. I haven't got long to save her.

I park at the edge of the woods and run. Winter has finally hit properly, and it's around sixteen degrees. I'd been in such a hurry when I left the house that I hadn't thought to grab a decent coat. I'm risking hyperthermia to save Romana, but it's worth it.

The last time I was in these woods, it had been Halloween. Now, snow covered the ground, making it all look the same. I hadn't paid attention last time, so I have no idea where I'm going, but still, I have to try.

I'm glad that I went with my boots today. They're keeping the snow off of my feet and providing a little bit of warmth to my already cold feet. I stumble as I catch my feet on fallen logs and branches that are cleverly disguised under the blanket of white snow. Thankfully, I manage to keep my balance.

I seem to wander eternally, growing colder by the second. I would try the teleportation spell, but I don't trust myself to focus well enough. I'm afraid that Romana and I would end up scattered into atoms and never coalesce again.

Looking skyward, I notice pink smoke rising from up ahead. It carries the scent of cinnamon and chocolate. *That has to be it!* A fresh batch of adrenaline kicks in and I run, the branches biting at my face and hands, but I don't care! I have to save Romana!

I fight through the army of trees and come out in the clearing. There, before me, is Malachi's log cabin. I cry out in relief and climb the steps to the porch. I bang on the door, my frozen hands barely feeling it. I knock again and again, with more urgency than I ever could have imagined myself mustering.

Malachi opens the door, wearing a hot pink hoodie and blue jeans. He's even taller than I remember. He registers me and then grins. "I knew you'd be back," he says.

"I need help," I interject. I hold Romana out toward him. "She was stabbed by a demon blade. It's been almost an hour. I don't know how much longer she'll last."

"How did your Familiar get stabbed by a demon blade!?" he asks

"The demon just appeared in my house."

"You haven't cast a protection spell around your house? *Tsk.*" He shakes his head disappointingly. "Still so much to learn, young one."

All day, I've tried my hardest to keep my temper from boiling over, but his patronizing tone tips me over the edge. The Beverly within me comes out. "Listen, princess," I seethe, "I am asking you for help in saving my cat. I'm not here to be condescended to, all right? You said you're a healing Druid, I'm in need of your healing powers; nothing else."

He takes a step back as if affronted, his hand to his chest. "Jeez, bitch, relax. I was just kidding."

"Not the time."

He opens the door wider and stands aside to let me in. "Put her on the table," he says.

I duck inside and am wholly overwhelmed by the scent of the chocolate and cinnamon that I smelled earlier. I look around at all of the eclectic décor. The kitchen—straight ahead—looks state of the art. Steel shines from the immaculate equipment and countertops. To my right, a fire burns fiercely in a stone fireplace. I feel sweat trickle down my back. To my left, there's a flat-screen TV snug against the wall, an Xbox attached. The area is closed in by plush leather sofas. I can see a hallway off from that room, guarded by an old suit of armor, aged with patina.

I lie Romana down on the nearest table. "You have a nice place," I say.

"Yeah, Tyler did a great job building the place. He's such a strong, manly man. It really turns me on," Malachi says, coming around to go into the kitchen.

"It smells like you're cooking dessert or something."

"I'm a pastry chef," he announces, grabbing herbs and other Druidic accoutrements. He comes back, his arms heaping with his wares.

"What can I do to help?" I ask, inactivity making me restless. I rub Romana's back.

"I need you to stay out of my way. This is going to get very intense, and I need to concentrate. If Tyler was here, I'd have him take you outside."

"Where is he?" I've heard a lot about his boyfriend, but I have yet to meet him.

"He's at work." *Right. Duh.*

I lean in and kiss the top of Romana's soft head. "Be brave now, baby. Malachi is going to make you better. I won't let this happen again, I promise." I force myself to step away, and I take a seat across the room, where I can see and hear everything.

Malachi goes past me and down the hall that I assume leads to the bedroom. He's gone a few moments before he comes back carrying a small vial. "This is rain water that has sat under a full cycle of the moon," he explains. "I've blessed it. It will help with the rituals."

"Whatever you have to do," I assure him, worrying my bottom lip with my teeth.

He pours the vial of water into a pan and places it on the stove. Within moments it's boiling. He opens a baggie and adds the contents to the boiling water. "Goldenseal."

After stirring until it looks sufficient, Malachi pours the concoction into a wooden bowl. He takes his long wooden spoon and drizzles a bit of the water onto Romana's wound. I wince at the thought of boiling hot water being poured on me, let alone her.

Malachi continues to add water to the wound, then, closing his eyes, he puts his hands upon her and starts to chant. The words are ancient, primal. I pick up a few words—Welsh—but not enough to string together. My knowledge of the Welsh language is still very basic; I stopped doing my online lessons when we moved.

The words hang heavily in the air as he continues to chant, growing louder with each refrain. *I never knew that Druidism was so involved!* The healing spell seems to go on forever, though the truth is that I'm more focused on an actual result than anything else. *Please let this work*, I pray.

I lose myself in prayer, drawing comfort from the familiar act. I've never been extremely religious, but I do believe in the power of prayer. As I've evolved in my study of witchcraft, I've come to realize that prayer and spellcasting aren't dissimilar. However, with spellcasting, you're more involved in the process.

After a while, I start to notice that Malachi's chanting has ceased. I finish my prayer and open my eyes. He's standing before me, Romana limp in his arms. *Oh, no! Is she dead?*

My eyes grow watery, and I stand, my legs quivering. "Is she...?" I choke out.

"She's asleep," he says softly. "The spell was a success."

"Oh, thank you!" I hug him, mindful not to squish Romana.

"She has a long road ahead of her, though. I was able to drain her of the demonic poison, but there was significant damage to her internal organs. The water and herbs I used should help regenerate the tissues within, but it'll take time. You need to keep her home and as sedentary as possible."

"I will," I promise, fighting back a joyous giggle. *She's going to be okay!* I take her sleeping form from his arms.

"Go home now, we all need to rest. That ritual took a lot out of me."

"I'm sorry." I hand him whatever is in my wallet, surely not enough for the enormous favor he has just done for me.

"It's fine. It's what I do." He takes the money and pockets it, his eyes looking bloodshot and heavy lidded.

I let myself out and run as fast as I can without jarring Romana too much. I follow my footprints in the snow back to the car. I'm grateful that it only takes a matter of minutes to warm up because, after the warmth of Malachi's cabin, I'm once again shivering uncontrollably.

I turn the key and crank the heat up. On the passenger seat, Romana lies, curled up. Instinctively, I reach out and pet her soft fur. She's back to her normal color; apparently, the spell cleansed her of the tar-like substance all together. Good. The last thing I want to do now is try to bathe her. I put the car into drive and head home.

****

When I come in the front door, Grandma is waiting for me, pale as a ghost. "How is she?" she asks, pacing.

"She's okay," I reply. "I had to enlist help from a Druid, but I got the job done."

"A Druid? How exotic!"

"Yeah." I hand Romana to her. "Will you take her upstairs? I need to attend to our demonic friend."

Grandma frowns, but nods and ascends the stairs. I wait until she's on the second floor before I go into the kitchen, break the salt circle, and yank the demon to his feet. Wordlessly, I drag him out into the garage and then fling him onto the cold cement. His flesh makes a wet *slap!* when it connects.

I straddle him, gritting my teeth. "You guys made a big mistake coming after my cat," I say. "You want to come for me? Sure. No problem. But you leave her out of it."

"She is your weakness," he croaks from his mouthless face.

"Wrong thing to say!" I snatch the blade from his belt and drive it through his throat until I hear the *shrink!* of the blade hitting the cement. I twist my wrist, making him writhe in agony. "Rot in Hell, fucker."

I wrench the blade free and walk away as his body erupts into multi-hued flames.

Chapter Twenty-Nine

No matter how relentlessly winter rages on, it inevitably ceases its frosty barrage. The snow stops falling, the ice melts, and, like a Phoenix rising from the ashes, the Earth begins its rebirth, new life from the remains of the deceased. Flowers begin to bloom, the grass grows, bright green with vitality and perseverance; everything seems inconsequential compared to the wonder of spring.

It was rough going with Romana at first, as her insides literally regenerated themselves. For the first few weeks, she barely ate or drank; all she wanted to do was lie on the bed and sleep. She did have a few accidents, but I couldn't be mad about it. Movement must have been excruciating for her. But, as spring fell upon us and life bloomed anew outside, so did Romana's good health. By mid-April, she was herself again. In the interim, I had performed a protection spell on her to keep her safe, as well as one around the house that would not let anyone who wished us harm to cross the threshold.

Erasmus was overjoyed when I'd called him that day. He was proud of how far I'd come in my self-defense lessons, and of my quick thinking. His approval means the world to me, though I won't admit it. When I was younger, I wanted approval from my dad and, yes, even from Don. I rarely got it. Erasmus' love is starting to fill that void for me, but not in a creepy way. I don't think of him as a father or anything.

Amethyst was the only one I could tell that I'd killed the demon, bent on revenge. I knew she wouldn't judge me or worry that I'd begun to succumb to darkness; she's a cat person and would gladly kill to protect her fur babies.

After the attack that wintery day in mid-January, things once again fell quiet on the demon front, which made me nervous. Each new attack had been more intense than the last one. *How long before I got completely overwhelmed and killed, or dragged to the Underworld? Which option was worse?* I poured my anxiety into studying the Craft. I took the black salt and poured it around the house, before taking a *besom*—a broom made of dried twigs tied to a stick—and swept the negative energies from the house. So far the salt has held up, but I can't help feel like it's only a matter of time.

Since my mom moved out, we have maintained careful contact. As long as neither of us baits the other, we do well. We're working on rebuilding our relationship. Of course, she doesn't want to hear anything about Erasmus or my witchcraft. I've spent the night at her new place a few times—it's not bad: a modest two-bedroom apartment. Willow's Crest doesn't have a ghetto, so there really aren't any unsafe neighborhoods. On the nights she has to work, she drops Brent off with us, which must just kill her pride. I try to go easier on her.

My dad called a few times, and I answered only because I knew it was expected, not because I really wanted to talk with him. Our conversations are always odd. All he's ever wanted to do is whine about how he's still paying child support. He once told me that the reason Mom had me start kindergarten a year later than normal was because she wanted to get child support from him for an extra year. Not true at all. I was a hyperactive child. I wouldn't sit still to color or read, and my mother felt it best to give me another year to calm down.

I haven't told my dad about Erasmus. I don't know how to. I don't know if he'll accept it or disown me. I remember, one summer I visited him when he was living with my Aunt Rita at her farmhouse, my cousin Ariana thought it would be fun to put lipstick and eyeshadow on me. I don't mind a laugh, so I allowed it. When he saw it, dear old Dad—drunk—got mean and had me in tears. I ended up calling Mom to come get me. Dad and I will never be close, I don't see how we possibly could. He's never been able to commit to being a father more than on a few occasions a year. He might as well be Santa Claus.

Ariana and I were never close when we were younger because I was very mean to her as a toddler. I'd get mad and pull her hair. Our poor Grandma… maybe that's part of the reason she had a heart attack and died so young. After that, Aunt Rita moved them to Canada; they didn't move back to Michigan until the early 2000s. When we met again as preteens, Ariana and I bonded over a shared love of video games, *Pokémon*, and other nerdy things. I haven't seen her in a few years, but we stay in touch via text and the occasional letter. *I should call her...*

The Sping semester is winding down, now—only a month left! Everyone has shifted their primary focus to the big party at one of the frat houses. I don't really want to go, but Erasmus thought it would be a fun time. He said that regrets that he wasn't in my life in high school, because he couldn't go to the prom with me, so he wants to make this like a prom for us. He even wants up to dress up to the nines.

I never went to any of my school dances back home, with the exception of a juvenile one back in first or second grade, when we lived in Port Huron. I'm not a dancer, and I'm not an ace socializer, either. Plus, there's the issue of Erasmus. I'm proud to be dating him, but I don't exactly want to blast our relationship for the whole campus to see. I'm not ashamed of being gay, but, once again, I don't want people to label me in their minds. And yet, a part of me does want to enjoy a college party with my hot, undead boyfriend, like any other college student.

****

I've been so focused on helping Romana with her recovery that I haven't attempted to try the sun protection spell again, but I think today is the day. My afternoon class got cancelled, apparently the professor was down in bed with a nasty flu. It's beautiful outside, with a gentle breeze, and the sun shining brightly in the cerulean sky. The last time that I was at Erasmus' house, I pocketed his ring. I don't want to be under so much pressure this time around. Besides forgetting an offering to the gods, I attribute rushing as part of the spell's failure last time.

Luckily for me, my Grandma is an avid wine fan. She's not an alcoholic or anything—I've only ever seen her have a half glass—but she always has a bottle or two at hand. Her favorites are Pink Moscato and White Zinfandel.

I walk into the kitchen, the air rich with the smell of Grandma's cooking. I find her at the stove, pulling loaves of Challah from the oven. She hears me and turns, smiling. "There you are, bubala."

"Here I am." I clap my outer thighs. I don't want to just help myself to her wine and have her think that I'm imbibing. True, I am becoming less of a goody-two-shoes, but I also don't want to piss off Grandma; she's a scary lady when she's mad.

"I'm making Challah, zucchini, and banana bread for Temple," she announces. Before living here, I didn't even know that you could make bread out of bananas and zucchini. I am clueless when it comes to things in the kitchen.

"Smells good."

"I made a loaf of banana bread for us, too. You like banana bread, right?"

"I've never had it."

She balks. "Well, when it cools down, try a little bit. I think you'll like it."

"Okay." I take a shaky breath as I try to muster up the courage to ask her what I want to ask her. I don't think about what it is I want to ask her, because I know that she'll just read my mind and beat me to the punch. I've been working on barricading my mind from telepathy.

She regards me again, squinting her eyes quizzically. "Is everything all right?" she asks, "You're as nervous as a kurveh in Temple."

I laugh. *God, I love Grandma's classic colloquialisms.* "Everything is fine, I just… have something to ask you."

"Okay." She turns to face me, folding her arms over her bosom. "I'm all ears, as you kids say."

"Okay." I fidget, my mouth dry. "Remember how I wanted to do that spell for Erasmus? The one to protect him from the sun's rays?"

"Of course."

"Well, I tried it a few months ago, and it didn't work."

"Why not?"

"I didn't know this at the time, but apparently, when performing a spell that invokes specific deities, you're supposed to provide an offering for the gods."

"Well, done! You're smarter than you give yourself credit for."

"I had help."

"Oh?"

"Lilja offered to mentor me, and said you asked her to do it. She says it's an honor to mentor a witch of my caliber, but I turned her down.

My grandmother sucks her tooth. "You've gotten so good at keeping secrets from me. I didn't know you knew, you haven't said anything."

"I just don't want to disappoint you. I'm sorry," I say. "Are you mad?"

"No, bubala. I just want us to be able to be open and honest with each other. I really think that you should travel this journey on your own as much as possible, but it's your choice. She's one of the most talented witches I know, and she could help you master the Craft."

"Have you known she's a witch the whole time?"

"Of course. We've been friends for decades. We once went to Stonehenge and tapped into the ley lines to try to regenerate the ozone layer."

"I thought you knew her from nursing school or something. "

"No, Witch school."

"There's a Witch school?" I exclaim. "Why haven't you told me?"

"There *was* a Witch school," she frowns. "Unfortunately, there was a great battle there, and it was destroyed. Our numbers were decimated. That's part of the reason there are so few of our kind left. I survived. Lilja survived, a few others did, too. But the deaths…" Her face grew dark as she recalled the scene in her mind. "So much death and destruction. Friends, sisters. I lost two sisters there. My brothers turned to the dark side and lost their lives, too. Lilja, the poor thing, she had to kill her own sister. It devastated her."

A tear works itself out of her eyes, leaking down her alabaster cheek. "I'm glad that Lilja is having an impact on you. Let's invite her to dinner soon. I'd like to have a witch night, just us girls."

"Sure." Lilja hadn't given any indication that she had family, but surely she must. *I guess this is another piece to the puzzle.* I feel myself forgiving her a little for drugging me; if she survived such a disastrous event, she had proven her loyalty.

"Anyway," she sniffles, "what did you want to ask me?"

"The spell requires an offering to the gods. Lilja suggested wine. I was wondering if you would be willing to let me take a little—for spell purposes only!"

Grandma smiles. "Of course, dear. You're of legal age, I don't care" She opens the fridge and takes out a wine bottle. She crosses to the cupboard and takes out a gold chalice. She pours a generous portion of wine into it and hands the chalice to me. "The chalice is spelled to keep the wine from spilling."

"Really?" I hold the chalice upside down, and miraculously, the white wine within it unswayed. *Wow!*

"I thought you'd like that."

"I was also wondering if I could borrow your car? I promise I won't drink and drive."

"I trust you." She smiles warmly, her eyes gleaming. "Now go! You've put this off long enough."

"Right. Thanks!"

I take the chalice and head out to the front porch. The sun is perfectly placed that it's been charging the ring the whole time. I'd cleansed it beforehand, so this can go as smoothly as possible. I set the circle of gold candles around the porch, placing the ring dead in the center and leaving enough room for me to maneuver. I sit cross-legged behind the ring and put the chalice of wine in front of it, so that the ring is between us. I take my cigarette lighter out of my pocket and light the candles. I make a mental note to learn how to make fire from my finger, take a deep breath, and close my eyes. I conjure up the words to the spell, recalling them from my obsessive cramming session last night and this morning.

Atum, Horus, Sekhmet,

Ra and Sopdu,

Hear my plea.

I call upon thee

To enchant this ring

To protect Erasmus from the sun

As long as he wears it.

Nevermore shall the sun harm him

So mote it be.

The air is heavy with energies again, but this time they're more powerful than before. I open my right eye and gasp as the chalice is lifted by invisible hands into the air. I lean back so that I can see as the wine within drains itself. *It's working!* The chalice floats back down to the pavement, and then I cover my eyes as the silver band glows a red hot gold, as if the sun itself were burning within it.

I wait until the brightness ceases and then uncover my eyes. The ring lay on the porch, still glowing faintly. *It worked!* I'm fairly certain, almost positive that it worked. "Thanks," I say to the deities. I'm assuming They are the ones who consumed the wine.

Bursting with excitement, I palm the ring and hurry back inside the house, candles, and chalice threatening to topple out of my arms. I put the candles back in the buffet in the dining room where we keep them, before taking the chalice back to the kitchen to be washed.

Grandma is waiting for me. "Well, did it work?" she entreats, nibbling on some yogurt.

"I think so! The chalice lifted into the air and emptied itself. Then the ring glowed brightly, it almost blinded me!"

"Sounds like a success to me!" She hugs me tightly. "You won't know for sure until you try it out!" She hands me the keys to her car. "Please be safe and have the car back by morning."

I give her a quick kiss on the cheek and then race out to the car.

****

I'm bouncing with energy as I make the drive to the posh side of town. I sing along to Jennifer Hudson—out of tune, off-key, and not caring! *This is it! I can feel it in my veins! I am going to make Erasmus so, so happy!*

I pull into his driveway and barely shut the engine off before I'm out and pounding the pavement as I hurry up to his door. I unlock the door with the spare key hidden in the top of the porch light and shut the door behind myself. It's two o'clock in the afternoon, so Erasmus is bound to still be asleep. *Time to get up!*

I find him in the bedroom, his torso naked. The blanket lies just below his stomach. A few black curly hairs peak out from under the blanket, enticing me.

I crawl across the bed and hold myself up above him, kissing his soft, cold cheek. He's not eaten in a while; otherwise, he wouldn't be so cold. It doesn't matter. I'd rather not kiss him and taste the iron tang of blood.

He stirs, slowly at first, and then he opens his eyes. "Graham?" His voice is heavy, raspy with sleep. He looks so adorable with his hair a mangled mess from sleeping.

"Hey," I say softly, grinning.

"What're you doing here?" He sits up, the blankets falling away from him, revealing his naked body. A wave of delicious lust shoots through me, but I quell it. *There will be time for that later. Now, it's time to give him a little something to show how much I love and appreciate him.*

"I have a surprise for you," I reply, sliding the ring onto his right ring finger.

"Is that where that went? I've been looking for it."

"I know."

"So, what's the surprise?" he sniffles. "Wait, is it time? Are you ready to let me—"

"Maybe later," I interrupt quickly, "but right now, we have to go outside." If he's disappointed, he once again hides it well.

"What time is it?"

"A little after two."

"Unless the sun is suddenly gone, you know I can't go out there."

"But you *can!*" I exclaim.

"What do you mean?" He knits his brow. "What did you do?"

I might as well tell him the truth at this point. "I enchanted your ring. You're safe from the sun now."

"Are you sure?"

"98%. Please, at least try. If it doesn't work, I promise I'll drop it, I just really want you to be able to enjoy the sun again."

He sighs. "If I get burned, you owe me."

"Consider your dick sucked." I quirk a suggestive eyebrow and waggle it.

"You could just do that anyway, it's part of being a good boyfriend."

"I will, later. But now? It's time to try this out!"

I pull him to his feet, and after he throws on boxers, we go down the hall to the French doors leading out to the cobblestoned patio. I part the curtains, and he instinctively shrinks back in fear. "I don't know about this," he says warily.

"Please try," I implore him, "for me."

He looks into my eyes and sees the desperation there. His hand touches my cheek and strokes it lovingly. "Even if this doesn't work, I want you to know that even *attempting* this is the nicest thing that anyone has ever done for me."

"It's my pleasure," I assure him.

He smiles at me and then, setting his chin, determinedly, he steps into the sunlight.

Chapter Thirty

As Erasmus takes his first steps out of the house, and into the bright sunshine, I hold my breath, my stomach twisting into sailor's knots. *What if I was wrong? What if the spell didn't work and he gets incinerated, reduced to ash? I don't want him to die!* I certainly don't want him to die trying to prove his love for me, either. I want him around for a long time.

He clears the house, and his pasty white skin is bathed in the golden glow from the sun. His naked torso is illuminated, making itself look even more appealing... and nothing happens. No smoke, no searing flesh, no screaming in misery, nothing. Regular old nothing.

He turns to look at me, his eyes wide in amazement. "You did it..." His voice is barely more than a whisper. "You really did it!"

"I guess so," I say, beaming. *It worked! It really worked!* Erasmus rushes to me, engulfs me in his arms, and lifts me, swinging me around excitedly. I laugh at the sheer joy of it all. I have never seen him look so happy before. I mean, he's hardly your stereotypical brooding vampire, but he's no poster child of exuberance, either.

"Let's go for a walk!" He sets me down, grabbing my hand firmly in his chilly one.

"You might want to put some clothes on first," I point out. He was naked—except for the tight black boxers accentuating his bulge and the tiny mounds of his butt cheeks.

Erasmus looked down and sighed. "Right, I should've thought of that. I'll be right back!"

"I'll be here."

He races into the house, and I sit down on the patio steps. I pull my pack of cigarettes from my jacket pocket and light one, inhaling deeply. *I cannot believe all the years I spent lecturing my mother and father about how they needed to quit smoking. Smoking is amazing! Thoughts of cancer, COPD, and emphysema are inconsequential; I'm twenty-one. Twenty-one-year-olds do not get either of those things from smoking. By the time I've caused enough damage to my lungs and body to worry about those things, they'll have found a cure, and it won't matter anyway. Plus, I'm an uber-powerful witch. I can probably just spell the cancer away.*

As I exhale the heavy smoke, I feel the pent-up tension of the last hour or so flee my body. They say that smoking doesn't calm you down, that it actually amps you up. Your brain just *thinks* that it calms you down, but I disagree. I think that may be true of some people, but everyone is different, and I am the epitome of different. It doesn't help that my mom smoked throughout her pregnancy with me, so I have an innate tobacco susceptibility ingrained in my DNA. Come to think of it, that's just another sign that she loves Brent more than me. She smoked while pregnant with me, but when she found out that she was pregnant with him, she quit. She didn't start smoking again until he was about two and a half, and we discovered he was autistic.

Erasmus comes back out and snatches the cigarette from my fingers. I've always been grossed out at the idea of sharing anything that touches my mouth with someone else, but I don't mind that we share cigarettes. I'm not sure how he can smoke though, given that he doesn't breathe. Perhaps, over the years, he's perfected the art of mimicking breathing so he'd blend in better with humans.

"So, where did you want to walk?" I inquire, smiling at him. Seeing a vampire out amongst the rest of us at high noon is a wondrous sight. Knowing how happy it has made him makes me feel accomplished inside. I might be a disaster when it comes to my family and friends, but at least I can make *someone* happy.

"Everywhere!" he exclaims. "I can *finally* do all the normal boyfriend things with you that mortals get to do with their partners."

"Like?" I prompt as we start walking through his backyard. His property is at the edge of town, but it leads directly to the park if you have the patience to walk along the beach long enough. Normally, I wouldn't have the patience, but today,

I would walk anywhere with Erasmus just to see the sheer joy on his face. It feels good to be able to do something relatively normal with him. My life has been so hectic this year, so any normality is a Godsend.

"Like... walking in the park during the day. No more hiding, no more living like a nocturnal recluse. I can help keep an eye on you—"

"Wait." I hold up a hand and stop walking.

"What is it?" He stops and turns to look at me, brow knit in confusion and worry.

"I didn't do this spell so you could follow me around and play bodyguard. I still haven't changed my mind on that. I don't need your protection, Erasmus. I told you how well I disposed of those demons in the bathroom. Your lessons have been helpful, thank you very much, but I need a boyfriend, not a bodyguard."

"Graham," he sighs. "You know I just want to keep you safe."

"I know that, and I love you for it, but I am not some dainty damsel in distress. I've learned how to handle this myself, so I got this. I did the spell so you wouldn't feel trapped anymore. Now, you're free to live a life of your own. One that includes me, obviously, but not one that is one hundred percent dedicated to me."

Erasmus pulls on his cigarette, letting the smoke build up inside before he exhales it into a puffy cloud. "I get where you're coming from; I really do. This spell, is the nicest thing that anyone has ever done for me. You must love me very much in order to attempt it."

"You know I do," I whisper. "I love you like crazy, but I'm also independent. My life doesn't revolve around you, and yours shouldn't revolve around me."

"I will never forgive myself if something bad happens to you," he extols.

"Some things are out of your control." I reach out and stroke his cool cheek.

"Like you?" he jokes.

"Definitely me."

We walk in silence for a bit, the sand giving way to dirt and grass. Eventually, we cross through the woods and into the beautiful park. I've never been before, but I've heard it is absolutely stunning. As we come out of the trees, the first thing I see is a little wooden bridge overlooking a duck pond. In it, gorgeous white swans glide effortlessly on the water, looking majestic.

"I've never seen a swan before in person," I confess, keeping my voice down so I won't scare them off.

"They're beautiful creatures," Erasmus agrees. "But not as beautiful as you are."

I roll my eyes with pretend frustration and lead him onto the bridge. I stop halfway across and lean over the stylish metal railing. Underneath us, the swan's peck at bits of bread passersby threw down to them. There are a few brown and green ducks floating nearby, too. *Who knew that nature could be so stunning?*

"I have lived in Willows Crest for ages," Erasmus says, "but I've never been able to see this place during the day. It's not as breathtaking at night."

"It's almost like you were waiting for me."

"I was."

I turn and look into his brown eyes, the eyes of this man I have come to love very, very much. A year ago, I never would've thought I would be so happy right now, so in love. I had always suspected that love and happiness would be denied my whole life, that love would never grace me with its spellbinding intensity. I didn't know it would completely unravel me before assembling me again into a wholly different person, forever changed. *Boy, was I wrong.* The love that was in store for me was greater than I had ever dared to imagine, in my wildest dreams.

I have always been afraid that if I did find someone who could put up with me, they'd be like my dad or Don, oppressive, controlling, dictatorial, soul-crushing. I have never seen my mother happy. I didn't want that life for myself, so I erected a wall around myself to keep even the closest of friends away from my inner sanctum, safe from hurt. The wall is still there, but, somehow, against all the odds, Erasmus has been able to work his way inside. Now, I can't imagine my life without him, and I don't want to. And yet... my inner doubts still whisper in my ear, telling me not to get too accustomed to it. They caution me not to let myself fall too deeply, because, after all, nothing lasts forever. How long will it be before this perfect daydream ends, only to be replaced with a devastating nightmare?

"Why do you love me?" I blurt, keeping my gaze on Erasmus' dark eyes.

"What?" he sputters, frowning.

"I'm twenty-one, Erasmus. You're... I don't even *know* how old. How can you tolerate me? I must seem so immature to you."

"Hey," he grabs my shoulders and turns me to face him. "You know that I love you."

"I know you do," I agree, "but what I don't understand is *why*?"

"You want to know why?" he challenges.

"Give me your worst."

"I love you because you're kind and caring, and despite the chip on your shoulder, you have the biggest heart of anyone I have ever met. You've been through a lot of shit in your life, yet you still persevere. No matter what life throws at you, you roll with it. You're adaptable. You're strong and independent yet still warm and open. I mean, who else would have even *attempted* to do a spell to let me be able to walk in the sun? Your innocence is matched with fierce loyalty and devotion. You're witty and artistic.

"You have the cutest laugh I've ever heard. I love the way your cheeks get red when you're angry, the way your eyes sparkle with childish delight when you're happy; the way you crinkle your eyes, and the dimples that result from those smiles. I love how you're willing to stand up for what's right, and you don't back down once you've set your mind to something. I love that Romana is your best friend. I've always thought you can tell a lot about a person by how they treat animals. You revere her as if she were a real person; you'd die for her."

"Absolutely."

"There are so many wonderful things to love about you. Graham, I just wish that you could see them for yourself so you wouldn't have to ever doubt my or anyone else's affection. If you let me, I will spend my life making you see those things."

"But you can't," I point out. "Are you forgetting about the other part of being a vampire? You'll live forever. I'll die and leave you behind, and I don't want to do that. I don't want to ever hurt you like that."

"We can figure that out. I'm sure there's a spell or something."

"I don't want to be immortal," I blurt. "Nothing should live forever."

"Who says that you'll outlive me? I have enemies, too. I could be gone long before you."

"Exactly! And then, I'd be devastated."

"Love isn't perfect. It has many advantages, but it also has its downsides. Remember that some things are worth enduring a broken heart."

I know he's right, but the thought of losing him makes my breath hitch. I don't know what would happen if he were taken from me. I'd probably go all Dark Willow and try to destroy the world. *Nah, I'm not that evil.*

"Are you… are you looking for a way out of this?" he asks, trying to keep the hurt from his face and voice.

"No!" I gasp, tears welling. "No! I'm not looking for a way out. I'm just… I'm trying to understand you, to understand this. Why do vampires always fall in love with mortals? It's a tried and true cliché."

"I can't vouch for those fictional vampires," he broaches, "but I love you for one reason and one reason only."

"And what's that?"

"Because you, Graham Norris, are incredible."

"Okay," I swat at his chest playfully, "now you're just pulling my leg."

"Nope, you are. Just because you refuse to see it doesn't make it any less true."

I nod and clear my throat. "I've really been thinking about what you said, about us going to that frat party together."

"Yes…?" He gives me his full attention.

"I want to go. With you. I want us to go together." *Why am I stammering like an idiot?*

Erasmus is my boyfriend, I shouldn't be having anxiety over this!

"You're ready for us to be out in the open? A real couple?"

"I think so, yeah."

"You think so?"

"I am," I correct myself, internally rolling my eyes.

"Are you sure?"

"I've never been more sure of anything in my life."

He nods. "Okay, then. Yes, I will be your date."

I jump up and down excitedly and hug him. "You're going to look so hot in a black tux."

"I was actually thinking of maybe red," he muses.

"Red's great, too. You'd look *killer* in red."

"When is it again?"

"Next weekend." I shoot him my most adorable, most pleading smile.

"*Next weekend? I was going to go on a blood run out of town...*"

"I know. I should have let you know sooner. I was just afraid."

"What were you afraid of?"

I sigh. "I'm afraid that I'm going to get too attached and then right when I get comfortable, you'll pull the rug out from underneath my feet."

"Graham, that is not going to happen, I promise."

"I'm so tired of everyone leaving me. I've never had someone here to stay before."

"I'm not going anywhere." His brown eyes stare deeply into mine. "I know you think nothing lasts forever, but I'm more optimistic. I know that we'll work through whatever bullshit we face."

"Okay." I don't know what else to say, but his answer is enough to calm my anxiety a little.

We start walking again, arm in arm. For the first time, I don't care that people look at us and know unequivocally that we are lovers, not brothers or friends. *Why did I spend so much time, waste so much time, caring what everyone else thinks?*

We walk for a long time, enjoying each other's company and the beauty of our surroundings. I don't know how long we walk, but I notice that by the time we are back in Erasmus' yard, the sky is no longer blue but rather a pinkish purple as the sun begins to set.

We go into the house. *I really should be getting home. I have class tomorrow morning, and Grandma is probably wondering where I am, but I don't want to go.* I want tonight to be the best of my life. I've crossed so many bridges with Erasmus. Now there's one more that we need to cross.

I lean against the wall, looking at him through my thick lashes. He picks up my vibe and crosses to me, blocking my exit. He lifts my arms and pins them to the wall. I shiver with lust and delight as he lowers his mouth to the sensitive skin of my neck. He brushes his sharp canine against the flesh, making me quiver with excitement.

"I want you," I gasp, rolling my head back as he teases my neck with his soft pale lips.

"I want you, too," he says. I reach back and find the front of his jeans, moving my hand along his penis within the skinny jeans.

"Fuck me," I rasp.

He stops and turns me around so that we're eye to eye. "Are you sure?" he asks patiently.

"I'm sure. Make me yours."

Erasmus doesn't need to be told twice. We rush back to the house, stopping for Erasmus to feed so he can function. After he brushes his teeth, we're in his room, on his bed. Our clothes are off, a tangled mess on the floor. We've done this so many times, but tonight we're going to do something that we've only ever attempted before, and only once.

I lie back against the pillows, and Erasmus moves so that he's kneeling before me. Gently, he lifts my legs onto his shoulders, exposing my most sacred, private part. He lowers himself down and kisses me on the lips and neck, making me moan. He kisses me for what seems like forever, and I lie there, tangled with him, lapping up his affection like a kitten laps up milk.

When it happens, there is pain and an awkward feeling like I need to go to the bathroom, but I breathe through it, putting my hand on Erasmus' lower back to encourage him to keep on. He watches me intently the whole time, making sure that I'm comfortable and not in too much pain.

The pain starts to blend with pleasure in an intense all-encompassing spiral, and I feel myself as an extension of Erasmus. We truly are one, in a way that we've never been before. It's overwhelming, but it's amazingly romantic and wonderful, too.

We finish at the same time, crying out in passion as we reach ecstasy together.

Erasmus kisses me deeply, his hair in his eyes. "Was that okay?" he asks, his lips swollen from our arduous making out.

"It was perfect," I pant, my heart drumming away in my chest.

Erasmus buries his head in the side of my neck, and I enfold him in my arms. Before long, we're both unconscious.

Gabriel Mero

Chapter Thirty-One

I sleep more peacefully than I ever could have imagined. I don't dream. There are no nightmares. Just peace. I've spent the night with Erasmus before, tangled up in each other's arms, but this is different. My last wall is down. I have completely let him inside, and all that fear and tension is gone. He loves me, and I love him; that's all there is to it. There's no drama or contention. It's simple.

When I awake, I feel more rested than I have ever felt before in my life. It's refreshing. I stir, and am immediately aware of Erasmus' wiry arms draped around me, as if shielding me from the evils and cruelties of the world. I need to use the bathroom, but I don't want to move and wake him or lose his touch.

It's hard to tell what time it is because the room is shrouded in perfect darkness. If I'm late for class, I really don't care. I haven't missed a day yet this year, so one won't kill me. However, I regret not calling my grandmother and letting her know I was staying the night here. She's probably apoplectic, taping up 'Missing' posters.

The urge to pee gets too great, and I'm forced to wiggle out from under Erasmus' grip. I move slowly, trying not to disturb his peaceful slumber. I assume he's sleeping. In all the time I've known him, I have never thought to ask about a vampire's sleeping habits. Do they sleep during the day, or do they simply go into a pseudo hibernation to keep them from being exposed to the deathly sunlight? I know so much about Erasmus, yet there are still so many unanswered questions.

When I have fully extricated myself, I use my hands to feel for the wall. It's so dark in the room that I can't make anything out. I take small, tentative steps, hoping I don't stub a toe or bump my shin into anything. *That shit hurts!* There is an en suite bathroom in the bedroom, but I want privacy and a few moments to myself, so I opt to use the guest bathroom instead.

My fingers eventually brush what I think is the wall, and I follow it until I feel the door. I reach down for the knob and slip out.

The guest bathroom is a few doors down the hallway. It's the one I usually use when I'm here since it's conveniently located off of the living room and kitchen, in the very center of the house. Normally, I'm incredibly germophobic when it comes to using other people's bathrooms, but I know that Erasmus does not need them. I know it's clean; not that I'd have a problem using my boyfriend's toilet, especially after what we did last night.

I quickly relieve myself and then remove my contacts, rinsing them of the eye gunk. I wasn't actually planning on sleeping here last night, so I hadn't been able to switch to my glasses.

Erasmus has a toothbrush and my favorite whitening mouthwash readily available for me. He likes the idea of me coming and staying the night with him. Part of me suspects that he wants to ask me to move in, but he's afraid that my stubborn, independent streak will rear its ugly head, and his feelings will get crushed. To be perfectly honest, he's probably right. I don't think I'm ready to move in with Erasmus or anyone. My living situation with my grandmother is almost ideal. She has company, and I get a whole upstairs to myself now that my mom and Brent have moved out. It's almost like my own fabulous loft apartment.

As I leave the bathroom, my stomach growls gregariously. As is typical of me, I cannot remember the last time I'd eaten. It's a wonder that I'm not dead, seriously.

I find a fruit bowl full of apples and bananas in the kitchen. I grab a banana and peel it before inserting it into my mouth.

"Didn't you get enough of that last night?" Erasmus' voice deep voice booms, making me jump.

"You scared me!" I exclaim, hand on my chest. I can feel my heart pounding away at the sudden surprise.

"Sorry." He leans over and kisses my neck. "I woke up and found you gone. I thought I'd come and see what you're up to."

"Just having some breakfast," I say, gesturing with the banana.

"And here I thought you were performing fellatio on it." His eyes twinkle with devilish mischief.

"Didn't *you* get enough last night?" I throw over my shoulder, biting off a bit of the banana and chewing it. Bananas are my favorite fruit, after grapes.

"How are you feeling?" Erasmus asks, sitting down at the island and again giving me his full attention.

"I feel fine," I answer. "I feel well-rested and stress-free."

"Are you sore at all?"

"A little."

"Not too badly?"

"No." I finish my banana and regard him intently. "Why?"

"I just want to make sure. I was afraid maybe I'd gotten too much into it last night and was too rough."

"You were perfect," I assure him.

"I'm glad to hear it." He shoots me a crooked grin.

I sit down beside him, clearing my throat. "So, I upheld my end up the bargain, so now it's your turn."

"I'm sorry?" He blinks in confusion.

"We made a deal a while back that if I let you top me, you'd tell me your story."

"Oh." He frowns, his face instantly going dark.

"What is it?"

"I'm afraid that you won't want to be with me anymore if I tell you about me, the whole story."

"Nothing you say could ever change my mind about being with you," I say with finality. "Whatever past transgressions you've committed are in the past. All that matters now is the present and the future."

"I've done some terrible things in my time..."

"Who hasn't? Just tell me."

"Why do you need to know so badly?"

"Because I want to know you, all of you."

"Even the bad parts?"

"Even the bad parts."

"Okay, if you insist." He takes a deep breath and launches into his story.

"I was born practically at the dawn of time. The world was a different place then, a harder place. I grew up in a wealthy family, along with my brother Aetius and my sister Iolanthe. We weren't close. We actually fought like wild animals. I was always a scholarly kid, interested in literature and my studies. I learned to speak several languages from the region, hoping to impress my father and make him very proud of me. He always favored Aetius, which didn't help our relationship. Aetius could do no wrong, and I was always second best."

In my mind's eye I can picture it: Erasmus, with a Caesar cut, wearing sandals, a skirt-length robe, without his tattoos. I bet his pale skin was olive colored, tanned from the Mediterranean sun.

"I already mentioned what happened to me when I was about ten... the rape. It wasn't a pleasant experience, but my duty was to fulfill it. I grudgingly took it on, and that experience opened me up to the possibility of same-sex couplings. It wasn't unheard of back then and wasn't the taboo issue as it has become in the last century. The Romans were very open about their lack of discrimination regarding bed partners.

"My first love was a beautiful girl named Simene. She had the most beautiful olive skin and the darkest hair I'd ever seen. Her round, almond eyes were captivating. I pledged my troth to her, and desperate to be a man, I asked her father for her hand in marriage. He laughed in my face and sent me home. It wasn't long before I caught Simene and Aetius having sex. Simene was reproachful, while Aetius was boastful. We fought, and it got heated, to the point where we drew swords. Aetius was always the better swordsman than me. He was always better at everything than me. He pinned me against the wall and was about to impale me, when I acted on instinct and grabbed the small blade from his belt and drove it into his stomach. I went in deep and fast, skewering his organs. Simene fled while I held my contentious brother as he breathed his last."

Poor Erasmus! I can't imagine killing Brent, even if he weren't Autistic. I know brothers fight, but I'd like to think that we've become more civilized since the days of Erasmus' humanity.

"When my parents found out what I'd done, they threw me out on the streets, wary of the shame that would befall our house. I was young and naïve, knowing nothing of the world or its complex machinations. I didn't know how to hunt or care for myself. I'd grown up a rich, spoiled brat, with slaves to jump at my every whim. I was totally lost.

"I met a charming older man named Sandor. He took me in and provided for me temporarily, but his intentions were not innocent. Once again, I found myself being raped, and when I tried to fight it, he beat me. One night, after he was asleep beside me, I slit his throat and took his money before fleeing.

"I traveled for days, trying not to use the money, but as you know, humans are weak. You need food, water, and rest. Before I knew it, the money was gone, and I was desperate. I took to selling my body for money—to men and women, it didn't matter. I didn't make much, but it was a start. I was especially popular amongst the wealthier clientele, as my thoroughbred upbringing made me more refined than the usual gutter trash that walked the streets. I always found a way to pocket anything of value that I could: coins, jewelry, you name it.

"One night, I met a mysterious woman, unlike any I had ever seen. She came from somewhere I had never heard of, a place called Nubia, and possessed the darkest ebony skin that I could ever have imagined. Her name, I learned, was Sarabé. She paid for my services and got me very drunk on wine. I thought she was beautiful, but also very dangerous. I don't remember drinking much, but I must have because I blacked out. I awoke the next night with an insatiable hunger for something I couldn't identify."

I feel a stirring of jealousy inside, but try to push it down. I hadn't even been born when all of this took place, so I don't have a right to be jealous of Erasmus' ex. I do admit, though, it's odd hearing him talk about women in a sexual manner; it's something he hasn't done since I met him.

"She told me that she took pity on me and gave me the greatest gift of all, the gift of immortal life," Erasmus continues. "I was instructed on how to feed and what my limitations were. My first victim was a baker who had stayed at his shop late. I drained him dry and then moved on to his wife. Their blood sated my thirst and warmed me within, making me feel all-powerful. I learned to like the killing, to drink past my fill of the blood because I could not get enough.

"Sarabé and I made our way through Greece, Rome, then Gaul, before heading throughout the rest of Europe. I fed on anyone I could get my hands on—men, women, children, it didn't matter. Blood is what mattered. Sarabé was impressed by my bloodlust, as it rivaled her own. I honestly don't even know the number of people we killed during our time together."

"What happened to her?" I can't help but ask. *If he had loved her so much, what made them part ways?*

"We were together for a few centuries, sometimes parting ways temporarily to get the lay of the land and test the blood pool. Sometimes we'd lure our victims into our insidious orgies before killing them, giving them the very height of pleasure. It was a nice thing to do. I thought of it as payment for their blood.

"The trail of blood that we left behind began to draw attention from others. One night, just after the sun went down, our cave was stormed by an angry mob, who quickly overtook us. They tried drowning and hanging us, but those methods weren't going to work. Instead, I was tied to a tree and forced to watch as Sarabé was beheaded. That worked. Her decapitated head rolled along the grass, coming to rest with her eyes toward me. A blood-red tear leaked from her right eye before her head and body collapsed in themselves, becoming nothing more than dust.

"My anger got the better of me, and I broke free of my restraints. I unleashed my vengeance upon the crowd, killing them as maliciously as possible. That didn't quell my rage, however. I was fuming inside, a maelstrom of fury and hurt. I set upon their town, murdering everyone in sight. It didn't take long before the entire village was nothing but smoking remains and blood-drenched ground."

My stomach turns and I want to gasp, but I don't want Erasmus to think that I'm judging him. It's hard to picture the sweet, loving man I know murdering people in cold blood. If he wasn't telling me this himself, I wouldn't believe it.

"I raged against the surrounding villages, too, decimating them within an hour or two. This continued for some time until the night when I thought I had ravaged the whole village but I was surprised when I heard a young girl sobbing. She watched me murder her entire family and village. She couldn't have been more than seven. Her skin was caked in dirt and dried blood. Before I could stop myself, I was upon her, teeth ripping the soft flesh of her neck open and lapping up her life's blood."

Bile rises in my throat, but I force it down. *Oh my God. A child!*

"Afterward, the realization of what I had done hit me, and I had an epiphany. Sarabé and I hadn't been the unjust victims of an angry mob. We had been rightfully punished criminals. We had no right to do what we'd done to those people. What's worse is that I hadn't even thought not to be a savage, blood-sucking fiend.

"I decided that night to stop feeding off humans unless they were already dead. I would not bear the weight of one more senseless murder upon my already tarnished soul. I starved for a night or two until my body began to decompose. I was too cowardly to do the right thing and let myself go. I began feeding on small animals, not that that did anything to assuage my guilt.

"I dedicated my life to doing the right thing. I found people in need of help, and I did everything I could to help them. Over the years, I amassed a considerable fortune. I used that money to build shelters, schools, and hospitals. I tried to erase the mark on my soul by doing good deeds.

"The years dredged on, and I continued to try to do the right thing. I came to America during the American Revolution and aided compatriots in their fight to free this county from England's oppressive grasp. In the Civil War, I fought for the north, helping slaves find a new home in the northern states. As the times changed, so did I. I helped educate people on their humanity, marching for civil rights and the oppression of women—all at night, of course.

"It wasn't until the last few years that I began to feel apathy for my life. I have seen so much evil, so much destruction, and loss. That's when I decided to leave my money to several good causes and end it. I stood atop the highest hill in town and waited for the sun to rise, reducing me to the same ash Sarabé had become all those years ago. But as I sat there, I felt... *something* compelling me to change my mind. It was you."

Tears burn my eyes, my heart breaking for him. He had told me about his suicide attempt before, but now, knowing the whole story, it seems so much worse. To think that he had been miserable enough to try to end his life is unconscionable to me. I've never seen him down, he's always been a beacon of positivity.

"The universe knew that what I needed most in all of this world was you. A companion that I could help, and who would love unconditionally. I needed someone who was willing to stand up to his mother's prejudice and was willing to perform an outlandish spell to harness the sun's energies into a ring, so that I could once again enjoy the feel of the sun on my cold, pale skin.

"What I'm saying Graham, is that you're it. You are the universe's reward to me for all the good things that I've done. You're my atonement. Just think, if you would have arrived in Willows Crest even a day later, I wouldn't be here now. I would've been turned to ash and scattered in the wind. But, instead, here I am, alive and well, because of you. You saved me."

He ends his soliloquy and looks up into my eyes. They're blurry from the tears shed while listening to his tragic tale. *Such a sad, empty life!* While Erasmus had certainly made some bad choices along the way, some of those choices were out of his control. He was just as much a victim as anyone else. In the end, he made a choice that has reaped bountiful goodness—not only for himself but for countless other people, too.

I blink the tears away and somehow find my voice, though it's husky. "I can see why you were afraid to tell me all that," I say.

"Yeah." Erasmus hangs his head in shame. "I'm not proud of the things that I did back then. If

I could go back in time and change them, I would, in a heartbeat, even if it meant having died millennia ago."

"But if you'd died, how many good things would be undone?" I challenge.

"Does the good outweigh the bad?"

"In this case, yes, I think it does. You didn't ask to become a vampire; that was Sarabé's choice. She influenced you into becoming a heartless monster; you were nothing but a scared, lost boy, Erasmus. You didn't know better than to follow instructions; that was all you'd known of life."

"I can still see all of their faces, hear their screams, when I close my eyes," he confesses.

"That I can't help with," I admit, "but I can assure you that while you did commit those heinous, unspeakable acts, that was a long time ago. You are not that man anymore. As you said, you've achieved atonement for those past transgressions, though I hardly think I'm your reward."

"But you are, can't you see that?"

"No." I shake my head. "I think your reward is still out there, Erasmus."

"If not you, then what?"

"Peace of mind?" I suggest. "A freedom from the guilt that weighs so heavily on you?"

"Maybe one day," he mutters.

"I'll help you," I promise, squeezing his hand. "I will never stop reminding you of what an amazing, caring man you are. Leave the past in the past. As far as I'm concerned, the man who did those things is dead. He died the night Sarabé was killed. The man I love would never do those things."

"I wish I could separate the two."

"You will, in time."

"I am so lucky to have you," he says, wrapping his arms around me.

"I'm the lucky one," I whisper, holding him tightly.

Chapter Thirty-Two

By the following weekend, my grandmother forgave me for not coming home and not calling. Believe me, when I got back to the house after Erasmus' revelations, I got a stern talking to. And I thought my mom was bad...

She lectured me about how worried she was and the dangers of me being out alone. Of course, this is worsened by the fact that I am public enemy number one in the Underworld. The attacks have grown more intense and dangerous. I'm not that worried, though; I've handled myself extremely well, especially last time, and I am confident in my abilities.

My grandma wanted to ground me until she realized that such an act would be futile at my age. I'm an adult, and I wouldn't actually be spending that much time miserable in my room, reflecting on my mistakes. The whole teleporting thing doesn't hurt my case at all, either. Being responsible is a hard cross to bear. Also, she's booked herself a plane ticket to go see her sister, Edwina, in Oregon, so I'll have the house to myself, anyway. It's almost as if the stars are aligned to make this the best weekend of my life. She won't tell me why she suddenly needs to see her sister, but it must be important if she's going to risk leaving me unsupervised right now.

I've saved enough money from the video store to get a very nice black suit. I know it would be more financially practical to just rent one, but I see it as an investment in my future. I don't plan on gaining a substantial amount of weight, and I'm pretty sure I'm done growing height-wise, so why not spend a little bit more and have a suit that I can wear for more than just one night? My old one fit me much better when I was fifty pounds heavier. I want to look good for Erasmus, not like a kid wearing his dad's clothes.

The suit is snug. When I picked it out, the sales lady warned against pairing it with a white dress shirt. She cautioned that simple black and white would make me look like a giant penguin. I didn't tell her that The Penguin is one of my favorite *Batman* villains. If I were to resemble the version of him from the *Gotham* TV series, that would hardly be a travesty. Ultimately, we agreed to go for the black suit, white dress shirt, and a red tie. I've watched countless videos on Youtube about how to tie a tie, but I can't wrap my head around it. I'll either ditch the tie altogether or ask Erasmus to do it. He's lived practically forever, so he knows how to do everything. I certainly wouldn't shy away from any excuse to get him close against me, hands on my neck...

Amethyst went with me to pick out my suit. We also spent part of the time dress shopping for her. She's forgoing the prom look, and settles on a nice dark purple off the shoulder dress that cascades down to her ankles. She said she normally wouldn't be caught dead at a frat party but since I was going, it would be okay. Alisha isn't ready for anything serious, so she and Amethyst have drifted apart. The thought of going without a date didn't deter Amethyst, either. She is literally my hero, so strong and independent. I definitely wouldn't have the courage to go to a party stag. Usually, a social event isn't exactly my thing, either, but I'm so excited to be able to be out and proud with Erasmus, and I want everyone to see that I'm happy and don't give a fuck about them or their bullshit.

Amethyst and I have to work at the movie store that night, but Vito took pity on us and has agreed to let us close shop at six-thirty, so that we can have dinner first. I'll be too nervous to eat, but it'll be nice for the three of us to do something together besides hang at Amethyst's apartment.

****

When I finally stir around noon, Grandma is arranging her luggage in the hall by the front door. I come down the stairs, and she glances up at me. "Oh, good, you're up. I was starting to think that you'd sleep up until you have to go into work," she says.

"I wish," I mumble, rubbing the sleep from my eyes. I have my blue polar bear bathrobe fastened tightly around my waist, and I nuzzle the fuzzy collar with my chin.

"I left my itinerary on the fridge, just so you know, in case anything should happen."

"Okay."

"The keys to the car are in the kitchen. Don't go crazy or anything with it, though."

"Darn," I say, snapping my fingers, "I was planning on driving to New York."

"If I didn't know what a good boy you are, I might be fearful of that," she returns, zipping up one of her suitcases.

"Do you need me to drop you off at the airport?" I ask, stifling a yawn behind my hand.

"No, I've called a taxi. It should be here any minute." She glances nervously at her watch. For some reason, she has an obsession with being on time. I shouldn't say being on time because that's a normal concern. She has to be at least a half-hour early, or she wigs out and gets all flustered.

"How long are you going for, again?"

"A week. Will you be all right here by yourself for that long?"

"I'll be fine. Worst case, Erasmus can come stay with me if I need a little extra protection."

"Mhm." I see her mouth tighten, and I know she has come to suspect Erasmus and I are having sex. Whether she's upset about it being gay sex or premarital sex, I can only wonder.

"Plus, Mom is just in town, one call away."

"Yes, yes." She nods, "I've paid up my bills as best as I can. There are some that aren't due quite yet, but I've left signed checks for them on my dresser. I'll need you to fill in the amounts for me and mail them."

"Okay."

"There's lasagna in the fridge and a pot of chicken noodle soup—it's fresh."

"Thanks."

I know she's stressing about everything, so she's infantizing me as if I don't know how things operate around here. I'm not in the mood to point this out, so I allow it. I don't want to rain on her parade, but even more so, I don't want an argument.

Outside, a horn honks, and she quickly grabs a few of her suitcases. For someone who is only going on a trip for a week, she has packed a lot of stuff. She has two full-sized suitcases, a carry-on bag, and her purse.

"Let me help you."

"Oh, thanks, bubala."

We open the door and find the yellow taxi parked in the driveway. The driver pops the trunk as I wheel the two suitcases out. What she needs two of them for, only God knows. I set the suitcases into the trunk and then help her with the carry-on bag. I shut the trunk, and she sighs.

"Well, I guess this is goodbye," she says.

"Only for a week," I remind her.

"Well, you never know, darling. Planes crash all the time."

"Okay, enough. This is a vacation; it's supposed to be fun. Don't ruin it by stressing."

"I'm not stressing; I'm simply pointing out the facts."

"Sure."

She laughs and pulls me into a hug. "Be safe and have fun," she whispers into my ear.

"You, too. Say 'hi' to Aunt Edwina for me."

"I will." Grandma glances down at her watch, then hugs me quickly again. "All right, I've got to go! Kisses!"

"Bye."

She gets into the cab, and I wave as it backs out onto the road and disappears from sight.

I head back into the house and sigh with contentment. Pure silence. Aside from Romana, I am the only living being here, and it feels amazing! I have not had the house to myself for more than an hour or two since we moved here. Before that, when we lived in Chesterfield, I often had the house to myself, as Don was working out of state and mom worked nights. Well, not *totally* to myself, Brent had been there, but he was asleep at eight most nights, so I had a few hours to wander and dream about what it would like to have my own place and not have to put up with other people.

I head into the kitchen for a bottle of water and see that Grandma has left a sink full of dishes. Typical. I've never understood people who don't wash their dishes behind themselves as they cook. *Why let them pile up and then have to do a bunch at the end when you can just wash them as you go?*

I run some dishwater and play some *My Chemical Romance* on my phone. I dance to the music as I meticulously clean the dishes. I've always been OCD when it comes to washing dishes. I don't get people who can't do dishes properly; it's not that hard, assuming you're willing to put in the work of scrubbing the dishes. I once had a friend whose grandmother didn't wash dishes—ever—instead, she just ran them under soapy water, so the plates would still have grease and chunks of food on them. My stomach turns at the thought of it.

After the dishes are done, I vacuum the entire house, sweep the kitchen, clean the bathrooms, and clean out the fridge. I don't want to do housework while Grandma is away. I'll have the house to myself, and I'd rather enjoy it with Erasmus instead of distracted with chores.

I take a long, hot shower before work and then load the car with my garment bag, suit and a small bag containing my toiletries. *I have to look perfect tonight, no ifs, ands, or buts.*

The Buick drives better than I remember. I've been thinking about saving up my money so that when the time comes for Grandma to get a new car, I'll be able to offer to buy it from her. I never expected her to just give it to me, though I would be deeply appreciative if she did.

When I get to work, Amethyst is buzzing with excitement. "I cannot wait for tonight!" she gushes, her eyes wild.

"Me neither. I just hope everything goes according to plan."

"It will; trust me, you've earned a perfect night."

"Maybe," I shrug, "and hopefully, we don't have to deal with any stupid people tonight. I want this shift to go by quickly and easily so we can enjoy tonight the way it should be enjoyed."

"Amen to that. I'm so over stupid people."

"Right?"

"So, are we riding to the restaurant together, or is Erasmus coming to pick you up?"

"He's supposed to meet me up at closing time. He'll follow me back to my house to drop off the car."

"Deal, then I'll head out whenever you send me home, and I'll see you guys there."

"Definitely." I think it's weird that although the manager promotion has been denied to me, I still have the power to send Amethyst home. Either Vito is not as upset me with as he wants me to think he is, or he's willing to sacrifice a little pride to avoid working doubles. Either way, it doesn't matter to me, I've always been a bit of a bossy, control freak, and with this job, I'm getting paid to do so.

The video store shelves have been cleaned recently, so I ask Amethyst to watch the store while I go out and clean the club room. It hasn't been used in a while and is usually cleaned before and after an event. Chances are, it's dirty and needs a cleaning, especially the bathrooms.

I fill a mop bucket with steaming hot water and roll into the club room, juggling the mop bucket, mop, broom, and dustpan. Then, I return to the supply room to get a hand bucket of bleach water and a towel to wipe down the counters.

The jukebox has five dollars' worth of credits left from its last use, so I turn on *Always Be My Baby*. I hum along, swaying my hips as I clean and sanitize the counters and the booths before sweeping the white tiled floors. *Yeah, it's definitely been a minute since this room has been cleaned.* I collect a mound of dirt and popcorn crumbs into the center of the room and sweep them up, dumping them neatly into the trash can. I make a note to make sure that this room gets a light cleaning at least every other week, if not every week.

I clean the bathrooms, which I absolutely hate doing. The plumbing is messed up, so the toilets don't flush properly. Instead of just using the handle, you have to hold it down, wait a few seconds, and then push it down again. Despite the signs above each toilet, the customers seem unable to understand. The men's toilet has a wad of toilet paper and bits of human feces in it. *You're getting paid*, I remind myself as I scrunch up my face in disgust. I use my foot to flush it all down.

The women's bathroom is a lot cleaner, though there is urine in that toilet. At least there are no bloody tampons, thankfully. My mom used to tell me horror stories about the bathrooms at Kohl's, where women would just leave their bloody tampons wherever. I'd probably projectile vomit if I had to clean that up.

Mopping takes the longest, but I concentrate on the music, and when I'm done, the club room smells like bleach instead of decaying dust and popcorn. I feel sweat trickle down the back of my neck and groan. *Great, I'm not going to have time to run home and shower, so now I'm going to stink like sweat. I'll have to rinse myself in the employee bathroom before we go.*

Amethyst is itching for a cigarette break when I get back into the store. "Thank God, I'm dying over here," she says, fanning herself dramatically.

"Go for a smoke," I tell her laughing, "and then it's my turn. That club kicked my ass!"

"I love that you smoke now. I'm such a bad influence."

"Only you would be proud that I smoke now."

"Why wouldn't I? Smoking is great! Now, we just need to get you drinking and smoking weed."

Gabriel Mero

"Perhaps tonight I'll imbibe a little." I wink suggestively.

"Yes! You know I'll be carrying."

"Always."

She dashes out the back door to smoke, and I lean against the counter, trying to catch my breath.

Business is slow for a Saturday, so I let Amethyst go at six. That'll give her time to get home, shower, and doll herself up to slay the dance floor tonight. I wish I could go home and shower, too, because even though a little sweat never killed anyone, I am paranoid that I stink.

"Are you sure you don't want me to stay?" she asks, hovering in the doorway.

"Yes! Go, get ready. Women take longer to get ready than guys, and that's a fact."

"Excuse me, bitch? You take longer to get ready than me," she points out with a sarcastic laugh.

"I'm a diva; what can I say?"

"You're a diva, all right. You're my diva, and I love the shit out of you."

"I love you, too."

"All right, call me if you need me."

"I will."

She starts to walk out but then pauses. "I'm really glad that we became friends," she says.

"Me, too. I'd be lost without you."

"I'd die without you."

"Well, luckily, we won't have to worry about that because neither of us is going anywhere."

"Sorry, I get emotional sometimes. I think my period is coming soon."

"Well..." I drawl, "you have fun with that."

"Over-sharing, sorry. Okay, I'll see you there."

"See you soon."

I watch her leave and then start putting movies away. That makes the next twenty minutes pass by, and then I'm back at the counter, tapping my feet impatiently as I stare at the clock on the wall. *Come on,* I urge, *move faster.*

At around 6:30pm, my phone rings, and a grin lights up my face when I see that it's Erasmus. "Hey, babe," I answer, the joy evident in my voice.

"Hey, darling. Should I head over there soon?" he asks.

"I'll be here until at least 7:15," I say, looking at my phone's clock, "so take your time. Once I shut the store down, I need to freshen up and change anyway."

"I can't wait to see you in your tux. You're going to look ravishing." His voice is heavy with lust, and I shiver with delight.

"I can't wait to see you in red. I've only ever seen you in black."

"Soon."

"Okay, well, I'll see you soon."

"I'll be there."

"You'd better. If you stand me up, I will kick your ass!"

"I wouldn't dream of standing you up."

"Good. I love you."

"I love you, too." When he says that, I actually feel it and know he's telling the truth. *He loves me. Erasmus Mayfair, gorgeous, rich, vampire playboy extraordinaire, loves me, plain old me. I am so, so blessed.*

I disconnect the call and slide my phone back into my pocket.

The next half hour crawls by, but at 6:59, I unplug the OPEN sign and turn the lights in the lobby off. I am beyond ready to get out of this dump and have fun like a normal person. I can't wait to see the look on everyone's faces when they see me walk in on the arm of a stud like Erasmus.

I leave the front door open, so Erasmus can let himself in when he gets here and grab the keys to the dropbox. I emptied it a while ago, but I always check it before shutting down, out of habit.

As I walk through the shelves, I'm preoccupied with thoughts of Erasmus' lips and his hands around my waist. I unlock the padlock and set it on top before opening the door. It's dark out here, so I can't see, but I place my hand inside and feel around. Inch by inch, all I feel is the cheap carpeting that Vito placed inside. *Typical. Oh, well, it's not like I'm wasting a substantial amount of time.*

I get ready to pull my hand out when suddenly, an orange light bursts from the bottom of the dropbox, and a clawed hand snakes out, latching onto my wrist. I groan at the sudden pain and try to wrest myself free from the grip of whatever it is. It tightens its hold, the claws of its hand digging into my wrist.

"Let me go!" I cry, grunting against the pain.

"Your time has come, witch!" a disembodied voice rasps. The pure evilness in the voice makes a chill creep up my spine.

The hand tugs, and suddenly, I find myself pulled into the dropbox. My head enters the portal, and instantly, the video store is gone.

Chapter Thirty-Three

The portal, or whatever it is that I've been dragged into, is warm, incredibly warm. I look around me at the red and black swirls that make up my surroundings, and I'm confused. *Where the hell am I?* This isn't something I've ever seen before, and now that I have seen it, I don't ever want to see it again.

I can just make out the shape of the thing that grabbed me. A red, clawed hand keeps a vice-like grip on my wrist as we float down, down, down, deeper into the red and black chasm. The temperature continues to climb the farther down we go, and I feel sweat forming along my hairline as my scalp starts to itch.

"Who are you? Where are we?" I demand, trying to keep my voice even.

"Soon, witch, soon," the deep voice replies, enshrouded in darkness.

I want to ask more questions, but it's hard to breathe, and I don't want to waste oxygen on futile attempts at conversation. Whatever I need to know, I will know when we arrive wherever it is we're going, though I do have a pretty good idea of where that is. There's only one place that has been longing for me all year: Hell. *I am on my way to Sitra Achra.*

Up ahead, I see the bottom of the portal open, and we drop out. I land—hard—on my shoulder, the rocky ground beneath me, making me bite my tongue. The air rushes out of my lungs when I land, and I splutter, gasping for air, eyes wild like a savage. *I'm going to die; I know it. Oh, hell....no one will know what happened to me. Erasmus is going to think that I stood him up. Grandma will think that I got kidnapped or murdered, and Amethyst will think I was playing her all along, using her.* My mind flashes to Romana, trapped up in my bedroom. She's safe from harm, but Grandma won't be back for a whole week; by then, Romana will have run out of food. *Oh, God...*

The pain subsides slightly, though my shoulder is still throbbing. Probably dislocated. I force air into my lungs and cough at the rough, sulfurous quality of it. My throat screams in protest, and I wish for a glass of ice water, to wash this nasty taste out of my mouth and clear my throat a little.

The demon—I'm assuming it's a demon—jerks me to my feet, and I cry out as his hand clasps my injured shoulder. I thought the worst pain I'd ever endure was rolling my wrist the first day of sparring practice with Erasmus, but this hurts like a motherfucker, and I feel tears of pain rolling down my cheeks involuntarily.

"Up, witch," the demon orders gruffly.

"Can you give me a minute?" I groan. "I think I've dislocated my shoulder or something." In response, he jabs my injured shoulder, making me cry out in pain.

"Get moving," he orders.

The light here is scant, and I know that we are underground. In the distance, I can hear wailing and sniffling, and I feel bile start to burn my throat, trying to work its way up. *We're definitely in Sitra Achra, and I am about to be subjected to excruciating pain.*

"What are they offering you to deliver me?" I ask, wincing as my shoulder continues to throb.

"I've secured a position for myself among Lucifer's elite army, thanks to you," my captor answers. His voice sounds familiar, but I can't quite remember where I've heard it before. My mind scrambles as I try to place it. Sabriel, maybe? Or Vito? No, this voice is closer to home; I can tell that, even though it's distorted.

I'm dragged along a rocky path, uneven and dangerous. With each step, a torch flickers to life by itself on the wall. I squint through the darkness, but all I can see of my captor is his black robes.

"What can I offer you that would convince you to let me go? Take me back to where you got me and forget this whole mess?" I query, stumbling along behind him on the path.

"Nothing you could offer me would make me go against my master," the demon says mirthlessly.

Great, I've always prided myself on being able to talk myself out of any situation, but I can't very well talk my way out of this trap when the thing holding me has no interest in bartering. "Are you sure? I'm pretty powerful, you know. I could... I don't know, restore your humanity, maybe? Or conjure you up a nice lady demon to share your bed. How does that sound?"

"I have no place for inconsequential amenities such as those. I live to serve Lucifer, and any honor he may bestow upon me, is just icing on the cake, as you mortals say."

Damn, yeah, there's definitely no reasoning with this one. I decide that my best bet is to wait until we come to a stop, use my telekinesis to knock him out, and run like hell back to the portal, hoping to God that it's still there. Worst case scenario, I'll have to perform the teleportation spell and pray that there isn't any interference down here.

I allow the demon to drag me along, focusing on the pain in my shoulder to keep my mind sharp. We must stop walking eventually.

I don't know how long we've been walking, but it seems an eternity. The sweat begins to pour down my face, soaking my shirt and making me wish that I'd worn shorts instead of skinny jeans. I don't think I have ever been so hot in all my life! I wonder if there are any water fountains or anything along the way. Then I remember what my grandmother told me back in the winter: if I were to get taken to Sitra Achra, I only have to last two days. If I don't eat or drink anything while I'm down here or give my powers over to evil, they'll be forced to release me. Not eating for two days will be a cakewalk, but not drinking anything; well, that's a different story entirely. *How am I not supposed to drink anything when I'm boiling alive?* At the thought of liquid hydration, my throat gets drier. *Fuck...*

Eventually, we come to an outcropping overlooking a river made of what appears to be liquid, hot magma. I am huffing and puffing by this point, fighting like hell to catch my breath. *Who can I speak to down here about turning the heat down?*

My kidnapper stops and sits on one of the rocks, exhaling sharply. "Sit," he orders. I don't have enough fight in me to argue with him. I do as I'm told, grateful for the rest. I don't know how much farther it is to wherever we're going, but I know that I won't be able to make it much longer if I don't rest now.

"What's your name?" I entreat, leaning my head back and closing my eyes against the stifling heat and the pain lancing through my left shoulder.

"That is of no consequence to you," the demon answers.

"Not one for conversation, huh? That's okay; I can talk enough for both of us. They didn't call me Gabby growing up for nothing."

The demon rises and flashes a sharp blade at me. "Keep talking, and I'll remove your tongue."

"I'm your hostage. Everyone knows you can't harm the hostage," I shoot back.

"Lord Lucifer wants your magic, not your tongue. Besides, if you're as chatty with him as you are with me, he'll thank me for the silence."

"Okay," I say, holding up my hands in surrender. I definitely do not want my tongue cut off. I'm in enough pain as it is.

The demon snickers and replaces the blade within his voluminous black robes. *How can he be wearing those in this heat?* I'm soaking wet with sweat in a t-shirt and skinny jeans, so he must be properly roasting. However, if he is a denizen of this hellish plane, I'd imagine he's either used to this extreme heat or immune to it.

We sit in silence as he pours some water from a canteen and gulps it down. He offers me a capful of water, and I want to accept it; I really do, but I can't. I will not damn myself to be trapped here for eternity.

"Drink," he coaxes, waving the cup before my face.

"No, thanks," I rasp, turning my head away.

"You much be parched. It's nice and cold. It'll feel great sliding down that throat of yours."

His words are tempting, I won't lie, but I have always been a stubborn son of a bitch. The more someone pushes me to do something, the harder I push back to do the contrary. Once, Don tried to force me into playing sports, so he signed me up for soccer. I couldn't give a rat's ass about soccer or sports in general, so I bitched and moaned about it. Don refused to let me quit, so I got even. While the rest of my teammates were busting their asses out on the field, I took it easy, walking instead of running and refusing to participate in the game. I can't say that I scored a single goal in the two years I was forced into soccer.

I draw on this stubbornness now to decline the offer of the cold water. The only way I will overcome this ordeal is if I stick to my guns and hang on to my humanity. Eventually, the demon gives up and replaces the cap on his canteen. "You'll break eventually," he promises me.

"Don't count your chickens before they hatch, buck-o," I snap. "I'm the most stubborn person I've ever met."

"I can tell."

"And don't think that just because you could pull a sly one and drag me here, you've bested me. I've fought stronger, smarter demons than you and ended them. Your time will come; I promise you that."

"With what weapon? I've seen you're fighting skills. You rely too much on fancy weapons and your sorcery. There's none of that here, and trust me, even if you were able to overtake me, you won't get my blade from me."

"Never say never."

"I'm surprised you haven't figured out who I am yet. I was hoping you'd have pieced it together by now."

"I can't place it," I confess, frowning. "Your voice is so familiar, and yet it's not... I don't know how to describe it."

"How disappointing. I guess I'll just have to spoil the surprise." He stands up and flips the hood of his robe down. At first, he's enshrouded in darkness, but then the light falls upon his face, and my stomach lurches.

I puke at my feet, yellow bile burning my throat and splashing on the rocks around us. "No, it can't be. No!"

Don stands before me, his features distorted in a malicious grin that no human being should ever be able to achieve. His frog-like brown eyes have been replaced by the creepy goat's eyes that all demons seem to have, and his mouth stretches beyond normal human capacity.

"Surprise," he sings, off-key as always.

"You're a demon?" I gasp, groaning as a fresh wave of vomit forces itself up and out.

"Oh, no, this body is just an appealing host. I chose it for its significance to you."

"What do you mean?"

"When I came to Earth, I knew my demonic body would not last long, so I bonded with this filthy mortal to buy myself more time. I thought I'd rid myself of it as soon as we got here, but I can access his memories and see how much he tormented you. I think it will make this much more enjoyable if I keep up the façade."

"Did you kill him?"

"Oh, no, he's in here, but I have control of his faculties."

The room starts to spin, and I lie down against the rock, squeezing my eyes shut and clutching my stomach, willing it to settle. I imagine that this is what being shit-faced drunk feels like. *This is not good, definitely not good.* As if this situation weren't bad enough, now I have to deal with a demon in my least favorite person's body, too?

"Are you going to kill him?"

Don shrugs, "Maybe. Maybe I'll give you the pleasure."

"I don't want to kill him."

"You can't fool me, witch. I know what he did to you, how he hurt you. Your feelings for him are pretty clear."

"I *do* hate him," I relent, "but that doesn't mean I want him dead."

"Well, if you don't, you're not as strong as I thought."

There, an insult that I shouldn't take to heart, and yet, I feel weak for not wishing death on my tormenting stepfather.

"He hates you, you know," Don continues casually, warming up to conversation. "He never loved you, even from the start. He tried, of course, but he just couldn't do it. You weren't his DNA, and he could never love someone as fucked-up as you are."

"Do you think you're hurting my feelings?" I grit my teeth as I say it, my anger rising.

"I don't think I'm hurting your feelings," he assures me, "I *know* I am. You've always cared far too much about what everyone thinks about you. Your biological father doesn't love you, step-daddy doesn't love you, your mother was going to abort you... poor little lost Graham, nobody loves him."

"I do have somebody who loves me. His name is Erasmus, and when he gets to the video store and finds I've mysteriously vanished, he'll figure out what happened to me. He'll come for me."

"And, what, he'll kick my ass?" The demon in Don's body shivers forcibly. "I'm not afraid. Vampires can't come here. No one can come here without the use of magic, and that blood-brain has none."

"I think you're forgetting that my grandmother is also a powerful witch. She'll find a way to get him here," I bluff. I'm hoping that the Don demon doesn't know that Grandma is currently arriving in Oregon.

"That old battle axe is useless," he guffaws. "Even if she could get him here, I'm hardly afraid of that walking skeleton. There's no blood for him to feast on down here; he'll either rot away before your eyes or give in to his insurmountable blood lust and drain you of your life's blood."

"So, you *do* want me dead," I note, filing that away for later.

"I do, yes, but it doesn't matter what I want. My job is to deliver you to Lucifer, keeping you safe until we arrive at his palace."

"But he doesn't want me dead?"

"He wants your power."

"Why? I thought it was Adrammelech who wanted my powers?"

"Adrammelech does want your powers; he wishes to harness them and curry favor with Lucifer. Lucifer has bigger fish to fry. He's planning something so big that once it happens, there'll be no stopping it."

"And what is that?"

Don seems to catch himself, and he stands up. "I've said too much." He jerks me back to my feet, tugging on my bad arm. I swallow the pain. "We don't have much further now."

"Yay," I mutter.

We follow the path down a winding staircase in the rock mountain. Whoever designed this place was actually quite an innovative genius.

Despite the heat and the smell, the architecture is pretty unique. I take a mental picture of it to tell Ariana if I ever get back home. The last time we talked on the phone, a few weeks ago, she'd told me that she's accepted an internship at an architecture firm. She's currently working on her master's degree in architecture. She possesses an incredible artistic gift far exceeding my own; I know she'll succeed in that field.

The stairs lead down, the air becoming a little more breathable the more we descend. I wonder if the whole heat-rises thing is true of Sitra Achra, too, because if the temperature were to drop even just a few degrees, I'd be ever so grateful. The irony is not lost on me that usually I'm bitching about the cold.

The closer we get to Lucifer's castle, the more intense the wailing gets. I imagine people shackled down, like in a medieval torture chamber, being dismembered and disemboweled, dipped in lava, and raped with pitchforks. From the shrillness of the screaming, I can only imagine what is truly happening around us.

After another long jaunt, we come to a tall gate fashioned out of bleached skulls. Their deathly grins make the hairs on the back of my neck stand up. Although I know I won't be killed down here, I can't help but fear that things will not go according to plan. *Who's to say that if Lucifer and Adrammelech don't get their way, they won't just kill me?*

Don knocks on the gate, the skulls staying in place with each thrust of his fist. *An impenetrable gate of skulls, that's not creepy at all.* After a moment or two, the gates creak open, and a high, black castle rises above us. *So, this is it, Lucifer's castle.* As soon as we're past the gate, the doors slam shut, the skulls rattling with the jarring motion. *No going back now...*

Don pulls me along the dead path and into the palace courtyard. I see goat-eyed demons regarding me with interest, their creepy eyes following me. This is the stuff of nightmares. If I'm lucky enough to get out of this, I'll have to find a spell to erase all of this from my memory. *There is no way that I want these images haunting me in my sleep for the rest of my life.*

The castle gates open as we approach. These ones are fastened from the rock that seems to make up the majority of the landscape down here. At least there are no more body part gates. I'm a fan of horror movies, so I can stomach a lot, but this is way too much, even for me.

I hear the gates roll shut behind us, and Don turns to look up at the highest tower, his grip slackening just a little. I jump at the opportunity and wrench my arm free, trying as hard as possible to ignore the pain spiraling through me. I back up a few paces and squint my eyes as I flick my hand at him. Nothing happens. *What?* I try again, focusing harder. Once more, Don remains firmly planted on the ground.

"Did you really think your powers would work here?" he asks, laughing. "Your powers were bound as soon as you crossed realms."

Great, so I have no weapons, no powers, and I'm in completely unfamiliar territory: great odds, wouldn't you say? I hold my hands up before me in a classic defensive manner. If I go down, at least I'll go down fighting.

Don launches at me, and I duck under his meaty arm, driving my fist into his gut. I wait for the impact but panic when I feel... nothing. I look up at him, fear really settling in. *How can I fight a non-corporeal entity?* He towers over me, cold eyes staring blankly at me, and I gulp. The last thing that I see is his fist coming toward me.

Chapter Thirty-Four

From darkness comes consciousness. The first thing I notice is a throbbing ache in my head. *Oh, no, not another one of my migraines. I haven't had one in years.* In my Freshman year of high school, I'd decided to get my gym requirement out of the way, and our teacher, Mr. Byle, would make us run laps on Wednesdays and Fridays. The deal was that if you ran the whole time on Wednesday, you got to relax on Friday and do whatever you wanted, but if you walked on Wednesday, you had to make it up and run on Friday. I decided to just bite the bullet and do my running. I didn't mind the physical activity too much, but it was the optical migraines that I got afterward that I detested.

They would start with optical disturbances, like when you rub your eyes and see the auras. The auras would expand and contract, making it hard for me to see very well. Next, the throbbing would begin. First, one side of my face would go numb, and the other would follow suit. Waves of nausea were roiling on my already unsettled stomach to make me even more miserable. When I got home from school, I'd go to bed and sleep for a few hours, waking up with a sore head but otherwise fine. I did eventually discover that if I ate a little something and/or threw up, the headache would cease. They were probably from low blood sugar and over-exertion. I haven't had one since the second to last day of Freshman year.

I groan as nausea washes over me, trying desperately to work itself up my esophagus. I absolutely loathe feeling nauseous. Thankfully, I don't often throw up, not nearly as often as I did as a child. I'd cry every time I puked, scared because I couldn't breathe.

I open my eyes and am relieved when I note that my vision is clear, free of auras. *Not a migraine, then.* I look around the scantly lit room, trying to piece it all together in my foggy mind. *Where am I?* This isn't my room back home, nor is it Erasmus' bedroom.

I sit up, and a light flares to reveal Don standing before me, and suddenly, it all comes flooding back to me. Some demon in Don's body kidnapped me, and I am in Sitra Achra. I remember approaching Lucifer's palace and attempting to overpower the Don demon, only to be knocked unconscious. *That explains the headache.* I've never been punched that hard before today, so it's an unfamiliar sensation.

I still can't see much in the scant light other than Don. I'm on a bed—not entirely uncomfortable—against a wall. Whether the wall is painted black or merely darkness encroaching upon me, I cannot tell.

Don is leaning against the wall but stands up straight and starts walking toward me, regarding me through his creepy goat eyes. I know that this isn't really Don, but I can't separate my tormentor from the demon that is currently inhabiting his body.

"Finally awake, I see," he chirps, staring down at me.

"How long was I out?" My throat is tight, my voice hoarse. I need water or something to drink. *But, no, I can't, not if I don't want to damn my soul to the underworld for all eternity.*

"Most of the night."

So, I've been here for at least half a day, only a day and a half left. I can do it. I have to do this. "Lucifer will be pissed at you when he hears that you cold-cocked me." Just talking makes my head hurt even more than it already does.

"He gave me strict orders to deliver you to him under any means necessary, short of murdering you. I'll be richly rewarded."

"Good for you. What will happen to me?"

The Don demon sits on the edge of the bed I'm lying on, and I'm reminded of the early years of our time living in Port Huron. My mom started working again, this time at Yonkers and didn't get home until after my nine o'clock bedtime. Don would pick me up after school, make us dinner as I did my homework, and then after a bit of playtime and a bath, he'd put me to bed. He would never sit and read to me from one of my comic books like Mom would. Instead, he'd make me read to him from one of my simple reading assignments.

"If you submit to him, it will be over. If you're a fool and resist, you'll be subjected to intense torture to sway you, and don't be fooled into thinking it won't be that bad. This isn't where you're from; there is no such thing as cruel and unusual punishment down here. You could be tied up and roasted over a fire like a pig. You won't die, of course, so every agonizing moment will radiate within you."

I shiver at the thought. I have always been deathly afraid of fire. I've thankfully only been burned a few times in my life, the majority of those times being when I was young and accidentally ran into the tip of my mom's cigarette. Another wave of nausea hits me. *Oh, God, please, no!* I silently beg. *Anything but fire, I can handle anything but fire.* "How will you keep me alive if I'm burned to a crisp?" I ask with the bit of courage I have left.

"The Dark Lord works in mysterious ways. He doesn't want you dead; he just wants your powers."

"Why? So he can become omnipotent?"

"Partly." Don sniffs. "He wants to use your powers to free himself from this treacherous place. He wants to corrupt the Earth, blackening the souls of every being. He wants to take revenge on God for exiling him from paradise, damning him to an eternity in a glorified volcano."

"And you're in line with this plan?"

Don stands up and starts to pace our small room as if nervous. *Why would a demon be nervous?* As far as I know, demons are immortal beings, so short of a war in which he could be mortally wounded, his life is safe.

I try a different tactic, buying time. *If I can get him talking, maybe I can delay the inevitable: my meeting with the Prince of Darkness.* "I heard a rumor that Adrammelech isn't entirely whelmed on Satan's plans. Apparently, he's planning a coup, to overthrow—"

"Quiet, fool!" he hisses, flying at me. I flatten myself against the darkness behind me—it's a wall. The sudden movement makes my head hurt even worse. It feels as though my brain is sloshing around inside my skull.

"What?" I ask, the sight of 'Don' lunging at me, recalling the scared boy within me.

"Where did you hear that?" His already bulgy eyes are bugging out of his head. In different circumstances, I'd probably find it comical, but right now, in this time and place, I can't find the humor in it.

The night Erasmus saved me from my first demon and revealed his true nature, he'd told me Adrammelech was vying for Satan's throne, that it wasn't exactly a secret. *Why does it matter to him?*

"Tell me!"

I decide to lie. If there's one thing I secretly enjoy, it's stirring the pot. "One of the demons that attacked me blabbed."

"Idiots!" Don rages, crashing his fists into the ground. The dirt cracks and breaks apart, the room shaking violently.

"Why are you so mad?" I ask, blinking dust out of my eyes.

"You still haven't figured it out?"

"Figured what out?"

Don suddenly jerks his head back, and a black gas mists out of his open mouth. The dark cloud filters out until it starts to coalesce into a body, and as soon as it is out of Don, his body collapses to the ground.

"Is he... dead?" I ask the cloud.

"Not yet."

"Who are you?"

The dark cloud starts to dissipate, and a figure struts out. When it comes out into the light, I blink in confusion. *What the fuck is this!?* The figure before me looks like something out of a Tim Burton movie. It has the head of a mule, a black man's ebony, ripped torso, and bird legs, complete with a colorful peacock tail. *What in the actual fuck?*

The mule's head blinks at me, then its mouth opens, a deep, rumbling voice announces, "I am Adrammelech."

I blink again, thinking that maybe I sustained a head injury when the Don demon hit me, and all of this is just a hallucination. Each time I blink, however, the figure before me remains the same, a macabre amalgamation of man, beast, and bird.

"It was you all along?" I gasp, trying to piece it all together in my head.

"Not all along," he corrects, "but you know the old adage: if you want something done correctly, you must do it yourself."

"But how? Why didn't you just come for me yourself before?" My scrambled brain fails to put all of the pieces together. *God, I'd kill for a Tylenol right about now!*

"Not all demons can travel back and forth between worlds," Adrammelech begins, strutting back and forth on his bird legs. It looks absolutely preposterous, but I don't say that.

"What about the ones that have been attacking me for months?"

"Only full-blooded demons are constrained to this realm. Half-bloods, the foot soldiers, can move about freely; but they're ever so weak and vulnerable, easily killed, as you have witnessed."

"And you're full-blooded?"

"Anointed by the Dark Lord himself."

"What do you have to do to become a full-blooded demon?"

"That honor is saved for the vilest, most evil beings, the ones who have given up all humanity within themselves."

"How do you do that?"

"I pledged my soul and eternal damnation to Lucifer and made a blood sacrifice."

"What is it with you demon types and your blood sacrifices? That's so tired."

"Blood is pure. It's life. There's no greater gift than one's own lifeblood. I'd gladly give mine, but I had none to give."

"So, what did you do?"

"I gave him the soul of an infant. It had been born with leukemia and lasted only a few short months before perishing."

I hate kids, I'm not going to lie. I find them annoying, needy, and useless, and I think that in most cases, having them is a huge mistake, but even I am saddened by what I hear. A poor, sick baby, dead and then damned to an everlasting afterlife here in a Hell dimension; what a tragedy. "You're sick," I say, scrunching my face in disgust.

"That's just your fledgling humanity talking," Adrammelech assures me, "once you've seen the light, you'll leave all of that behind."

"I won't join you," I say determinedly. "I'd sooner die."

"They all say that."

I scowl. "What's your stake in all of this? Is it true? Are you planning to overthrow your beloved Dark Lord?"

Adrammelech's mule head grins—a truly disturbing sight—and he crosses his muscled arms over his sculpted chest. "Well, I might as well tell you. I'm your only ally in this dump, so if you throw me under the bus, you'll condemn yourself. Once you've come to your senses, you'll see that I am your friend."

"Sure. Just tell me." He's suddenly so chatty. He was mute and stoic the whole way here, and now he's like a gossipy woman.

"It's all true. It's far beyond time for a regime change. Lucifer, I love him, I do, but he's so short-sighted. All he wants to do is hurt his creator to get revenge. How petty. My plans are far more sinister."

"Why?"

"Let's just say that what I've got planned would never even cross Lucifer's mind."

Why isn't he disclosing his plan to me? "Tell me," I urge.

"Oh, no," Adrammelech laughs, "not all at once. I can't have you trying to parlay a deal with Lucifer against me."

I must admit, that is something I would have thought of doing. Maybe Adrammelech is smarter than I've given him credit. A part of me though, is genuinely interested in these mysterious egregious plans he's concocting. *Is he planning on killing*

Satan? Can Satan be killed?

Adrammelech yawns. "I'm sorry to cut our *tête-à-tête* short, but I've got a Senate meeting to attend now, but I'll be seeing you later. Enjoy your cellmate. I'm sure you both have loads to talk about." He waves his hand, and light spills from an opening in the darkness. He steps through, and it closes behind him, the light vanishing. *So I'm in a cell of some sort. Good to know.*

Below me, Don stirs and jumps to his feet. "What's going on? Where am I?" he gasps, pawing at the walls like a caged cat.

"You want the truth?" I ask, ennui heavy in my voice.

He looks at me for the first time, and realization dawns on him. "Of course, it's you!"

"I didn't bring us here," I assure him.

"Where are we?"

"We're in Hell."

"AKA marriage to your mother," he grumbles.

"Being around you isn't exactly a treat," I shoot back, rolling my eyes.

"Am I dead?"

"Not yet."

"What's *that* supposed to mean?"

"It means stay down and keep quiet. I'm trying to think," I bark. I've never seen Don out of total control. It's kind of off-putting to see.

"Like you're going to get us out of here?"

I turn to him. "I am the only person who *can* get us out of here. So, drop the attitude, or maybe I'll just leave you here. After all, you should get acquainted with where you'll spend your afterlife."

"You're the gay one."

"You say that like it's a bad thing."

"Well, it's not a good thing!"

"God, you're so repressed! You're probably a huge fag, but you're too afraid and too boring to experiment with it." I find myself saying it and suspect that maybe it's true. Could it be that the whole reason that he tormented me all of my life is that he knew I'd end up gay, and he was conflicted about his own clandestine gay feelings? I don't know; maybe I'm reaching too far in order to make myself feel better.

"Me? A fag?" Don laughs bitterly. "I'd rather kill myself than make out with a dude."

"Your loss. There's nothing quite like getting down with a guy."

He shoots me a dirty look, and I giggle. It's fun torturing him. That dark part of myself that's been rearing its gorgeous head lately is out to play again.

"I want to make something perfectly clear right now," I say, regarding him down my long nose. "I *am* getting out of here. I don't care what I have to do to do it, but I'm doing it. You, on the other hand, are nothing but collateral damage. I don't care if you get out or not, but know this: if I do decide to help you out, you're going to disappear. You're going to stop making my mother unhappy. You're going to drop the lawsuit and move to... Germany, maybe? Somewhere far, far away, where we will never see or hear from you again."

"Fuck you! I'm not leaving my son."

"Taking him away from my mom will kill her."

"I'm what's best for him,"

"You're what's best for him from a financial standpoint, yes, but a mother should never be separated from her child. You'll live."

"I won't abandon him," he reiterates.

"Then you'll be spending the rest of forever in this oven. Enjoy."

Any further conversation is cut off by another opening in the wall. I fix my attention on the figure that comes through. She's pale, dark circles ringing the skin underneath her eyes. Her black hair falls in intricate waves around her hips. "Come, Graham," she says softly.

I don't know who she is, but I can sense the gentility inside her. This woman is nothing but a pawn; I won't hurt her unless absolutely necessary. I rise and shoot Don a dark look as I follow her through the hole in the wall.

Gabriel Mero

Chapter Thirty-Five

The hole in the wall seals itself behind us, and the woman starts to lead me down a corridor. Despite the intense heat that hangs heavily in the air here, this woman appears to be completely composed—no sweat, no frizzy hair—except for the dark circles under her eyes. *What's that about?*

I haven't seen my reflection, but I know I must look a disastrous sight. My hair—normally high and dry—has collapsed and hangs in greasy strands in my eyes. My skin has that nasty, oily feel that excess sweating creates, and I don't know how long I've been down here, exactly, but my mouth feels gross, too. My teeth have a fine coating of plaque, and I can taste the rancidness of my breath. Basically, this is my worst nightmare come to life.

"Who are you?" I ask, following her at a respectful distance. I don't know if she can smell or not, but I don't want to assault her nostrils.

"I'm not supposed to talk to you," she answers in a quiet voice. She reminds me of a battered woman, with her quiet voice, frightened demeanor, and avoidance of eye contact. If there's one thing I hate, it's the abuse of women. Real men don't hit women.

"Please," I implore, grabbing her cold hand and stopping. "I'm scared and alone here, I need *someone* on my side."

Her mouth scrunches up as she fights the urge to tell me, but with a sigh, she relents. "My name is Persephone."

"Persephone? You're not... *the Persephone*?" I balk. Greek mythology has always been an area of interest for me, especially once I got into *Xena: Warrior Princess*. If memory serves, Persephone was the wife of Hades, and, having been kidnapped by the God of the Underworld, Persephone gave in and ate a pomegranate seed. She was then forced to spend the winter months in the Underworld, being allowed to return to Earth for the rest of the year. I'd always thought it was just a fun little myth conjured up to explain the changing of the seasons, and once again, I have been proven wrong.

"The one and only." Persephone casts a nervous look over her shoulder, as if Hades or Lucifer himself is waiting just ahead to punish her for talking.

"It's all real," I whisper, perplexed. *So, are Hades and Lucifer the same person, then? If ancient Greek culture predates Judaism and Christianity, that would make Hades older than Lucifer.*

"Come, we must hurry."

"Wait," I call, rushing to catch up to her, as she motors along the corridor, her sandaled feet scuffing the ground, "Why are you here? I thought you spent the winter months in Hell."

"I do, I was recalled for this momentous occasion."

"What momentous occasion? Me getting captured?"

"Yes."

"This is sick."

"I'm not your enemy," she says, "but I'm not your friend, either. I'm just a bystander. I feel bad about what's happening to you, I really do, but I can't help you. I need to do my duty so that I can go back home. Surely you can understand that."

"Yeah," I admit, "I understand. I don't agree with it, but I understand."

Persephone halts in her tracks and turns back to me. "Do not think ill of me, I'm as much a victim in all of this as you are. This is never what I wanted, not the life that I dreamed for myself. I was kidnapped and brought here against my will, just like you. I was terrified, especially when faced with him. The only advice I can give you is to not eat anything, I foolishly gave in and sought comfort in pomegranate seeds, and now I'm damned to spend four months a year here. He rapes me, He beats me, He makes my life... well... He makes my life a living hell. I wish I was mortal because I'd have died centuries ago and be past all of this, but I'm not. I'm immortal, and thus my sentence drags on eternally, constantly haunting me."

"I don't think badly of you," I assure her. "I know you're a victim, too. I just think that if anyone can relate to what I'm going through, it's you. There must be a way out of here, you're one of the only people here who has come and gone. Do you know of any portals that can take me back to the surface?"

"The portals are created by Lucifer himself, using primal dark magic. I know of no way for you to escape. You've got a day left of your sentence; if you can resist the temptation of food and drink until then, you'll be transported home automatically. You must be strong, Graham."

"If there's one thing that I've learned this year, it's just how much strength I possess, though I've never known it."

"Good. You'll need to draw on that strength. Lucifer is the master of illusions, too. He'll say and do anything to get you to bend to his will. You have to keep your mind clear."

"I'll do my best. Thanks."

"Don't thank me. I'm not helping you, just warning you of what you're about to face."

"Understood. You're as much an enemy as Adrammelech is." I know this isn't actually true, but I can't risk alerting Persephone. Until she shows a sign of dissension, I have to pretend to treat her as an enemy.

"For all intents and purposes, yes."

The corridor opens up into what would be a pretty garden if this were Earth; instead, the atmosphere here is not compatible with life. Where plants would grow, only dead vines and weeds poke from the ground.

I spot a boy huddled amongst the weeds. His clothes are worn and tattered, though vaguely dated. The jeans that he wears aren't modern low-rise jeans; they're the unflattering style of the 70s and 80s that made everyone look like they had a big, square ass. The young kid looks to be about ten. His blond hair is all disheveled, and his face is caked with what looks to be dirt or soot. His clothing is ripped and hanging in tatters. Obviously, he's been here for a long time.

The more I stare at this ragtag vagabond, the more I feel… something, an intense connection of sorts, as if I know him. I know that I don't, I know that, but I feel as though I should. I break away from Persephone, and, despite her protestations, I approach him. He sees me and jolts to his feet, poised to run away.

"I won't hurt you," I say, holding my hands up in surrender. "I'm here against my will, too."

The kid looks at me through frenzied blue eyes and stands down a bit.

"My name is Graham. I know this sounds insane, but I feel like I should know you ."

"I don't know you," the boy snaps. "Leave me alone."

I examine him more closely, and I start to see a resemblance. He has the same blueberry blue eyes as I do, though the shape is different, smaller. We have similar big noses, and share the same face shape and features, even down to the pinched, angry look that naturally rests on our faces. *Who the hell is this kid?*

"My name is Graham," I repeat, stepping closer. "My mother's name is Beverly. Her mother's name is Ginevra." I see him tense, his wild eyes going wider. *Is that it? Is that the missing piece of the puzzle? Are they somehow related to me?*

"I know them," the kid says, stepping forward.

"How? How do you know them? Please tell me, this is not making sense at all."

"Your mother is the one that sent me here."

This hits me like a punch to the chest. *What? Mom did this!? How? Why!?*

"Who are you?" I demand, bile burning my throat.

"I'm Julian, your uncle."

My mind whirls at this sudden revelation. *Mom has a brother? And she sent him her? Why? So that's why she and Grandma hate each other!*

Julian looks like he's about to say more, but then suddenly shrinks back and darts away, like stray cats when approached. *That's weird, why would he be so afraid of me?* I turn around, and my breath catches in my throat.

The figure before me is menacing, standing over seven feet tall, with razor-sharp teeth, thick black claws, and ram's horns jutting from his forehead. His body is well-muscled, the black skin luminescent. I've often wondered what Satan would look like. Part of me mused that he would look just like a normal guy; after all, he is supposed to be an angel that betrayed God and got punished for it. On the other hand, I couldn't help but be influenced by pop culture. After seeing the movie *Legend* as a kid, I kind of assumed that he would look like the Lord of Darkness from that movie. While I wasn't entirely wrong, the whole red skin thing was definitely off. I even considered something closer to Darth Maul from *Star Wars Episode 1: The Phantom Menace. Boy, was I wrong.*

He's not wearing any clothes, not that I can see, but I also can't see any genitalia or anything among the blackness of his skin. His flesh looks as though all life has been leached from it, leaving only a dark husk in its wake.

Lucifer towers over me, staring down at me through the same creepy goat's eyes as the other demons I've encountered. I gulp, my heart kicking into overdrive. *This is it, he's got me trapped. I can't outrun him, that's for sure.*

"Hello, Graham," he says, his voice deep and gravelly.

"Hi, Satan."

"Lucifer," he corrects me, voice booming.

"Sorry, Lucifer."

He regards me again, his tongue scouring his razor-sharp teeth, mechanically. "So, at last, the witch is before me."

"Against my will, but, yeah," I say as nonchalantly as I can muster.

Lucifer laughs and claps his giant hands together in amusement. "It's been so long since I've had someone who wasn't terrified of me. It's refreshing to trade barbs with one of my *guests.*" I know that by *guests,* he means victims, but I don't correct him. What would be the point in pissing off my captor already? I try to cast a glance behind me to see if Julian is still nearby, but it's as if he was never even there. *Where could he have run off to? Will I see him again before I get out of here?*

"You wandered off from your guide," Lucifer continues, drawing my attention back to his insidious presence.

"Yeah, sorry. I was distracted by something."

"Hasn't anyone ever taught you that it's rude to keep your host waiting?"

"Don't take it out on Persephone," I interject. "It wasn't her fault."

"That useless hag has been dealt with," he replies ominously.

Oh, no, I hope that I haven't gotten Persephone into too much trouble. Fuck!

Lucifer grabs my arms and steers me back toward his palace. I don't want to go, but I have no choice. So far, he's been pretty nice, but I can't help but wonder just how long that will last. You don't get to be the ruler of a hell dimension by being kind. Chances are that his niceness is a façade. He's trying to get me to give my powers over to him willingly. *Well, that's not going to happen.*

We walk in silence until we're inside the palace proper. A winding staircase leads us up, up, up. It seems to go on forever. *I guess demons don't have to worry about sleeping or anything, so why would an infinite staircase be a bother to them?*

After what feels like years, we come to the top of the stairs and push through heavy wooden doors. They open into a room with a long wooden table bearing a variety of foods to stir the appetite. I can smell roast beef and chicken, pizza, orange chicken, lasagna, all of my favorite foods. My stomach turns at the scents, and it rumbles furiously. *I am starving.*

"Sit," Lucifer commands, pushing me down into a chair that pulled itself out. As soon as I'm seated in it, it pushes itself back up to the table. Lucifer sits at the head of the table and waving his hand, fills his goblet. "Eat."

"I'm not hungry," I lie, turning my face away from the table.

Lucifer laughs again and swallows some of his wine. "Stubborn, I see. That's fine, I shall enjoy breaking you. I love a challenge."

"Don't get too excited about it," I tell him. "I'm not exactly planning on staying here. You've got me for another day and a half, and then I *am* going home."

"Do you think so?" His dark lips curl up into a sneer. "Well, it's nice to have dreams, I suppose."

"You can't keep me here," I challenge, "I know the deal."

"Scholarly as well, good for you! You've saved me a lot of unnecessary talking."

"You played dirty to get me here. Don't act so surprised that you've finally got me in your clutches."

"Did I?" Lucifer looks affronted. "You were ignoring all of my other invitations, killing my messengers, in fact. How else was I supposed to get you to stop in?"

"If someone ignores your 'invites' that usually means that they're not interested."

"Such fire!" He grabs a chicken leg and devours it—bone and all—in one bite.

Damn! "Why do you look like that?"

"Don't you like it?" Lucifer looks down at his dark skin, regarding it. "I wasn't sure what to wear, so I went with intimidating. I can change it if you like." He snaps his fingers, and sitting in his seat is Erasmus. Well, not Erasmus, but Lucifer masquerading as Erasmus.

I feel a pang in my chest as I look at my boyfriend's image. I wish that I could tell him where I am, so he wouldn't be hurt and think that I abandoned him. I'd give anything to be safe with him now, in his arms, kissing him. *Soon, babe, I silently tell him.*

"Does this form suit you better?" Lucifer taunts.

"Looking like my boyfriend won't get you what you want," I say. "I'm not giving you my powers, nor am I pledging my soul and powers to evil. I may not be lily-white, but I'm not evil. You're wasting your time with all of this. You're going to piss me off badly enough that when I get home, I'll find a way to destroy you forever."

Lucifer leans forward in his seat. "Oh, sweet, Graham," his voice is Erasmus' and I try my best not to take comfort in it, "I would *love* for you to end my miserable existence. Do you know how depressing it is to be stuck here for all eternity? I love being evil, I do. I love torturing these poor souls and making them scream, but even that gets old after a few centuries. Quite frankly, I'm bored. I want more."

"Like?"

"With your powers, I'll free myself from this domain, and I'll set about causing chaos in your world. Killing the good, letting the evil triumph, shaping your world to resemble mine. There's an infinitesimal supply of souls to feast upon where you come from, and not just the rotten ones I'm forced to consume here. I want the good ones, the ones that my *Father* gets his hands on. Once I've destroyed his Earth, I'll exact my vengeance on Him and end His reign."

I fight the urge to puke. Lucifer is even more sociopathic than I could have ever imagined. *All of this is a ploy to get revenge on God for punishing him? So, Adrammelech was right, after all. I don't like Adrammelech any better than Lucifer, but maybe I should ally myself with him. At least his plan involves destroying Lucifer.* "That's not going to happen," I spit out, shaking in anger. *This is so pathetic!*

"You say that now," Lucifer crows. "You have no idea what's in store for you."

"You can torture me all you want, I still won't let you do this! You got yourself into this situation, Lucifer, don't blame anyone else. This is your fault! Pay the consequences like any other adult."

"It wasn't my fault!" he roars, slamming his hand down on the table and making all of the food platters shake. "Who is He to decide who is good and who is evil? I gave Him *everything!* It wasn't until I saw how short-sighted He is that I was damned. He likes to think He's perfect, but He's not. You follow Him blindly, like a sheep, but you don't even know Him, I do. He doesn't have your best interest at heart."

"Spare me." I shake my head. "I don't want to hear it. You want to destroy the world and get revenge like a petulant child. In my book, that makes you the bad guy."

Lucifer—still in Erasmus' body—chews the gristle from some roast beef, as if forming his next words carefully. "If you won't join forces with me, you will be subject to torture beyond your worst imagination."

"Bring it."

"I should also warn you that I can tap into your innermost fears. Each torture will be designed from your own fears."

Shit, that doesn't sound good. Still, I can't let evil win. I can't, and I won't. I set my chin determinedly and cross my arms over my chest in defiance.

"So be it," Lucifer growls. "Guards!"

The doors burst open, and hideous winged demons grab me. They smell like rotting flesh, and their touch leaves behind an inky substance on my skin,

Lucifer throws back another goblet of wine. "Take him to the Well of Sorrow."

Oh, no, this doesn't sound good. I'm yanked from the room, and I feel trepidation setting in with each step. *This is definitely not good.*

Chapter Thirty-Six

The demons that have hold of me, are not being gentle at all; they're definitely not here to play. They mean business and their claws digging into my arm prove it. *Well, I've really gone and done it now. I've pissed Satan off to the point where he's sentenced me to egregious torture.* I've toughened up a lot in the last few months, sure, but the idea of being tortured makes my knees tremble.

I'm dragged out of the dining room and down the hall. We come to a large wooden door and then crossing the threshold, we're in what appears to be a medieval torture chamber. *Of course, why wouldn't the King of Hell have a brutal, primitive torture chamber in his castle?*

"Come on, guys, can't we talk about this?" I say, my voice trembling a little as I'm slammed back against a wooden post, and my hands are jerked behind my back, tied tightly so that I can't move. *Oh, God, what's happening? What hideous torment am I about to endure?*

Lucifer strides in, still looking like Erasmus. This must be some kind of psychological maliciousness. *Does he think that if he hurts me wearing Erasmus' face, that I'll sour toward my beloved vampire? Well, I won't, nothing could ever make me not love him. The bond that we've developed over the last six months can never be broken.*

"Are you sure you won't comply?" Lucifer asks, coming to stand before me, leering at me.

"I'd sooner die," I reply.

"Unfortunately for you, I can't test that theory, but I can do some things that will make you wish that you were dead."

"I'm not afraid of you." *Okay, I'm totally lying.* I am absolutely bloody terrified of what Lucifer has in store for me, but I will not, under any circumstances, let him know that. I will not give him that upper hand over me. The Beverly in me rises to the surface; *I'll be strong, I have to be.*

"You say that now, but we'll see how you feel after a few rounds of my... *persuasive techniques.*" He laughs and rubs his hands together in sinful delight.

"Do me a favor?"

Lucifer quirks an eyebrow and leans in. "I'm intrigued," he admits.

"Change again, into anyone but Erasmus."

Lucifer guffaws and takes my face in his hand. "Poor little witch doesn't want to see his lover hurt him, eh? How quaint!"

"It's not that." I try to wiggle my face out of his vise-like grip.

"Then what?"

"I want to see you, the real you. I want to see the face of the thing that I'm going to kill when I get out of here."

Again, the gregarious laughter, deep in his chest. "You amuse me, witch. I will yield on this request, but only because you amuse me so greatly." He waves his hand in front of his face, and the image of Erasmus is gone. Now, in his place is a clean-shaven man with long, light brown hair that falls around his shoulders. White feathery wings plume out from behind him, swiping at the air harmlessly. His piercing blue eyes bore into mine as he awaits my reaction.

"Is this... the real you?" I inquire, blinking to clear my vision as my left contact shifts out of alignment on my eye and the astigmatism takes over.

"This is how I looked before, yes," he answers. "This is me as I was before I was ostracized from Paradise."

I'll never say it out loud, but the old Lucifer was not a bad looking man... angel.. whatever. His thin lips quirk as he watches me watching him, assessing his face, inch by inch. Under different circumstances, I would definitely be open to attempting seduction, but I know that the being before me is immune to my charms. This demon lives only to cause pain.

"I thought you'd be taller," I say, finally, playing aloof.

"Do not think that you can appeal to my vanity," Lucifer warns gently, "all that remains of the angel I was before is the shell outside."

"If this is how you normally look, what was the black demon thing you appeared to me before?" I'm staling, buying time before the immense pain to come.

"I know you mortals usually perceive me to be a big, red, muscular creature, and that amuses me. I just prefer black to red."

"I'm glad we mortals amuse you so."

The Prince of Darkness turns toward a table next to him and starts eying up the buffet of blades laid upon it. There are the normal sharp blades, a curved sickle-like one that looks particularly wicked, and a pair of *kukri* blades. Also, there's something resembling a dentist's forceps and pliers, and rusty nails and needles. *This is definitely not going to be fun.*

He picks the sickle and runs the blade along his finger. I see the skin split easily, and blood start to well up. He places the finger to his lips and sucks at the blood, closing his eyes in exaltation before coming back to stand before me. The sickle shines menacingly in his grip.

"Pledge your eternal life to me, Graham," he says, swinging the blade.

"Eat shit and die." I muster up more courage than I'm feeling. If it's the last thing that I do, I will not show weakness before him. I'll be strong and unwavering, I'll make my mother proud.

"Have it your way."

In one swift motion, he thrusts the blade tip into my stomach, below my navel. I twitch as the pain lances through me, and I bite my tongue to keep from crying out. *This hurts worse than I ever could have imagined.* Tongue jutting out from his even white teeth, Lucifer juts the knife in deeper and then forces it up, splitting my stomach and chest open.

I feel vomit in my throat as my intestines unravel onto the floor below me. My eyes tear up, and I blink past the wooziness. *Is this what severe blood loss feels like, or am I just in shock?* I force myself not to look down at my entrails, and I meet the demon's icy blue eyes. "Is that the best you've got?" I groan, blood overtaking my mouth and dripping out with each word.

"I'll admit, I'm impressed," Lucifer pontificates, pulling the blade out of my body and tossing it onto the table. "You'd be dead now if this was happening on Earth. I was kind of hoping I'd get to see you cry, or at least beg for mercy."

"I wish I could say that I'm sorry to disappoint you, but we both know that I'm not." I swallow the puke down, closing my eyes against the miserable feeling of it all.

"Don't worry, this isn't the best that I've got; I'm just warming up, witch."

I feel myself starting to drift off. *Is this what death feels like?* I wonder, my eyelids growing heavy. Maybe I'll get lucky, and death will take me. I don't want to leave Romana, Amethyst, or Erasmus, but I also don't want to be subjected to hours of excruciating pain, either.

Lucifer waves his hand majestically, and I feel a tug inside of me. I open my eyes to see my intestines folding back into my body, like a fishing pole being reeled back in. *Okay, this is far too weird of an experience; no one should ever be disemboweled and then stay conscious afterword.*

Once everything is back inside of me, the wound seals itself cleanly, no scar in sight. At least I have that in my favor. The only scars that I'll retain from this unfortunate episode are emotional ones; the physical ones wash themselves away, apparently.

"Now," he muses, pacing back and forth in front of me, "what shall we try next?" He taps his strong chin, really mulling it over. "I'm sensing so many fears within you. Perhaps..." he grins and stamps his foot. "We should heat things up a little, what do you say?"

I want to beg him not to do what I suspect he's about to do, but I somehow keep myself from saying it. There's only one fear of mine that involves heating things up. *Being burned alive is going to suck tremendously!*

Back in middle school, I developed an interest in Joan of Arc, the French heroine who claimed to hear the voice of God, spurring her to help save France from the English. That she was captured, and after being betrayed was burned at the stake fascinated me. I've always had a morbid fascination with death; not in a psychotic, serial killer way, but I just find it interesting how brutal methods of execution used to be.

The local video store had a VHS copy of *the Messenger: The Story of Joan of Arc*, and after several weeks of waiting for it to come back, I snatched it up, and as soon as I got home, I put it in. I was not prepared for the level of brutality depicted in the movie. From rape and murder, to graphic language, I was in awe of it all. What really irked me was the graphic death scene where you see Milla Jovovich as the heroine, tied to the stake, the flames burning brightly about her. Then, we see her bare feet on fire, and then the flames devouring her whole body, her dress blowing up as her face is burned away.

Needless to say, after that movie, I have had an incredibly irrational fear of being burned alive, particularly to be burned at the stake like poor Joan. People have informed me that the nerve endings would be gone before the pain could get too intense. That, once they're gone, you'd feel nothing, I still could not bear the thought of suffering through such an abominable ending.

From the wicked smile on the Devil's face, I know that this is precisely what he's plotting for me now. *Please, God, no! Not this! Anything but this!*

My prayers fall on silent ears as my shoes are torn off with a flick of his hand, and the demon henchmen return with stacks of brush. Where they got it from, or how they knew to come now, I have no idea, but that's the least of my worries at the moment. I feel my feet being secured to the stake, and I know that I'm done for.

"Are you sure you won't reconsider my offer?" Lucifer presses, as the brush is piled up around my bare feet.

I don't answer right away. This is the point in the process where I want to give in and say anything, do anything, to spare myself the hell that I'm about to face, but I know that I can't. As badly as I want to, I can't abandon my morals. *Is this how Joan felt in those moments leading up to her terrible end?*

My silence is taken as a negative, and a flaming torch appears in the demon's hand, the orange flames burning brightly, clawing at the air above them. Impulsively, my stomach clenches, and I vomit up a puddle of yellow bile. *Oh, dear God, help me, please!*

Satan throws the torch into the dry brush that enfolds my feet, and immediately they go up in flames, the first few rows are gone almost immediately. *This is definitely happening a lot more quickly than it should.* Thick black smoke swirls past my head, stinging my eyes. I take deep breaths of it, hyperventilating. I once read in a book that chances are that Joan passed out and died from smoke inhalation before the flames got her too badly. I pray the same will happen to me. I cough as my sensitive lung tissue is assaulted by the acrid smoke.

In under a minute, I can feel myself sweating, and I squirm, trying to get my feet as far away from those flames as possible. My attempts are futile as there is no slack in the ropes or whatever it is that's binding me to the stake. I pant as I feel the flames grow closer, hungrily devouring the dry brush.

"You're a sick twisted fuck!" I scream, beyond caring if I keep my composure.

"I think that's the nicest thing that you've ever said to me," Satan taunts.

I cry out as the flames find my flesh, licking the skin and incinerating the muscles and tendons underneath. If I thought that the disemboweling was bad, this trumps that by a lot. I scream, again and again, trying to awaken the adrenaline within me to miraculously free myself from the stake and end my misery. I try again and again but to no avail.

The smell of searing flesh assaults my nostrils, and I puke again; the vomit lands at my feet and hisses as the flames evaporate it. I hear snapping and popping as my blood vessels burst, and my nerve endings die out down there. *Kill me now*, I beg Lucifer quietly, *please, please just end this. End my misery.*

The flames climb up my legs, destroying my jeans and settling into the soft flesh of my thighs and groin. "Fuck!" I gasp, panting. *Why can't I just have peace and fucking die!?* As bad as the real people burned at the stake had it, at least they got a merciful death eventually. I am damned to suffer this whole ordeal totally conscious. *What did I ever do to deserve this?*

In almost every account of Joan of Arc's life, I remember that her only request upon her execution was that a cross was held up before her as she died. I assume it was so that she could focus on God and be reminded that no matter how badly she was suffering, that soon she'd be welcomed into the arms of her Heavenly Father and be beyond all pain and suffering.

I think of Erasmus, of his dark brown eyes, the same eyes that captivated me from the first time I saw him back in August. I think of his adorable smile and the way that his lips feel as they brush mine. *Oh, God, what I wouldn't give to be in his arms now, instead of being immolated.* My mind focuses on my lover, his taste, his touch, the feel of him.

Despite preoccupying my mind with Erasmus, I can still feel the flames climb up to my chest, neck, and face. My hair goes up quickly. I cry, I sob, I scream until my voice is horse and only mangled cracks come out of my hollow throat. I scream until the flames incinerate my lungs and throat, and nothing but darkness surrounds me.

****

At first, I think that this has all been a dream, some terrible nightmare that was a result of my overactive subconscious. I open my eyes, and my stomach drops when I see that I am not in my room, nor am I at Erasmus'. I'm in Sitra Achra . *It's all real.* Flashes of my body burning come back to me, and I dry heave. My stomach repeatedly convulses, trying to purge itself despite there being nothing left.

Gabriel Mero

After a few minutes, I compose myself and look around the room for Don. Sure enough, I find him sitting in the corner, eyes wide as he watches me. I sit up and groan, My skin feels weird... almost like I got a really bad sunburn. Technically I got burnt pretty badly, but I shouldn't be in pain.

"How are you alive?" Don demands, mouth open.

"It's demon magic," I answer. "I can't die, not yet. They were torturing me, trying to get me to give in to them, but I didn't."

"When they brought you back, you were nothing but a pile of ash. I watched as you grew out of it; bone, muscle skin. You looked like one of those goddamned anatomy drawings!"

That explains the pain. After the fire, everything had to regrow, and my skin was the last to come back. I anxiously reach up and heave a sigh of relief at the comforting feeling of my full head of hair on top of my head. *At least I grew back whole.* "How long was I out?" I ask, wishing for the life of me that I could have a sip of ice water. Between the dry air and then being burned alive, my throat is beyond desert level dry.

"It's hard to tell how time passes here," Don replies. "There's no sun to tell day from night. According to my watch, we've been here for thirty-six hours."

Thirty-six hours of forty-eight, not bad. All I have to do is suffer twelve more hours in this barren cesspool, and then I'll be free to go home. Twelve more hours...

"Not much longer now," I mutter.

"Huh?"

"I have twelve more hours, and then they can't keep me here anymore. As long as I don't eat or drink anything, they can only keep me for forty-eight hours."

"What about me? I didn't do anything to piss these people off! I don't even know why I'm here!"

"Just sit tight," I say, irritation setting in. *I'm a decent human being, Don is not. How is it fair that I'm the one being subjected to all this pain, while he's just sitting here on his fat ass, wiling the hours away? Where's the justice in that?*

"Sit tight? I have nothing to do with this... this nonsense! I want to go home so that I can see my son."

"And you will, soon, I promise. Twelve more hours, and then we're out of here."

"That rule applies to me, too?"

"I don't know," I admit. *I've kind of been wondering about that this whole time. Can Don eat or drink anything and still leave with me? Can he leave at all?*

"You don't know!?"

"Hey, I didn't bring you here," I remind him. "A demon took you over because you were in Willow's Crest. I don't want you here. I can't stand you, I never could. The last thing I want to do is be forced to sit in a glorified jail cell with you."

"The feeling is mutual," he snaps.

That should hurt my feelings, but strangely, it doesn't. Somewhere along the line, I stopped caring about Don or what he thinks of me. It's a weird sensation after wasting so many years scrambling for his elusive approval.

"Have you had anything to eat or drink?" I ask, trying to lighten the mood a little. *As much as I don't like it, Don is innocent for once. If we're going to get out of this, we're going to need to work together.*

"No, I haven't been offered anything." He won't look at me, and he has his arms crossed over his chest like a petulant child.

"Good. As long as you don't eat or drink anything, you're fine."

"Why? Why can't I eat or drink anything?"

"I don't suppose you're familiar with Greek mythology?"

"What?"

"Never mind." I lie back on the cot and close my eyes. *I can do this. I can. It's only twelve more hours. I've survived being disemboweled and burned at the stake. If I can survive those things, I can handle anything else these fuckers throw at me.*

Chapter Thirty-Seven

I must have dozed off because when a portal opens in the wall, I jerk up on the cot, my body in full fight or flight mode.

Persephone steps through the portal, carrying a tray of food and drink. She keeps her eyes downcast, and there's a livid red welt on her cheek. No doubt, when she 'lost' me, Lucifer punished her with a punch. *What a vile piece of shit.*

"How long was I asleep?"

"I suggest you eat," she says, her voice soft and submissive. The tray has bananas and grapes; seeing them makes my mouth water. *What I'd give for just one bite.*

"You know I can't do that, Persephone." I wince as I take in the mess of her pale face. "Did he do that to you?"

"It does not matter."

"It does." I cross to her and gently grab her shoulders, staring intensely into her dark eyes. "He's going to pay for what he's done to you, okay? I promise you that."

"You can't kill him."

"Who said anything about me? You know as well as I do that Adrammelech wants to stage a coup. If I can join forces with him, that'll instigate drama between them. If Lucifer gets killed in the process—"

"You can kill his body, but not the manifestation of Evil."

"What?" Lucifer has a body just like everyone else.

"When God cast him from Heaven and condemned him here, he became the physical manifestation of Evil. You can't kill Evil because it's in the hearts and souls of everyone, it's omnipresent. If you killed him, your soul would take his place."

Fuck, well, that certainly puts a damper on my plans. I wonder if there's a way that I can free this innocent woman from having to come back down here. She's no more than a pawn in all of this, and I sincerely hope that nothing terrible befalls her. Enough innocent people have been dragged into this fight; I won't stand for anymore.

"How much longer do you have to stay down here?" I ask, changing the subject.

"As soon as your time is up, I'm free to return home."

"What do you do when you're not down here?"

"As the daughter of the Goddess Demeter, I have eternal life on my side. I live amongst nature, in a pocket universe, slightly out of sync with your reality. In my home, there have been no technological advances. We exist as we did all those years ago. My mother and I live in peaceful harmony with nature and all its creatures."

"That sounds nice," I admit. "I hope that you can return there soon."

"I wish I could stay there forever. Even after millennia of coming to this place, I still loathe it. I'll never grow accustomed to being here."

"When I get home, I'll try to help you. There might be a spell in my *Grimoire* that can relieve you of your sentence."

Her eyes widen in excitement, and for the first time, I see her pink lips tug up into a smile. "You'd do that for me?"

"My fight isn't with you. You're as much a victim in all of this as I am, Persephone. I don't want this for you, you've been very good to me."

"I won't hold out for it, but if somehow you're able to do so, I'd forever be in your debt."

"First things first, I need to get out of here and get home."

"Not long now," she says with a conspiratorial wink.

"I'm so confused," Don interjects, watching us from across the room.

"About what?" I ask. *What could he possibly be confused about?* He has not shown much interest in what is really going on here.

"What the *hell* is going on here!? None of this is making any sense at all! You were brought in here as ash and somehow regrew yourself, she claims to be immortal and a goddess... what kind of drugs are you people on? What did you slip me?"

Oh, poor, Don, too simple to think outside the box. He's convinced himself that this is all the effects of drugs. Of course, he has, why not?

The portal suddenly opens again, and two demon thugs cross over. "What is the meaning of this?" Persephone demands, skirts whirling as she spins to face them.

"Quiet, whore! We do not explain ourselves to you. You're nothing more than the Master's concubine," one of the demons hisses angrily.

Don is snatched up by one of the demons, and he starts to kick and buck like an anxiety-ridden horse. "Hey! What's going on!? Let me go!" he cries. The angry demon backhands him with a meaty *slap!* Don falls prone in his arms. The other demon jerks me to my feet and holds me tightly.

I don't need to ask what's going on; I already know. Time is running out, and Lucifer is getting desperate to claim his prize. The gloves are off.

Persephone follows us as the demons drag Don and me from the cell and down the hall again. The hall leads to an opulent staircase that takes us out into the area outside of the castle. I frown when I see a crowd assembled around us, like witnesses at an execution. *What the fuck is going on!?*

Lucifer and Adrammelech stand off to the side, watching as Don and I are brought into the center of the courtyard. Don is thrown to the ground, and I am released, I rub my wrists where they ache from the tightness of the demon's grip.

Adrammelech's grotesque body trots over to Don and me, his mulish eyes bearing not even a trace of humanity within them. "I'm sorry that it has to come to this," he says, "but you're pressing our hand. You won't give us what we want, so we have to get more aggressive." Despite his soft words, I know that they're a warning. There is no kindness in demon-kind, I've learned that already.

The guards suddenly turn and grab Adrammelech by the arms. "Let go, fools!" he cries! "Unhand me at once! What is the meaning of this?"

Lucifer walks around to face Adrammelech, once again adopting his demonic guise with the charcoal black skin and menacing horns. "Do you think me a fool, Adrammelech?" he purrs.

"What do you mean?" Adrammelech tries to play dumb, his animalistic eyes rolling here, there, and everywhere desperately.

"I know of your plan to overthrow me," Lucifer spits.

"Master, forgive me." Adrammelech drops to what equates to his knees, despite having his arms held behind him. Apparently, he knows there is no sense in feigning ignorance in this instance. Despite his secretiveness, somehow, word got out to Lucifer of his scheming. "I would never betray you, my Liege. You can't see how dangerous your plan is. I mean, what... what if you're killed on Earth? I'm simply looking out for you! I merely meant to give you a rest from your duties! I wish you no harm!"

Adrammelech definitely knows how to bullshit. I don't believe him, but part of me wants to. How could anyone argue with sound logic?

The King of Hell shakes his big head. "I am not a fool, Adrammelech, you have always been a treacherous viper. I've tolerated you all these years because of your brutality in the Senate. But one thing I will not abide is betrayal."

"Please, Lord!" Adrammelech begs, his voice reedy.

"Guards," Lucifer presses. The two demons holding Adrammelech start to ravish his macabre body, breaking the arms and tearing at the flesh. Adrammelech said that demons don't have blood, and I see he's telling the truth. Nothing comes out of the wounds. *Satan must be different, because he wasn't born a demon.*

Adrammelech cries out and then throws his head back, his mouth open. A familiar black cloud swells from his gaping mouth and sways in the air as if weighing its options. Don looks up and gasps. The cloud, sensing its opportunity, lunges at Don, invading his mouth and nostrils until his eyes turn black.

"Good," Lucifer says, grinning. "You've trapped yourself in a mortal body. Now, it's time to pay for your betrayal." He turns to me and holds out a red hilted blade inscribed in an unfamiliar language. "The only blade that can kill a true demon," he explains, "use it to kill the traitor. Kill him and take his place at my side."

"I don't want to serve at your side," I argue, shaking my head emphatically. "I want to go home!"

"Don't ignore the wickedness inside of you for the sake of your precious soul. You're not strong enough to resist it, just give in, let it wash over you and forget your petty anxieties."

"Never!"

Lucifer sighs. "Very well, then. I have no choice but to prove just how evil I can truly be."

That statement makes my heart skip a beat. *Uh, oh, what now?* I thought that being burned alive was bad enough, but now I'm starting to suspect that was just the overture to a symphony of pain.

He approaches me, and before I can react, he yanks my mouth open, and although he doesn't move an inch, I feel him pushing himself inside of me. I cry out at the invasion, this spiritual rape. Darkness, pure evil, enters my body and floods my veins, attacking all that is good within me.

I try to fight this fresh onslaught, but after everything I've suffered in the last day and a half, I am weak, far too weak to combat this enemy. I am not trained in spiritual strength, either, so I stand no chance of winning.

"Give in to me," Lucifer's voice whispers in my head, echoing again and again, piercing my ears despite the quietness of it. He's inside of me, and I can't help but wonder if I'll be able to get him out, and if I can, just how much of him will be left?

"No!" I scream, hands over my ears and my eyes squeezed shut, anything I can do to keep him out of me.

"You can't fight me, so don't even try. Just give in to the evil within you; you've always wanted to."

His words carry a sweet, seductive quality to them. I'd be lying if I said that I didn't have darkness inside of me. *Maybe he's right.* Maybe I have been wasting my life fighting the inevitable for all of these years. I've tried for so long to do good, to be good, and for what? Where has it got me? I have always believed that good things happen to good people and bad things happen to bad people. Considering that mostly bad things have happened to me, I must not be a good person.

In my mind's eye, I see myself at Lucifer's side, leading an assault upon the Earth, raging vengeance for all of the crimes committed against me. I see myself making Don sorry that he ever hurt me. I see myself destroying my real dad, the one who never cared enough to make me a priority. All of the assholes who bullied me in school, I see them splayed and flayed before me, their cries of misery like a symphony in my head.

It comes to me so easily. This is who I am, who I have always been. There's no struggle, no anxiety. This is me. "Okay," I moan, my legs quivering under the assault my body is experiencing.

"Okay?" the King of Hell presses, wanting to hear me say the words.

"I'll do it," I say. "I'll join you."

There's a tug inside of me, and then I feel as though my body is an airplane, and someone has opened the emergency exit door while in mid-flight. I drop to my knees from the force of it, and my head sways, making me dizzy. *What a rush!*

Slowly, I regain my feeling of internal normalcy and struggle to my feet. I am so dizzy, my vision swimming before me as the room appears to spin.

"Good choice," Lucifer continues, holding out the demon blade toward me. "Take it."

I reach out and take it. The handle is warm in my hand, inviting. It fits my hand perfectly, as though it was made just for me. I test its weight, and I am delighted that I can wield it easily.

"Kill him." The black, pointed finger motions at Don, or rather, Adrammelech hiding inside of Don's body.

"Please!" I don't know if it's Don or Adrammelech speaking; maybe it's an amalgamation of both. Either way, it doesn't matter. I have to do what I have to do. It all makes sense to me now.

"Don't do it!" Persephone cries, her voice surprisingly forceful.

I whip around to face the direction that her voice came from. *Where is she? Why is she speaking up?*

"Silence!" Lucifer roars, whirling around and smacking her in the face hard enough that she drops to the ground, weightless as a rag doll.

That snaps me out of my reverie, *and I feel an unburdening in my soul. What am I doing? Why am I holding the demon blade?* I feel violated, as if I've been used as a receptacle of evil and then dumped.

"No," I say, trying to drop the blade, but it stays firmly in my hand.

"Too late now!" Lucifer exclaims, turning back toward me. "Kill him! Kill him!"

"No, I won't do it!" I shake my head profusely.

I hear Persephone cry out and turn to see that Satan has her by the throat, holding her above the ground so that she cannot breathe. Her dark-lidded eyes are wide in panic. Her pale skin is slowly growing purple.

"You can't kill her," I say, mustering up the remainder of my compromised courage. "She's an immortal."

"Who said anything about me killing her?" he challenges. "That blade you hold can kill demons and immortals. All it will take is one more rape, and I can make you kill her with your own hands. Do you really want that on your conscience?"

Just when I thought that this fallen angel could not get any more insidious, he proves just how wrong I am. He's laid the gauntlet down. I either kill Adrammelech—and Don in the process—or under his influence, murder Persephone. *Fuck me gently with a chainsaw.*

"Are you that desperate?" I ask, my face crinkled in disgust.

"I think you'll find I'll stoop to any level necessary to get what I want." And with that, he changes form again to look like Erasmus. *My poor Erasmus.* I hope he's doing all right without me and that he's not blaming himself for all of this. It's not his fault any more than it's my fault. *Sometimes, evil happens.*

"I can't," I moan.

"Choose. Or I'll make you kill both of them."

I stand in the middle of two losing choices. Do I kill an innocent woman who has been good to me or kill a demon in the body of my tormenting stepfather? I look into Persephone's pleading eyes and then into Adrammelech's bestial eyes.

Gritting my teeth, I raise the blade and dart over to Adrammelech. Crying out, I drive the blade right into his chest, stopping only when the bone within stops the knife from going deeper.

The animalistic eyes widen in shock and then roll back into his head. Don's body falls to the ground and starts to convulse. Multihued flames materialize out of thin air and begin devouring the seizing body. Once again, the sickening smell of burning flesh makes me queasy, and I fight the urge to dry heave.

"I'm sorry," I say, my voice cracking. "I had no choice."

Adrammelech and Don disappear into the flames and leave charred stains on the rock beneath where they lay. *There, it's done.*

"Wonderful!" Lucifer claps Erasmus' hands excitedly. "You did so well for your first kill. I can't wait to hone your skills."

"Let her go." I jab the blade in Persephone's direction. Tears spring from her eyes, and she is as purple as a cartoon octopus now.

"Deal." He lets her go, and she drops to the ground, sputtering and coughing. She gasps as her bruised windpipe is opened again, and air rushes in.

"Are you okay?" I ask her.

"I'll be fine," she gags.

"All is done now, except for one final thing," Lucifer continues. He snaps his fingers, and an enormous old-fashioned leather-bound book appears in his hand. I know without being told that the leather is actually the dried flesh of his victims. I shiver in disgust at the thought.

He brings the book to me, and the knife moves of its own volition, slicing my palm open. I wince at the sharp pain. "Sign your name in my book, Graham, pledge your allegiance to me with your very lifeblood."

I look down and see that my feet are starting to shimmer, becoming translucent. *Oh, my God! It's my time! My time is up, and I'm going home! I did it!*

"Go fuck yourself," I say, with a newfound zest of confidence.

Lucifer's wicked smile vanishes, and he growls low in his throat. "Do it!"

"Sorry to disappoint you there, bud, but my forty-eight-hour sentence is up. I haven't had anything to eat or drink, and I haven't signed your book. You lose!"

"Noooooo!!!!" he roars, stamping his foot so hard that everything starts to shake, and the ground splits. *Somebody is pissed!*

"Persephone, see you up top!" I call, looking past him to Persephone. She, too, is transparent.

"See you there."

The crowd behind me starts whooping and clapping. I turn to see Julian grinning broadly and jumping in excitement. "I don't know how," I call to him," but I'm getting you out. Do you hear me? I am getting you out!"

My body is replaced with pins and needles, and everything about me fades away as I am atomized and scattered throughout the dimensions.

Epilogue

I coalesce onto the street outside of the video store. I feel the solid ground beneath my feet and gasp. *I did it. I got home.* It's early morning, and the sky is a beautiful purple-orange color that makes me think of my mother; purple is her favorite color.

I notice that the parking lot is empty. Grandma's car is gone. I'm sure that when he got here to pick me up and found me nowhere in sight, he rallied together the troops to try to rescue me. Grandma probably flew back from Oregon on a redeye to be here for me. Thankfully, it's only a few blocks back home.

Despite having not eaten or drunk in over two days, the only thing I want, the only thing I need at this moment is a bloody cigarette. I pat my pockets, hoping beyond hope that my pack has somehow survived the ordeal of the last two days. I can't say I'm shocked when my ripped pockets turn up empty.

I quickly search my person and find that my wallet is gone, too, and that my phone's screen is cracked. In my reflection from the glass door by the dropbox, I can see that I am covered in soot and blood, my bangs are limp in my eyes, and the top of my hair is in disarray. I look like a cockatiel. *Okay, first things first, I need cigarettes.*

Just around the corner is a gas station that is open twenty-four hours. I know I look like I have just survived *the Texas Chainsaw Massacre*, but I don't care. I need some nicotine. I stroll into the store, squinting my eyes against the bright halogen lights. The lady behind the counter looks up from her fashion magazine and does a double-take when she sees me stumbling toward her. My shoes are gone, and the skin on my feet is broken and bloody from being barefoot in that treacherous place.

"Can I help you?" she asks, not disguising her alarm very well.

"Can I get a pack of the Camel Crush menthol, please," I rasp.

"Uh, ID?" she stammers.

Oh, shit. I don't have any ID because my wallet is missing. "Listen, I've just been to hell and back—literally—can't you cut me some slack? I know I look young, but give me a break, okay?"

As if by magic, the woman's demeanor instantly changes. She stands up ramrod straight, and her worried countenance is replaced with a chipper smile. "Okay, I'll give you a break this time." She reaches up to the cigarette shelf above her and grabs a pack of Camel Crush.

"This, too," I say, grabbing a purple lighter and setting it on the counter next to the pack of cigarettes.

The lady rings them both up and fixes her eerie smile on me. "That'll be ten dollars, please."

"Ten, why so expensive?" I ask, confused. The cigarettes should be six-fifty, the lighter, a dollar, plus tax, I should be at around eight dollars.

"That's the cost of smoking," she says, grin still glued in place.

I instinctively reach for my wallet, and I am once again reminded that I do not have it, nor any money. *What am I going to do?* My face beams red with embarrassment as I meet her friendly gaze. "I, uh, lost my wallet," I say. "I don't have any money." *Shit!*

"No money?" She asks this as though this idea is totally alien to her. Considering that she works at a gas station, being broke should be a relatable experience for her.

"All my cash is in my wallet. I don't know where that is," I reiterate. "I don't suppose you could... you know... cover me for now? I live a few blocks away. I can run the money over later."

"Sure. Take it." She pushes the pack of cigarettes and the lighter toward me with that same creepy smile.

"Thanks..." I say, brow knit in confusion. *What the hell is going on?* I hope that I haven't been returned to some crazy parallel universe or something. With my luck, anything is possible.

Before she can change her mind, I hurry out the door and take off down the street. My fingers peel the plastic wrap off the pack and shove it into my shoddy pockets. I do not condone littering. I open the pack and fish out a white filtered cigarette. I quickly crush the menthol capsule in the butt and put it into my lips, flicking the lighter to life.

That first inhale is amazing, making my eyes roll back into my head with delight. *Oh, God, I have missed this!* I take another deep lungful, holding the minty smoke in my lungs for as long as I can. *Amazing!*

I continue to puff on the cigarette as I make my way home. After everything I've just been through, I don't care who sees me smoking and what they may or may not have to say about it. I finish the cigarette quicker than usual and grind it out on the sidewalk before tucking it into the palm of my hand. I'll toss it in the trash when I get home.

The early spring morning chill hits me hard after the sweltering heat of Sitra Achra, and I hug my arms around myself, shivering slightly. *Not too far to go now.*

I cross a few streets and come at last to mine. Before me, my grandmother's beautiful home looms, comforting. A part of me believed that I would never see it again, that I would cave in and be stuck in that place forever. *Guess again, sucker!*

I go up the driveway and onto the front stoop. My hands freeze before the doorknob. No, I'm not ready to go in yet. I am not ready to discuss what has just happened to me, especially since I haven't even had time to process it all myself.

I sit down, light another cigarette, and let my mind go. *I killed a man. I killed an evil, but still, an innocent man possessed by a demon to save the life of an innocent woman. Is that justifiable? Murder is still murder, regardless of the proposed intent. How much have I tainted my soul in doing so? Am I a bad witch now?*

The truth is, I don't feel as bad as I should about killing Don. He was awful to me for years, and getting to end him once and for all had elicited a feeling of intense satisfaction and accomplishment. *Is that the dormant evil within me talking?* I have no idea how much residual evil is in me after Lucifer raped my soul. Maybe none of this is my fault. Maybe I can eventually stop feeling numb to the act and seek forgiveness from the guilt that will ultimately wrack me. *Perhaps I'm still in shock. I know what will be on my mind on Yom Kippur.*

What am I going to tell my family? Brent? Don's disappearance is going to raise a lot of questions. Should I be honest and say that I killed him, choosing the life of an innocent over his? Should I even mention that he was ever there with me at all? In the real world, people go missing and are never heard from again. Perhaps Don pissed off the wrong person and was fed to the pigs or something. The possibilities are endless.

It's going to be weird seeing Erasmus again after Lucifer deliberately masqueraded as him to torment me. I know that Erasmus would never intentionally hurt me, but still, I don't know if I'll be able to be as open with him as I was before, at least not for a little while. Even though it will hurt him, I know he'll understand and not begrudge me. If anything, he'll blame himself for being unable to save me from my torment.

I don't notice that the cigarette is gone until the butt falls from my hand. I blink and look down at the yellow-stained butt. I'd smoked a whole cigarette while being in my head.

I decide against lighting another. Now that I'm in familiar, safe territory, my body and mind ache with exhaustion. I need to sleep for a little bit before I can begin working through all of this.

I rise and try the door, though I'm not surprised to find it locked. Of course, it is; it's like five o'clock in the morning. My house key is MIA, but thankfully, I know where Grandma keeps the spare. I reach down into the bush in front of me and feel along the branches until I come to the plastic Easter egg that she cleverly uses to hide the spare key.

I crack the egg open and take the key out, sliding it into the lock and turning it until the door slides open. I step inside, enshrouded once again in almost darkness. *Yes, darkness. I need sleep.* Like a zombie, I shamble up the stairs, using the railing as a crutch. I'm so weak from starvation and dehydration that I don't trust myself not to fall and plummet to my death.

It takes a while, but I eventually make it to my room. Upon opening the door, my heart swells when I see Romana lying on the bed, facing me. At the sight of me, she brightens up and runs at me. Blinking back tears of joy, I crouch down and pick her up, raining kisses down on her head as she rubs against me, purring delightedly.

"Daddy came back for you, Romana," I whisper. "Daddy will always come back for you, I promise." I have missed my baby girl so very much, and I am so relieved that she somehow survived the two days without me with little to no food. I quickly fill her bowl and rub at my burning eyes.

I should take a quick shower and brush my teeth, but I'm too tired. Instead, I strip out of my soiled clothes and climb into bed, switching on my electric blanket. The extra warmth feels good, and I remove my contacts, throwing them in the trash next to my bed before rolling onto my left side and closing my eyes. Romana comes and lies by my hands, her purring lulling me off to sleep.

****

It's like I died because, for the first time in a long time, I don't dream. I don't wake up several times to check the time or assess my surroundings. I just sleep. The world around me ceases to exist for those glorious hours.

When I come round, Romana is still lying beside me, her purrs bringing me back to consciousness. Without my contacts in, I can't see anything. I remember packing my glasses in my duffel bag for that night, just in case I ripped or lost a contact. Where that bag is now, I have no idea. Through my blurry vision, I find Romana and kiss her before padding to the door and across the hall to my bathroom.

I switch on the light and stand before the toilet, emptying my screaming bladder. How there is any fluid to need evacuation is beyond me, but it's definitely there. I wash my hands before taking my boxes of contacts out from behind my mirror and sliding in a new one for each eye. The world is suddenly clear again.

I look at my reflection in the mirror. Although I don't look any older than the night of the party, my eyes seemed to have aged. The sparkle of innocence that has always resided there is gone, replaced by a coldness.

As much as I want to just crawl back into bed and relax, I can no longer ignore the aching rumbling in my stomach. I need food. I'll eat a little bit, and then I'll let Erasmus and Amethyst know that I'm all right, and then I'll go back to sleep. I should be in class right now, I imagine, and I realize that I have no idea what time it is or how long I was asleep.

I take a long, hot shower, washing the dirt and grime and some of my sin from my body. I scrub hard at it all, stopping only when my normally pale white skin is a furious red. I watch as the water below me—which should be clear—rolls off me in rivulets of brown and red. The hot water feels amazing on my tired, aching muscles, and I close my eyes, letting it cleanse me.

My teeth feel like they've become Chewbacca's, and my breath is tinged with tobacco smoke and decay. I hurriedly floss, brush until my gums start to bleed, and swish some mouthwash until I feel human once more.

I didn't bring any clothes with me, so I step back into my room and throw on a pair of skinny jeans and my Wesley Crusher-inspired sweater. It's a dorky look, I know, but I am a huge nerd. Romana chirps at me from the bed, and I scratch her chin. "Daddy's not leaving you again, baby, I promise," I coo. "Daddy needs to eat, though; I'm starving. You'll be okay for fifteen minutes or so."

Fully dressed and refreshed, I go downstairs and into the kitchen. I'm so hungry now that anything and everything sounds good. I don't want to go overboard, but I need something. I open the fridge and pull out the carton of eggs. I check the date—Grandma has a bad habit of not doing so—and see that they are good until June. A few weeks, then.

I scramble four eggs and devour them before they've even cooled down. My empty stomach readily accepts this, grateful to be replenished again. I consider making more, but opt against it, wanting to get back to Romana.

I'm just finishing washing up my dishes when I hear the front door open and close and slow footsteps coming toward me. *Well, here we go; time to face the music.*

Grandma rounds the corner, a Styrofoam coffee cup in one hand and her purse in the other. She's looking down into her purse at first, so she doesn't see me, but I can see her. I frown when I notice her usually dark hair is now completely gray. She'd never let it go gray; she always told me that gray was for the commoners. Her small mouth is also lined with deep wrinkles, which I don't remember ever seeing before. *Just how worried was she?*

She looks up, and her eyes meet mine. At first, she does nothing, but then she gasps, and the Styrofoam cup drops out of her hand and hits the wooden floor, steaming hot coffee everywhere.

"Oh, my God, bubala!" she whispers, hand flying to her mouth.

"I made it, Grandma; I'm okay," I say before she can fuss over me. It's bad enough knowing that the psychological scars from my ordeal could linger forever. The last thing I need is pity.

"But... but how?" she stammers, staying firmly rooted in place. She looks me over as if I am a celebrity, as if she can't believe what she's seeing or that she's seeing me for the very first time. Maybe she does have dementia or Alzheimer's; it would explain a few things...

"I waited my allotted time and, since I didn't do any of the stuff that would keep me there, I was brought back. I made it."

"Two days?"

"Yeah, two days. You know the deal."

"You weren't gone two days, bubala."

"I know. It feels like I was gone for a hundred years. I can't even begin to tell you what I was subjected to—"

"You were gone for ten years, Graham."

Her words hit me like a brick wall. I stumble back as if I'd hit that wall. "What? No!" I laugh. "I was gone for two days, two misery-laden days."

"We all thought you were dead!" I can see now that genuine tears are welling in her eyes.

"I got kidnapped! But I made it; it's okay."

"We looked everywhere for you. We even tried spells. Poor Erasmus was absolutely heartbroken. He blamed himself, you see."

"Grandma, stop," I beg in a quiet voice. "Please stop teasing me."

"I'm dead serious."

I spy a newspaper on the counter and pick it up. I shiver when I see the date printed along the top: May 23rd, 2021. *What.The.Fuck!?*

"Ten years…" I gasp.

"Oh, bubala, this must all be so confusing for you!"

She reaches for me, but I shake her hand off, my mind scurrying to take in all of these new details. *Ten years… I've been gone for ten years. How? How the* hell *could that be!?*

"Ten years…"

"We had a funeral for you and everything. Your poor mother was beside herself. I thought she was going to have a stroke. Turns out that losing you was just the beginning of her woes. Brent has been so sick in the last few years. She's a total mess."

"What?"

"Brent started having seizures when he got to be about eleven. His first one was on Halloween night while they were out trick or treating. He collapsed and stopped breathing. Your mother was scared shitless. The ambulance ride alone ate up her meager savings. Since then, it's been frequent trips to the hospital and specialists, not to mention his medications…"

"What's wrong with him?"

"Seizures are common with Autistic kids. When they start reaching puberty, their hormones go haywire. He's lucky he's made it this long. I can't tell you how many times he's stopped breathing."

"Oh, God." I clutch my stomach and fight the urge to puke up my breakfast. *This all has to be a dream. A terrible dream.*

"Breathe," my grandma urges.

"Where is Mom?"

"She lives across town. I'll call her for you. She'll be so happy that you're okay. Losing you destroyed her. You've always been her favorite."

"Call her," I murmur, my head spinning. "If I was gone for ten years… why is Romana still alive? She doesn't look like she's aged a day since I left."

My grandmother sighs and begins her story.

****

Ginevra stood in the doorway to Graham's room, holding onto the wall for support. He'd been so safe for so long. How could this possibly have happened to him?

She received a frantic call from Erasmus, who was mad with rage. He went to the video store to pick Graham up, and he simply wasn't there. They found his phone and the car but absolutely no trace of him whatsoever.

Ginevra knew the truth, they all did, though no one wanted to admit it yet. Graham was gone. The demons had managed to snatch him and drag him to Sitra Achra. He was strong, a fighter, sure, but Ginevra wasn't sure that even her grandson could withstand the pressures of Hell. If he did come back, it wouldn't be as the Graham they all knew and loved, but as a Dark Witch, bent on destruction.

From Graham's tidy bed, Romana mewled anxiously. Ginevra entered the room in a swaying of skirts and saw that the food and water dishes were not empty; Romana was upset because her master was gone.

"It's okay, old girl," Ginevra said, her voice tight with emotion. "I miss him, too. He loved you more than life, you know?"

She sat on the edge of the bed, and Romana scampered over, butting her head against Ginevra's arm. Cat specialists say that act is the cat's way of marking the human with its scent as if claiming ownership of them.

"He's not coming back, is he?" she asked, blinking back tears.

As if in response, Romana yowled loudly and started kneading Ginevra's lap.

"Oh, I can't bear to watch you wither and die," she exclaimed, "I know he loved you so much. It doesn't seem fair that either of you should have to live without the other." Ginevra inhaled sharply. "I could do a time lock spell on you, so you'll never age another day. You'll be frozen in this exact moment just in case...well, just in case he comes back. How's that?"

The cat started rubbing on her again, this time more fervently as if she could truly understand the words coming out of Ginevra's mouth.

Slowly, the old woman got to her feet and closed her eyes, centering herself. She waited for Romana to lie down and get comfortable before beginning the spell.

Mighty Chronos, hear my plea

Render your gifts unto me

'Til Graham returns, freeze Romana in place

Everlasting 'til the end of time and space.

As she said the words, Ginevra felt a cool breeze through the room, and suddenly Romana stopped moving and stopped breathing. She was frozen in time, perhaps forever.

"It's the best I can do," she said with a sniffle. She leaned down and pressed her lips to the cat's *golden head. "Let's pray he returns to us."*

Tears in her eyes, she made her way from the room and shut the door behind her.

****

"Your room is exactly as you left it,'" Grandma finishes.

"I noticed."

"I'm so glad to have you back!" She hugs me, her thin shoulders quaking as she cries.

"Where's Erasmus?"

"I haven't seen him in ages. He took your... disappearance... particularly hard. Like I said, he blamed himself. The last time I heard anything about him, he was still living in his mansion across town. He's become somewhat of a recluse, I imagine. You were the love of his life. You *are* the love of his life."

"I have to go to him," I declare, shaking my head. "I need to see him right now."

"But what about your mother?"

"Call her and get her here. I'll be back in a little bit."

"Here," she hands me the keys to her car. They're different than the ones that I'm used to. Apparently, she no longer has the Buick. *A lot can change in ten years...*

I climb into her purple Impala and start it, throwing it into reverse immediately and roaring down the street. I speed the whole way to Erasmus' place. It's early enough still that the police are not out in force, so I don't have to worry about getting pulled over.

As I drive, I take in the surroundings. Willow's Crest hasn't changed much since I've been gone. Perhaps that's the downside of living in a small town; no matter how long you're away, whatever changes there are, are minute and go practically unnoticed.

I pull into Erasmus' driveway and kill the engine. I leap from the car and rush up to his front door. I know from experience that he keeps it locked. Without hesitation, I start pounding on the door furiously, like a person in a horror movie with a psycho killer hot on their heels.

"Come on, come on," I urge, pounding harder and harder. "Come on, Erasmus."

Over my knocking, I make out the sound of bare feet on the floor coming my way. *Yes, yes, about time!* After all this time, I can see Erasmus again and tell him that this wasn't his fault, that he can stop torturing himself because I'm here, and I'm okay, and I love him. *I love him so very much.*

I continue to pound until the door opens, and there's nothing for me to hit anymore. I stumble back when I see not Erasmus, but a pale blonde woman at the door. She appears to be naked except for a tight dress shirt, buttons straining against her ample cleavage. "Can I help you?" she asks, an edge to her voice.

---

610   **Gabriel Mero**

"I'm here to see Erasmus." My voice sounds tinny. *Who is this bimbo?* I wonder.

"Babe?" I hear Erasmus' voice call.

I crane my neck to see past the bimbette.

"It's for you," the woman says, crinkling her nose in distaste.

Erasmus appears behind her and kisses her neck softly. My heart catches in my throat. *Is he with her?* He casts a glance at me, and the smile vanishes from his face. If it were possible, I'd say he grows even paler. The coffee mug he's carrying slides from his fingers and crashes to the floor. It shatters, and the blood within starts to pool on the hardwood, staining it.

Erasmus and I lock eyes, our expressions perfect reflections of shock.

About The Author

Gabriel Mero has been writing for as long as he can remember, getting his start in fan fiction. He has always loved the supernatural... witches in particular... and cats are his life. He jokingly refers to himself as the male equivalent of a "crazy cat lady": He lives in a small town in Michigan with his cats, Valerie, Clara, Alistair, Romana, and Cersei. When he isn't making pizzas, he can be found at home embracing his Jewish heritage, cuddling with his cats, or reading.

Connect with Gabriel:

INSTAGRAM

https://www.instagram.com/wandering_jew90/

FACEBOOK

https://www.facebook.com/akjdfkalsjdflkafd

YOUTUBE

https://www.youtube.com/channel/UCQEb koAyjNg9Lw0EKjs7E6A

Books by Gabriel Mero

Witch'd

The First Of A Four-Book Series

Dark and Theatrical

A Poetry Collection

www.ingramcontent.com/pod-product-compliance
Lightning Source LLC
Chambersburg PA
CBHW051927020726
47501CB00001B/20